The Test of Love

E. D. E. N. Southworth

THE TEST OF LOVE

BEING THIRD AND LAST PART OF "THE TRAIL OF THE SERPENT"

BY MRS. E. D. E. N. SOUTHWORTH AUTHOR OF "NEAREST AND DEAREST," "LITTLE NEA'S ENGAGEMENT," "THE LOST LADY OF LONE," "THE STRUGGLE OF A SOUL," "WHY DID HE WED HER," ETC.

CONTENTS

CHAPTER I
A GIRL'S TRAGEDY

ONCE more Hamilton Gower read the little pink note that had come with the manuscript which his beloved, Seraph Elfinstar, had given him to read:

"Before you begin to read my narrative you must know this in explanation: Mr. Elfinstar is not my father, but my grandfather, and I am Margaret Campbell."

He sat stupefied with amazement and sorrow.

One idea possessed and overwhelmed him—that Seraph Elfinstar, the good and beautiful girl whom he loved and worshiped for her angelic attributes of person and character, could be one and the same individual with Margaret Campbell, the convict murderess, whom he had learned to loathe and abhor for the cruelty of her nature and the atrocity of her crime.

He could not understand this. He could not believe it. The terrible revelation crushed, but did not convince him.

He sat there paralyzed by the stunning blow, utterly incapable of reasoning upon it.

Seraph Elfinstar and Margaret Campbell one and the same woman! It was incredible! it was impossible! even though she herself had said it!

He felt a sudden sense of suffocation. Rising and staggering like a drunken man, he tottered to one of the windows and raised it, drew a deep inhalation of the fresh air, and then sank down on a chair beside it and rested his elbow on the sill.

Margaret Campbell and Seraph Elfinstar one!

Oh! this was a nightmare from which he would presently be relieved! He had talked too much and thought too much of this detestable Margaret Campbell, and her sinister influence on the life of Seraph Elfinstar, until at length he had blended them in his dreams! He would pinch himself severely and wake up.

He did so, but without effecting any change in his surroundings.

Here was still the hotel room, with its whitewashed walls, its straw matting on the floor, its white-curtained windows, and its white-draped bed. There was the little pink note that had stung him like an asp lying on the floor, and here was the roll of manuscript in his hand!

No, he had not been dreaming! He was wide awake, and face to face with a hideous, a ghastly, reality. Seraph Elfinstar was Margaret Campbell, and a convict for life! Seraph herself had written it! Seraph, whose word was truth!

Since she was Margaret Campbell, of course, she was lost to him forever and ever! There could be no thought of marriage with her, a convict for life in the penal settlements of Tasmania!

But was she guilty?

Impossible!

Seraph Elfinstar must be as innocent as an angel, even though Margaret Campbell had been convicted under overwhelming evidence, and the two names represented but one woman.

Yes, Seraph Elfinstar was innocent! He felt absolutely certain of that! He could not have been intimately associated with her for six weeks without recognizing the purity, tenderness and sincerity of nature which would have rendered such guilt as had been ascribed to Margaret Campbell utterly impossible to her.

How, then, had such a net of circumstantial evidence involved her in its meshes?

Would her narrative explain that?

He was scarcely capable of examining the manuscript as yet. The terrible excitement of the last half hour had almost exhausted his strength. He felt as weak as a child.

He was very abstemious in the use of wine; yet now he felt the need of some stimulus.

He stretched out his hand and rang the bell, whose pull was within his reach, summoned a waiter and ordered a glass of wine; and when he had drunk it he settled himself in his large armchair, unrolled the manuscript, and read:

"THE STORY OF MARGARET CAMPBELL

"Dear friend, who have been so good to me,

I feel that I must be true with you.

"Now, standing in the shadow of death, I must tell you the whole story.

"I preface my narrative by confessing that but for my own fault I should never have been placed in the awful position in which I stand to-day—doomed to die for a crime that I never was capable of committing.

"Dearest of dear friends! you knew so little of me, of my circumstances, before my dire extremity brought you to my help, that I must recount something of my early life in order to explain what is to follow.

"I am the only child of Duncan Campbell, second son of Duncan Campbell, of Rose Hill, and of Seraph Elfinstar, only daughter of Theobald Elfinstar, of Thorncliff, Yorkshire.

"I have no memory of my parents, having lost them both in the first two years of my existence.

"My infancy and childhood were passed happily under the guardianship of my father's elder brother, Mr. Stuart Campbell, of Rose Hill.

"My uncle was without children, and I, in right of my father, was the recognized heir presumptive of the estate.

"I was the adopted daughter of the house, petted and spoiled by both uncle and aunt.

"I loved my uncle, who was my uncle by blood; but I actually adored my aunt, though she was my aunt only by marriage.

"She loved me with more than a mother's tenderness, and I worshiped her with more than a daughter's devotion.

"The bond of affection between us was a perfect bond.

"She was a most accomplished woman, and when, in the seventh year of my age, the question of providing a governess for me arose in the house, and I—spoiled child that I was—rebelled at the idea, with a storm of sobs, and tears, and protestations that I would never let a stranger take possession of me, and separate me for ever so many hours a day from my dear auntie, she, in her self-sacrificing love, came to my rescue by declaring that she herself was perfectly competent and perfectly willing to take full charge of my education, and would henceforth do so.

"Yes, the lady of the manor, in her love for the little alien child who was not of her blood, readily assumed the duties and responsibilities which are usually considered very onerous and oppressive even by those who are trained to undertake them as a profession.

"My uncle, with an incredulous smile, remarked that he hoped that my aunt would not find cause to regret her undertaking.

"If she ever had such cause she never expressed the least regret.

"She was the most patient of teachers, and I was to her, what I might not have been to any other human being, the most docile of pupils.

"We were both much happier for this new and close companionship established between us; she found in it occupation and amusement, I employment and pleasure.

"In this way several happy years passed, when at length my aunt's health began to droop. She was now about forty-five years of age, my uncle being ten years her senior, and I a well-grown girl of twelve.

"My dear aunt had no especial disease, nor do I think she need have died, had not heart-break been added to other causes of decline.

"Yes, heart-break! You shall know all about it now.

"About this time, when my dear aunt was failing in health and beauty, there came to visit us a very distant cousin of my uncle — an impecunious widow, aged about thirty-two or thirty-three — in person beautiful and attractive as an angel; in character selfish and subtle as a demon.

"Using and abusing her privileges of relationship, she gradually appropriated and absorbed all my uncle's time and attention.

This was not all accomplished in a day, or a week, but in the course of weeks running into months.

"She talked, read, or played cards with him in the house; she walked, rode, or drove with him in the park; while my aunt, confined to her own room by indisposition, was utterly neglected, and left to pine in solitude, or with no other company than myself, or her maid, Stockton.

"While these follies were going on under my eyes I did not at first recognize them as improprieties. I was too young. I knew too little of the world. I thought that it was my uncle's duty, and a very hard duty, under the circumstances, to entertain the lady guests, and I was sorry for him and vexed with her, especially when my aunt, looking at me with anxious, pathetic eyes, would ask:

"'Meg, darling, where is your uncle?'

"And I would be compelled to answer that he was with Mrs. Mattox.

"Sometimes I would grow impatient at seeing how my aunt was neglected, and how despondent she was becoming, and then I would exclaim:

"'I wish that Mattox woman would go home, if she has any home to go to! I should think she might see that she is a nuisance, especially to poor uncle, who wants to spend some time in the day with his wife!'

"But my aunt would only answer by the saddest smile, that always ended in a sigh.

"One day I was suddenly enlightened. I happened to be alone in my aunt's boudoir, arranging some of the first wild violets of the spring in little vases on her table, when Stockton entered with a silk quilt to lay on the sofa in readiness for her mistress, who intended to lie down there that day for a change. As she was arranging the silk quilt and cushions she suddenly exclaimed:

"'I hope my master will find time to-day to come and sit a while with my mistress.'

"'Why, he cannot, Stockton. He is going by rail to Tynemouth to show Mrs. Mattox the ruins of the old abbey she is so anxious to see,' I exclaimed.

"'Humph!' muttered the maid, with a decided expression of scorn and detestation.

"Encouraged by this tacit sympathy, I cried out sharply:

"'I wish to the Lord in heaven that woman would go about her business—that I do!'

"'She is about her business, Miss Margaret! Never you doubt that!'

"'What do you mean by that, now, Stockton?' I demanded, feeling annoyed and made vaguely anxious by something very peculiar in the woman's tone and manner.

"'She knows her business pretty well, Miss Margaret, and she has set herself about it in earnest. I am sure my poor mistress sees that as well as I do, although she says nothing.'

"'Stockton, why can't you speak out? What is her business, then?'

6

"'To become the second wife of your uncle, and the mistress of Rose Hill!' curtly replied Stockton.

"At these words I fell into a perfect whirlwind of fury. I uttered many wild, mad threats, which were afterward produced against me on my trial.

"Yes, I did say the words reported of me. I did say:

"'That she shall never be! I will kill her first—the snake! I will kill her with my own hands before she shall succeed to my aunt's place in the house, even if she has supplanted her in the heart of her husband! I will kill the crawling, venomous reptile first! I will kill her with my own hands!' I repeated many times, and in my blind fury and passion I meant what I said.

"Two housemaids, who were passing the door on their way to the upper chambers, paused and stood aghast at my state of rage.

"'For the love of the Lord be quiet, dear Miss Margaret, or we shall have the house about our ears! Look at the maids, how they stare! Go about your work, you minxes! What are you loitering here for?'

"The two young women passed on, pale with dismay.

"I raged on, unheeding Stockton's prayers and remonstrances, until at last she said:

"'Now, there is your aunt's bell, and I should not wonder if she had heard you and is frightened out of her senses.'

"That stopped me at once. I would not have hurt, or in the least degree startled, my aunt on any account.

"I had never liked Mrs. Mattox; but from that hour I hated her with a bitter hatred, and I pitied my aunt with an intensity that nearly broke my heart. I would look at her sweet, pale face and hollow eyes and gray hair, and have to run out of the room to hide my tears. I would then encounter the round, rosy cheeks and beaming, black eyes and golden hair of Mrs. Mattox with a burning rage that nearly consumed me. Oh! I thought, if I could only strike her dead with the glance of my eyes! Or if I could breathe a pestilence over her and wither her freshness and beauty with leprosy or smallpox, how gladly I would have done it!

"The whole household saw the intensity of my hatred and shuddered at it, and were compelled to testify to it when they were forced to appear as witnesses against me on my trial.

"But, now, was there no excuse for me?

"This woman Mattox had deliberately won my foolish old uncle's affections from his invalid wife! She daily flaunted her fresh and blooming beauty and elegant and bewitching toilets, in contrast to the pale, gray, failing lady whose heart was breaking even faster than her health!

"She was killing my sweet and gentle aunt! How could I help hating her unto death?

"Once I ventured to ask my aunt:

"'Why does not Mrs. Mattox go home? She has been here for four months now, and her children must want to see her, if she does not care to see them.'

"'Her children are at boarding school, dear, and can only see their mother at stated intervals,' replied my aunt.

"'But, why, then, does not she go home?' I persisted.

"'I do not think she has any settled home. I think, while her daughters are at boarding school, she visits around among her friends.'

"'Then why in the world doesn't she go to some other friend now? It must have been somebody else's turn at least three months ago! She must be defrauding some admiring friends out of their proper share of her pleasant society!'

"'I suppose she finds her quarters here more agreeable than elsewhere,' said my aunt, with a patient smile.

"'I wish I could make them very disagreeable to her! I wish—'

"'Hush, darling,' said the gentle lady.

"'Auntie, dear, why do you not write her a note, and say that it is not convenient to entertain her any longer? Oh, auntie! do write that note, and I will take it to her myself—with pleasure.'

"'No, dear, I cannot do that. It would do no good. It would rather do harm, for it would displease your uncle,' she patiently replied.

"'Displease my uncle? Who cares if it would? You have the right to send away the woman who takes up so much of his time that ought to be passed with you!'

"'Hush, hush, my love, and listen to me,' she said, impressively. 'I am going away from this earth, dear Margaret; I am going away very soon; and I want to go—I want to go to that love which never disappoints, or wounds, or fails; but I want to go in peace, dearest, in perfect peace with all the world.'

"'Oh, auntie; oh, auntie, what do you mean? Do you mean to let that woman kill you, and never say a word?' I broke forth, in burning indignation.

"'Hush, my darling; hush! I mean only this—that the few remaining days of my life on earth may be passed in peace, so that in leaving it I may depart in peace. What, my Margaret, shall I mar with discord this sacred time, when earth is fading on my vision and heaven is brightening? No, dear child; no.'

"I looked at her and made up my mind, if she would not write that note to send Mrs. Mattox away, I would speak to that woman myself.

"I was terribly excited. I did not dare to trust myself in the creature's presence until I could command myself; for I required perfect calmness in order to speak to her as I intended to do. But how or when I should attain such calmness I could not know.

"I went to Stockton, who was busy in my aunt's dressing room, to consult her.

"'Stockton,' I said, 'I am so very nervous. My heart is throbbing up toward my throat, as if it would choke me; my brain is beating as if it would burst; my limbs are trembling so that I can scarcely stand; and you can perceive for yourself that I cannot speak steadily.'

"'I can see you are in an awful way, Miss Margaret; and now what has put you into it?' she inquired.

"'That woman, of course!'

"'Now, Miss Margaret, you must not think of her, or you will be growing crazy! Just to see that state you are in!'

"'Stockton, I know it! And I do not wish to betray myself. I am going downstairs now. Give me something to quiet me! You know what to give. I have seen you give it to auntie when she has been very nervous. What is it? Give me some!'

"'It is laudanum I gave my mistress, by the doctor's directions, my dear Miss Margaret. I would not like to fool with it without orders.'

"'How much do you give auntie, then?'

"'Eh twenty-five drops; but she is used to it; twenty-five drops might lay you out. No, Miss Margaret, I can't even give you so much as one drop without the doctor's orders. It might kill you, and I don't want to be hung for poisoning, not at my time of life!'

"I turned away from Stockton and went straight to the little cabinet in which the medicine bottles were kept, and I deliberately dropped ten drops of laudanum in a teaspoon and swallowed it.

"I had never taken laudanum in my life before, and the effect was prompt and potent. My turbulent blood suddenly fell as calm as the stormy sea at the divine command.

"I went downstairs as firmly as if I had been fifty years old instead of twelve; and I went into the library, where Mrs. Mattox sat reading poetry aloud and making eyes at my uncle, who listened, and leered, and sighed over the traitress, in a way to have put me in a rage, if it had not been for the laudanum.

"'Uncle,' I said, 'I have something to say to Mrs. Mattox, if you will please excuse me, and leave us alone for a few minutes.'

"'Indeed! A message from your aunt, perhaps,' he said, rising, while Mrs. Mattox closed her book, keeping her thumb in her place.

"I did not reply to my uncle's theory, and he, taking it for granted that he had guessed the truth, left the library.

"We were alone together-the snake woman and myself.

"'Have you a message from your aunt to me, my love?' she sweetly inquired, bringing her black eyes to bear caressingly on me.

"'No, madam, I have no message from my aunt to you. It is scarcely likely that my aunt would send a message to you,' I replied, with a calm dignity not at all natural, but due entirely to the laudanum.

"'But you have something to say to me, my dear? she murmured in the most mellifluous of tones.

"'Yes, madam, I have this to say: You have been here nearly five months; you have so completely engrossed the attention of my uncle that he has had no time, days nor evenings, to give to his invalid wife. Everybody notices this and blames you. The attendant physician, the servants in the house, all talk about it. Some one ought to tell you what is said. I do it. You should go away, and leave the husband to his wife.'

"She did not lose her temper at those plain words, as any one might have supposed she would have done. Oh, not in the least. Her wonderful powers of dissimulation served her as well as the opiate did me. So that what might otherwise have been an unseemly war of words became a quiet discussion.

"'But, my little love,' she said sweetly, 'I cannot go away and leave the family at such a distressing time. I would willingly have gone three months ago, or any time since that. I came only to spend the Christmas holidays. I had promised January to the Countess of Rockland; February to the Countess of Grassmere; March to the Marchioness of Widelands; April to the Duchess of Wincaster; and to all these ladies I have had to send excuses because my duties kept me here at Rose Hill, and I have had to forego all their pleasant country parties for the sake of staying here in this afflicted family, and doing my little best to supply the place of its lonely invalid mistress. I am sorry people are so absurd as to talk; but that should not prevent me from doing my duty.'

"That I did not fall upon her, tooth and nail, for her hypocrisy was due only to the calming influence of the laudanum.

"'So you will not go?' I said.

"'No, sweet one, I must not.'

"'You will stay here as a guest until you are sure of remaining here as the mistress of the house?

"'Is that what the wicked people say of me, my dear?

"'It is just what observers think of you, madam.'

"'How unjust they are! How little they know me!'

"This woman knew that she was not deceiving me. She did not even wish to do so. I saw through her. She wished at the same time to avoid a scene which would have compromised her, and to defy and taunt me under the cover of her sweet words and looks.

"I, a child of a dozen years, was powerless in the hands of such a woman.

"'You will not go, then! You will not go! Very well! I shall pray day and night to the Lord to deliver us from you, as from the greatest evil that afflicts us!'

"I spoke passionately, notwithstanding the opiate, and I left the room.

"I never told my aunt of this conversation, nor did Mrs. Mattox complain of me to my uncle. She would not have done that. Her tactics were to avoid all disturbance; to keep all in apparent harmony.

12

"My dear aunt faded gradually, and about three weeks after my interview with Mrs. Mattox she passed quietly away.

"Then I think my uncle was seized with a sudden remorse, for he shut himself up in his room and refused to see any visitor, leaving all necessary arrangements in the hands of his solicitors and steward.

"On the day of my aunt's death, Mrs. Mattox came to me, and said:

"'I must leave you, sweet love! I grieve to do so; but you must be aware that it would not be proper for me to remain in the house of a widower where there is no lady at the head of the establishment.'

"'Oh, go, go,' I answered passionately. 'Go! you have finished your work here! You have won the heart of the husband and broken the heart of the wife! You have killed her! Go, and may the Lord judge you!'

"'You are excited, dear love! You will be more just to me when you are calmer,' she said, as she stooped to kiss me; but I started and turned away, and she left the room, and, a few hours later, the house.'

CHAPTER II
AN OLD MAN'S FATE

"AFTER the funeral of my aunt, my uncle continued disconsolate for many days.

"All his fondness for myself was revived, and he kept me much with him, and made me talk about my aunt. He never dreamed that she had known of his devotion to her rival, and that she had secretly broken her heart over it, for no word or look of hers had ever betrayed her feelings on that subject; nor did I ever drop a hint to my uncle that could have enlightened him.

"I had too much veneration for the delicacy and dignity of my dear aunt's character to show the death wound that she had covered.

"Nor was the name of Mattox ever mentioned between us. Remorse, no doubt, kept my uncle silent, and pride and hatred restrained me.

"I hoped and believed that we should never see or hear any more of that woman. Ah! I knew so little of human nature!

"In a few more weeks my uncle grew restless, and took a journey, telling me that he was going away on business. He was absent a week, and returned in much better spirits.

"A month later he made another journey, and stayed away another week, and came home accompanied by an upholsterer and decorator, who was engaged to fit up and refurnish the whole house.

"Still, I had no suspicion of what was soon to follow.

"If my aunt's maid had been with us she might have enlightened me; but Stockton had left to take another service.

"The whole interior of the house seemed to be turned topsy-turvy, and the utmost confusion prevailed for several weeks; but, at the end of that period, the work was complete, and the house was elegantly decorated and refurnished.

14

"Then my uncle went on a third journey, without explaining his business to any of us.

"When he had been gone four weeks he wrote from Paris to our housekeeper, telling her to have everything in readiness to receive her new mistress, as Mrs. Campbell and himself would arrive at Rose Hill at six o'clock on the ensuing Saturday evening.

"This news was a terrible shock to me! My ravings on that occasion proved the malignant hatred I bore toward the second Mrs. Campbell.

"When the newly married couple arrived at the stated time, I refused to meet them.

"While madam was in her dressing room, my uncle came in search of me, and would have embraced me had I not broke suddenly out upon him.

"'You shall never kiss me again as long as you live! You have brought that woman home here to take the place of the lady whom you and she killed between you! Yes! You killed my dear aunt between you, and you know you did, and I hate you both! I hope the Lord will punish you both!'

"My uncle said if I could not behave myself he would have to send me to school, and so he left me.

"Well, it turned out that I really could not behave myself, and so I was sent to school. I was very glad to go, so as to be rid of the sight of the woman who had as surely killed my aunt as if she had stabbed her through the heart.

"I entered the school early in January, and remained until the end of the term early in June. Then my uncle came in person to bring me home for the midsummer holidays; but I utterly refused to come, and spoke of the new woman in such terms as to leave him no option but to return to Rose Hill without me.

"I remained at the school another half year, which ended with the Christmas holidays. Again my uncle came for me, for he loved me as his child, and was always good to me. He pressed me to return home with him. He told me that I had a little baby cousin, a little boy, who, to be sure, was born the heir of Bose Hill, so that I was no longer the heiress, but that I should be so richly provided for by his will that I should never be the worse for the loss of the estate.

"I replied that I neither wanted the estate nor the money; that all I wanted was never to set foot within limits of Rose Hill again, and never to set eyes on the murderess of my aunt, or on her son.

"Strong and bitter words these, yet they scarcely expressed the strength and bitterness of my feelings.

"My uncle replied, with some dignity, that he should certainly never ask me to come to Rose Hill again, or even allow me to do so, and thus he left me.

"But we did not either of us keep our words. Circumstances controlled us. I stayed another year at school, then I got a letter from my uncle, written in a faint and feeble hand, and asking me to return with the end of that school term and spend with him at Rose Hill the last Christmas he would ever see on earth, for that he was on his death-bed!

"On reading this letter, every line of which revealed the dying hand, my long-cherished resentment melted away like snow under the sun, and I wrote back, begging him to forgive my undutiful conduct to him; expressing the greatest sorrow for his illness; assuring him of my devoted love and gratitude for all his patient goodness to me, and promising to return to him at once, and never leave him as long as he would permit me to stay with him.

"I sent off this letter, and as soon as the school broke up for the Christmas holidays I hurried off to Rose Hill.

"I found my poor uncle much nearer death than I had anticipated.

"I found also in the family three members that I had not left there— the infant heir, now aged about thirteen months, and Lavinia and Malvina Mattox, the two daughters of Mrs. Campbell's first marriage.

"I found, also, an entirely new set of servants, from the butler and the housekeeper down to the youngest maid. All these had been engaged by the new mistress, and were devoted to her.

"The young heir was the idol of the whole household. The two stepdaughters of my uncle were the recognized young ladies of the family, but with a difference: Lavinia, the eldest girl, aged seventeen, was a youthful image of her mother—a black-eyed, golden-haired blonde—and she was always elegantly dressed, and affectionately caressed.

"Malvina, the younger girl, aged about fifteen, was very plain, having a pale, sallow face, dull, flaxen hair, dim, blue eyes, and a fragile figure, with one shoulder a little higher than the other. She had, also, a very feeble mind, and a very uncertain temper. She was dressed shabbily, and snubbed constantly. For all these reasons I became at once much interested in the poor girl.

"The new Mrs. Campbell was very devoted in her attentions to her dying husband. She was, also, very sweet in her manner. It was her cue to be so, and, therefore, I did not appreciate her superficial amiability.

"I was my uncle's constant companion. It was his wish that I should remain in his room and sit by his bed as much as possible.

"He assured me that he had never ceased to love me as a daughter, and that I was well provided for by his will, and he hoped, he said, that I would try to get on with my new aunt, who was really very amiable, and desired to make me happy.

"I could not contradict or oppose my dying uncle. I promised all he wished, and I even treated Mrs. Campbell decently in his presence for his sake.

"My poor uncle lingered a few weeks longer, and then died, with my hand clasped in his own.

"After my uncle's funeral his will was read. He had made ample provision for me, but had constituted his widow the guardian of my person and the trustee of my property.

17

"Those were bitter pills!

"And, ah! from that day how much changed for the worse my life became!

"Mrs. Campbell threw off her mask forever!

"She no longer affected any kindness of feeling or conduct toward me. I, who had been brought up in the house as the heiress presumptive of the estate, and treated with the tenderest affection by the master and mistress, and with the highest respect by all the servants of the establishment, was now made to feel as if I were a poor dependent on the bounty of a widow, and a barely tolerated intruder in the home of my ancestors. I was treated with contempt by the new mistress, and with insolence by the new servants, who were her creatures.

"My own beautiful suite of apartments, consisting of boudoir, bedchamber and dressing room, was taken from me and given to Miss Lavinia Mattox, and I was put in a small apartment in the attic, with the poor, sickly, half-witted Malvina for a roommate, and even for a bedfellow. And I was ordered to watch over her and take care of her, for it was not safe either to herself or to others that she should be left unguarded.

"I told you that at first view this girl had excited my compassion, but when I came to know her more thoroughly she inspired me with fear and dislike. She was not quite an idiot, but she was sly, cruel and vindictive, as idiots often are. She was cowardly, also, and secretive to a degree I have never seen equaled.

"She saw that I, equally with herself, was a butt for the ill usage of the household, and she divined that, equally with herself, I resented the bitter injustice.

"She confided to me, in secret, her hatred of the whole family, and of her mother most of all.

"This shocked me so much that I felt compelled to tell her how wicked it was in her to hate her own mother.

"Then she laughed in my face, and told me that she gave hate for hate, that her mother was ashamed of her, and would like to have her dead and out of the way, and she knew it!

"Yet it was only to me this unfortunate girl confided her real feelings. She had inherited her mother's powers of dissimulation, and she openly fawned upon the relatives whom she secretly hated.

"This creature had, among her other infirmities, the troublesome and dangerous habit of sleep-walking.

"Now, though I feared and disliked her, yet I pitied her, and I was often anxious lest she should come to harm during her fits of somnambulism; and whenever I awoke in the night and missed her from my side I always rose, lighted a candle, and went in search of her, usually finding her loitering aimlessly about the upper corridors of the house, when I would gently awake her and lead her back to her bed.

"We two were almost inseparable companions; and we were so, not of choice, but of necessity. For such was the will of Mrs. Campbell. We slept together in the little attic room, and we ate together at the second table. We were not allowed to sit down with the family at the first.

"But the catastrophe was approaching.

"It happened one long, dreary, drizzling season in mid-winter that Mrs. Campbell and Miss Mattox both lost their spirits and their tempers; nothing could please them, and they tormented each other.

"It was during this season that one day, in a climax of insolence, Mrs. Campbell, who had been out walking in the wet park, sent for me to her room, and ordered me to take off her muddy boots.

'Of course, I flatly refused to do so, telling her that it was the duty of her maid to perform that service.

"A disgraceful scene ensued, such as I cannot even recount here, but will merely say that she finished by declaring that she would use her power, as my guardian, to punish and degrade me; and that the very next day she would give me a mistress, by binding me out to a tailoress, to learn the trade, even if she had to pay a high premium with me.

"I flung myself out of her presence in a fury of passion, and used the wild, mad words that have since been brought up against me on my trial.

"My violent excitement continued so long that one of the maids carried word to the housekeeper, who came to me and brought a sedative draught, and coaxed me to go to bed.

"I did so, and the last that I remember of that maddening day is that I fell asleep in the arms of Malvina Mattox, who had undressed herself and lain down beside me to try to console me.

"Poor creature! I was the only one in the house whom she did not hate, and whom, perhaps, she even loved a little.

"The reaction from the extreme excitement and the influence of the sedative combined to cause me to sleep long and deeply.

"I was aroused in the morning by the tremendous confusion that rolled through the house from cellar to attic. I was still folded in the arms of Malvina, as if neither of us had moved during the night.

"It was one of the housemaids who had burst into the room, with her eyes staring and her dress in disorder, and with the news that the infant heir was missing from his crib in the nursery, and could not be found anywhere, and that the mistress was beside herself with grief and terror. And did we know anything about it, she inquired, or had we seen anything of the dear little master?

"We were both too much startled by the rude awakening to understand the full force of what was said; but I answered that we had seen nothing of the child since the preceding day; while Malvina, with the most stolid indifference, yawned, turned over, and closed her eyes as if to go to sleep again.

"I arose at once; for, notwithstanding my hatred of the mother, I had a really tender love for the poor baby, who was an affectionate and winsome little laddie.

"You, my dear friend, as well as the public, know all the hideous details of the domestic tragedy that followed. I need not repeat them here.

"I think I was suspected from the very first, though this suspicion never got into the papers.

"It was not, however, until the remains of the poor, dear baby were discovered at the bottom the dry well that I was openly accused.

"And to my intense amazement, the first witness against me at the coroner's inquest was my half-witted roommate, Malvina Mattox, in whose arms I had slept the whole night of the murder.

"Amid tears and sobs that seemed to prove her reluctance to tell the story, which was dragged from her by questions, she testified that about three o'clock on the night, or rather on the morning of the murder, I arose from our bed, drew the key from our chamber door, and taking it with me, left the room and went downstairs; that I was absent about an hour, and returned to the chamber a few minutes after the clock in the tower struck four.

"This testimony, false and incomprehensible as it was to me, was the first link in that fearful chain of circumstantial evidence which was forged for my destruction.

"You have seen how link after link was found and fitted until the whole fatal sequence was complete!

"The coroner's jury brought in a verdict in accordance with the evidence, and I was committed to prison on the charge of having murdered my infant cousin, there to await the action of the grand jury.

"That first night in my lonely cell I lay too stunned for thought or feeling. I seemed to have not a friend in the world, for no one came near me but the prison officials.

"But the next day, when the turnkey unlocked my door, and the bright morning sun streamed into my cell, you entered with that light, a fitting halo for the benignant face that shone upon me there.

"You sat down on the cot beside me, and took my hand, and told me that you were Theobald Elfinstar, of Thorncliff, my grandfather and my mother's father, and that you had come to help me, and, if possible, to save me.

"I had never seen your face before! I had never heard your name before! I had never even known of your existence before! Nor of the bitter feud—most bitter on the part of the Campbells—which had kept my father's and my mother's people apart, and had hidden from me the knowledge of the Elfinstars.

"But I loved you from that moment with a. love that filled my whole soul.

"You came to me like an angel from heaven. You told me that in face and form, in voice and manner, I was the counterpart of what my mother—your own, only child—had been at the time when young Duncan Campbell fell in love with her, against the will of his whole family.

"You believed my unsupported declaration of innocence—you said it was impossible that I could ever have imagined, much less perpetrated, such a crime.

"You said that you felt perfectly sure of my innocence, and would move earth and heaven, if possible, to prove it.

"And, oh! my dearest dear, you kept your word!

"You have spent a fortune on my defense, and, though you could not secure my acquittal in the face of the tremendous falsehood of that circumstantial evidence which has convicted me, yet you have paved the way to a commutation of my sentence, and you say that if I am spared from death and sent for life to the penal colonies, you will spend another fortune to go out there and make me a home!

"Was ever human love like yours?

"I know not what the end may be; but, if it should be death, it is due to you, dearest dear, that I should leave this record of the truth behind me.

"And whatever my fate may be, in living or dying, oh, most beloved, my heart is bound to you by the strongest bonds of love and gratitude and veneration. I have done, and I sign the name that never was sullied by a sinful charge—the name that you say you will give me when we shall have passed through this *via crucis* and reached some home of peace—my angel mother's—your angel daughter's name,

SERAPH ELFINSTAR."

"She is innocent!" exclaimed Hamilton Gower, when he had finished this manuscript. "My martyred love is innocent! But she is none the less lost to the world, and to me, unless I can prove her to be so! I will henceforth devote my whole life and fortune, if necessary, to the one sacred object of the vindication of her name and fame!"

CHAPTER III
"AS A SPIRIT"

"YES! here and now do I pledge my life and fortune and 'sacred honor' to this most sacred cause!" earnestly repeated Hamilton Gower, as he once more lifted the manuscript of Seraph Elfinstar from the sofa table on which he had laid it.

There were a few supplementary pages added to the end. They were dated on the morning of that day, and were as follows:

"You will see by the foregoing narrative, my friend, that it was written in those dark days that immediately followed the conviction of the writer.

"It is scarcely necessary to add now that my dear grandfather, by almost superhuman efforts, succeeded in procuring a commutation of the death penalty to that of transportation for life to these penal colonies.

"He did all that man could do to ameliorate my condition in the prison where I was confined while waiting for the departure of the convict transport ship in which I was to sail.

"He sent confidential agents in advance to select a site and begin the building of a home here.

"He let his own patrimonial home and bought and shipped furniture, books, pictures, statuary and all that was required to fit up and embellish a comfortable and refined home.

"He saw me every day, and kept up my spirits by telling me the progress that he had made in his preparations for emigration, and picturing the quiet, peaceful haven we should reach after these storms, and the harmonious life we two should lead in that far-off island of the southern sea—which, though some parts of it had been given over to demons and their drivers, was yet, in the beauty and sublimity of its scenery and the salubrity and delightfulness of its climate, a paradise fit for the dwelling place of angels and good spirits.

"And, meanwhile, so diligently did he work, that by the time the prison ship was ready to sail his own arrangements were all completed.

"He saw me off. He commended me to the care of the ship's captain, and he did all the 'regulations' would permit him to do to soften for me the hardships of that voyage in the convict ship. He urged me to keep up my courage, to pray when my heart failed, and to believe that he would be at Hobart Town ready to receive me, to take me at once out of the penal station, in the only way he could, as his 'assigned servant,' nominally, but really as his dear and cherished daughter. And so he blessed me and bade me good-by an hour before the ship sailed.

"I do not wish to speak of that sad voyage. The convict transport ships are notorious for being the worst in the service, and that in which I sailed was old, slow and unseaworthy. Some unfortunate Irish patriots, whose only crime had been love of national liberty, and whose death sentence had, like mine, been commuted to transportation to the penal colonies for life, went over in the same ship.

"I have heard that they were penned with the worst of the convicts, and suffered unimaginable tortures; but I never saw one of them; for, by the intercession of my uncle, the influence of the chaplain, the fact that I was the only female prisoner on board, and, I think, through the pity of the officers and their wives for my childish and harmless personality, I was treated with great kindness. I was taken out of the convict quarters of the ship and appointed to assist the stewardess in waiting on the officers' wives.

"When we reached Hobart Town, my dear grandfather stood upon the dock.

"I see him now as I saw him then—his tall, spare figure clothed in black, with a white necktie, his venerable head bare, his long, white hair waving in the wind, his broad-brimmed black hat held in his hand.

"I was allowed to land before the band of convicts did. The chaplain and one other detailed officer were my custodians.

"When we stepped on the wharf my grandfather me and took me in his arms and warmly embraced me.

"He had a carriage waiting. We four—my grandfather, the chaplain, the sergeant and myself—entered it, and were driven immediately to the residency, and ushered into the presence of the superintendent of convicts.

"There the necessary forms were gone through and the documents signed, and Margaret Campbell, life prisoner of the crown, was transferred to the guardianship of Theobald Elfinstar, Esq., as his 'assigned servant.'

"The chaplain and the sergeant then left us, and my grandfather put me in the carriage and directed the coachman to drive to the Royal Victoria.

"While we were on our way he opened a bundle, in which there was a large, handsome cloak, which he wrapped about me to hide my prison garb. Next he took from a box a hat and veil, which he gave me to put on my head.

"Then he told me that he had sailed from London two weeks after I did, and yet he had reached Hobart Town a month before I arrived, and had been busily engaged in overseeing the completion of our house, which was now habitable, if not finished.

"When the hack drew up before the Royal Victoria, my grandfather got out, paid the hackman first of all to get rid of him at once, and then hurried me, closely veiled as I was, into a private suite of apartments and rang and ordered breakfast.

"When we were alone he said to me:

"'Go into the adjoining room, my dear, where you will find clothing suitable for a young gentlewoman. Dress yourself in it. Then make up your present garb into a parcel. We will throw it away when we get out of town, as we will throw away the name of Margaret Campbell forever! You are no longer a Campbell, my dear! You are an Elfinstar in name as you certainly are in face. And you are not my grandchild, but you are my daughter, my dear Seraph, restored to me again. Go make your toilet, Seraph Elfinstar. You are now all my own; for I have plucked you out of the fire.'

"Was ever love like this? I asked myself again. I threw myself into his arms and burst into a flood of tears, and wept and kissed and embraced him until he gently led me to the door of my chamber and put me through it with a repetition of his words:

"'Go and make your toilet, Seraph Elfinstar.'

"I went in and closed the door behind me, and found myself in a clean, spacious, comfortable apartment, that seemed to me—after my prison and ship experiences of the last seven months—to combine every imaginable luxury—the greatest of which was the bathroom.

"I took a bath, and dressed myself in the black silk suit that had been provided for me, and added the little white linen collar and cuffs, and the blue silk necktie that came with it. Nothing had been forgotten, not even the white linen pocket handkerchiefs.

"I took one and passed into the parlor, where the table was already set and my grandfather was waiting for me.

"'Now, be at perfect peace, my love,' he said as we sat down to the table. 'No one in this house knows anything about you. The past is past. In a few minutes I expect my faithful servant, Jonas Stackpole, here with our private carriage, which he is to bring to meet his master and his master's daughter, who is just arrived from the old country.'

"I assured my grandfather that I was at perfect peace. Every state is relative to other states. After my terrible peril and suffering, and the intermediate sea voyage, sad enough, but ameliorated by kindness and by hope, I felt I had now reached a fair haven of rest. I was in a state of calm delight.

"My grandfather recognized this, and smiled with benignant pleasure.

"After breakfast he led me, closely veiled, out to the carriage, which was waiting for us before the door.

"The tallest, gauntest and reddest man I ever saw was seated on the box. He got down, touched his hat and opened the door for us.

"My grandfather put me in, followed me, and we were soon bowling along the New Town Road on our way to the Hermitage.

"How well I remember that delicious ride! After my long, long confinement, and longer sea voyage, that ride was life and joy to me; deep, calm joy, for I was not yet capable of jubilant exultation.

"But on that glorious morning the sun, which shone, flooding the azure heavens and the green earth, the waving forests, the undulating hills, the distant, towering mountains, whose opal-hued tips blended with the golden and ruby-tinted clouds along the horizon—the exhilarating fresh air, and even the rapid motion of our carriage, all combined to give me delight.

"After a few hours of this delicious drive we entered upon a very rough, new road leading into the wilderness of jagged rocks and thorny trees that surrounded the base of Mount Wellington, like the enchanted, impenetrable thicket of the fairy tale.

"'I had this road opened, but it is not yet completed,' said my grandfather, as the carriage was stopped for a moment, while Jonas Stackpole got down from his box and went to the horses' heads to lead them.

"In this manner we went on for a mile or two, winding up the mountain, until we came to a place beyond which we could go no farther in the carriage.

"Here several rude-looking men in yellow jackets were at work on the extension of the road, and they stopped work, leaning on their picks and shovels to gaze at us.

"Here, also, was a rough building of boards, for temporary use as stable, carriage and tool shed.

"We left the carriage and mounted saddled horses, that were waiting for us, and so we ascended by a bridle path that wound up the mountain, until we reached the plateau where stands the Hermitage, with which you are now so familiar.

"It was not then complete. The grounds were still half wilderness, and only the rooms on one side of the hall had been finished.

"But when the horses stopped at the main entrance the servants were all there waiting for us.

"My grandfather helped me to dismount, and led me up the stairs, saying to the domestics:

"'This young lady is my daughter, and your mistress.'

"The women courtesied and the men touched their hats as we passed by them and entered the house.

"My grandfather called a rosy-faced young girl to us, and said:

"'This is Jones, your lady's maid, my dear. Now, Jones, show your mistress to her own apartments. My dear, I ordered dinner at six.'

"I followed my new maid upstairs, and to an elegant suite of apartments that had been especially fitted up for me, and that outshone every place I had ever seen before in splendor and luxury.

"Such was my reception at the Mountain Hermitage.

"No one in the house knew any better than that I was Miss Elfinstar, the daughter of their master.

"They had never been in any manner interested in Margaret Campbell, and most likely they had never heard of her or of her imputed crime; or, if they did, they had passed it over and forgotten it in the multitude of more recent, if not more sensational, newspaper items.

"My life at the Mountain Hermitage has been calmly happy.

"My grandfather goes down to the residency once a month to make reports of his 'assigned servant,' Margaret.Campbell, life prisoner of the crown, and his reports are always so satisfactory as to the conduct of the girl that there are faint, distant hopes that he may obtain for her a conditional pardon, but never the slightest possibility that she will be allowed to return to her native country.

"Now you know why I may not ever marry.

"Go home to England, and take with you my life-long gratitude and affection.

"I do not ask you to forget me, but to remember me as one who has passed away from this earth. Think of me only as a spirit, and of the Mountain Hermitage as a home of the spirit world which you have seen in a dream.

Goodby. God bless you!"

"Think of her 'only as a spirit, and the Mountain Hermitage as a home of the spirit world seen in a dream!'" said Hamilton Gower to himself, as he folded the manuscript. "I shall do nothing of the sort! I have flesh and blood myself, and so has she, and we have half a century of material life on this planet yet to endure! No; it is a quixotic adventure to undertake, but I will do it! I will vindicate her fame, and restore her to the world!"

He fell into deeper thought.

"Let me see what I have to do: It is now March-the first day of March, really. In six months it will be the first of September—my birthday—when I shall be of age. Why—I have not got more than time to rally my witnesses and return to England to claim my inheritance!

"Ha! ha! ha! What an unpleasant shock my appearance will be to the worthy Mr. Lewis Manton, who stepped into my shoes, assumed my rank, and married my sweetheart! And what a sensation in the quiet village of Hawkeville! Ah!

"But I must look after my witnesses. To be sure, it would never do for me to go to Hawkewood and claim my rights unsupported by witnesses! The excellent Mr. Manton is quite capable of disputing my identity.

"Let me see. Delaplaine and Gow must accompany me to Hawkewood, or meet me there. They both promised to meet me at the Hall on the first of the next September. But that promise was given eighteen months ago, and may have been forgotten—at least by Delaplaine—for it is not likely to be so by Gow, from whom I parted only a few months ago.

"However, I must write to both. Gow, I know, is still at Dead Maiden's Brook. But where is Delaplaine-the dandy!—where is he? Ah! In the hair-dressing line of business in the Rue du Rivoli, Paris; but I have lost my memorandum and forgotten the number.

"But a letter will find the fellow, no doubt. I must write to him at once. The *Norfolk* is expected to touch here on her return voyage from Melbourne to London, to-day or to-morrow. I wish I were ready to return by the *Norfolk*; but I am not. I must see Seraph Elfinstar again, and have a final understanding with her. And I must notify Ham Gow. He must return with me by the *Labrador* a month hence."

As Mr. Hamilton Gower formed this resolution he went to his valise, unstrapped it, and took from it his writing case, which he laid upon the table, opened and arranged.

Then he sat down and wrote two letters. The first was directed as follows:

M. HENRI DELAPLAINE, *Barbièr et Coiffeur, Rue du Rivoli, Paris, France.*

The second one was addressed to:

MR. DUPLICATE HAWKE, *Gold Diggings, Dead Maiden Brook, Via Melbourne, Victoria.*

Having sealed these letters, he put them in his pocket, took his hat, and went out to post them.

This was Hamilton Gower's first walk through Hobart Town.

When he had first arrived in the city that morning he had been too deeply absorbed by the mystery of Seraph Elfinstar, and his curiosity and anxiety to read her manuscript and solve the enigma of her life in the wilderness, to feel the slightest interest in his surroundings.

Now, however, he stepped out upon the clean and well-kept street, flanked by its neat and tasteful dwellings, with the bright, blue waters of the Derwent flashing in the morning sunlight on his right, and the vivid, green-wooded hills, and the distant cloud-capped opal mountains on his left, his mind was penetrated and exhilarated by the beauty and brilliancy of nature surrounding this quaint little city of the Antipodes.

He did not know the way to the post office, but he meant to ask the first man he should meet.

"Good-morning, Mr. Gower. How do you do?"

This salutation came from Dr. Briggs, who suddenly joined him.

"Ah! good-morning, doctor. I am glad to meet you," returned the young man cordially.

"Fine morning. Glorious weather, this!"

"It is, indeed."

"When did you reach town?"

"Only this morning."

"I hope you left our friends at the Hermitage well?"

"Quite so."

"By George! a strange household, that!" remarked the doctor, as the two gentlemen walked on together.

Hamilton Gower said nothing.

"A very strange household," continued Briggs. "The idea of a man of his age coming out to this colony and spending a mine of money to build a palace on a mountain! Why, sir, the cost of building that house on Mount Wellington was at least ten times what it would have been to have built it on the banks of the Derwent, or on those of Sullivan's Cove, where the villas of our wealthiest colonists are located! Why, sir, the engineering of that mountain road leading up to the house cost a fortune, cheap as convict labor is!"

"I have no doubt of it," said Mr. Hamilton Gower, by way of saying something.

"Do you know what people say about it?" inquired the surgeon, looking up suddenly.

"No," replied Mr. Gower uneasily, for he feared that some suspicion or even knowledge of the identity of Margaret Campbell, the convict servant, and of Seraph Elfinstar, the daughter of the master of the Mountain Hermitage, had got abroad.

"They say that no man but a man whose eccentricities had reached the verge of insanity would have selected such a site for a home!" explained the doctor.

"Yet it is a beautiful home," replied Mr. Gower, with a sense of relief in discovering that no knowledge or suspicion of the truth had crept out.

"Oh, yes, a beautiful home in the wilderness; but no society, or possibility of society," growled the doctor.

"I do not think he wants society," ventured Mr. Gower.

"Maybe he does not; but the young lady, sir, his daughter. Do you not suppose that it is natural she should want society?"

"Oh, well, she may marry some day, and then she will get it."

"Marry? By Jove! I should like to know whom she could be likely to marry up there, unless, indeed—oh!" suddenly exclaimed the doctor, stopping short and staring at the young man by his side.

"Or, at least," said the latter with an embarrassed smile, "the old gentleman, who is turned three score and ten, may die very soon—

must die before very long, and then his daughter will be at liberty to leave the Hermitage. She will not grudge a few years of her early youth to him."

"A few years, quotha ? Why, if the man has only turned seventy, he may live ten, twenty, or even thirty years longer, until the young girl shall grow into an old woman. Which way are you going?" suddenly inquired the doctor, as they came to a crossing.

"To mail letters; but, really, I do not know but that I am going away from the post office! I meant to inquire, but your conversation interested me so much that I forgot to do so," replied the young man.

"Well, I am going there myself. It is around this corner."

The two gentlemen turned and walked to the post office together, mailed their letters and came out.

"Which way now?" inquired the doctor.

"Well, I hardly know where to go, or what to do with myself to-day," replied the young man frankly

"Quite so, and so much the better. Come home with me to a bachelor's early dinner, and afterward I will take you around and show you the town—the government offices, military barracks, convicts' barracks, county jail, female house of correction, prisoners' hospital—such is the enlivening program! Oh, I assure you, life at Hobart Town is a criminal drama and a penal panorama! You'll come?"

"Thank you! Willingly," replied the young man.

They turned into Macquarrie Street, the surgeon leading the way.

"Hello!" he exclaimed, "whom have we got here?"

CHAPTER IV
AN EMBARRASSING ENCOUNTER

A SLENDER young girl, dressed in black, was flying to meet them—a delicate, thin young girl, with a fair, thin face, large, light blue eyes, and pale, yellow hair. Her colorless countenance was radiant with surprise and delight as she flew on toward them, and—regardless of the presence of a third person—threw herself, sobbing for joy, into the arms of the astonished and horrified Mr. Hamilton Gower, and clung tightly around his neck.

"My good girl! my good girl!" remonstrated the young man, while the surgeon of convicts stood and laughed.

"Oh, my dear Ham! Oh, my darling Ham! Do I you at last!" cried the young woman, hugging for dear life.

"But, my good girl! Really, now, you know! Indeed now! Really, now!" cried Mr. Hamilton Gower, blushing furiously and trying gently to release himself from this overpowering and embarrassing embrace.

"Oh, Ham! Precious, precious love! I have come so far to see you! I have sailed so many thousands upon thousands of miles across the ocean, and was seasick, and got the quinsy among the icebergs, and was scared almost to death when Neptune came on board crossing the equator, you know—though he was nobody but the bo's'n, after all! And when I got here and couldn't find you—oh, Ham! But it is all over now, Ham, my darling! And I am so happy! so happy!" she exclaimed, with another bear's hug of her slender arms, to which excitement had lent unnatural strength.

"But, young woman! you are—you are—this is—this is—" cried Mr. Hamilton Gower, crimson with confusion, as he tried to unwind the clinging arms from about his neck, while the doctor stood and laughed silently.

But Lona Pond was deaf and blind to everything except the presence of her supposed betrothed, and she went on with her hysterical exclamations:

"Oh, Ham, dear, I was so disappointed when I first got here! I came with Mrs. Belle Isle, as lady's maid, you know! Mrs. Belle Isle, who was Miss Isoline Irvine, my own young mistress, and she married Lieut. Belle Isle and came out here with him, and brought me to wait on her; but I never would have come, dear Ham, if it had not been for your sake," she added, with a tighter rivet of her arms around his neck.

"Young woman, this is really and truly—" he began; but she went on without hearing him:

"Oh, I was so disappointed and heart-broken when I got here and couldn't find you, and when my mistress told me you must be three or four hundred miles away from me! Oh, Ham! I didn't know that, you see, or maybe I might not have had the courage to come out here ! Lord love you, dear Ham! I always had thought that Sydney and Melbourne and Hobberton, and all these outlandish Bottomy Bay places were close together, just like Hawkeville and Demondike and Bowling Green, and so on, at home in England."

"But see here!—I say! You are—"

But she only squeezed him tighter, and continued:

"Oh, Ham! you'd have pitied me if you'd seen how done for I was when I couldn't find you! Oh, I like to have died! My mistress could tell you! And once, Ham, I saw a convict in the chain gang working on the new road that I took for you—and that almost did for me too! Not that I believed that you had been guilty of any crime, dearest Ham! but, then, I knew that innocent people sometimes get convicted by the courts. And he was the very image of you, dear Ham!" she concluded, with another squeeze.

Mr. Hamilton Gower found that he could not release himself from those slender, clinging arms without hurting them, and so he ceased to struggle and resigned himself to the situation, while the surgeon stood laughing silently, and the girl continued her monologue:

"He was an awful man whom I mistook for you! Oh, I beg your pardon for mistaking him for you, dear Ham! But he was the very image of you! I—-Why don't you speak to me, Ham? You haven't— you don't seem to be glad to see me!" said Lona Pond, suddenly coming to her lover's irresponsive mood, as she withdrew her arms and looked at him.

He stood before her cold and calm, for he had now recovered his self-possession, notwithstanding the surgeon's irritating, silent laugh.

"No, indeed, you don't seem a bit glad to see me!" said Lona Pond, in mournful resentment.

"Who are you, young woman?" quietly asked Mr. Hamilton Gower.

"Who am I? Is that the way you speak to me, Ham Gow? Who am I, do you ask? You know very well who I am! I am Leonora Pond! your promised wife! and this is your engagement ring I wear upon my finger! Who am I, indeed! Oh! Oh! Oh, dear! Oh,dear!" she exclaimed, beginning to groan and wring her hands.

"Here is some huge mistake, and I think I understand it," murmured Mr. Hamilton Gower.

"I should think you might understand it! But the mistake was all mine in thinking you would be faithful, and loving you, loving you in your absence as if you were already my— Ah, me! Ah, me!" groaned the girl, wringing her hands.

"You are Leonora Pond, you say? Now, then, whom do you take me for?" he inquired.

"Whom do I take you for? That is a pretty question to ask me, Ham Gow. I don't take you for the King of France, nor yet for the Emperor of Russia. I take you for Ham Gow, of Hawkeville, as have been engaged to be married to me for three years and more. But I do suppose you have made your fortune in the gold mines and you are looking higher now! looking to marry a lady!" she added in bitter scorn.

"You take me for Ham Gow —"

"I know you are Ham Gow! What do you mean?" resentfully demanded the girl.

"You are utterly mistaken! My name is Hamilton Gower!"

The girl gazed at the speaker, and burst into a weak, contemptuous laugh, saying:

"Oh, indeed! Ham Gow wasn't a good enough name for the grand gentleman that made his fortune in the gold mines, so you must tack two or three more syllables on to it! Mr. Ham-ilton Gower. But," she said, with a sudden effort at self-assertion, "you needn't be afraid, Mr.Hamilton Gow-er! I do not mean to force myself on you! I'd die sooner than force myself on any man, even if he was my lawful, wedded husband! much less only my engaged one! I would have thrust both my hands into the fire before I would have put them around-before I would have touched you with them, if I had known that you had changed to me! Yes, I would! I would, and you know I would!" she passionately exclaimed, as she suddenly turned and walked away.

"But you are mistaken, my good girl! You are indeed! I am not Ham Gow, but I know who is, and I dare say he is as true as steel to everything he ever promised you! Come back and listen to reason!" said the young man, stepping quickly after her.

She turned fiercely upon him, drew the betrothal ring from her finger and threw it down on the ground, exclaiming:

"You want that back again, I suppose! Take it!" and walked swiftly away.

He stopped and picked up the ring and put it in his vest pocket to keep it from being lost, and then he would have followed her; but the street was no longer private—a group of officers coming out of the barracks walked slowly down it.

The young man retreated and rejoined the surgeon, who was still noislessly laughing.

"What amuses you so much, I should like to know?" inquired the former gravely.

"Oh, Mr. Gower! Mr. Gower!" exclaimed the surgeon, shaking his head.

"Do you really think that I knew anything about that young woman?" resentfully demanded the young man.

"She thought so " replied. the surgeon, with his silent laugh.

"She was mistaken," said the first speaker.

"Oh, now, come, come! Come, come, my young friend; I am a graybeard and—a physician!"

"What in the deuce has that got to do with it?"

"I know that young men will be young men! I don't expect them to be saints and angels! Mrs. Belle Isle's little maid really is a pretty creature! Only it is a pity—only it is a pity that she should have taken any nonsense you may have talked to her in such dead earnest as to have followed you out here—by Jove!" laughed the surgeon.

"I never saw that girl in the whole course of my life until to-day! I never talked 'nonsense,' as you call it, to any girl at any time! and I never will!" exclaimed Mr. Hamilton Gower, flushing with honest resentment.

"Eh!" cried the surgeon, struck at last by his earnestness, and stopping and staring at him.

"I am serious," said the young man.

"I see you are, and I believe you, of course! but how in the mischief came that young person to make such an absurd mistake?" inquired the doctor.

"She mistook me for another man to whom I bear a wonderful resemblance. I know the man she mistook me for! I have known him from my boyhood. And we came from the same neighborhood, Hawkewood, in Cornwall, England! I could have explained to that young woman—if she would have stopped to hear me-that her lover was probably faithful and that he would be here to answer for himself in about a month from this; but you saw that she would not listen to reason!"

"Ha, ha, ha! No! she was too much confirmed in her belief that you were her recreant lover! Very awkward for you! I don't think anything would convince her of the truth but the visible presence of Ham Gow at your side and before her face!"

"Perhaps not! Well, the poor girl can have that evidence in a few weeks, if she does not choose to receive any other testimony sooner," said Mr. Hamilton Gower.

"Here we are at my quarters! Come in," said the doc- tor, leading the way into a small house adjoining the prisoners' barracks.

About the same hour Mrs. Belle Isle was sitting alone in her parlor, when the door opened and her maid entered and dropped down at her feet in great agitation.

"What is the matter, Lona?" inquired the lady.

"Oh, madam, it is all over! all over!" cried the girl, bursting into tears and weeping wildly.

"What is all over? What do you mean, Lona?"

"Oh, madam, it is all over between me and Ham Gow! He has made his fortune in the gold mines, and he has turned against me! I know just how it is! He is rich and he wants to marry rich! and so he is false to me!" wildly wept the girl.

"I do not believe it, Lona. What makes you think so?" inquired the lady.

"Oh, madam, I would never have believed it of him either, if I had not heard it out of his own lips!"

"Have you seen him, then?" demanded Mrs. Belle Isle, in surprise.

"Oh, yes, madam! He is in the colony! He is in the town!"

"Where did you see him?"

"On Macquarrie Road, as I was coming home with the Berlin wool yarn you sent me to buy for you. He was walking with another gentleman. I think it was the surgeon of convicts, and I spoke to him. Oh! I was so overjoyed, so crazy with delight when I saw him, that I'm afraid—I'm afraid I behaved very improper! But he denied that he was Ham Gow, and he pretended that he did not know me! Oh! Oh! Oh, dear me! Oh, dear me!" cried Lona, bursting again into a passion of tears.

"Try to be calm, my poor girl; and try to think now whether you are quite, quite sure that this man was Ham Gow," said her mistress kindly.

"Oh, madam! Oh, madam! as if it was possible for me to be mistaken in my own Ham Gow!" exclaimed the girl. Then dropping her voice, she moaned: "My own Ham Gow! Ah, me! Ah, me! My own Ham Gow no longer! Never again! Never again!"

"You were mistaken once, you remember, Lona, when you mistook a convict in the chain gang on the public road for your betrothed," said the lady.

"'Oh, my dear ma'am; but that was such a different thing!" said Lona Pond illogically. "That man was a convict, and couldn't have been Ham Gow at all; and this man looks respectable, and certainly is Ham Gow."

"But you thought at the time that Hice was Ham Gow."

"Yes, ma'am; but Hice wasn't, you know, because it was proved that he wasn't. But this man is. I know he is," replied Lona, with stupid persistency.

"My poor girl, you are probably as much mistaken in this instance as you were in that. You are unsound on the subject of your lover. You have mistaken some other man for Gow. Really, Lona, you must not go about the town laying claim to every man who happens to bear some resemblance to Gow! Consider, child, that Gow would never have denied his own identity, or his knowledge of you. I could never believe that of him."

"Nor could I ever have believed it of him if my own ears had not heard his own lips speak it!" sobbed the girl.

"Mr. Belle Isle shall find out if Gow is in town, if that will satisfy you," said the young matron, who seemed really at a loss how to comfort the "foolish virgin" at her feet.

"Oh, ma'am, he is in town, fast enough; there is no doubt about that! But I won't distress you any more with my going on, ma'am. You are very good to me, anyway—much better than I deserve," said Lona at length, rising and wiping her eyes as she left the room.

Later in the day, as Mrs. Belle Isle sat alone in her parlor, an orderly entered with two cards on a waiter.

Mrs. Belle Isle took them, and read in succession:

"George Briggs, M.D."

"Mr. Hamilton Gower."

"Show these gentlemen in," said the lady.

The orderly saluted and threw open the door, and Dr. Briggs and Mr. Hamilton Gower entered the room.

Mrs. Belle Isle arose to receive them.

"Good-morning, madam! I have taken the liberty of an intimate friend to bring you a visitor—a forlorn young man just arrived, a stranger in the town—Mr. Hamilton Gower—of—Cornwall, England—Mrs. Belle Isle," said the surgeon, presenting his companion in an offhand manner.

"I am glad to see you, Mr. Gower. Doctor, you have had a pleasant day for your usual walk," said the lady, as the two callers seated themselves, and she resumed her place on the sofa.

"Yes; and a rather amusing adventure—of which more presently. You have been out to-day?"

"No, I have been lazy and remained indoors, and there-fore 'I have lost a day,' as some sage or hero said, long ago, when he had missed doing a good deed," said Mrs. Belle Isle with a smile.

"I have been doing good deeds, then, and have not lost a day! I think I have made two in one! After getting through with my patients, I fell in with Mr. Gower, here, wandering about like the Wandering Jew, and I took him under my protection and have been showing him around our town—into the cheerful and exhilarating jails, hospitals, convict barracks and so on."

"Ah!—and what do you think of it all, Mr. Gower ?" inquired the lady, turning to her younger visitor.

"I think of it, madam," said the young man with a thoughtful smile—"under your ticket-of-leave system—very much as some people think of purgatory, with this difference, that its convicts are quite as likely to sink down into utter perdition as to rise into the comparative heaven of honesty and respectability."

"That is but too true," assented the surgeon. Then addressing his hostess, he said, quite suddenly: "Speaking of convicts, ma'am, you remember that desperate fellow Hice, in whom Mr. Belle Isle showed so much interest at one time?"

"Oh, yes! It was because—because my maid, poor girl, saw him in the chain gang on the new road, and imagined that she recognized in him an old acquaintance of hers," replied the lady, speaking with some hesitation.

"He afterward bolted, you know."

"Yes, I know; and he threw the whole community of women here in such a state of terror by his outbreak that not one of us would dare to take a walk or ride beyond the limits of the town."

"Ah! he was not half as black as he was painted! He is gone, poor fellow, to render his account to the only just Judge! Did you hear the particulars of his capture and his death?"

"No; I only heard that he had been taken and, dangerously wounded, and lately that he had died at the Mountain Hermitage."

"Our young friend here was his captor," said the surgeon, turning with a smile to Mr. Gower.

"Ah, indeed!" exclaimed the lady, glancing at the young man with a new interest.

"Yes! it is rather a queer story altogether. Shall I tell you about it ?"

"Yes, if you please; I should like to hear it."

"That boy, there, is the hero of the adventure, you know—by the way, he is rather in that line of business, I think. He had a notable one this morning; but more about that presently. Now I am going to tell you a moving tale about his rescue of a beautiful young lady from the hands of a brutal ruffian in the wilderness, at the foot of Mount Wellington!"

"Doctor, I beg you to spare me," laughed the young man.

"I am going to do so, my dear fellow! I am going to spare you and to laud you," persisted the surgeon.

And he told the whole story of Hamilton Gower's adventure in the wilderness, including the rescue of Seraph Elfinstar, the capture of John Hice, and all that followed, ending with the recovery of the wounded convict and his assignment, through the intercession of the chaplain, to the private service of the master of the Hermitage, and his subsequent sudden death from congestion of the brain.

"Poor soul! I am glad he had a few weeks of peace at the last, and a quiet death in a Christian house," said Mrs. Belle Isle with a sigh.

"And such was the end of the man your maid raised such a coil about because she took him to be an old neighbor from her native village! But tell me, madam, is this girl rather"—the doctor touched his forehead significantly—"on the subject of this old neighbor of hers?"

"I fear so," admitted the lady.

"Rather given to imagine this, that and the other man to be the old neighbor in question?"

"I think so; but why do you ask?"

"Because this morning she met us on Macquarrie Street and suddenly threw herself into the arms of this young man, to his amazement and my entertainment," laughed the doctor.

"How shocking! She told me of it. She took him to be Ham Gow. She still believes him to be so," replied Mrs. Belle Isle.

"Oh, she told you! Well, she made quite a scene. Fortunately, at that time there was not a soul on the street but ourselves—at least there was no one in sight or hearing. Gower could not convince the girl that he was not her own recreant lover, and she overwhelmed him, first with caresses and afterward with reproaches. Finally she left him in bitter anger."

"I know. I am very sorry, Mr. Gower, that you should have been so annoyed," said the lady, turning with a vivid blush toward the young man.

"Oh! I beg you will not disturb yourself, dear madam. The incident was rather comic than otherwise, and as soon as I discovered the precise nature of her misapprehension I could have explained it to her and satisfied her; but she would not stay to listen."

"Flung Ham Gow's engagement ring at the feet of Mr. Gower and fled away in a fury!" added the doctor.

"We could not but feel some compassion for the young woman in the midst of all our amusement, and also some responsibility for my resemblance to her lover, and some obligation to give her satisfaction."

"That's why I dragged him here. He said he should be intruding, but I made him come," put in the doctor.

"And I am very glad to have made your acquaintance, Mr. Gower," added his hostess kindly.

"Thank you, madam. On my own part I am very grateful to the circumstance that gives the privilege and pleasure of knowing you," responded the guest with a bow.

"And what my amiable young friend wishes further to say is this— that he knows this Ham Gow, who is his personal double; that this is not the first, nor the second, nor the third time that they have been mistaken for each other, though let me add, on my own account, one is a gentleman and the other is—not," explained the doctor.

"This Gow, however, was the favorite playmate of my childhood, and the companion of my boyhood. He is the betrothed husband, as I know from his own telling of this girl. He is in Victoria at present, but I expect him here within the month, for we are to return to England in company by the *Labrador*, and I think, from what I know of him, that when he finds his betrothed here he will wish to marry and take her with him. This is just what I wanted to explain to the girl if she had given me an opportunity," concluded Mr. Gower.

"And it would be kind of you, ma'am, to let this poor fool know how the case stands. It would save her from breaking her heart, or cracking her brain, and it might save Mr. Gower from being assaulted or embraced in the public streets," laughed the surgeon.

"I will tell her," said Mrs. Belle Isle.

Then the two gentlemen said good-by and went their way.

CHAPTER V
AT THE GOLD DIGGINGS

DEAD MAIDEN'S BROOK had changed very much since the first great "rush" to its newly discovered gold fields.

Then it was but an extensive, disorderly encampment along the banks of the gully in the deep ravine through which it ran.

Now the scene presented every appearance of a prosperous settlement—a new, strange town such as may only be found in the Australian gold fields—a town of only one street, if street it could be called, where a loosely strung chain of dwelling houses, shops and taverns ran along for miles, on the east and west side of the gully, facing each other across it, and having the mountains at their backs.

These houses presented the most novel and curious aspect, being constructed of the most unusual and various material—some of cedar logs set upright like palisades, some of bark nailed on a framework of wood, and some of canvas-lined green baize or red cloth.

They were nearly all roofed with bark, or canvas, and lighted by one or more glazed windows.

Behind many of these houses were gardens where cabbages and potatoes and other common table vegetables were raised, and tended by the women and children.

Here and there was also a cow to be seen under a shed; but that was a luxury.

And the shafts, windlasses, pans and cradles of the diggers were to be seen everywhere—between the houses, along the banks of the gully, behind the houses, under the mountains, before the houses of the gully, and scattered up and down through the great ravine as far as the eye could reach in any direction.

The two principal hotels were—the "Queen's," on the north end of the east bank, and the "Prince of Wales," at the south end of the west bank. These were good-sized, well constructed frame buildings.

Besides these there were several other smaller and less reputable public houses, and more than a dozen "all sorts" stores, where everything, or a little of everything, was sold, from an ounce of tea to a pound of Epsom salts, and from a straw hat to a canvas tent.

There was also a post office, and a weekly mail from Melbourne.

Our friends, the numerous Joneses, had greatly prospered, some of them still engaged in working out the inexhaustible treasures of their first lucky leads, some engaged in the almost equally lucrative trade of the town, and one, the head of that fortunate tribe, enjoying himself in literally "taking his ease in his inn" as landlord of the Queen's, with a good staff of assistants in his own sons and daughters to take all the hard work off his hands.

Mr. Duplicate Hawke had also prospered in the beginning of his gold digging.

To sum up his fortune briefly, the first nine months had brought him very nearly ten thousand pounds.

But after that his luck declined. His "lead" yielded less and less, until at length it was worked entirely out.

He sunk other shafts, but found little or no gold. He was still persevering, however, under discouragement and a growing homesickness.

He had a little room on the second floor under the roof of his friend, Mr. Jones, the landlord of the Queen's.

There he slept and took breakfast and supper; but he spent his day beside his shaft, where his partner had a hut, and where they took "turn and turn about" working at the windlass, or digging at the bottom; but as yet they had raised nothing from this shaft but "dirt."

One afternoon he returned to his lodgings much earlier, and in a much more despondent mood than usual.

After supper he sat smoking a pipe with the landlord, on a bench in front of the house.

Before them yawned the great, deep gully that formed the bed of the low brook.

Across the gully was the row of cedar post, bark or canvas houses.

At this hour the street was quiet but for an occasional miner sauntering home to his supper.

The young man sighed.

"Give it up, lad!" said the landlord of the Queen's—"give it up! Luck has turned! And when luck has once turned, be it for good or for bad, it seldom or never turns back again! Give it up! Invest your money in some safe business. Take the place of barkeeper here. My boy has a mind to set up for himself, on the 'all sorts' line, and is only waiting for me to get a good substitute before he starts off."

"Want to go home," murmured Mr. Duplicate Hawke, almost unconsciously.

"Oh, you do! What for? You could not invest your capital to one hundredth part of the advantage at home as you can here. Don't you know that?"

"Yes—want to go home," muttered the young man demurely.

"Left a sweetheart there, maybe?"

"Yes—want to go home."

"Well, why in the deuce don't you go, my boy? You are able to afford it now. You must be worth about ten thousand pounds! Go home and marry your sweetheart and bring her out here with you, if you want to become a millionaire, or stay there with her if you decide to content yourself with a modest competency. Do anything rather than stay here and mope, mope, mope, until you are likely to be going mad instead of going home!" exclaimed Mr. Jones of the Queen's.

"How willingly, how gladly, would I have gone long before this, if it had been possible; but I cannot go," the young man mournfully replied.

"Can't go? I should like to know why; you are rich enough, as I said before."

"But for all that I cannot go back to England," sighed Mr. Duplicate Hawke.

"Whe-e-e-ew! Is that it?" said Jones, with a long whistle and a troubled look.

"No! that is not it!" energetically responded the young man. "It is not what you think! I never committed a crime in all my life! I—I might almost say I never did a wrong act in my life!"

"You can say a great deal more than most sinners, or saints either, for that matter, if you can say that; and really you look as if it might be true," replied the landlord.

"Look here, Mr. Jones, I don't consider myself worthy to be called a Christian! No, I don't, when I read my Bible and see what the life and example of the Divine Founder of Christianity was! But I'll tell you this: when parson was reading over the Commandments at morning service in your parlor last Sunday morning, I couldn't help feeling that I had kept them all 'from my youth up'—except the one about keeping holy the Sabbath day; but I have been loose in that respect—not going to church as I ought to have done. But as to my positive wrongdoing—no, Mr. Jones! no! your first opinion of me was the true one; I am not unworthy of your confidence."

"I know it, lad! I know it! I did but waver one second when you said that you could not go back to England! But why, now, if you will satisfy a good friend—why can you not go back to England?" affectionately inquired the landlord.

"I would tell you, if the secret was only my own, but it is not; however, my exile is not a lifelong one; but I cannot show myself in England, or even in any civilized part of these colonies, before the first of next September," said the young man.

"Ah! I begin to see! You are kept out of the way of being a witness in some case in which some one doesn't want you to testify."

"No, that is not the case. That would be wrong, and I told you that I had done no wrong."

"Well, then, I give it up."

"And you believe in me?"

"Yes, I believe in you, chap! But see here! If it will be safe for you to appear in England on the first of September, you have not more than just time to get there if you start now!"

"I know that, but I cannot go until I hear from a friend of mine who is out here in the colonies. By George! You are so confiding that I feel just as if I ought to give you an inkling of how the case stands!" suddenly exclaimed Mr. Duplicate Hawke.

"That is just as you please, lad " heartily responded Mr. Jones, though it was easy to see that he was full of curiosity.

"I will, then! It can do no harm, now and here. I will just give you an idea. Well, you see, there was a young nobleman who was left an orphan in his childhood to the care of a crabbed, narrow-minded, tyrannical old tutor, who made his life a burden that grew heavier and heavier year after year, until the youth got to be about nineteen years of age, and had but two years more of that bondage to bear; but he felt that he could not endure it any longer. So he planned to gather up all his money and jewels, and cut and run for the uttermost parts of the earth, and stay two years, and then return home only when he should be of age and could defy his tutor. That young nobleman is now in these colonies, and he will be of age on the first of next September."

"Oh! Oh, ho! I see! I perceive! I understand!" exclaimed the landlord of the Queen's, beaming radiantly. "You are the young nobleman in question, my lord! I beg your pardon for not recognizing your lordship's dignity at once, as I should have done intuitively if I had not been one of the stupidest of men!"

Mr. Duplicate Hawke burst into a peal of laughter, and when it had subsided said:

"Mistaken again! Did I not tell you that I had never in my life done a wrong act?"

"Yes, my lord; your lordship did."

"And was it not very wrong in the young nobleman to run away from his tutor?"

"Ah—hum—ha—I do not know, my lord. Your lordship is the best judge," replied the landlord of the Queen's, in a noncommittal manner.

"Well, then, I judge that it was very wrong in a young nobleman to run away from his tutor; and as I insist that I never did any wrong, consequently I was not the young nobleman who ran away from his tutor."

"I beg your lordship's pardon," said Jones of the Queen's, in some little confusion.

"Nor am I a lordship, either. Come to your wits, my friend, and understand that I am no more nor better than the honest fortune-hunter you have hitherto known me to be."

"Yes, sir," said the landlord, a little, but a very little, resentfully. "And that being so, what has the young nobleman's tantrums—which I must say are very unbecoming of any young man, not to say a young nobleman—to do with your exile to foreign countries until the first of next September?"

"Only this—that having been in his lordship's confidence, and having been the last person known to be with him before his disappearance, and having a net of circumstantial evidence thrown around me, I was accused of this young nobleman's murder, and if I had not fled for my life I should, doubtless, long ago have been hung for it."

"Whe-e-e-w! Couldn't you have told people that he had run away?"

"Oh, yes; I could have told them that, easy enough, but they would not have believed me, and I could not have proved the fact, and so I should have been hung, all the same. So I thought it best to follow the example of my lord, and cut and run. We are both in the colonies now."

"Seen him since you have been out here?"

"Oh, yes. Do you remember the man we picked up at the other side of the mountain the day before we reached these diggings?"

"And you introduced as your brother?"

"Yes; and I guess I didn't tell a story that time. I guess he was my brother, by a gypsy marriage; at least I have been told so," laughed Mr. Duplicate Hawke.

"I remember him. And he was the absconding young scamp, was he?"

"He was the absconding young scamp. I say-it was very wrong in a young nobleman to run away from his tutor, was it not?"

"Oh, very wrong! Quite unpardonable! And to get an honest lad like you into such a mess, too! Now, what are you going to do about it?"

"Wait here until I get a letter from him fixing the day of our embarkation for England; for by our latest arrangement we are to return home together—he to claim his inheritance, on his majority; I—who have been in his secrets from the first—to prove his identity in case the man who, since his supposed death, has held his title and estates, should attempt to dispute it. And when I show them the young nobleman alive and well I hope they will stop calling me a murderer, and wanting to hang me."

"But, now, suppose this young lord should not write to you? Suppose something should have happened to him—that he should have perished in the bush, or have been killed by the blacks? What would you do in that case?" inquired Mr. Jones.

"I should have to stay here for the rest of my natural life, I suppose."

"And give up your sweetheart?"

"And give up my sweetheart."

"That would be blamed hard."

"Yes, it would be hard; but I hope it will not happen to me. It is true, I have not heard from my lord for the last two months; but then he was going to Van Dieman's Land, which would account for my getting no letters."

"There'll be a mail in to-night. Perhaps you may get a letter."

"Perhaps I may; but there is no special reason why I should," said the young man in a despondent tone.

But he did get a letter that very evening.

Half an hour later the mail wagon came running into the town, and past the Queen's, on its way to the post office.

In another moment the whole street, and that means the whole town, was alive.

Men, women and children whirled out of the houses on both sides of the gully, and surged up in the rear of the wagon on its way to the post office.

Many of the impatient people did not wait for the opening of the mails, but eagerly questioned the driver.

"Has there been a ship in from the ould country, Mick, boy?" was the question put with but little variation from more than a dozen different persons.

"Ay, sure! The *Labrador* is in, with mails from England and likewise from Hobbyton! My bag be nigh bursting wi' 'em!" was the satisfactory answer that put new life and lightness into the hearts and feet of the anxious crowd.

Mr. Duplicate Hawke and Jones of the Queen were by no means the hindmost in the rush. They pushed their way to the front, though once or twice they were very nearly being forced over the bank and down into the gully.

Being. the most impetuous of the crowd, they were the first to push themselves into the post office, and the first, when the mail was opened, to get their letters.

The landlord of the Queen's hurried home, happy in the possession of a joint letter from his own and his wife's mother, and a bundle of London and Penzance newspapers.

Mr. Duplicate Hawke hastened after him, equally well pleased with the solitary epistle postmarked Hobart Town, and directed in the familiar hand of Mr. Hamilton Gower.

On reaching the inn he hurried to his little room on the second floor, lighted his tallow candle, placed it in the neck of an empty bottle on his little table, and sat down to read his letter, which was this:

"ROYAL VICTORIA HOTEL, HOBART TOWN,
"March 1, 18-. "DEAR Gow:

If I have not written to you for some time past it has been because I had rambled out of the reach of mail routes.

"I arrived in this city only this morning.

"I write this letter for the *Labrador*, which arrived here yesterday morning from London, and will sail for Melbourne with the first tide to-morrow morning.

"I suppose she will remain at Melbourne for a few weeks.

"She will touch here again on her homeward-bound voyage.

"Now, Ham, it is high time that you and I were on our way to England. If you can possibly make your arrangements to do so, I beg that you will leave Melbourne by the *Labrador*, and I will join you on board from this port, and we will return home together.

"If you should be at any pecuniary loss, dear friend, you know that I will make it up to you, as in common justice I should be bound to do; for your company on the voyage home, and your support when I shall present myself as one risen from the dead to claim an inheritance, will be all important and most valuable to me.

"You need not feel the slightest uneasiness in the prospect of presenting yourself here under your real name. You will not be arrested for the murder of the late Earl of Hawkewood. Not—mind you—because it has been discovered that he never was murdered at all, for no such discovery has yet been made; but because an unfortunate convict, one John Hice, being dangerously wounded, and believing himself to be near death, made a full confession of his crimes, acknowledging, among the rest, the murder of the Earl of Hawkewood, which homicide, he said, lay heavier on his soul than all his other sins, though he never meant to kill the earl, but only to strike him a stunning blow in self-defense.

"(I so entirely believed that statement to be true that I afterward asked and obtained the privilege of a private interview with the convict, in which I explained to him that he had never had the opportunity of killing the young earl, either intentionally or otherwise, and that he had only stunned another man with a harder head, when he had intended to stun the earl. My explanation, when I had convinced him of its truth, made the poor wretch positively happy. He is gone now, but not from the effect of his wounds, thank Heaven! However, this is aside from the purport of my letter.)

"The confession of Hice, duly taken. down in writing from his lips, signed, witnessed and attested, is on record, and fully exonerates you from the charge of murder. You can come to Hobart Town a free man, under your own name.

"Whether I shall assume mine before I reach England I have not yet decided. But I will, for once, indulge myself in the luxury of signing it here as

"Your true friend, HAWKEWOOD.

"P. S.—I have written to Delaplaine at Paris, to remind him to keep tryst on the first of next September, at Hawke Hall. H."

"Well, well, well, well," slowly ruminated Mr. Duplicate Hawke, or Ham Gow, as we may as well call him, now that the ban is taken off from his name. "What a letter! Here is food enough for thought to keep me awake all night. My unknown assailant discovered in a Tasmanian convict! Blest if I did not always believe it to have been that fellow Lewis Manton who tried to murder the earl to succeed to his estates!—I am blest if I didn't!—and now it has turned out to be an ordinary sneak thief that dealt me that stunning blow! Well, his confession is on record, and I am cleared. Ah, I am glad to know that!

"By Jove!" he exclaimed with a laugh, as a new aspect of the case struck his sense of humor. "It was I myself who was assassinated and half murdered, and as if that were not 'enough for the monkey,' it was I myself who was charged and all but hanged for that same assassination and supposed murder! Now I wonder if the like of that ever happened to mortal man before!

"Life's a conundrum, and I give it up!

"Well! We will keep the tryst at Hawke Hall on the first of September, and have some fun there! But how about the good Mr. Delaplaine? My lord says that he has written to him to join us at Hawke Hall. Good gracious! Has my lord forgotten that Mr. Delaplaine was accused with me of being an accomplice in his murder, and that therefore the worthy Mr. Delaplaine never could have carried out his purpose of buying that little business? My lord has forgotten that the excellent Mr. Delaplaine must be in hiding somewhere, and unless the valet, or himself, should remember the tryst to keep it at all risks, my lord must, do without his support. Well—I think we can do without it. And now to make glad the heart of my kind host, who will rejoice with me at this speedy prospect of happiness," said Ham Gow, as he blew out his candle and went downstairs in search of the landlord.

All the quietness that had prevailed throughout the hotel during the day was at an end now. The taproom and the parlor were as full as they could be with the miners, who were drinking, smoking, playing cards, singing songs, reading the newspapers that had come by the *Labrador*, or exchanging private intelligence that had reached them in letters by the same ship.

The landlord was not among them; but the landlord's son, young George Jones, who was tending bar, called out to the newcomer, saying:

"If you wish to see father, Mr. Hawke, he is sitting with mother in her little back parlor, and he will like to see you, I know."

"Thank you, George, we'll find him," replied Ham Gow, as, glad to escape from the noisy scene, he passed through the crowded taproom and public parlor to the little apartment in the rear, to which the landlord retreated when he wished to enjoy a quiet hour with his family.

He found Mr. and Mrs. Jones seated at a small, round table in the middle of the room, with its top covered with letters, pamphlets and newspapers.

The faces of the man and the woman were beaming with happiness.

They both looked up at the same moment, and welcomed him with smiles.

"It is easy to see that you have received good news—so easy that I congratulate you before knowing what it is," said the young man, with a responsive smile.

"Oh, yes, lad; thank you kindly; the very best of news! Draw a chair up to the table here with us, and listen to it. You'd hardly believe it, but the two old lasses are really coming out to us!" exclaimed Mr. Jones, with tears of joy in his honest blue eyes.

"The two old lasses?" repeated Ham Gow in some perplexity, as he made himself comfortable by sitting down and leaning his arms upon the table.

"Oh, ay! Her mother and mine! Our fathers have gone to their rest. Our mothers are widows; but they have always been fast friends, living near each other in Market Street, Penzance. It was our mothers' close friendship that brought Jane and me together in one of the happiest marriages—though I say it—that ever was made! And now the two old folks are coming out to us to complete our happiness—as why should they not, when they have neither kith nor kin in the old country to keep them there?"

"It must be a great undertaking for them, however," said Ham Gow bluntly.

"Not a bit of an undertaking for them! Lord love you, lad! they are two hale old girls, a trifle rising sixty, and have been at sea the best half of their lives—having both been stewardesses on the coasting steamers until they had saved money enough to set up shop—my mother kept a thread and needle shop, and hers a pastrycook's."

"I am glad that they are coming out to you, then."

"Thank you, lad. So are we. They are coming by the *Golden Path*, that will be due here in about a month from this. So, you see, they are on the ocean, and three-quarters through their voyage, even now."

"As near as you can calculate, keeping in mind the great uncertainty of the time made by these sailing ships," put in Mrs. Jones.

"Ay, Jenny, and that is true, too. But I declare that you and I must go to Melbourne by the first of the month, and stay there until the ship does come, if we have to stay for months. It would never do for the old lasses to arrive and we not be on hand to meet 'em."

"But the house—the business? Hadn't one of us better stay here to look after things, and the other go to meet the old folks?" suggested Mrs. Jones.

"No, Jenny, lass, no! Let our boys and girls run the house for a while, or let it run itself, or let it stand still—I don't care! But your good mother shall not miss seeing you when she first sets foot in this strange land; and I'll be doggoned if my dear old mammy shall miss seeing my face among the foremost on the wharf; so that is settled."

"When will we go?" inquired Mrs. Jones.

"A fortnight from this will be time enough for us to start," said Mr. Jones.

And then turning to his guest, he said:

"Now we have been talking so much about our own affairs that I have forgotten to think about yours, Mr. Hawke. You were anxiously looking for news from Hobby Town. I hope you got it, and that it is good."

"Thank you. I got it, and it is good," answered Ham Gow with a cordial smile.

"And you go back to the old country soon?"

"Yes, as soon as possible. I shall leave this place by the mailwagon that starts at daylight to-morrow morning for Melbourne, and I shall take passage in the *Labrador* for London. She will stop at Hobart Town, as usual, and there my friend will join me, and we will go to England together."

"That will be very fine for you and your mate. But it is quite a sudden blow to us. I'm blest, if it wasn't for the thought of having the two old gals over so soon, I'd feel quite knocked over at the loss of you, lad!" said Mr. Jones.

"I do thank you for feeling so much interest in such a vagabond as I am! But I do not think you will lose me altogether. "I think I shall come back here—that is-is—is"

If the 'girl you left behind you' consents to emigrate, eh?" put in the landlord of the Queen's, with a wink.

"Just so," frankly admitted Ham Gow. "If she will come out with me I shall return, and I don't see why she shouldn't do so, for she has really no one belonging to her in the old country except a crabbed stepmother whom she will be glad to get away from. And now, my friends, I must leave you for the present. I have got a great deal to do to-night. I must go back to my claim and make some arrangement with my partner, Traverse, and get my pile and pack my valise."

"I should think you would have a great deal to do to get ready on so short a notice," said Mrs. Jones.

"And so I will bid you good-night," added Ham Gow rising.

"We will see you again to-morrow morning," said Mr. Jones kindly, rising and holding out his hand, which Ham Gow took and pressed.

"And you shall have a good, hot, comforting breakfast before you start, be it ever so early," said Mrs. Jones.as she pushed her plump fingers into the hand of the young man, who clasped them warmly.

"And now get along with you, lad, for the night is passing, and seeing as you have so much to do, it would not be kind in us to keep you," said Mr. Jones, with practical good sense.

Ham Gow laughed and left the room, and quickly made tracks for the claim over which his partner, George Traverse, kept the night watch.

This claim was situated at the base of the mountains, about a mile north of the Queen's Hotel, and there was no other claim very near it.

There was no moon, and the sky was clouded over so that when Ham Gow had left the lighted houses behind him his way was very dark; but the low, distant light in the hut, like a glowworm on the ground, was a beacon to guide his steps.

He found George Traverse seated in the door of the hut, smoking a pipe, and not at all startled by the sudden announcement that his senior partner was going to leave by the mail wagon for Melbourne the next morning; such impulsive departures were too common in the mines.

The arrangements for the dissolution of partnership were of the simplest kind. Ham Gow was to take his clothing and his "pile," and leave George Traverse in possession of the hut, the claim and the tools.

He spent the night with Traverse, who walked back with him to the Queen's the next morning to see him off by the mail wagon.

The landlady of the Queen's kept her promise and had ready the good, hot, comforting breakfast, in which George Traverse joined Ham Gow.

At daybreak the mail wagon was ready to start, and Gow, after taking an affectionate leave of his partner, of the Joneses and of all friends and neighbors who were astir at that early hour, mounted to his seat, and waving a final adieu to all, started for Melbourne.

He reached that city in the highest health and spirits, had time enough there to purchase a comfortable outfit for his long sea voyage, and a week later he sailed in the *Labrador* for Hobart Town and London.

CHAPTER VI
THE LOVERS

"HAM GOW will answer that letter in person, if I know the fellow " said Mr. Hamilton Gower, as he went home to his hotel that night, after having spent the day in sight-seeing and the evening at the barracks. "In fact, he will have to answer it in person and come with the first mail, that leaves the diggings if he wants to be in time to secure his passage in the *Labrador*. He will be here in two or three weeks, and I must be ready to join him. To-morrow I will go and have an understanding with the Elfinstars,"' he concluded, as he composed himself to sleep.

Early the next morning, in accordance with his resolution, he arose, ordered his horse, took his breakfast in a hurry, threw himself into his saddle and started for the Mountain Hermitage.

It was but seven o'clock when he cantered briskly out upon the New Road, where the chain gang of convicts, in their yellow jackets and ferocious or despondent aspect, were already at work under their drivers and guards.

He rode rapidly past these with sinking spirits, until he got out of sight and hearing of them and into the solitude and freshness of the green and dewy country, where he breathed more freely.

It was but nine o'clock when he reached the base of the mountain and began to wind up it by that wonderful road engineered by Mr. Elfinstar's enterprise and the convict labor.

It was ten o'clock when he reached the plateau on which the beautiful house and grounds of the Mountain Hermitage were situated.

He rode around by the foot of the lowest terrace and up a graded road leading to the stables, where he found old Jonas Stackpole sitting down in his armchair outside the door, smoking a short pipe.

"You didn't expect to see me back so soon, Stackpole, eh?" gayly inquired the young man.

"No, sir; but I am all the happier in having the un- expected honor," replied the old coachman, taking the pipe from his mouth and rising respectfully.

"I will leave my horse here and walk up to the house," said Mr. Hamilton Gower, as he dismounted and threw the reins to one of the grooms.

"All right, sir! He shall be well looked after," said old Stackpole, touching his forehead.

Mr. Hamilton Gower walked on toward the house.

As he drew near the upper terrace he saw Seraph Elfinstar at a distance. She was coming from the rear of the cultivated grounds, evidently from the rocky and thorny wilderness infected by noxious weeds and infested with venomous reptiles, that lay at the foot of the precipice, and that she haunted in her hours of morbid despondency and called her Gehenna.

She seemed, as she drew nearer, to be in one of her most despairing moods. Her radiant light hair was all gathered up in a dark net under a dark straw hat. She wore a dark-brown dress and shawl. Her face was very pale, and her eyes were fixed upon the ground as she slowly and languidly approached.

She did not see her lover until they met face to face, and he spoke to her.

"Seraph!"

She started as violently as if she had received a shock.

"You are back, then?" she said in a fainting voice as she looked up at him and leaned against a tree for support.

"Yes, I am here! here to renew my pledge to love only you of all women in the world! to marry only you, if you will be my wife, or— never to marry at all!" he answered, with earnest love and faith expressed in every tone of his eager voice and in every look of his eloquent face.

64

"And—Margaret Campbell?" she faltered.

"Was a child-martyr as good and pure as were the St. Agnes and St. Rosalie worshiped of Christians!" warmly replied the young man.

"Ah! no, no, she was not! She did not commit any crime, or break any human law; but she was jealous and vindictive in temper. If she had not been so, don't you see, this fearful chain of circumstantial evidence could never have been woven around her for her destruction," said Seraph mournfully.

"'Jealous and vindictive,' do you call her? A helpless and harmless child, goaded into cries of pain and anger by wrongs that might have maddened older and more self-governed people!" earnestly responded the young man.

"You defend Margaret Campbell now as eloquently as you denounced her—once," said Seraph with a slight smile.

"I know her now. I did not know her then; and I would beg her pardon, at her feet, for the rash misjudgment by which I so greatly wronged her," said the lover reverently.

"Oh, you need not. It was so natural, so inevitable. It was a misjudgment also which you shared with the wisest judges and the sharpest jurors; with the press, and with the public," murmured Seraph.

"By all my hopes of heaven I will make them all change their minds!" eagerly exclaimed the youth.

"Ah! I do not know how you will manage to work that miracle!"

"The truth must prevail, if it has but one earnest advocate! And it shall prevail, for I am such a one! I shall return to England by the next ship. I shall devote all my time, fortune and energies to the vindication of your name!"

"Would you indeed do all that for me?—for me-lost, forlorn, despairing as I am—" Her voice broke down in emotion.

"Yes, all that, and more! for your misfortunes are mine and your unhappiness is mine; in serving you I serve myself. All that man or angel can do for you, I will do!"

"Ah! where can you ever begin? Your enterprise will be—a phantom hunt!"

"No, no! I believe I have a clue!"

"A clue!"

"Yes! I was too anxious in reading the narrative not to be on the lookout for clues, and I believe I have found one."

"You—suspect—some—one?" she inquired in a low, hesitating, almost breathless voice.

"Yes, I suspect some one."

"Whom—whom ?"

"That deformed, half-witted malignant who was your roommate and your accuser."

"Great Heaven!" breathed Seraph, gazing at the speaker in amazement.

"Seraph, is it possible that you never suspected this girl?"

"Never."

"And yet you knew that she was half-witted, malicious and a sleepwalker!"

"Yes."

" And you knew that only she, besides yourself, had command of that key of your room, which was also the pass-key to the nursery, and which was on the inside of your locked door on the night or early morning of the child murder!"

"Yes!"

"And you never suspected her!"

"Oh, no! I never even thought of her in that terrible light. I should never have deemed it possible that she could have perpetrated such an atrocious crime. I do not believe it now!"

"Who did, then?" significantly inquired the young man. "You did not; that is certain to my mind. And there was but one other who could possibly have done it-that half-witted deformity who was your only companion in the room, and who was your first accuser. I shall follow up this clue. I shall set detectives privately to look up her antecedents and watch her present conduct."

"Oh, do not, do not have another guiltless one accused and punished," pleaded Seraph.

"She shall not be falsely accused or unjustly punished. Even if I should be successful in vindicating you and fastening the guilt where I believe it belongs—on her-still she will not be punished. She is half-witted, and, therefore, legally irresponsible. She would, if convicted, only be sent to the Hanwell Asylum for Criminal Lunatics, where she would be much better off than in her mother's house—judging from your narrative, Seraph; a fate much better than she deserves. By Jove! it will seem like a reward instead of a punishment for her guilt!"

"She is most unfortunate in her bodily deformity and mental derangement," said Seraph.

"Why are you so tender in your feelings toward her? She was your first accuser."

"I thought she believed the story that she told me, and wept because she was compelled to tell it."

"She probably wept because she was not altogether an unmitigated devil, and felt the terrible wrong which, in order to shield herself, she was doing to one who had always been kind to her. Seraph, I believe that I have got the right clue, and I shall follow it up. If the girl is innocent, my investigation will not hurt her; if she is guilty, it would vindicate you without really injuring her. Will you let me lead you to the house? You look really faint."

"Thank you. I think we had better go in," assented the young lady, as she took the proffered arm of her lover.

When they reached the entrance they found Mr. Elfinstar sitting in his armchair on the piazza engaged in reading.

"So you are back, young sir!" he said, rising to meet his guest.

"Did you not expect to see me back?" inquired the latter with a smile, as he placed his companion in a seat and took another himself.

"Well, frankly, I did; for I know well the persistence youth in such matters."

Mr. Hamilton Gower then spoke earnestly of Margaret Campbell's unjust conviction and cruel fate, and unfolded his own theory of the murder and plans of detecting the guilty and vindicating the innocent.

Mr. Elfinstar was penetrated by the fidelity and devotion of the young advocate and impressed with the plausibility of his opinion. He said but little, however, until Mr. Hamilton Gower, having finished his explanation and declined an invitation to dinner, arose to depart. Then the old gentleman warmly grasped his hand, saying:

"You are an enthusiast in this cause, my dear young friend, but— enthusiasts often succeed."

CHAPTER VII
A LOVER'S FAITH

MRS. BELLE ISLE was very glad of the power put into her hands to relieve the mental distress of her foolish maid, but not until after breakfast on the morning succeeding the visit of the surgeon and the traveler did she get an opportunity of speaking privately to the girl.

When the lieutenant had gone on some business to the commissariat and the lady sat alone in her parlor, she summoned her maid to her presence.

Lona Pond came in, pale, red-eyed and dejected.

"Sit down; for you look as if you were about to sink through the floor. How silly you are, child, to distress yourself for nothing," said Mrs. Belle Isle kindly.

"For nothing! Oh, ma'am, do you call it nothing, after I have followed him so many thousand miles out to this dreadful country, to have my young man as I was engaged to be married to turn his back on me?" said the girl, bursting into tears at her own words and sinking down on a hassock at her mistress' feet.

"But he has done nothing of the sort, you stupid child!"

"Oh, ma'am! but his own words and looks and my own eyes and ears to prove it, ma'am," persisted the girl.

"Look here, Lona! You were equally credulous to the testimony of your own eyes and ears when you mistook the convict, John Hice, for your betrothed, Ham Glow!"

"Oh, ma'am, but that was very different."

"Very different, indeed, Lona! for whereas you mistook a chain gang prisoner for Gow on that occasion, you now mistake a gentleman of wealth and position for him!"

"And this time I am right, ma'am! He may be 'a gentleman of wealth and position' now, for aught I know to the contrary. He looks it, and I'll not gainsay that he is! 'Wealth' is sometimes soon won in the gold mines, ma'am, and 'position' always comes with it in these colonies! Yes, and the two together often turn men's heads, and hearts, too, for that matter, as they have turned the giddy head of my wild Ham and set his heart against his own true girl that crossed the big seas for his sake!" sobbed the girl.

"Oh! what a tiresome idiot you are, Lona!—I cannot help saying it! Now, listen to me and don't speak a word until I get through. The gentleman whom you met and embraced yesterday—"

"Don't throw that up against me, please, ma'am! I'll never do it again!" sniffed Lona.

"I hope and trust and pray that you will not; but I can't feel sure about it," smiled her mistress.

"I'll never, never, never kiss Ham Gow again as long as I live in this world! No, not if it was to save his neck from being stretched or his soul from being burned!"

"Hush! hush! you must not say such shocking words!"

"Not when I have been scorned and cast off by my young man who was engaged to be married to me, and for whose sake I crossed the seas! Beg pardon, ma'am, for speaking so strong in your presence; but I said it and I meant it!"

"Lona, your lover has never scorned you or cast you off—at least, to your knowledge, and you have no right to say that he has! Now, then, listen to me! Did I not tell you not to utter a word until I had finished?"

"Yes, ma'am, and I will be silent."

"Very well, then; now keep your promise and attend. The gentleman you seized upon in the street was Mr. Hamilton Gower," began Mrs. Belle Isle.

Lona Pond muttered something under her breath to the effect that she knew that he had added two or three syllables to his honest name since he had made his fortune; but Mrs. Belle Isle took no notice of her interruption, and went on to say:

"He is from Cornwall, and knew this Gow intimately from boyhood."

"I should rather think he did," mumbled Lona.

"It is not the first time, he says, by many that he has been mistaken for Gow and Gow for him."

"Tell that to the horse marines," muttered Lona under her breath.

"What are you saying, child?"

"Nothing much, ma'am."

"Mr. Gower, so far from resenting the mistake you made in regard to him, actually feels a kindly interest in you raffairs—"

"I thank him for nothing, and wish he would let me and my affairs alone."

"Eh?"

"Nothing, ma'am."

"Mr. Gower wishes to relieve your mind from doubts and misgivings. He has a very good heart."

"Ah, yes, 'a very good heart!'"

"What is that?"

"Not anything particular, ma'am."

"He says that Ham Gow, his own old acquaintance, came out to these colonies about the same time that he himself did—"

"Ah I guess he told the truth there, anyway."

"Lona!"

"I was only thinking something to myself, ma'am."

"They did not come out in the same ship, however."

"Didn't they?"

"But they met quite incidentally on the road of the great rush to some new gold fields that were discovered just before their arrival, and they spent a few weeks together."

"No doubt they have spent a good deal of time together—have Ham Gow and Mr. Ham-ilton Gow-er!"

"Lona, if you continue to interrupt me by such remarks I cannot go on."

"I beg your pardon, ma'am."

"Mr. Gower left Gow at Dead Maiden's Brook—for that is the name of the new diggings. Mr. Gower has been traveling since that time, and has constantly corresponded with Gow, who has remained at the diggings, where he has made quite a large fortune already."

Lona gazed at her mistress in silence, seeming no longer to have the slightest inclination to contradict her.

"By a long-understood arrangement Mr. Gower and Ham Gow will return to England together. Mr. Gower has written to Gow to notify him of the time set for sailing. Gow is expected to arrive here by the *Labrado*, which will touch here on her voyage to London, when Mr. Gower will take his passage back to England with Gow."

"Dear me," said Lona Pond, putting her hand up to her head in a helpless sort of way.

"You will then have an opportunity of seeing the two men together, and knowing 'which is which,' concluded the lady with a smile.

Lona Pond did not answer her, but slowly shook her head, muttering to herself:

"Dear me! dear me! I wonder if I am growing silly?"

Mrs. Belle Isle could not reassure her by saying that she was not going in that way.

"And is it really and truly the case, ma'am, that I have mistaken a gentleman for Ham Gow, after going and mistaking a convict for him, too?" sighed the girl.

"I thought I had convinced you that you had. But when you see the real Ham Gow you will believe the evidence of your own senses."

"No, ma'am, no! I never shall! I never can believe my own eyes and ears and sense again as far as Ham Gow is concerned—never! I am gone daft on that subject, I know!" persisted Lona.

Mrs. Belle Isle thought it very likely that the girl spoke the truth of herself, and said no more.

Mr. Hamilton Gower became rather a frequent visitor at Lieut. Belle Isle's quarters, where he was always cordially welcomed; but he never encountered again the girl who had so vehemently embraced him, for Lona Pond, convinced at length that she had made a mistake, was so thoroughly ashamed of having kissed the wrong man that she kept carefully out of his sight.

Mr. Gower and Lieut. Belle Isle became great friends; but the former often caught the eyes of the latter fixed on him with a strange and wistful expression.

One evening when he was passing an hour in Mr. Belle Isle's parlor the young lieutenant, being present, suddenly said to him:

"By Jove! it is very strange!"

"What is strange, my dear fellow?" inquired Mr. Gower.

"The likeness."

"Oh! my close resemblance to the estimable Mr. Gow!" laughed the guest.

"No, not at all. I never saw Mr. Gow, to my knowledge, much as I have heard of that gentleman. No; I mean your likeness to the late unfortunate young Earl of Hawkewood. I knew the very first time I ever saw you that I had seen your face, or one exactly like it, before—somewhere or other."

"Very likely you have," laughed the visitor; "for I have been there or elsewhere—occasionally."

"At first," gravely continued the young lieutenant, "I could not locate the likeness—so to speak—but now I can do so—with the late Earl of Hawkewood."

"Ah ! you knew the young earl, then ?" said Mr. Hamilton Gower.

"No, not at all, except by sight. Few people knew him in any other way, I fancy. He was kept very secluded from all society by a dreadful old dragon of a doctor of divinity, who was both his guardian and his tutor. No one ever saw him except at church. It was at Hawkeville's old church that I first saw his lugubrious lordship."

"Ah!"

"And I always thought his dark, sad face foreshadowed a tragic end. I did not dream of a death by assassination, however. I thought of—suicide. He looked like it."

"Humph!"

"You are from Cornwall, I understand?"

"From Cornwall, yes."

"Then perhaps you may have known the late young Earl of Hawkewood?" suggested the lieutenant.

"I think I knew him—slightly," replied Mr. Gower with some hesitation.

"'You think,' my dear fellow? Are you not sure whether you knew him or not?" laughed Belle Isle.

"No, indeed, I am not sure; for though I was in his company a great deal, I cannot say that I knew him well, or that I ever addressed a word to him directly in my life; or that he ever spoke to me," gravely replied Mr. Gower.

"Oh! Ah! I see! You met him in mixed companies—in churches or lyceums, or something of that sort—for he never went into society at all."

"No."

"But did you not notice, as I did, the profound melancholy of the young man?"

"A melancholy bordering on despair. Yes, indeed, I did notice it, more than any one else, I think; and I was more impressed than others with the doubt whether it would not end fatally," gravely responded Mr. Gower.

"Well, you see, it would seem that 'every face is a history or a prophecy.' His face was a prophecy of his tragic end."

The entrance of a servant with a tray of chocolate and cream cakes changed the current of the conversation.

After these refreshments had been discussed, Mr. Gower arose and bade good-night to his new friends.

Hamilton Gower was also a very frequent guest at the Mountain Hermitage; usually on the occasions of his visits leaving the Royal Victoria as early as six o'clock in the morning and reaching the Hermitage at nine, and there spending the whole day, and sometimes the night as well.

There he was received by the venerable master as an honored guest and as a beloved son, and welcomed by the young lady of the house with the calm delight she had come to feel and show in his presence.

He had inspired both the father and the daughter with his own strong faith in "a happy issue out of all their troubles."

So much of his time was passed at the Hermitage that whenever he spent a day and night with the Elfinstars, and left them after an early breakfast, it was always with the promise to return the next morning, so that they knew when to expect him, and on this expectancy Seraph Elfinstar vegetated until she saw him again; for she seemed now really to live only in his presence.

One morning, after having spent a day and a night at the Hermitage, having taken leave of his beloved, with the promise to come again early the next day, he went out and saw another saddled horse waiting beside his own.

"I will ride with you a little way," said his host as he mounted the second horse.

They cantered along slowly down the graded carriage way leading from the house and sweeping half around the foot of the lowest terrace.

When they had turned out of the grounds into the winding bride path that led down the mountain side, the old gentleman spoke:

"I have been wanting to talk to you for a long time to talk privately, I mean—but I could not ask you for a *tête-à-tête* without giving some explanation to Seraph, and I did not wish even to hint to her the subject which I must discuss with you."

"What subject?" uneasily inquired the young man.

"This. You see, I have not interfered with your conditional engagement to my daughter, and have even warmly welcomed your frequent visits and long stays, because all these have made her happy, as well as given me pleasure; and she has had so much woe, so little joy in this world, that I cannot bear—I have not the heart or the moral courage to deprive her of any enjoyment that comes in her way, or to inflict upon her the pain that its deprivation would cause," slowly answered Mr. Elfinstar.

"But why should you deprive her of this natural pleasure?" anxiously questioned Mr. Hamilton Gower.

"Because of the uncertainty of the future. You are, as you have secretly confided to me, the Earl of Hawkewood; your family one of the oldest and most honored in England; your connections among the highest nobility in the kingdom. And—" The old gentleman paused, and sighed profoundly.

"Well! Well! sir, what of all this?" impatiently inquired the young man.

"I must put the subject in its plainest, and, therefore, its most painful aspect. You wish to marry Seraph Elfinstar, my adopted daughter, who appears to you as she really is, a beautiful, amiable and cultured young girl—but—whom you now know to be one and the same with Margaret Campbell—"

"I beg you will cease!" exclaimed the young man, wincing.

"No, I must go on! Margaret Campbell, a convict, a life prisoner of the crown! Now, suppose that your most sanguine expectations are fulfilled, and that you succeed in vindicating the name and fame of this much-injured girl, and that you restore her to freedom and to her native land; I ask you, can you, a man of your rank and position, an earl, the grandson of a duke—can you marry Margaret Campbell, in the face of all her hideous antecedents? What would your relatives, say? What would your world say? The' Countess of Hawkewood an ex—"

"Silence, sir; in the name of Heaven!" cried the young man, stung by the words.

"I am answered," gravely murmured old Elfinstar, nodding his gray head several times in affirmation; "I am answered; and I think, my lord, and I say it without the slightest surprise or resentment, that it is best you should not come again to the Hermitage. You see that you cannot marry my daughter—how much soever you may love and esteem her—you cannot marry her, in view of her horrible past.

"You mistake me! You misjudge me! You wrong me bitterly! What have I ever said or done to lead you to suppose that I could be recreant to my plighted faith? Yes, I do love Seraph Elfinstar—for by that name only have I known her, and by that name only will I call her. I do love her, I do honor her, and I will marry her, if she will do me the honor to become my wife."

"But your rank?" mildly suggested the old gentleman.

"As to my rank, I am not at all indifferent to it, I assure you, Mr. Elfinstar! I should rather be the Earl of Hawkewood than to be a costermonger, or even a county clerk; but I am not the slave of my 'rank'! I will not bow down and worship my 'rank' as an idol! I will not sacrifice on the altar of my 'rank' all my heart's holiest affection! No! sooner than do that I will continue dead to the world, which for nearly two years has supposed me to be really so. I will leave my title and estate in the possession of my heir presumptive, who now usurps them, and I will live a true life here with the woman who is to be my mate forever. But it will not be necessary for me to sacrifice my rank, and my love shall share it with me! Come, Mr. Elfinstar, dear friend, we shall all be home in England within one year from this time—a happy household in Hawke Hall."

"But your relatives?" meekly queried the old gentleman.

Hamilton Gower broke into a soft and silvery laugh.

"'Relatives'!" he echoed. "Bless you, I have none whatever! I have not even acquaintances! And if ever I lamented the want of family and social ties, I now rejoice in it! There is positively no one to interfere with me! My only living kinsman is the man who now usurps my title, and he is so very distant a cousin that no one on earth but Sir Bernard Burke, who runs 'The Peerage,' could trace the connection. And the only humiliation he will feel must attend his being turned out of Hawke Hall. So you see my 'relatives' are as little likely as my 'rank' to be an impediment to our happiness."

" Finally—your world?"

"I haven't any, my good sir! I have lived so secluded from society that I have no world, outside of this colony. So much for my world. Have you anything else to urge?"

"In objection? No! but I have this to suggest. It is that, in case you succeed in vindicating the name and fame of Margaret Campbell, and thus restoring her to liberty—if you should still be determined to marry her, you marry her privately by her name of Margaret Campbell, and then, when we all get back to England, you receive her from my hand as my daughter, and marry her publicly as Seraph Elfinstar, and let this public marriage be attended with all the ceremonies

"'That wait on princes' nuptials.'
Will you do this?"

"I will do anything in my power to please you and Seraph."

"I wish this plan adopted to save you and yours from unmerited reproach. My granddaughter was but a child when she was caught and crushed in this terrible machinery of circumstantial evidence—a pale, thin, little girl of fourteen. She is now a tall and handsome woman of nineteen. You will marry her privately, under her first name, in order to make your union legal beyond all possibility of doubt. You will marry her publicly, under her second name that I have given her by adoption, and do this to throw a veil over misfortunes which the world must never know; and no one will ever recognize in Seraph Elfinstar, or the Countess of Hawkewood, the crushed and martyred child who was sent out to these colonies four years ago. Do you understand?"

"I understand."

"And now I will bid you good-by, and turn back home with a somewhat lighter heart than I brought," said Mr.Elfinstar.

"And with more faith in me, I hope, sir," smiled the young man.

"It is faith that has lightened my heart. Heaven bless you, my boy," said the old gentleman, as he turned his horse's head and rode slowly up the mountain path.

Hamilton Gower, smiling to himself, cantered briskly on toward Hobart Town.

CHAPTER VIII
ANOTHER MAD MEETING

THE month of March drew to a close, and the arrival of the *Labrador* was daily expected.

This prospect did not prevent Mr. Hamilton Gower from going as usual to spend a day and night at the Mountain Hermitage. He was not afraid of being left behind by the ship, in the event of her arrival during his absence. He knew that she was expected to remain for a few days in port.

And so it happened that, on the morning of the thirty-first of March, Mr. Hamilton Gower rode out to the Mountain Hermitage to spend a day and night with the Elfinstars.

And that same afternoon the *Labrador* sailed up the Derwent, and dropped anchor.

The news spread like wildfire through the town, causing considerable excitement—the arrival of a ship was such an important event at Hobart Town, even though it was a ship from Melbourne on her voyage to England, instead of a ship from "home," bringing news of friends and relatives.

The *Labrador* had brought such news on her voyage out, and now she would carry back answers to letters that had come by her mails some five weeks previous.

These answers, which had been begun soon after the reception of the letters and continued in the form of installments, had been waiting in many households to be dosed up and sent "home" by the *Labrador* when she should stop at Hobart Town on her way back to London.

Now she was in port, and the letters must be finished in time for her next departure.

It happened that Mrs. Belle Isle was among the busiest letter writers. She had written long epistles to the Rev. Dr. Irvine, to Lady Victoria Belle Isle, and to Miss Olive Ball, and she wished to add to each a postcript; but having used up her stock of thin, foreign note paper, she sent her maid, Lona Pond, out into the town to procure a new supply.

Lona walked down Barracks Lane into Macquarrie Street, and thence into Queen Street, where she intended to make her purchase.

She walked with her eyes cast down upon the ground, for she could not bear to look at or speak to any one since her misadventure with Mr. Hamilton Gower.

Suddenly she heard her name called in a voice that ought to have been familiar.

"Lona! Lona Pond! Is it possible! You here?"

She started in terror, and raised her eyes, to see standing before her, barring her way, a fine, stalwart-looking man, with good features, dark, sunburned complexion, dark eyes, dark hair and a full, heavy, dark beard.

He wore a sailor's suit, and held in his hand a tarpaulin hat.

She uttered a faint cry, and covered her face with her hands.

"Lona! Lona Pond! Is this really you? I can scarcely believe my eyes! How came you out here? Speak to me!" exclaimed the newcomer.

But she only held her hands before her eyes and trembled.

"Are you Lona Pond? Speak to me! I cannot have made a mistake! Speak to me! Are you Lona Pond?" pleaded the stranger.

"Ay, I'm Lona Pond fast enough; miserable, demented girl that I am!" muttered the young woman from behind her trembling hands.

"You are Lona Pond! Of course, I knew it! I was sure of it! Dear, dearest Lona! It is such a surprise, such a delight, to meet you so unexpectedly! When did you come out here, and with whom?"

"I came out about a year ago, as lady's maid to an offi- cer's wife—Mrs Lieut. Belle Isle; but I wish you would let me pass, and not bar my way!" said the girl in a shaking voice.

"But, Lona! Why, Lona! Why do you speak to me in that manner? Don't you know me? Can it be possible that you don't know me?" demanded the young man in a voice of surprise.

"No, I don't know you at all! Let me go by, if you please," said the girl, trying to push past him.

He stopped her gently.

"Perhaps it is because you don't want to know me," he said in a tone of pain and displeasure.

"No, I don't want to know you, and, what is more, I won't know you—so there, now! I have been fooled just once too often, and I will never be fooled again! Stand out of the way and let me pass!" she exclaimed in a shaking voice as she tried to push by him.

"One moment longer," he answered, breathing hard, as he continued to bar her path; "just one moment longer, and one question more. You don't want to know me, you say! Perhaps you have another sweetheart? Perhaps you have a husband?"

"No!" vehemently exclaimed the girl, "I have no husband and no sweetheart, and don't want any but my own ,dear Ham Gow! My own dear Ham Gow as I crossed the high seas to come to, but as I shall never find in this world! No, never! I have found only his doubles and his fetches, as have deceived and fooled me until I'm almost demented; but I'll never be fooled again! Let me go on, sir! I am out on an errand, and my mistress is waiting for me," she persisted, trying to pass by him.

But he blocked her way with the most affectionate words.

"Dearest, dearest Lona, you have found your faithful lover at last! I am your own, true Ham Gow !"

"I don't believe it! You can't fool me! Let me go by!"

"But I am, indeed, Ham Gow!"

"You are nothing of the sort!"

"I am Ham Gow—"

"You are a fetch!"

"Look at me, then! Look me straight in the face and assure yourself that I am he."

"Oh, yes! I looked at the others! at the convict in the chain gang, and at the gentleman on Macquarrie Street, and by looking at them I was fooled. They were neither of them Ham Gow! They were his fetches!"

"But I am no 'fetch'! I am he!"

"You may be the Emperor of China, for aught I know! but if you don't stand out of my way and let me pass I will give you in charge! Here! Constable! Constable!" she cried, hailing an officer that was passing on the opposite side of the way.

"You are certainly crazy!" exclaimed the stranger as he stepped aside and let her pass.

Lona Pond hurried along Queen Street until she had put a hundred yards or so between herself and the stranger, and then she suddenly paused and put her hands up to her head in a bewildered manner, muttering:

"He was wonderfully like Ham Gow! wonderfully! But I know he wasn't Ham Gow! He was only another fetch, the third fetch! and the proverb says, 'Beware of the third time!' And I promised my mistress—solemnly promised her—never, never, never to take another man for Ham Gow! And I never will! And now I must hurry and get what she sent me for!"

She quickened her steps and walked rapidly on for a few paces, and then paused again and put her hands up to her temples with an expression of perplexity.

"Now, what was it my mistress sent me for? That man has knocked it clean out of my head! Let me see! What was it? Berlin wool? No! Cologne? No! Oh I cannot remember to save my life! I shall have to go back and ask her! Such a loss of time! And she in such a hurry, too!"

Lona Pond turned and retraced her steps to the barracks in a hurry, and presented herself before her mistress in heat and agitation.

"You have walked too fast, Lona! You should not have done so," said Mrs. Belle Isle. Then: "Have you got the paper?" she inquired.

"Oh, it was paper! So it was! Dear ma'am, please forgive me; but—I had forgotten what you sent me for; and—I had to turn back!" replied the panting girl.

"Forgot my errand, Lona! That was very strange! But sit down and recover your breath! You are not fit to stand. How came you to forget?" gently inquired the lady.

"Oh, ma'am," breathed the palpitating creature, as she sank down on a footstool at her mistress' feet, "it was all along of a great shock I got on Queen Street."

"What sort of a shock, Lona? I hope—"

"Oh, dear, ma'am, it was another Ham Gow!"

"Lona!"

"I mean another fetch of his, ma'am!"

"Oh, my poor girl! are you quite losing your senses? "sighed the lady.

"Oh, no, dear ma'am, I am getting them back again, sure! for I would not allow this fetch to be Ham Gow, although he was the image of him—as perfect an image of him as the other fetches were, and even although he himself owned up to being Ham Gow, which the other two fetches didn't; but, on the contrary, denied that they were so."

"Lona!" suddenly exclaimed the lady. "You say that this third man declared himself to be Gow?"

"Yes, ma'am, he did, the deceiver! And he was the first to speak to me, calling me his dearest Lona, and asking me if I didn't know him, and a lot of other questions! But I wasn't to be fooled by him! I wouldn't allow him to be Ham Gow for one single minute!" said the girl, emphatically shaking her head.

"I think you have made another mistake, Lona," said the lady.

"Oh, no, please, ma'am, I haven't! No mistake this time! I remembered my solemn promise to you, ma'am, never to take another man for Ham Gow as long as I should live in this world! And I didn't, ma'am! For when this third fetch kept on trying to fool me, I just called a constable to him and come away!"

"What! You had the man arrested?"

"Oh, no, ma'am, not that; for when I called the constable he got out of my way and let me pass. And then I hurried down Queen Street to do your errand, and then found out that I had forgotten what it was! Now, dear ma'am, wasn't it enough to make me forget?" pleaded Lona Pond.

"Yes, and I excuse your forgetfulness," laughed the, lady. "But, Lona, I have reason for believing that this last man was really your lover!"

"Oh, ma'am !" cried Lona, catching her breath.

"Do you not remember that I told you Gow was expected to arrive by the *Labrador*, due here about the first of April?"

"Yes, ma'am, I know, but—"

"Well, the *Labrador* has arrived."

"The *Labrador* arrived, ma'am!" exclaimed the girl, staring.

"Yes, this afternoon, as I should have told you if I had thought of it. The *Labrador* has arrived, and Gow with her, no doubt! So it must have been he whom you met and flouted in Queen Street just now."

"The Lord have mercy upon me! Now I have it!" exclaimed Lona Pond, with a look of utter despair.

Mrs. Belle Isle laughed, and said:

"Don't distress yourself, Lona. Mr. Hamilton Gower promised to bring Gow here to see you as soon as the ship should reach port, and he will certainly keep his word; and when you meet your lover you can explain to him how you happened to deny him, and it will be all right."

"Oh, ma'am; but to think that after taking two fetches for him I should take him for a fetch!"

"Never mind, Lona! You are sure of seeing your betrothed now, and that should be a great consolation! Go, take off your bonnet. I shall not send you out again today. I can call at the stationer's myself, when I go out for a drive," said the lady, gently dismissing her agitated maid.

The next morning Mr. Hamilton Gower returned from his visit to the Mountain Hermitage. The first news that met him at the Royal Victoria was that of the arrival of the *Labrador*.

"And there's a—an individual come by her, stopping here and inquiring for you, sir," said the head waiter, hesitating whether to designate said individual as "a man" or "a gentleman."

"Ah, yes, I expected him! Where is he?" anxiously inquired Mr. Hamilton Gower.

"He is in the coffee room at present, sir, taking his luncheon."

When he gets through, show him up here," said Mr. Gower, dismissing the waiter by a gesture,, and then going into his bathroom to wash the dust of his ride from face and hands.

He had just got through, and was standing before the glass in his bedroom, brushing his hair, when the door opened and Ham Gow entered the room, ushered in by the waiter.

Mr. Hamilton Gower dropped the brush and wheeled around, eagerly exclaiming:

"Ah! Ham Gow, old fellow, I am so glad to see you! If I were a Frenchman I should embrace you," and he shook his hand heartily.

"Glad to see you looking so well, my l—" began the visitor, but Mr. Gower stopped him with a:

"Hussh-sh-sh! Stow that until we get back to England! I would not have a rumor of my existence to reach Lewis Manton before my arrival at Hawke Hall upon any consideration. Come! Come with me into my snuggery here,. and let us have a good talk," said Mr. Hamilton Gower, as he hastily drew on his morning coat and led the way into the front sitting room which overlooked the street.

When the two men were comfortably seated each in a resting-chair, Mr. Gower was the first to speak.

"Well, how have you prospered on Dead Maiden's Brook?"

"Fairly. The first six months I thought I was going to make an enormous fortune, hand over fist! But then my lead began to give out, and yield less and less, until it failed altogether. And I never struck another lead that did more than pay expenses. Luck had turned, and when luck once turns for good or for evil it seldom turns back again; so, upon the whole, I thought it was about time to quit, when I got your letter."

"How much did you make in all?"

"Stated in round numbers, about ten thousand pounds."

"I am glad that my summons occasioned you no loss"

"Not a bit! I had made up my mind to go home. I was only waiting to hear from you. I was aching all over to get home. I wanted to see my girl. I had not heard from her, sir, for more than a year," said Ham Gow with a deep sigh, given more to the memory of his unlucky encounter with Lona Pond on Queen Street than to the thought of their long and silent separation.

"Ah! Then I have a delightful surprise in store for you. You did not know that your faithful sweetheart had taken service with a lady, Mrs. Belle Isle, the wife of an officer whose regiment was ordered to this place, and had come out here for the hope of finding you?" said Mr. Gower gayly.

But his communication was not met with the looks of surprise and delight he had expected to see. On the contrary, Ham Gow sighed more deeply than before, and answered:

"No, sir; I did not know it till yesterday afternoon, when I met her on the street, and she pretended not to know me."

"Impossible!"

"Yes, she did, sir. I suppose she has found another sweetheart out in this place," sighed the lover.

"No, indeed; she has not! I know the poor girl well, through knowing the family she is at service with, and her fidelity to the lad she 'followed across the high seas,' as she puts it, is a subject of sympathy and some amusement to her mistress and master.

"But she wouldn't own me when she met me, sir. She called me a fetch, an impostor, and an evil spirit, who had taken the form of her lover to fool her."

Mr. Hamilton Gower laughed aloud, and said:

"I understand it all, Ham. There were two men in this colony that bore so strong a resemblance to you that either of the Nans who brought you up might have mistaken either of these men for yourself. One—the first 'fetch'—was a convict, John Hice—"

"Oh-h-h! The very man who was arrested for me in the old country!"

"Exactly. And this young girl saw him working in the chain gang on the road, thought he was her own Ham—"

"I'm much obliged to her, I am sure!"

"She thought her 'own Ham' had been unjustly and cruelly convicted of some crime that he was incapable of committing; went into hysterics over his fate; insisted on her employer taking him out of the chain gang and into their private service as an 'assigned servant,' and went under the protection of the chaplain to visit him in jail, when at length she was convinced of her mistake."

"Poor Lona! What a terrible trial!"

"The second 'fetch' was myself. She met me on Macquarrie Street on the first day of my arrival in this town, and, poor innocent! threw herself in my arms with a burst of joyful tears! And when I tried to convince her of her mistake she bitterly reproached me with infidelity, threw her betrothal ring in my face, and left me in boiling anger!"

"Poor Lona!"

"That very evening I happened to make acquaintance with the people where she was at service, and in the course of conversation my strange encounter with the girl came to be spoken of, and an explanation ensued. Later on I heard that the mistress gave the maid a serious lecture and warning against making such another mistake."

"Poor, dear Lona!" murmured Ham Gow.

"So, you see, you cannot blame her, when at last she met the real 'Simon Pure,' yourself, that she should have taken you for a third 'fetch' and repudiated your acquaintance!"

"No, indeed, I cannot. But who are those Belle Isles with whom she came out? Any connections of the Duke of Grand Manors?"

"Yes, of course; the lieutenant was a nephew and ward of the late duke, and used to be a good deal at the Castle Belle Isle, I understand. And, by the way, he detected a very wonderful likeness between myself and 'the late unfortunate young Earl of

Hawkewood' whom he says he used to see at the parish church at Hawkeville!"

"Ha! ha! ha! that must have amused you, sir. You have been staying here quite a good while, my lor—sir."

"Yes, quite a good while. I—have been interested in the colony," replied Mr. Hamilton Gower. Then a sudden impulse came upon him to take Ham Gow, his old playmate and companion, partly into his confidence, not in regard to Seraph Elfinstar, but in regard to Margaret Campbell.

"Gow," he said, "do you remember a celebrated trial that occurred in England about four years ago, in which a young girl, scarcely past childhood, was convicted of the murder of her infant cousin?"

"You mean the case of Margaret Campbell, of course, sir?"

"Yes," said the young gentleman, wincing a little at the name, "I mean that case."

"I should think I did remember it, sir! I should think I had good cause to remember it," so solemnly replied the tramp that the young gentleman gazed wonderingly into his face as he asked:

"What do you mean? What special cause have you, more than any one else, to remember that case?"

"Because, sir," said the tramp, lowering his voice and turning pale even under his dark, bronzed complexion, "because I—I saw that deed done!"

CHAPTER IX
WHAT HAM GOW SAW ONE NIGHT

HAMILTON GOWER sat back in his chair, and stared at his visitor in blank amazement for a moment, and then slowly repeated the words:

"You-saw—that-deed—done?"

"Yes, I did, sir! to my great misfortune! for, though I have been through a great deal of evil things, I never witnessed anything so horrible, so heinous, as that night's work!" said the tramp with a shudder.

"You saw that foul murder committed?" persisted Hamilton Gower, still amazed and incredulous.

"Yes, sir, I did; I told you that I did—to my sorrow!"

"Then, why, in the name of Heaven, did not you interfere to prevent it?" sternly demanded Mr. Gower.

"Good Lord, sir, I could not! It was done in an instant, before I knew what was going to happen!"

"Then, why did you not afterward give the alarm? The child might possibly have been rescued!"

"Because, sir, I did not understand what had occurred until it was too late."

"When did you first discover the dreadful import of 'what you had seen?"

"Not until the day that the body of the murdered child was found at the bottom of the well. Then the scene that I had witnessed at Rose Hill in the dead of night came back to me like a nightmare with a new and horrible meaning. Ugh! I see the night sky; the black mass of the stables, the dark trees, the well, and the wild-eyed girl, and I hear again the deep, soft thud when that which she dropped in struck the bottom!" shuddered the tramp.

"You saw the girl's eyes? You must have seen the girl's face very distinctly!"

"I did. I was right there—I saw her face right before me as she turned, after having dropped something down the well!"

"Then you could have sworn to the murderess?"

"Yes, indeed! Hers was a face never to be forgotten!"

"Then, why, in the name of justice and mercy, did you not appear before the coroner's jury to testify to what you had seen?"

"Because I could not bear to go and help to convict and hang a young girl; who, in fact, was but a child, and evidently a luny child at that!"

"And yet, by your morbid sentimentality in withholding your testimony, you have caused irreparable injustice, unutterable sorrow to another and a most innocent young girl, and to all who are interested in her!" bitterly exclaimed Mr. Hamilton Gower.

Ham Gow stared at the speaker in dismay.

"I cause injustice and sorrow to an innocent girl!" he exclaimed.

"Yes! the most atrocious injustice, the most cruel sorrow!" bitterly repeated Mr. Gower.

"I do not understand you the least in the world! Please tell me how I have done this, sir, if I have done it?"

"Do you not already know? Can you not see what you, have done?"

"Indeed, I cannot, sir, in this case."

"You have, by your culpable reticence in withholding your testimony from the coroner's inquest and from the courts, shielded the guilty at the expense of the innocent. You have allowed the murderess to go free and Margaret Campbell, the innocent victim of circumstantial evidence, to be tried, convicted and only saved from a felon's death for the sake of her childish years, to be sent to this penal colony for life! Oh, Gow! it was a cruel and wicked course."

"I swear, by all my hopes of salvation, that I don't know what you are driving at, sir! I don't, indeed!" exclaimed the tramp, with an utterly puzzled and helpless look.

"You acted at first, no doubt, under a good impulse. It was merciful in you to withhold the testimony that might have consigned so young a girl, however guilty, to a felon's ignominous death!"

"That was the only reason why I held my tongue, sir!"

"And at first you might have been right. But when you saw another girl, a most innocent young girl, accused of this heinous deed—indicted, arraigned, tried, convicted, condemned to death for a crime you knew she never committed—why, I ask, in the name of justice and mercy, did you not, at some stage of these proceedings, go forward and give the testimony that would have vindicated the innocent, even if it had to convict the guilty?"

"I am all at sea, sir!" exclaimed Ham Gow in utter confusion. "Whom are you talking about, anyhow, if you please, sir?"

"Why, Margaret Campbell, of course!"

"Well, she was tried and convicted of the murder, wasn't she, without my evidence, either?"

"Yes, but—"

"And she was the one that did the murder, as they proved without my help! So where is the innocent girl that I allowed to be convicted? I let an innocent girl be convicted? I, Ham Gow? Surely, you don't know Ham Gow!"

Mr. Hamilton Gower sank back in his chair, overwhelmed and pale as death.

"There was no other girl tried for that crime except Margaret Campbell, who was convicted, was there, sir?"

"No," breathed Mr. Gower in the tone of a sigh.

"Then what did you mean by saying that I let the innocent suffer while I shielded the guilty? There must be some great misunderstanding between us," said Ham Gow in a perplexed manner.

"I think so, too! But tell me distinctly who was it that you saw drop the parcel—which afterward proved to be the body of the murdered child—into the well?"

"Margaret Campbell, of course! I thought you knew that!" said Ham Gow, raising his eyebrows.

"I know to the contrary! I know it was not Margaret Campbell, and could never have been she! She was falsely, foully accused! I am very glad that you did withhold your testimony, since you believed her to have been the criminal! But what led you to believe such a falsity?" asked Mr. Gower in an agitated voice.

Ham Gow shrugged his shoulders with a perfectly helpless look, and said within himself:

"One of us two must be demented! I wonder if there be anything in the climate of Hobart Town to turn people's 'wits? There was my old sweetheart, a sensible enough girl when I left her in England, talking and acting like a lunatic here in Hobart Town! And here is my old friend, the earl, who used to be considered an intelligent young man in the old country, carrying on like an idiot here! It must be the air of the place that don't agree with Cornwall wits! I'm glad we shall leave it so soon!"

"Gow, I asked what led you to believe that the girl you saw at the well that night of the murder was Margaret Campbell," demanded Mr. Hamilton Gower in a troubled voice.

"Why, the witness of my eyesight."

"But you had never seen her before, and you never saw her afterward, perhaps?"

"No; but there were corroborating facts."

"Lying, circumstantial evidence!" exclaimed Mr. Gower.

"And there was the printed description of the girl, which tallied exactly with her appearance at the well!"

"The printed description!" repeated Mr. Gower.

"Yes—I'll tell you! The girl I saw at the well seemed just at the turning point between child and woman-say about thirteen or fourteen years of age, small and slight, thin and pale, with delicate features, large eyes and a great quantity of long, light yellow hair."

"Was that the true personal appearance of the girl you saw?"

"Yes, it was! Under the circumstances is it likely that I could ever forget her looks? I speak from memory of what I saw! And now I will tell you the description I read of her in the paper, as she appeared when arraigned at the bar. It tallied so exactly with her looks at the well that I can repeat it nearly word for word. You see, the whole thing made such a deep impression on me."

"You need not repeat it. I am familiar with the description. I acknowledge that it does tally with what you say you saw of the girl at the well! But I tell you again that you are utterly mistaken in supposing that girl to have been Margaret Campbell!"

The tramp shook his head dubiously.

"The agreement between the printed description of Margaret Campbell and the personal appearance of the girl you saw at the well is the most convincing proof to your mind that they were one and the same person, is it not?"

"Yes, sir, it is! It can't be got over, you know!"

"And yet consider how superficial that description was, and how many young girls it would suit who might be very dissimilar in minor features—'fourteen years of age, small and slight, thin and pale, with delicate features, large eyes and light hair!' Why, there might be a dozen young girls whom that description would suit, and yet every one of them have different shaped foreheads, noses, mouths and chins, so that no two of them might be the least alike! Don't you see that?"

"Yes, sir, I see that; but I think the girl at the well that night was Margaret Campbell, all the same!"

"Will you tell me how you came to be on the premises of Rose Hill Manor that particular night, Gow?" somewhat impatiently inquired the young gentleman.

"Of course, sir! Willingly! I had been on the tramp through the North Riding of Yorkshire, and had been very unlucky, scarcely getting jobs enough to do to keep body and soul together. Indeed, I was at my very lowest ebb of luck—as near starving as a man could be—not to starve."

"Those evil days are over forever now, Ham, if you invest your money well."

"I hope they are, sir. Well, at the close of a dismal winter day I found myself, footsore, cold, hungry and half fainting, in the neighborhood of Rose Hill Manor. In that wintry weather, and at that late hour, none of the outdoor servants seemed to be about, so I crawled into a cow shed, where the

"'Milky mothers of the herd'
were lying down in clean, warm straw. I lay down among them, between a fat, comfortable old cow and a yearling calf, who laid its innocent, velvety head against my cold face in the most affectionate manner, and consoled me very much, I tell you."

"Poor fellow!" breathed Mr. Gower.

"Oh, I was happy then! I was under shelter, and warmed by the contact of my four-footed hostess, and cheered by the sympathy of her daughter, the calf, and so deliciously tired that I fell asleep to the music of the pattering rain on the shed roof."

"All happiness is comparative, Ham."

"Yes, I suppose it is. I know I slept deeply and sweetly for several hours. It must have been near day when I was awakened by the movements of my bovine hostess, who was struggling to her feet; the calf at the same time moved its gentle, witless head from my face. I remembered where I was, and at the same time I felt the sharpest pangs of hunger."

"My poor lad!"

"A sudden impulse seized me—to milk the cow, if she would let me! I opened the door of the cow shed to get a little light from the stars, if possible, and I fumbled through my pack and found the small tin pannikin that had been my companion in my tramps over the four quarters of the globe. By the time I had found it my horned and hoofed hostess had walked out of her house, intent upon some business of her own. I followed her, and found her at a little pile of fodder, helping herself to an early— —But perhaps I am wearying you with these details, sir?"

"No; I follow you. I wish to have a picture in my mind of the scene and circumstances of your discovery."

"I wish I could banish the picture forever from my mind!" sighed the tramp.

"Go on!" urged Mr. Gower.

"Well, I had some experience in the rural art and mystery of milking cows, and so I went to this milky mother and began to pat and coax and caress her. She was a very gentle creature, and she allowed me to milk her and fill my little pannikin and empty it until my hunger and thirst were fully satisfied. When this was done I arose to my feet, and then—"

"And then?" eagerly questioned Mr. Gower.

"I witnessed the scene that I have spoken of. The rain had ceased even before I had left the shed; now the moon was shining in the west, but was near her setting. As I arose to my feet I saw over the back of the cow the old well about three yards off, with the stables and a clump of dark trees at some little distance behind it. And stooping over the well I saw a white figure with a white bundle—the figure of a young girl clothed in a white gown and having long, fair hair hanging down her back. A superstitious thrill passed through me—the hour, the scene, the form, were all so ghostly. She stooped over the well and dropped something into it! I heard the low, soft thud as it struck the bottom! Then the girl turned and came toward me. She was within three feet of me before she saw me. Then we stood face to face with each other for what seemed to me one dreadful moment, her pale, thin face, white and wan in the moonlight, her large, wild eyes blazing as from an inward fire! She seemed to scan me half questioningly, half defiantly, as if she wished to know whether I had seen or suspected anything wrong in her errand to the well. But as she found neither suspicion nor danger in my looks, she turned and limped away as fast as her halting limb would permit her."

A great cry burst from the lips of Mr. Hamilton Gower.

"Now, what in the deuce is the matter with you?" exclaimed Ham Gow, forgetting his respects in his dismay.

Mr. Gower had started to his feet, and was shaking with excessive emotion.

"Say that again !" he exclaimed in husky, guttural tones.

"Say what again? Are we both gone daft together? demanded the sorely tried tramp.

"About the girl's limping! You said she limped! Did she limp?"

"Why, of course she did! Her right leg seemed to be shorter than her left, and her right shoulder lower than the left one."

"Heaven be praised!" exclaimed Mr. Hamilton Gower in great excitement.

"What for in this special instance?" questioned the disgusted tramp.

"For that which will now bring the truth to light, and vindicate the innocent. For if that child murderer was a deformed cripple, we shall be able to prove that which I knew before—that she was not Margaret Campbell!" exclaimed the young gentleman exultingly.

"How so, sir? How can you prove that?" inquired the tramp, with the tone and manner of one humoring and drawing out a lunatic.

"Because Margaret Campbell was not a deformed cripple! Margaret Campbell was as straight as an arrow, with a form as perfect as beautiful, and as well proportioned as that of the famous Medician Venus, with a step and movement as graceful and stately as that of an antelope! Ah, Gow! if you had only given your evidence in regard to this deformed cripple before the coroner's jury, what unutterable woe you would have saved Margaret Campbell and all who love her! But, thank Heaven! though the past cannot be recalled, the future may be redeemed! Your tardy testimony will even now restore her to liberty and to her native country. Thank Heaven! she will be saved! Did you linger long in the neighborhood after your discovery?" rather suddenly inquired Mr. Gower.

"I never lingered long anywhere, sir. And about the same time the girl limped away, I saw a man, who had come out of the stable with a lantern in his hand and was looking about himself. I thought he had been awakened by the cow; and not wishing to be seen, I slunk away into the clump of trees. I left as soon as it was daylight, and without the slightest suspicion that there was anything amiss about the place, or of the terrible tragedy that had been enacted there! Why, sir, if I thought anything of what I had seen I only thought it was a bundle of rubbish the girl had dropped into the dry well, and dismissed the subject from my mind until it was horribly recalled to me by the publication of the tragedy at Rose Hill. I was 'then down near Liverpool, and a few weeks later I left the country and was gone two years—after which I re- turned to England and went down to Cornwall, arriving at Hawkewood on the day of your *fête*, sir."

"Thank Heaven, she is saved!" exclaimed Mr. Gower, whose thought seemed to have wandered off from the narrative of Gow's travels to the subject of the unjustly condemned girl.

"You are very much interested in this case, sir," said the tramp.

"Profoundly interested in it," answered the young gentleman.

"And you really think, sir," said Ham Gow gravely and even sorrowfully, "that through my failure to reveal what I had seen the guilty party escaped and an innocent girl was condemned?"

"I am as sure of it as that I live! I have seen this girl in the colony," said the young gentleman cautiously, for he did not intend to take the tramp into his confidence in respect to Miss Elfinstar. "She has been assigned to private service in a gentleman's family in the country, where I am acquainted, and from all that I saw of the girl I felt sure that she could not have committed that crime. Your revelation has confirmed my faith in her."

"It is an awful reflection for me, sir, that by my silence I suffered an innocent young girl to be convicted. But I thought to a dead certainty that she was the one I saw—and the printed description suited her so well!"

"But that description said nothing about a halting gait, or a humpback, did it?" sarcastically inquired Mr. Gower.

"Well, no; but I did not think that omission of any consequence; for, you see, I was already confirmed in my belief that the accused girl was the same whom I had seen. Besides, there was another witness—the stableman who had been disturbed by the cow and had come out in time to see the girl at the well—who testified that she was Margaret Campbell."

"He saw the girl from a greater distance. He was mistaken in her as well as yourself."

"Yes, sir, I must believe that now. But, then, there was the market gardener, who saw her near the house, you know."

"He saw the figure of a young girl, clothed in white, near the house at an unusual hour, but he did not pretend to identify the girl as Miss Campbell, I think."

"And there was other testimony that went to confirm me in my opinion."

"All the merest circumstantial evidence, that could have been blown away by a breath of the testimony you were able to give concerning that deformed cripple whom you saw at the well."

"Oh, if I had only known! If I had only come forward and testified! But, sir, who could that little monster have been?"

"One whom I strongly suspected of the crime before I heard your story—a deformed, malignant idiot, who was a member of the Rose Hill household, but of whom it is not yet time to speak further. When we get back to England, we will work up the case until we can fix the guilt where it belongs, and vindicate the innocent."

"Heaven knows I will be with you heart and hand in that, sir."

"I am sure of that. When does the *Labrador* sail?"

"The captain hopes to get away by Saturday."

"And this is Tuesday. There is something to be done in the meantime. We must be busy. At least, I must. And now about your faithful betrothed, Ham. What are you going to do? Leave her here?"

"Oh, no, sir! My greatest wish in returning to England was to rejoin her! It was an unlooked-for joy to find her here; though that was soon turned into grief by her conduct toward me."

"Which I hope I have explained to your satisfaction, Ham."

"Oh, yes, sir, I thank you; quite so."

"And you will take her back to England with you?"

"Oh, yes, sir!" laughed Ham Gow. "Though I certainly did not expect to find a wife out here and take her home, yet I shall rejoice to have Lona, if she will come with me. You see, I must take her on every account, for I don't want to have to come back here after her. A six or eight months' voyage is no light undertaking."

"Indeed, it is not. Well, since you have to arrange preliminaries with your sweetheart, I think you had better see her at once. I will take you around to Lieut. Belle Isle's quarters."

"Thank you, sir; I am ready," said Ham Gow.

And the two men walked out together.

CHAPTER X
REVIVING HOPE

As Mr. Hamilton Gower, accompanied by Ham Gow, turned into Macquarrie Street on his way to the barracks, a question of etiquette arose to perplex him.

How was he to dispose of his companion on reaching the lieutenant's quarters?

Was he to take the tramp up into Mrs. Belle Isle's parlor?

Scarcely.

And that parlor and the dining room beyond were the only apartments in the house with which he was acquainted.

It is true, Mrs. Belle Isle had said to him:

"When this wonderful Ham Gow, with the innumerable doubles, arrives at Hobart Town, bring him directly here.

"But, then, did that lady mean that he was to take the tramp upstairs into her presence?

"I wish," said Mr. Gower to himself, "that my worthy tutor, in teaching me much Greek, and Latin, and Hebrew, and mathematics, had given me some chance of learning the ways of the world!"

When he rang the bell at the lieutenant's quarters, an, orderly opened the door.

"Is Mrs. Belle Isle at home?" inquired Mr. Gower.

"Yes, sir; walk upstairs, if you please," politely responded the man.

"Stay; you may take this card up first," said the young gentleman, drawing his ordinary visiting card from its case and writing one line:

"I have brought Gow with me, according to orders."

The man took the message upstairs, and in two minutes returned, saying:

"Madam's compliments, and you bring your friend up, if you please, sir."

"Come, Gow," said the young gentleman, going upstairs preceded by the orderly, and followed by the tramp.

They found Mrs. Belle Isle seated alone in her parlor and engaged upon her favorite Berlin wool work, which she laid aside as she arose and came forward to meet her visitors.

Hamilton Gower greeted her with warm respect, bending low over the hand that he held.

Then he presented his friend, whom the lady received with cordial kindness.

"You have had a pleasant voyage from Melbourne, I hope," she said, turning to Ham Gow when they were all seated.

"Yes, madam, a very quick and pleasant voyage, I thank you," responded Ham Gow, whom all Mrs. Belle Isle's kindness failed to place at his ease.

At length she said to him:

"You wish to see some one who is in the house here, I believe?"

"Yes, madam, if you please; a young girl whom I understand to be in your service at present, and to whom I have been long engaged."

"Lona Pond?"

"The same, madam, thank you."

"You shall see here at once," said the lady, rising and ringing the bell.

Ham Gow fidgeted, and felt more uneasy than ever. He did not certainly wish to meet his sweetheart in that parlor in the presence of the lady and the gentleman.

When the orderly answered the bell, the lady said:

"Show Mr. Gow into the dining room, and send Lona Pond up to see him."

The orderly saluted, and opened the door.

Ham Gow, much relieved, blithely sprang up and bowed and followed his conductor to the adjoining apartment where he seated himself in a high-backed chair to await the coming of Lona Pond, whom the orderly went to send.

In a very few minutes the girl entered—more shyly than she had ever before come into the presence of her lover.

Ham Gow, seeing this hesitation and confusion on her part, and attributing both to the right cause, sprang up, hastened to meet her and fold her to his honest heart, murmuring in her ear:

"My love! my dearest! I know all about it now, and so do you. You will not take me for my 'fetch' now?"

"Oh, Ham, dear I took two other 'fetches' for you first; and then I got so discouraged from disappointment, and so mortified by—by—by—taking a gentleman for you, that I couldn't believe it was you when I did see you at last!"

"I understand how that could be, my dear! And so, my true-hearted girl, you really crossed the seas and came this long, long, long voyage for the sake of finding a poor, good-for-nothing fugitive like me!" he said, looking tenderly, penitently, into her pretty face.

"You are not good for nothing, Ham, and you shall not call yourself so! You are good and true, Ham! Yes, as good as gold, and as true as steel! If you had not been so I should never have come so many thousand miles to find you!" she gently replied.

"Ah, my dear! I wish, I wish that I were all you take me to be! But I will try to be so! I will for your sake, Lona! And you have crossed the sea once for love of me! Will you cross it again for my, sake?"

"What do you mean, Ham?"

"I came here to-day to ask you that question. Will you cross the sea again for my sake? Ah! I see you don't understand! I am going back to England by the *Labrador* that is to sail on Saturday. Will you marry me between now and then, and go with me?"

They were by this time seated in two high-backed chairs that were drawn as closely together as such uncompromising seats could be persuaded to come, and as he asked this question he stole his arm around her waist.

"Will you, Lona? Will you?" he repeated, seeing that she hesitated to answer him.

"Oh, Ham, can you be in earnest? It is so sudden!"she said; but the light of joy beamed from her face.

"I am in dead earnest, of course, Lona. And as for its being sudden— you can't call it that after such a long engagement! Besides, we have no time to delay, Lona, dear. The *Labrador* sails on Saturday, and I am obliged to go with her on the most important business that cannot be put off! And the alternative is that we marry and go together, or that I go alone, and leave you here alone. 'It may be for years, and it may be forever,' as the old song says, and says truly. Now, can you doubt which alternative to choose? Speak, Lona, dear!"

"Well—then—Ham," she began, hesitating and blushing, "since— such is the case—I suppose-'What can't be cured must be endured,' and I shall have to go with you."

"My own true-hearted love, you shall never, never have cause to regret it!" warmly responded Ham Gow, sealing the promise on her lips.

"Mr. Hamilton Gower is going home, too, by the *Labrador*, is he not?" uneasily inquired the girl.

"Yes, he is."

"You know I hugged that gentleman by mistake for you! I hugged him hard. Oh! I hope I won't see him on the ship!" aspirated Lona, with such a genuine dismay that Ham Gow laughed aloud, saving:

"I think he forgave you, my dear! Indeed, I don't think he minded it one bit! And no more do I, seeing that it was all meant for me! And so neither need you, you know! Just try to forget all about it, Lona!"

"I wish I could!"

They talked some time longer—so long, indeed, that Ham Gow's conscience began to accuse him of trespassing though he could not tear himself away from his so recently recovered sweetheart, until a servant entered the dining room and began to lay the cloth for dinner.

"I think you had better go now, Ham, dear," said Lona gently. "I hate to send you away, but I think you had better go."

"And when shall I see you again ?" he inquired, rising and taking his tarpaulin hat from the floor where he had dropped it.

"Any evening you please. I am engaged all day, but in the evening I am free."

"May I come this evening?"

"Yes, and take me to a concert at the Lyceum."

"All right. What time?"

"Half-past seven."

"I will be on time !" said Ham Gow, and-the servant being busy at the cabinet, with his back toward the lovers—they kissed and parted.

Ham Gow went into the parlor, where, on his appearance, Mr. Hamilton Gower arose to take leave.

When they had left the house and found themselves on the street, Ham Gow, with boyish frankness and delight, told his friend and patron of his reconciliation with Lona and of their approaching marriage. Mr. Gower congratulated him, and inquired on what day the auspicious ceremony was to be performed.

"Before we sail, of course, sir; but only just before, Lona says. So, as the *Labrador* leaves on Saturday afternoon, we'll get the knot tied on Saturday morning, quietly, you know, sir, by the chaplain of the regiment. And I hope you will be on hand, sir, to—to—to—"

"Give the bride away? Of course I shall!" laughed Mr. Gower.

"To wish us good luck, I was going to say, sir. I hadn't thought of such an honor as the other."

"Never mind! I have a fancy for giving the bride away, and I shall do it."

"You are very kind, sir," said Ham Gow.

When they reached the Royal Victoria, Mr. Gower paused before entering the house, and said:

"Gow, I am going to take a ride a few miles out into the country to a house where I know I can make you welcome for as long as you would like to stay; but we cannot get back to-night. Will you go with me?"

"Well, no, sir, I thank you very much, if you will excuse me. I have an engagement to take Lona to the Lyceum this evening."

"Ah, to be sure! Well, go in the house, there's a good fellow, and order dinner to be served for us immediately in my apartment. I am going around to the stables to take a look at my horse."

They separated there, Mr. Gower turning off toward the stable, and Ham Gow passing into the office of the hotel.

A quarter of an hour later the friends met at a *tête-à-tête* dinner in Mr. Gower's apartments.

"What are you going to do with yourself until it is time to go to the Lyceum?" inquired Mr. Gower, when they finally arose from the table.

"Saunter around the town and see the sights," replied Gow.

"Well, you will not see me again until tomorrow morning. My horse is at the door."

"I will see you into your saddle, then, at all events," said Ham Gow.

Mr. Gower took his hat, gloves and whip, and led the way downstairs.

A few minutes later the young gentleman was cantering briskly out of town on his way to Mount Wellington.

He had left the Hermitage only that morning, and certainly he was not expected back there that evening.

Yet he could not resist the impulse to hurry to the presence of Mr. Elfinstar and Seraph, and tell them the glorious news that a witness had providentially turned up whose testimony would clear Margaret Campbell from every imputation of guilt; and that the vindication of her character and the restoration of her liberty was no longer a matter of anxious hope, but of positive certainty.

Never had Mr. Hamilton Gower ridden along so gaily as on this bright afternoon.

The sun set before he reached the foot of Mount Wellington and began to wind up the ascent to the plateau by the shorter bridle path.

The moon and stars were shining with the glorious light they shed over the nights of the Southern hemisphere, when he finally reached the Hermitage. The father and daughter were sitting out under the veranda enjoying the beauty of the hour. As he rode up and threw himself from his saddle the old gentleman arose and hurried to meet in some trepidation. He was made anxious by the untimely visit.

"Oh, I understand it too well! The *Labrador* arrived while he was here yesterday, or this morning, and she is to sail for England immediately! He has come to bid good-by!" said Seraph, turning pale and faint.

As he hastily shook hands with Mr. Elfinstar, his lover ears caught the purport of her murmured words, and he hastened to reassure her.

"No, love, no!" he exclaimed, catching her hand and carrying it to his lips. "I have not come to bid you good-by, but to bring you the most glorious news that could possibly reach you! I could not keep such news until to-morrow!"

Father and daughter gazed on his face in anxious, vague expectancy.

"It is not—it cannot be—a full pardon from the queen!"breathed the old gentleman in a sudden fever and ague of hope and fear.

"Better than that! Oh, infinitely better than that! It is a full vindication! What is a full pardon compared to a full vindication? Come, Mr. Elfinstar! Come, dear Seraph! Let me sit between you, while I tell the glorious news!" he exclaimed, as he seated himself on the bench, with the old gentleman on his right and the young lady on his left.

And there, in an eager, rapid, but distinct and graphic manner, he related all the particulars of Ham Gow's adventure at Rose Hill on the night of the murder.

"And now, you see," he said in conclusion, "that your full vindication is no longer 'the fair illusive dream' that you have called it, my Seraph; but it is the 'sober certainty of waking bliss'! I shall sail with this witness for England in the *Labrador* on Saturday. Be you as happy and as hopeful as possible, my love, during my absence! As soon as I reach London I shall lay the facts of this case before the home secretary, and the next returning ship shall bring out to you the order of your discharge."

"Oh, can this be possible? Can this, indeed, be possible? Oh, my dear father, answer me!" pleaded Seraph, fearful of believing too easily in the promised happiness.

"My dear, it is true, true " replied the old gentleman, laying his hand caressingly on his daughter's head.

"And you, you who expatriated yourself to share your child's exile; oh, my more than father! You will return to England to spend the rest of your life in your own home! Oh, that thought makes me happiest of all!" she cried, throwing herself into the arms of the old gentleman and fervently embracing him.

"Let us go in, my love; the night air grows chilly," he said at length, gently disengaging his child's arms from about his neck. "Come, Mr. Gower."

The three entered the house together.

Mr. Elfinstar rang and ordered a tray of refreshments brought into the drawing room.

"You have had a long ride, Mr. Gower, and you must have something before you retire," he said in explanation.

When these refreshments had been served and discussed and the evening prayers and thanksgivings had offered up, the small party bade each other good-night, separated and retired to rest.

The next morning, at the breakfast table, it was arranged that Mr. and Miss Elfinstar should accompany Gower back to Hobart Town, and remain at the Royal Victoria until the following Saturday night, in order to see the voyagers off in the *Labrador*.

This had been done at the earnest solicitation of Mr. Hamilton Gower, supported by the mute entreaty of Seraph Elfinstar's soft blue eyes—influences to which the spirited old man easily yielded.

"I think there can be no serious objection to this course," he explained, when his daughter had left them to prepare for the journey, and he and his guest were walking up and down the front piazza. "No objection, because no soul in the town—no soul on earth, except you and me and Seraph—know her identity with Margaret Campbell, for not only in these three years and a half that she has here has spent here she developed from the thin, pale, sallow, broken-hearted child into the beautiful woman that you see in her now, but every officer in the colony who was here when she arrived has been changed. We have an entire new civil and military administration. Some of the officials of course, knew that Margaret Campbell is in my house; but they think that she is there as a domestic, and every one who has seen or heard of Seraph believes her to be my daughter. I shall be glad to give her this change. She has not left the Hermitage since her arrival here."

"I thank you so much for giving us this happiness of being together for these last few days, and I look forward with the deepest delight to the time when I may be instrumental in bringing you both the best change that could come to you—the change from exile back to your native land," said the young man earnestly.

The appearance of Seraph Elfinstar, dressed for her journey, interrupted the conversation.

"I have only had a few articles put in a couple of valises, father, dear; but I have ordered Jenny to pack a trunk to send after us," said the young lady.

The carriage was coming up toward the house, and seeing it, the two gentlemen stepped back into the hall to get their hats and gloves.

"Suppose you take a seat in the carriage with us and allow one of the boys to ride your horse back," said Mr. Elfinstar.

"With great pleasure," assented the young man.

And in a few minutes later the three friends, seated inside the coach, and having Jonas Stackpole on the box, were driving slowly down the mountain road, attended by Peter, the groom, mounted on Mr. Gower's horse.

Hamilton Gower, with Seraph Elfinstar by his side on the front seat, and the kindly old gentleman opposite to them, thought that this was about the most delightful drive he had ever enjoyed in the whole course of his life.

They reached Hobart Town about noon, and were provided with a fine suit of apartments on the first floor front of the Royal Victoria

Hotel—immediately across the hall and opposite to Mr. Hamilton Gower's room.

Ham Gow was nowhere visible about the house, but, might be supposed to be in attendance on his bethothed.

After luncheon the three friends walked out into the town together, and Seraph Elfinstar was as much delighted as any child could have been at the gayety and variety of the shops—the bookstores, the picture dealers, the fancy bazaars—all had the attraction of novelty for the young girl who had not been shopping for nearly five years.

It will be easily understood that the public buildings—which consisted principally of the government offices, military and convict barracks, jails and hospitals—objects of interest to most strangers visiting Hobart Town, had no attractions, but, on the contrary, a strong repulsion for Seraph Elfinstar. She avoided them with horror, and kept away as much as possible even from the streets that led to them.

In the evening she went to a concert with her father and her lover, and enjoyed the music, the lights and the gay crowd with the keen delight of one long deprived of such pleasures.

In the auditorium Mr. Gower caught sight of Ham Gow and Lona Pond, seated side by side.

He pointed out the tramp to the old gentleman, saying:

"That man is your witness!"

Mr. and Miss Elfinstar both gazed at the man with the deepest interest.

"I never set eyes on him before," said the old gentleman.

"He has a fine face—a very familiar one-Why, he is like you!" whispered Seraph, turning suddenly to her lover.

"Yes, very like you, Mr. Gower!" added her father, who had overheard her remark.

He saw that Ham Gow was also regarding him and his party with the greatest curiosity and interest.

But the commencement of the music soon attracted all their attention.

When the concert was over Mr. Hamilton Gower missed Ham Gow in the crowd that was pouring out of the hall; but that night, after he had reached the hotel, left his friends at the door of their apartments and had retired to his own room, the tramp came to him.

"I have been looking for you all day," said Mr. Gower.

"I have been most of the day with Lona Pond," replied Ham Gow.

"You saw the lady and gentleman who were with me?" said Gower.

"Oh, yes. The angel and the gentleman, you mean, sir! How heavenly beautiful she is, sir!"

"Yes; did you never see her before?" inquired Mr. Gower, with an affectation of carelessness.

"Never in my life, sir! Where was I see her? I never was in Hobart Town before."

"Did you ever see any one who looked like her?"

"Never, sir. I do not believe there is another lady in the world like her!" exclaimed Ham Gow enthusiastically.

"Neither do I," frankly admitted Mr. Hamilton Gower, whose questions to the tramp had been dictated not by any faintest suspicion that the latter had seen her at the well on the night of the murder, but by the desire to bring out in the strongest manner the fact that Gow had not set eyes on her anywhere before, and could not, therefore, be mistaken in the person of the girl at the well.

"And now, if you please, sir, as I only dropped in to pay my respects, and it is late, I will bid you good-night," said Ham Gow, moving to depart.

"Good-night, and much obliged," replied Mr. Gower, as he closed the door after his visitor.

The next morning Mr. Hamilton Gower proposed to take Miss Elfinstar for a drive along the beautiful banks of the Derwent. Before the young couple left the hotel, and while Seraph Elfinstar was in her bedroom putting on her bonnet, Mr. Hamilton Gower took Ham Gow into Mr.Elfinstar's parlor and introduced him to the old gentleman, and then said:

"Now, Gow, I wish you to relate to my friend here the particulars of your adventure at Rose Hill on the night of the murder. But you need not begin until Miss Elfinstar has left the house. You can entertain him with the story during the absence of his daughter and myself."

"All right, sir; I will do it."

The lovers went for their drive, and were gone three hours.

When they got back to the hotel and Seraph Elfinstar had gone to her room to change her dress, leaving her father and her lover alone together in the parlor, the old gentleman said:

"I have heard the whole story from Gow—and, if there had been any doubt in my mind—which there was not—his narrative must have dispelled it! My daughter is saved!"

"Undoubtedly! But here she comes! Let us change the subject."

Seraph came in, looking fresh and blooming from her drive, and the three friends sat down to luncheon.

On the following Saturday morning, Ham Gow and Lona Pond were quietly married in the little chapel of the barracks, Mr. Hamilton Gower acting as groomsman, and Lieut. Belle Isle giving away the bride.

The Elfinstars were not present at the wedding; for though no one knew the identity of Margaret Campbell and Seraph Elfinstar except the three friends, they deemed it best not to attract too much attention to the father and daughter.

The bridegroom and the bride, after an affectionate leavetaking of their friends, went immediately to the ship.

That afternoon Mr. Hamilton Gower, having lingered to the last safe moment in the close carriage that had brought his friends and himself down to the wharf, bade a mournful but a firm and hopeful good-by to his love and her father, and went on board the boat that was to take him to the ship just one second before the gangplank was drawn in.

Half an hour later, before a fair wind and outgoing tide, the good ship *Labrador*, with all her canvas spread, sailed for England.

CHAPTER XI
ON THE TRAIL

THE *Labrador* made a rapid, prosperous, and, therefore, uneventful voyage, leaving nothing for the narrator to chronicle, unless it were the changes of the weather, of the seasons, and of the bill of fare, which would scarcely make an interesting chapter of accidents.

She reached her landing at the East India Docks, London, early on the morning of the first of August.

"And now, Ham," said Mr. Gower, as they stepped on shore, "we will have a whole month before us, you see, for it would not do for me to go down to Cornwall and present myself at Hawke Hall until I shall be legally qualified to act for myself, which will not be the case until I shall have attained my majority, which I shall not do, as you well know, until my twenty-first birthday, which will come round on the first of next September."

"Yes, sir. I am aware of that," replied Ham, who was busily engaged in elbowing and pushing a way for himself and Mrs. Gow through the crowd.

"You know, of course, that I do not wish to show myself at Hawke Hall until I can take command of affairs there in my own proper person," continued Mr. Gower.

"Of course; quite so, sir; but what do you intend to do in the meantime?"

"Just what I have been talking about doing ever since I began to suspect that we should make an early arrival, and have some weeks on our hands before it would be time to go down into Cornwall! I intend to stop in London and work up the case of Margaret Campbell."

"You, you keep to that plan."

"Decidedly! See here! Here is a cab stand. We had better take a cab and go at once to some good inn. Do you know of one near?" inquired Mr. Gower.

"The Crown and Anchor is not far off, sir. It is clean and quiet, or it used to be so when I knew it; but it might not suit you, sir."

"We'll try it," said Mr. Gower, as he signaled a cabman, who immediately touched his cap and turned his horse toward the party.

"To the Crown and Anchor!" said Mr. Gower, when the three were comfortably seated in the vehicle.

The cabman touched his hat again and started his horse, and in about fifteen minutes they drew up before one of the oldest inns in London.

It was a substantial building of dark-red brick, and small twisted chimneys, and broad windows with iron sashes and small, diamond-shaped panes, and with a high, brick arch-way leading to the courtyard, at the back of which were the substantial stone stables and coach houses.

From this "hostelry," in the good old times, a line of mail coaches to or from Dover started or arrived twice daily; and here, in still older times, knights and squires and "lords of high degree," as well as farmers, teamsters and men of low estate, fed their beasts and regaled themselves.

Mr. Gower paid and discharged the cab and led the way in to an antique taproom, presided over by a short, stout, middle-aged man in a fustian suit, with a red waistcoat and a redder face—a man who might have stepped out of one of the old English comedies.

To this functionary Mr. Gower made known the wants of his party — a suite of rooms with two chambers and a parlor.

The man in the red waistcoat handed the mug of foam- ing ale to the customer for whom he had been drawing it, and then called a waiter in a white apron, and said:

"Party wants two beds and one sitting."

The waiter in the white apron touched the top of his low forehead and summoned a chambermaid in a cap with blue ribbons, and instructed her to show "this lady and gents into the Griffin and the Dragon and the Salamander."

Mrs. Ham's brows went up and her chin dropped down at this alarming command; but her husband calmed her fears by whispering:

"It is only the names of the rooms, my dear, and nice, cozy rooms they are, if I may judge of what I have seen of the place before!"

And "nice, cozy rooms" they were truly found to be, when the friends had followed the chambermaid in the cap trimmed with blue ribbons upstairs.

There were three rooms in a row on one side of a quiet passage.

The chambermaid unlocked the door of the middle which was labeled Salamander, and invited the guests to enter.

They did so, and found themselves in a large, square, antique parlor, whose floor, walls and low ceiling were all of dark oak wood, and whose one wide window was glazed with small, diamond-shaped panes, and whose broad fireplace was lined with Dutch tiles and adorned with bright brass andirons, shovel, tongs and fender, and decorated with a jar of paper flowers—for there was no fire at this warm season. The furniture was upholstered in dark-red serge; but the floor was bare except for two Turkey rugs, one of which lay before the fireplace and the other before the red sofa that stood below the red-curtained window.

A door on the right and one on the left led into the adjoining bedrooms.

"This gives one the feeling of being in a large wooden box, does it not?" said Ham Gow.

"It does so! And it smells so old !" answered Mrs. Ham, sitting down in the large red serge-covered easy-chair.

"The bedrooms open right and left from this, ma'am. Any orders, ma'am?" inquired the chambermaid, addressing the "lady."

"I don't know! Ham, dear—Mr. Gower, please, sir!" said Mrs. Ham, helplessly appealing to her two companions.

"Yes, breakfast in this room as soon as it can be served," said Mr. Gower.

"What would you like, sir?" inquired the girl.

"Anything at all, so that it is cleanly and quickly served!" said Mr. Gower.

The girl left the room, and the young man turned to his fellow travelers, and added:

"You see, I am in a fever to get to Scotland Yard."

"I know you are, sir," replied Gow.

"You must go there with me, Ham!"

"Of course, sir! Little use your going without me, I reckon."

"And you must get some papers for Mrs. Ham to read while we are gone. By the way, let your wife take a look at the bedrooms and select one for yourselves."

"Hadn't you better take your choice first, sir?"

"As if I had a preference! No, I will take the one that shall be left."

"I dare say there isn't any difference between them! Lona, lass, take a look at the two rooms, will you?"

Mrs. Ham arose and went into the room on the right, which seemed to satisfy her; and then, actuated by curiosity rather than by fastidiousness, she went into the room on the left, and came out looking so evidently disappointed that Ham laughed and remarked:

"Not so good as the first one, eh?"

"They are both exactly alike, even to the ugly, old-fashioned, four-post bedsteads, and heavy chintz curtains, and the hideous china images on the mantelshelf. But, as I have to take one or the other, though there is no choice. I'll take this last one," said Mrs. Ham, as she turned and re-entered the room to lay off her bonnet.

The waiter now entered the parlor to lay the cloth for breakfast on the round oak table that stood in the center.

The meal was promptly served, and as soon as it had been discussed Mr. Gower and witness went out and took a cab and drove to Scotland Yard.

On arriving at the police headquarters Mr. Gower asked to see the chief on important business.

He was shown at once into an inner office, where, beside a table covered with heavy books and bundles of documents, sat a tall, portly, gray-haired and gray-bearded man, who looked more like one's idea of an archbishop than a police officer.

Recognizing a gentleman in the manner and appearance of Mr. Gower, he arose and bowed, requesting his visitors to be seated.

"And I must beg you, sir, to dispatch your business with me as promptly as can be convenient, for time is valuable," he said, with more politeness in his tone than was expressed in his words.

"I will not trespass, sir. I want the services of the most skillful and experienced detective officer on the force. I want to employ him in a case that I am perfectly willing explain, if you have leisure to listen to me—"

"That depends. If you have important information to lodge I must make time to hear it—but, otherwise—" said the chief.

"It is otherwise, at present. I am not quite prepared for so decided a measure. I want your most skillful and experienced detective officer. I am aware that there are men to be found who call themselves private detectives, but they are not always to be relied upon; so I prefer to get one from you."

"You think ours are, then?"

"I think they are more likely to be."

The chief smiled in a peculiar manner, and said:

"I will send you Hutchings. He can be relied upon at least for sharpness, discretion and experience. What address?"

"Mr. Hamilton Gower, Crown and Anchor Inn, near East India Docks."

The chief took it down, and said:

"Hutchings will wait on you in the course of the morning."

Mr. Gower thanked the chief, and left the office, attended by his friend.

When they returned to the Crown and Anchor, Mr. Gower left word with the barkeeper that if anyone should call to inquire for him the person should be sent up to his apartment.

Then the two men went upstairs to while away the time as best they could while waiting for the detective officer.

It was twelve o'clock before Hutchings made his appearance.

He was a small, spare man, about forty years of age. He had rather a large head, the back and sides of which were covered with short, black hair. He had a large, bare, projecting forehead, and bushy eyebrows overhanging a pair of deeply set, keen, black eyes; a thin, sharp, turned-up nose, and a heavy, black mustache and beard that covered his mouth and chin. He wore a black cloth suit and a white necktie, and he looked like a dissenting clergyman.

"A natural born as well as a regularly ordained detective," whispered Ham Gow to himself as he took stock of this physiognomy.

"I have the honor to speak to Mr. Gower," said the detective, when he had shut the door and advanced into the room, instinctively addressing himself to the right man.

"My name is Gower," said the latter. "And yours?"

"Hutchings, at your service, sir. The chief sent me to this address."

"At my request. I have a very important case upon which I wish to employ you."

"Quite so, sir. I am ready."

"It is understood that all which passes in this room is to be held as private and confidential?"

"Just so, sir," assented the detective, with an inquiring glance toward Ham Gow.

"Oh, that man is connected with the case," explained Mr.Gower.

"Ah!" exclaimed Hutchings.

"But, Ham, where is Mrs. Ham?" inquired Mr. Gower, in an aside to his companion.

"Oh, she has gone out in a cab, shopping. She didn't come through the parlor, which is the reason why you didn't see her," replied Mrs. Ham's lord and master.

"Then we can proceed to business," said Mr. Gower, and the three men drew their chairs to the table.

"Mr. Hutchings," said the young gentleman, coming directly to the point," do you remember the notorious Rose Hill case?"

"Of the child mysteriously missing from its nursery for several days, and then at last found dead at the bottom of a dry well? Yes, sir, I remember it. It occurred between four and five years ago."

"Yes, you were perhaps on that case."

"No, sir, I was not on it," replied the detective, with an emphasis of denial that seemed to indicate offense taken at the question.

Mr. Gower looked at him sharply, but discovered nothing more from his guarded face.

"I was down at Liverpool, sir, looking up a bank robbery," added Hutchings.

"Oh, excuse me; I had hoped that you had been on that case."

"I was not, sir."

"Then you know nothing about it?"

"Nothing but what I read in the newspapers and heard and saw at the trial; for I did attend the trial, sir."

"I had hoped that you had been on duty at Rose Hill at the time of the search and investigation—which would have afforded you better opportunities of forming a just opinion that either the reading of the newspapers or attending the court would have done; for it is on this very case, observe, that I wish to employ you," said Mr. Gower.

Hutchings looked up with awakened interest.

"Some new facts have come to my knowledge in regard to that child murder," added Mr. Gower.

"I am not at all surprised to hear it, sir."

"How! You are not surprised to hear it?"

"No, sir, I am not."

"Why are you not, may I ask? Had you already formed an opinion different from the verdicts rendered at the inquest and at the trial? Remember, Mr. Hutchings, that it is this very case that has brought us together to-day, and that our relations are now confidential. Speak freely to me! Did you differ in opinion from the judge and jury that tried that case?"

"Well, sir, I can't say that I absolutely differed from them; but I have, and I had from the first, the strongest doubts as to the guilt of that child they transported for life!"

"Ah! you had! You were right! We hope to be able to prove her innocence of that crime," said Mr. Gower.

Hutchings looked up with more interest than before.

Mr. Gower continued:

"You say that you had the strongest doubts of the condemned girl's guilt. Had you, at the same time, any suspicion as to the identity of the real criminal?"

"No, sir, I had not—unless— But, indeed, I prefer not to express my suspicion," said the detective, correcting himself.

"Let me express it for you! Let me finish your sentence 'unless'—it was of the half-witted, deformed girl who was Miss Campbell's roommate and first accuser!" solemnly added Mr. Gower.

"Sir! How came you to arrive at that conclusion?" demanded the detective.

"Because that girl, Malvina Mattox, was really the guilty party, as we shall soon be able to prove! There was an eyewitness to the murder; but as, for certain reasons, that shall be explained hereafter, he did not appear as a witness at the time of the murder, his testimony might not be sufficient to clear the innocent, unless it was supported by corroborative evidence, and it is this evidence that we wish you to discover."

"Tell me all the facts that have come to your knowledge, sir, and produce your eyewitness, if you please," said Hutchings.

"Here he is!—Mr. Gow. He will give you all the facts. He was on a pedestrian tour at the time, and being caught in the rain on the night of the murder he took shelter under a shed near that old well where the body of the child was found. Gow, tell the story as you told it to me."

125

The Test of Love

The young "pedestrian" nodded, and began his narrative.

The detective was a most attentive listener. He drew a capacious notebook from his pocket and took down in shorthand the words of the narrator.

Sometimes he stopped to ask questions or to make a comment.

When the story was finished he closed his notebook and put it, with his pencil, into his pocket, remarking:

"It is a pity you had not given in this evidence at the time. But I appreciate your motive. Thinking that the law had got hold of the right party, and that she was only a half-witted child, you did not wish to help to put the rope around her neck."

"That was it, of course," assented Gow; "but now I know that my holding back caused an innocent girl's conviction, I do feel guilty of all her misfortunes, and I shall never feel easy until I have atoned for my fault. Would not my testimony alone be sufficient to clear the young lady, sir?"

"It might if you were a doctor of divinity; but as you are not, your testimony will be all the better for being corroborated by other evidence."

"What is your advice in the premises?" inquired Mr. Gower.

"To put the suspected girl—"

"The 'suspected' girl, indeed! The criminal girl, you should say!" exclaimed Mr. Gower.

"To put her under secret surveillance, then! It cannot be, if she has committed this crime, that she has not at some time betrayed herself and does not continue to do so."

To put her under secret surveillance! That is exactly what I wish you to do!"

"Where is the girl now?"

"I do not know. You had best go to Rose Hill and make secret investigations. When could you start for Yorkshire?"

"To-night."

"Very well, then. Here are a hundred pounds to begin with. Spare no expense in the quest, and write to me daily at this address," said Mr. Gower, putting a roll of bank notes into the hand of the detective.

"I will write a receipt for this money, sir, and keep an exact account of its expenditure," said Hutchings, as he counted over the notes.

Pen, ink and paper being supplied to him, he wrote out an acknowledgment for a hundred pounds, gave it to Mr. Gower, and took his leave.

"Will you want to see us for any further purpose before you start?" inquired Mr. Gower.

"Not again. Oh, no—not at all. You will next hear from me at Rosedale, where I shall make my headquarters while investigating Rose Hill," answered the detective as he walked out of the room.

"Now what on earth shall we do with ourselves, while waiting for news?" inquired Hamilton Gower, disconsolately.

"I propose that we just run down to Hawkeville and see how the place looks. We need not discover ourselves prematurely—at least you need not," suggested Ham Gow.

"But our going seems incompatable with the business we have taken up," replied Mr. Gower.

"Oh, I don't think so at all! We can go and return before we shall be wanted on this business. Listen: It is now two o'clock. There is a train leaves Paddington at four," said Ham Gow, with all the eagerness of a confirmed vagabond, who could not rest long in any one place, as he fixed his eyes on a page in the Bradshaw he had been consulting through the morning.

"Well, there's a train leaves Paddington at four-what then?" inquired Mr. Gower.

"We can leave by that train, reach Hawkeville by day-light, run down to Demondike and see the Nans, and learn all the news at the Hall, and leave again by the afternoon train, and reach London on the following morning in full time to receive the first letter that Hutchings could possibly write you from Rosedale. Don't you see?"

"Well-yes! the plan seems practicable enough! But how about Mrs. Ham? Would you leave her here until our return?"

"Leave her here, sir? Not a bit of it! Why, she would be sure to come to grief, if not to ruin, if she were to be left here alone! I would not leave her any sooner than I would leave a child five years old."

"So I supposed! But how are you going to take Mrs. Ham, if she has not returned?" inquired Mr. Gower.

"Humph! I— But she has returned!" exclaimed Ham Gow, breaking off from his first answer as the door opened and Mrs. Ham entered the room, radiant from her ride.

She was immediately informed by her husband of the proposed expedition to Hawkeville, and she was as pleased as a child with the prospect.

She hurried into her room to pack a small valise for the journey.

While she was thus engaged Mr. Gower rang and ordered luncheon to be served as quickly as possible.

When she came out she found the table set, but as there was no luncheon on it as yet, she proposed to go into Mr. Gower's room and put up his necessaries for the journey.

"I have packed a bag for Ham and me," she said, "and now I would like to pack a bag for you, Mr. Gower."

"My dear, I never take anything but a hair brush, a tooth brush and a clean shirt when I go a journey—and those I roll up in a newspaper.

And here is luncheon, so that you will have. no time to pack even if there was anything to put up!" said Mr. Gower, as the door opened and a waiter appeared staggering under a large, heavily laden tray, which he contrived to strike and jar at every favorable opportunity of doing so as is the custom of awkward waiters.

As soon as the luncheon was arranged upon the table, the friends sat down to it with good appetites.

But they did not linger over the meal, and half an hour later they were in a four-wheeler cab, bowling on toward Paddington.

CHAPTER XII
BACK TO HAWKEWOOD

THEY reached Paddington Station just in time to secure their tickets and hurry into a first-class carriage on the four o'clock express to Southampton en route for Penzance and Hawkeville.

They traveled all the afternoon and reached the first stage of their journey at Southampton near sunset.

They had time to enjoy a comfortable tea at the Southwestern Hotel before taking the train for Penzance.

It was long after midnight when they reached this "most westerly town in England," where they were delayed an hour, and improved the time by taking a late supper or an early breakfast of hot coffee, muffins and mutton chops, at the railway restaurant.

After this refreshment they entered the train for Hawkeville, where they arrived at about daybreak.

"Now, then," said Ham Gow, "if it was not for my wife, you, sir, and I could walk on to Demondike; but we shall either have to take a fly to convey her or leave her at the Hawke Arms Inn. What do you think?"

They were standing on the platform of the station, whence the few passenger who had left the train at this point had already departed on their several ways, and the train itself was puffing and blowing as it "slowed" out of the station on its way to Land's End.

"I think you had better leave the matter to Mrs. Ham herself," said Mr. Gower, with a laugh.

"What do you say, Lona?"

"I say, Ham, and if you please, Mr. Gower, sir," began the young woman, addressing her companions in turn, "that if you leave it to me, I would rather not stop at the inn by myself, nor get into a fly neither. I am that cramped up with sitting so long in the train that I feel as if I would like to begin to walk and keep on walking to the end of my life!"

"Ha, ha, ha! Your life would be a very short one if that were the case!" laughed Ham Gow.

"Do you really think you will be able to walk the three miles between this and Demondike?" considerately inquired Mr. Gower.

"Yes, sir, indeed, please, I could so, with pleasure-but—I would like to wash the dust and cinders out of my eyes first."

"Well, there's a ladies' dressing room in the station! And I reckon we would all be better or the cleaner for a little soap and water. Eh, Mr. Gower?"

"Decidedly," replied the young gentleman, leading the way into the station, where they separated, Mrs. Ham going into the ladies' dressing room, and the two men into the gentlemen's.

As Mr. Gower stood before the looking-glass brushing his hair, after having washed his face and head, he turned toward Ham Gow—who was vigorously using a crash towel upon his own neck and ears—and said:

"You remarked, when persuading me to this journey ,that 'we need not discover ourselves prematurely.' I would like to know how we are to avoid doing so, if we walk through the neighborhood.

"I said so; but I added, on second thoughts, that you need not do so, at least. And you need not, sir. You will never be recognized until you declare your identity and prove it! You are dead, sir, as dead as Julius Cæsar, who was killed near two thousand years ago! As dead as the well-known 'door nail' that never lived at all! You were murdered in your bed, sir, two years ago come the first of next September. And your successor reigns in your stead. It would take a vast deal of ocular demonstration and hard swearing to convince people to the contrary. Once in, a fixed idea and malaria are the hardest things in nature to get out of men's systems. And the people of Cornwall have a fixed idea that you are dead and—no, not buried, but more completely done for—that is, dissected!"

"Well, it may be that I pass unsuspected, especially as I have really grown since my nineteenth birthday-when I was murdered. I have grown, in these two years, about two inches in height and six in breadth, besides having my complexion tanned some shades darker, and wearing a full and heavy beard, such as I never sported then. I fancy you are right, Ham. I shall pass unchallenged!" laughingly replied Mr. Gower.

"But as for me, sir, it is difficult. I never was reported dead, but only as absconded in three or four different directions; and, no doubt, people are still on the lookout for me to nab me and get the reward offered for my apprehension. Nor have I changed so much as to elude detection. I have not grown a hair's breadth in any direction, having attained my full stature about three or four years ago; and I have the same sunburned skin, and the same rough, black hair and beard, familiar from sight to all who knew me personally, and from description to all who read the posters advertising me. It would be a funny thing if I were nabbed and committed to jail on the old charge of having murdered you, sir — wouldn't it?"

"Not to you, I should think!"

"Well, no, not to me; but you would not allow me to remain in prison until the first of September, would you, sir?"

"I am afraid I should have to do so, Ham, for you know I cannot very well declare myself at Hawkewood until the first of September shall give me my majority and with it the power of acting for myself. Therefore, my good fellow, I advise you to be cautious and keep out of the way or arrest!" laughed Mr. Gower.

"Humph! and if on the first of September, or afterward, yon did not choose to come forward and show yourself, I might chance to get hanged for the murder of a man who had never been hurt!"

"You might so, Ham! Such things have happened before this. But I would not permit matters to proceed so far! On the first of September I shall declare myself, if it is only for the pleasure of turning Mr. Lewis Manton out of Hawke Hall and witness his astonishment and discomfiture! But I advise you to 'keep shady' until the first of September."

"I'll try to! But all the same I expect to get nabbed and spend the next four weeks in Hawkeville jail," said Ham Gow.

"Well! It was your doings! You would come down into this neighborhood, you restless tramp! I really do think the only place where you could be kept quiet would be a prison cell, or a strait-jacket!" laughed Mr. Gower.

"I shouldn't be quiet there! There'd be broken bars and broken bones, if not broken necks !" exclaimed Ham.

They were by this time ready to leave the dressing room.

As they entered the ladies' waiting room, Mrs. Ham, looking much refreshed, advanced toward them, saying:

"The ladies' maid tells me that we can get breakfast at the restaurant here if we want it, and I would like a cup of coffee and a roll before we start on that long walk!"

"What do you say, sir? Shall she be gratified?" inquired Ham Gow of his friend.

"Why, of course! Why do you refer the question to me? "demanded the young gentleman.

"Because you are our chief, sir! It is all right, Lona! We will go in to breakfast, since you wish it! Let alone a delicate young woman for being a gormandizer! Now, we could have fasted until we got to Demondike, and there we could have breakfasted on Old Nan's coffee, tea, or chocolate! None better, in the three kingdoms, for a reason that I suspect, but will not betray! So on, Lona, we follow!"

She led them into the ladies' division of the restaurant and there they made a good breakfast.

A few minutes later they were on their way to Demondike, following the line of the coast.

"Did you notice how hard the people looked at me in the waiting room?" inquired Ham Gow, on the first opportunity he had for private speaking, which occurred when Lona strayed a little in advance of them to pick up bright bits of seaweed, or shells, or pebbles—after the manner of children or young people walking on the seashore who gather up these attractive little objects only to throw them away again.

"Did you notice how the people stared at me, Mr. Gower?" repeated the tramp, seeing that his absent-minded companion had not answered his question.

"Yes, I did notice! Ham, you are in danger!"

"And yet I didn't know anybody there, except ourselves!"

"But they evidently knew you by sight, or suspected you from the printed description! Ham, I repeat, you are in danger!"

"I shouldn't wonder! Look here, sir! I don't want to rusticate in prison for a month; but if I thought there was a dead certainty of my being nabbed, I tell you what would do! I would give myself up to poor old Proddy, the cobbler, and let him turn me over to the police and get his two hundred pounds reward! I would! It wouldn't hurt me much, you know; only four weeks' retirement from the world, and that retirement cheered by your frequent visits solaced by all that money could buy, and supported by the certainty of deliverance in the first week of September! For I do not think that even red tape could prolong my incarceration for more than five or six days after you shall have resurrected yourself, sir! That will not be so very much for me to endure, sir, and think what a fortune to old Proddy! Why, the old fellow would be richly provided for for the rest of his life, sir! and think—only think of the laugh we should have at the expense of the authorities! Ah! it is worth it! I declare the fun is worth the imprisonment! I have a mind to give myself up to old Proddy, sir!" concluded Ham Gow, with a laugh.

"I would not do anything of the sort rashly, if I were you! Remember Mrs. Ham!" suggested Mr. Gower.

"I do! I would take her partly into my confidence, and let her enjoy the joke."

"I don't think she could be persuaded to enjoy it! Remember, also, the cause of justice in another case in which your testimony may be required any day."

"Now, that is a good argument, so I guess I will not be over meddlesome in giving old man Proddy a fortune to retire upon yet a while! Ah, old man! You don't know what you have neared and what you have missed in the last ten minutes!"

As he spoke they came up to Mrs. Ham sitting on a fragment of rock, with her lap full of "ocean treasures."

She hastily tied them up in her handkerchief, and arose to accompany them, so that there could be no more confidential conversation between the two men.

The three walked on, talking on indifferent subjects, until, in turning a point on the coast, they came in sight of Demondike, about a quarter of a mile ahead of them.

"How natural it all looks! It seems to me as if it was only yesterday that I left it!" murmured Ham Gow, gazing almost fondly on the old ruined tower.

"Old Nan is getting breakfast. See what a smoke is coming out of the chimney!" exclaimed Mrs. Ham.

"You don't want another breakfast, do you, little woman?" demanded Gow.

"I shouldn't mind," responded. Mrs. Ham; "breakfasts at railway restaurants are not so very satisfactory."

"Ah, sir, you see I had need to go to the gold mines!"said Ham, with a look of comic appeal to his "chief."

As they drew near to the ruin they perceived that there was no life stirring outside of the tower, but the sound of voices came from within.

Ham Gow stepped before his companions, went up to the door and knocked; but the earnestness of the discussion within seemed to prevent the speakers from hearing the summons—and not only voices, but words, reached the visitors without.

"I shouldn't wonder to hear of the earl's arrest any day. The whole neighborhood is talking of it. They say all that is wanted to bring him to trial, ay, and to the gallows, too, is some one bold enough to make the charge against him," said the voice of Young Nan.

"Ay, but where'll that bold man be found? It'll take a bold one, I'm thinking, to bring the charge of murder again' the Yarl of Hawkewood," replied the voice of Old Nan.

"What in the de—octors is up now?" muttered Ham Glow, turning in amazement to his astonished companions. Then, being too honorable to play the part of an eavesdropper, he knocked loudly— so loudly that he startled the inmates, one of whom was heard to rise and come forward to open the door.

It was Old Nan, who started and looked aghast at the sight of her visitors.

"Hello, mother! don't you know me? I'm not a ghost! I'm solid flesh and blood! Ain't you glad to see me?" exclaimed the tramp, holding out his hand, and laughing at the old woman's dismay.

"Ham Gow!" she exclaimed, staring at him, and changing color. "You have no consideration—to come dropping down upon one in this way! I'm that weak I must sit down!" she sighed, sinking into the nearest chair. "Gimmy a drop o' brandy, lass!" she said to Young Nan, who, attracted by the name of her beloved vagrant, had hurried to the door.

But Nan, instead of running for the brandy, suddenly threw up her arms in a burst of joy, exclaiming:

"Ham! Ham Gow! Oh! My dear boy! Is it you? Is it indeed you?" And she clasped her recovered treasure to her bosom.

"Yes, indeed, it is I, Nan! and ever so glad to see you, old gal! And here is my wife. You remember Lona!" said the tramp, gently

136

extricating himself from the woman's embrace, and presenting Mrs. Ham.

"Oh, yes, I remember Lona—Lona Pond! To be sure I do! She was lady's maid at Stony Fells and afterward at Hawke Hall. And she was your true and faithful sweetheart! And she went out to the colonies with Mrs. Belle Isle on purpose to find you out there! And she did find you, and she has brought you back, else you might never have come! And I bless Lona!" exclaimed Young Nan, warmly embracing Mrs. Ham, who blushingly returned her caresses.

"And here is a dear friend and patron of mine, a gentleman who came over in the same ship—Mr. Hamilton Gower," said the tramp, turning to indicate his fellow traveler, who had withdrawn a few paces from this family meeting; but who, on hearing his name uttered, came up and permitted himself to be presented in form.

"But come in, all of you, and make yourselves at home! Don't stand out there a moment longer! Take seats!" said Young Nan, hospitably, bustling about, dusting chairs and handing them to her visitors.

"Are you going to gimmy a drop o' brandy? Or are you going to lemmy sink and die here for the want of it?" querulously demanded Old Nan Crook of her daughter, as she glared around upon her visitors.

"Ugh! she's a trial! If she wasn't my own mother I couldn't stand her! She gets queerer and queerer everyday, Ham, lad!" whispered Young Nan, confidentially, to the tramp, as she dusted a chair for Mrs. Ham.

"But you must stand her, Nan, dear, because she is your mother and because she is old. Stop! I will get the brandy for her! I know the old hiding place of the bottle—or I ought to know it!" laughed Ham Gow, as he went to the furthest end of the strong room, drew away a movable wooden cupboard and displayed a deep black hole in the thick wall of the tower, from which he took a bottle of brandy; then from the cupboard he got a glass, and he turned to cross the room, when Old Nan screamed at him:

"Push that cupboard back again' the wall, you officiousing, interfering interloper, you!"

Ham Gow laughed, replaced the cupboard, and carried the brandy bottle and the glass to the old woman.

"How much shall I give you, granny?" inquired the tramp, as he drew the cork with his teeth, while he held the bottle in his right hand and the glass in his left.

"Fill it up full, you fool!"

Now as the glass was a half-pint tumbler, the young man naturally hesitated to obey the order.

"Fill it up full, you idiwut! Do you think as I'm a babby to be hurt by a little likker? And there's good likker, good brandy, made outen honest grape juice! None of your mannerfactored pizens! None of your bensins, norkerosins, nor no other sort o' 'sins, spiced up and sweetened up to deceive the people! Gimmy a glass full, or lemmy have the bottle myself" exclaimed the crone, fast losing temper.

"Oh, let her have it, Ham, for peace sake! It won't make her tipsy! If that is proof brandy, she is brandy proof!" said Young Nan.

"Oh! Since when have you taken to punning?" laughed Ham.

But he did not fill the tumbler for Old Nan; he was not very particular, but his conscience really would not allow him to administer half a pint of brandy, even to a fireproof old crone. He placed the bottle and the glass on the table near her, and was turning away, when Old Nan accosted him:

"Who is that with you?"

"The young woman is my wife, Lona Pond that was. Let me bring her to you, granny. You knew her?"

"Oh, yes! I don't mean her so much, either! I heard you interdooce her to Young Nan. I'll kiss her presently, because she went out yonder after you and brought you home to us," said Old Nan, speaking of Lona Pond's voyage three-quarters around the globe as if she had only gone out of doors to call her lover in from an apple orchard or a turnip field. "I don't mean her; I mean the gentleman."

"Oh—he is—is a friend and benefactor of mine-came over in the same ship," replied the tramp.

Old Nan bent her beetle brows and brought her sharp blue eyes to bear upon the stranger, and then asked:

"His name?"

"Mr. Gower—Mr. Hamilton Gower," replied the young man.

"'Mr. Gower—Mr. Hamilton Gower'—is that his name?" inquired Old Nan, sipping the brandy to which she had bountifully helped herself, while still sharply scrutinizing the visitor.

"Yes, that is his name," replied Ham Gow.

"Humph! Well! Maybe he is Mr. Hamilton Gower! Maybe he is; but—I don't believe it," said Old Nan, and she swallowed the rest of her brandy at a gulp.

"What do you mean, granny?" inquired the tramp.

"Never you mind what I mean! Fetch your wife here! Don't bother your brains about what I mean! It is none of your business! Fetch your wife here! And after I have kissed and done with her, you may fetch him to me—out of politeness, you know."

Ham Gow went to Lona, who was sitting by the side of Young Nan, with the woman's arms around her waist, and took her by the hand, and saying:

"Come, speak to the old woman," led her up to Old Nan.

"Well, my lass, you went and fetched him, didn't you? And you married him, out of hand! And now you'll steady him, I know! Come, gimmy a kiss! So! that was as hearty as if it had been gin' to Ham! Ah! my lass! if you knew what you had married in him! If you knew his rale rank, and yours as his wife!" said Old Nan, as she warmly kissed and embraced the young woman.

"There! Now fetch the other fellow to me—the impostor!—Mr. Gowilton Hammer, is it? Yes! fetch him."

The tramp went to the gentleman, and said:

"I beg pardon, but will you humor the old woman, sir? She wants to speak to you. And will you please to excuse her whatever she may say? She is very queer. I think she is falling into her second childhood, and is going to be a very bad child indeed."

"Why, of course I will go to her! What, my hostess? Certainly! I was only waiting her convenience and permission to pay my respects to her!" said Mr. Gower, with a smile, as he arose and followed his friend to the "presence."

"How do you do, Mr. Howilton Gammer? I am proud to make your acquaintance," said Old Nan, without waiting for the stranger to be formally introduced.

Mr. Hamilton Gower bowed with as much ceremony as if he had been presented to a duchess.

"I think I have seen you before, Mr. Gammilton Hower," she added, looking sharply into his eyes. "Yes, I'm sure I've seen you somewhere."

"Quite likely; I have often been there," solemnly replied the visitor.

"And your father, also!"

"Just as probable! I once rejoiced in an honored relative of that denomination who was in the habit of 'walking to and fro on the earth, and going up and down in it,'" coolly replied the young man.

"Humph! humph! humph!" mumbled Old Nan, with a nod at every "humph." "Eggsactly! You couldn't have hit it closer, Mr. Howilton Gammer! You struck the pupil of the bull's-eye that time! And now I won't keep you any longer, Mr. Howdoyou Gammon!"

"Then I will bid you good-by, ma'am," said the young gentleman, with another ceremonious bow.

"Good-by, Mr. Howdoyou Gammon!" responded the sarcastic and inhospitable Old Nan.

"Why, you are not going to leave us, sir?" anxiously inquired Ham Gow, as they left the "presence."

"I shall take a walk over to Hawke Hall. I shall return here before night. Meantime, dear Ham, be cautious."

"Oh, I am safe here. I have a sure hiding place. Nor can I be taken by surprise!"

"Well, but be very cautious," replied the young gentleman, and then he bade good-by to the two women, explaining that he was going out for a stroll, but would return before night.

And Mr. Hamilton Gower left Demondike and took his way toward Hawke Hall, never dreaming of the strange developments that awaited his discovery in the ancient seat of the Earls of Hawkewood.

CHAPTER XIII
AT HAWKE HALL

WHEN Mr. Hamilton Gower stepped forth from the Ruined Tower upon the rocky beach, the vast expanse of the blue sea spread out before him, shining with dazzling radiance in the sunlight of that bright August morning.

But he turned his back on the flashing and blinding scene, and, following the course of Demondike on its left or west bank, walked in an inland and northerly direction toward Hawkewood Park.

He saw the Hall dimly outlined on the background of its woods in the extreme distance of the horizon before him. But between him and the Hall lay three miles of rolling downs, now covered thickly with the golden gorse and glistening in the morning sun like veritable gold.

Mr. Hamilton Gower paused for a moment to contemplate this scene.

"To judge from appearances, these should be the 'gold fields,' and the harvest should be reaped with scythe and sickle, and not gathered with pickax and shovel," he said, with a smile, as he resumed his walk along the rude path on the brink of the chasm and pursued it until he came to the bridge.

It was a safe bridge now, defended by strong walls.

He crossed it to the east side of the chasm and entered upon the turnpike road leading from the village of Hawkeville to the manor of Hawkewood.

As he walked on, meditatively looking from right to left and back again upon the familiar scenes of his childhood, and whose pleasantest memories were associated, it must be confessed, with Ham Gow, the boy tramp, he saw three men before him in the distance on the road, walking slowly, so slowly that without the slightest effort to do so, he soon overtook them.

They were old acquaintances. He recognized them at once—Phil. Penn, the locksmith; Jim Tree, the tanner; and little gray old Tommy Proddy, the cobbler—the constant cronies concerning whom Hawkeville made a bull by saying that:

"Them three always hunted in couples."

"Good-morning," said the young gentleman, pleasantly, as he overtook them.

The three men turned about and stared stupidly. Only old Proddy returned the salutation by taking off his very ragged old hat and bowing low, and saying, reverently:

"My sarvice to your honor."

"Do not let me detain you," said Mr. Hamilton Gower to the two silent men, who thereupon gave their forelocks a pull by way of an obeisance, and slouched on their way.

Old Proddy lingered respectfully, hat in hand, until the young gentleman joined him, when they walked on, not quite side by side, for the old cobbler kept meekly a step in the rear.

"My mates there, sir," he said, nodding toward the two men, "don't mean to be noways oncivil, sir, but they have that on their minds as e'en a'most makes idiwuts of 'em, and so naterally they forget their manners and wot's jew to the honorable gentry," sold Old Proddy, partly recognizing the rank of his chance companion.

"Have they troubles?" inquired Mr. Hamilton Gower, ready enough to draw the old man into conversation.

"Troubles, is it, sir? Ah, sir, your honor may well ask! Look at 'em, sir; that long, dark man, all skin and bone, as looks as if he'd tanned hisself in his own bark vats and dried hisself on his own stretchers, him is Jim Tree, the tanner, the father of eleven children, the oldest a gal of fourteen—a honest, hard-working man as ever lived, yet they be all well-nigh starving."

"I am very sorry to hear that!" said Mr. Hamilton Gower.

"And look at t'other un, your worship; that little red-haired feller, so thin and white and vapory as he minds me of nothing so much as a crystyliss, arter the moth have gone outen it—half gone in a consumption hisself, sir, and a sickly wife and seven little uns; yes, and an old, helpless feyther and mawther! Him's Philly Penn the locksmith, as honest and hard-working as Tree, and his folks a-starving as bad!"

"This is terrible! And how is it with yourself, my friend?" inquired the young gentleman.

"Pretty bad, sir! Pretty bad, though all my children being growed and gone to do for themselves, me and the missus can manage to knock along somehow or another."

"What is the cause of this suffering?" inquired the young gentleman, with growing interest.

"Why, the new lord, sir, for certain! You be a stranger to these parts belike, sir, and you don't know but the new lord ain't one of the old anshunt r'yal nobility o' Hawkewood, sir; not one of the r'yal Hawkes, sir; but a new man wid a new name, a sort of a use-upper, sir, as we none of us don't have no reverence for."

"Is he a hard landlord?"

"Oh! hard, your honorable worship; flint, cast iron, neither millstones ain't no harder nor that use-upper's heart! He riz on us all, sir, soon's ever he come inter the estate."

"How did he do that?"

"Oh, every way, sir, every way except the wages! He didn't riz on them! He riz on the rents and lowered on the wages."

"That was certainly very unjust and cruel."

"It was, sir; and he had the power to do it. The Arls o' Hawkewood own the willage of Hawkeville, as well as every inch on ground between the forest and sea! But the old, anshunt r'yal nobility never grinded the faces of the poor like this use-upper does! You'll excuse me speaking so free, your honor?" inquired the old man, with an humble, deprecating yet keen glance into the face of the young gentleman.

"I am very willing to hear you speak. I am interested in what you are saying," kindly replied the wayfarer.

"And, I don't know how it is, sir, but my heart seems to warm to you like—I hope your honor'll excuse me saying so!"

"I am very much pleased to hear you say so."

"Thanky, sir! Well, sir, as I was a-saying, the old, an-shunt r'yal nobility of the Arls of Hawkewood never grinded the faces of the poor, but cherished us wid good wage and low rent, so that we wa'n't starved, but was comforted wid full and plenty, and able to lay by a penny for a rainy day. Yes, your honor! Such was our happiness and prosperity under the rule of the old, anshunt r'yal nobility of the Arls o' Hawkewood!"

"And this new man, you say, cat down your wages and raised your rent?"

"He did, your honor! He riz on us as soon as ever he came inter the property. And for the first year, your honor, we managed to keep from suffering, because our savings as we had saved under the old, anshunt r'yal nobility eked out our wage, and helped to pay our rent; but them savings wouldn't last forever, and so, last winter, which it were an uncommon hard winter, the most on us run behindhand in our rents, and now we be t'reatened wid ejectment!"

"This is a frightful injustice! But your friends there cannot have suffered from having their wages cut down, however they may have been injured in having their rents raised. They are not laborers on the Hawkewood estate. They are mechanics—I think you told me one was a locksmith and the other a tanner."

"That is so, your honor, and I, myself, am a cobbler, and not one of the trree on us in the empl'y of the use-upper! But we rent of him, and we have all had our rents riz to a ruinous rate! And, besides, your honor, when wages on the great Hawkewood estate goes down, while rent goes up, it do hurt all other sort o' work."

"In what manner? I wish to understand these matters," said the young gentleman, showing much interest.

"Well, this way, your honor! Take me, Tommy Proddy, for an example. I'm a cobbler. I mend shoes and boats for a living! And Penn and Tree and dozens of other workingmen, both on and off the estate, used to give me their custom; but now that most on 'em have no more money than enough to put bread in their children's mouths and keep a ruff for a little while over their heads, they can't afford to have their boots and shoes heeled and toed, you know, and so the people go barefooted, and the cobbler doesn't get any work."

"I see; it is shameful to grind down the poor in such a way!"

"It is, sir! Now, there's Phil Penn! Look at the poor fellow, sir! One foot in the grave and one out'n it! Last winter, when the snow was on the ground, his shoes was so far gone as his heels and toes were all out, as likewise was all his children'. And I begged and prayed of him to let me put 'em all in order free, gracious, for nothing! But no, he would go barefooted before he'd go in debt or take a sarvice as he couldn't pay for."

"But that was carrying an idea to extremity, wasn't it?"

"Well, sir, he calls hisself a Wesleyan Methody, but I calls him a fanny tick! He says: 'Owe no man anything; but love one another,' according to the Scriptures; but I say, how can he love me, or how can I love him, when he won't let me heel and toe his shoes nor his children's shoes, though I should just enjoy doing it if I never got paid for it."

"You like your craft, then?"

"Yes, your honor, I like my craft, and I like my friends! Why, your honor, when I'm going 'long the road and sees a man or a 'oman or a little chile wid a bad pair o' shoes on, I just longs to get hold of the shoes and heel and toe 'em, or do both, if the shoes 'quire of it, just for the satisfaction of seeing the broken shoes made whole again."

"How long a time," inquired Mr. Hamilton Gower, reverting to the "previous question," "will your landlord give you before proceeding to extremities?"

"How long—why, sir, the order were for ejectment in ten days if the rent wa'n't paid! Eight of the ten be gone, your honor, and to-day is the ninth day, and to-morrow is the last of grace! Me and my two neighbors be a reputation from the tenants wot can't pay to ask a few days more."

"Do you think you will get it?"

"Lord knows, sir; I don't!" replied the old man, in a despondent tone.

"Or if you should get ten days more, do you think you will be able to pay at the end of that term?"

"No, your honor, we know we won't be no more able to pay then than we are now!"

"Then why do you ask for the extension?"

"Well, your honor, let alone our being anxious to keep a ruff over our heads and over the children's heads as long as possible, we feel pretty sure that though we won't be able to pay the rent by that time, our landlord won't be in a sitteration to turn us out of our homes," solemnly replied Old Proddy.

"Why, what do you mean?" demanded Mr. Hamilton Gower, struck by the deep gravity of the old man's manner "Is—the new earl threatened with illness?"

"The use-upper is t'reatened with worse than that, your honor," whispered Old Proddy, with deep significance.

"What is he threatened with, then?" inquired the young gentleman.

"With the loss of his liberty and life, your honor. 'Tis said, here and there, that the sword of Damascus hangs over his head,'" replied the old man, in a voice of deep solemnity.

"What do you mean?" inquired Mr. Hamilton Gower, as his thoughts flew back to the words he had overheard uttered by Old Nan Crook in the Ruined Tower.

"Well, sir, 'tis an awful thing to say; but 'tis said, here and there—and you might be told of it anywhere—that"—here the voice of the old man dropped to a hoarse whisper—"that the present use-upper did felinishly make way wid the late arl!"

Mr. Hamilton Gower started, and stared at the speaker.

"Who says that?" he demanded.

"His own lady wife was the first to say it, your honor; and there's been enough to say it after her."

"His own wife! What—the countess?"

"Her as was Lady Gaylante Belle Eyes, the duke's darter; but she did not know what she was saying, poor lady, or maybe she'd never 'a' said it. Ah! it was the day the heir, was born, and died, sir; and she was very ill and belirious in her lunatics, and she raved about the innercent baby's death being of a judgment on its father for that night's work when he slew the young Aarl of Hawkewood in his bed."

"Lady Hawkewood said this when she was delirious?" demanded the young gentleman, in amazement.

"Ay—she did, sir; and much more to the same purpose, too. They tried to stop her, but they might as well ha' tried to stop the rush of Demondike's torrent arter a heavy rain! She raved about seeing him come out of the arl's room the very hour of the murder, and of his pale and white face, and his guilty looks, and suspicious conduct afterward. And the doctors heard her, and the nurses, and the servants; and 'tis said my lard tried to get everybody out'n the room, but didn't get to do it until they had all heern too much. And the next day she died; and 'tis said that before she died she lay for an hour or more like one stone dead, 'cept that the breath hadn't quite left her body, when all of a sudden she riz right up out'n that, and fixing her eyes on the arl, as stood at the foot of the bed, and stretching out 'her arm and pointing to him, she said:

"'There stands the man that murdered Horace Hawke, Earl of Hawkewood'

"And with the words on her lips she fell back on her pillow and died."

"Is it possible! Can that be true? What could have put such a horrible thought in the poor lady's head?" inquired Mr. Hamilton Gower.

"No knowing, your honor, unless it was true wot she said in her belirious lunacy—that she saw the use-upper come out'n the young arl's room the very hour when 'tis said the murder was done."

"And has this story obtained much credence in the neighborhood?" inquired the young gentleman.

"Beg pardon, sir," said the cobbler, with a look of perplexity.

"Do people believe it?" inquired Mr. Hamilton Gower, simplifying his question.

"Believe what, sir?"

"That the late countess spoke the truth of her husband!"

"Yes, sir; they do. More believes it nor disbelieves it; and 'tis said, now and then, that it only wants a man bold enough to bring an ackessation agin' the use-upper before one of the honorable nobility of the magisters of the peace to have him 'rested for the murder."

"How long has it been since Lady Hawkewood died?" inquired the young gentleman.

"Well, it must 'a' been a matter of eight months, sir."

"And this affair has been talked about ever since, without any steps having been taken to investigate it?"

"Yes, your honor, and it is a-going to continny to be talked about till that use-upper is 'rested and dealt with according to lawyers."

"You people of Hawkewood seem to be a slow community."

"That we are, your honor! Slow and sure, and sartin!" exclaimed the cobbler, as if accepting a just tribute to his native town.

"But how do you know that it may not be eight more months before anything is done in the case?"

"I shouldn't know at all, sir, 'cept that it is said here and there that something new have turned up wot will compel the noble magisters of the peace to look inter this matter, and as how the use-upper must be 'rested before many days, and some say before many hours."

"And what is this that is said to have turned up?"

"I don't know, sir. It is a dead secret among them as knows, it seems, and will never be told 'til the trial. Here we are at the park gate, your honor! Tree and Penn have gone in. Beg pardon, your honor," said the old cobbler, stopping and glancing furtively into the face of his companion.

"Beg pardon for what, my friend?" smiled the young man.

"For saying as I never did in all the days of my life!" exclaimed the old fellow.

"You never did—what?" laughed Mr. Hamilton Gower.

"See such a likeness as your honor do bear to the late demented young Arl of Hawkewood! Why, sir, your honor's face, from the top of the forrid down to the bottom of the nose, is a perfect similar to hizzen! I don't know about the mouth and chin, because it is hidden under a heavy beard, which he never wore, sir. His lordship's chin was as bare as a peeled potato Beg pardon for my freedom, your honor! Be your honor coming in to take a look at the park?"

"I think I will. There is no objection, I hope?" said Mr. Gower.

"Not as I knows on, your honor! There didn't used to be when the place was under the rule of the r'yal nobility of the Hawkes; but I don't know how it is under the use-upper," cautiously replied the cobbler.

"I think I will take the risk. I will stroll around the grounds for an hour, and then wait for you at the gate here. I feel rather anxious to hear the result of your interview with the usurper, as you call him," replied Mr. Hamilton Gower.

"Very well, sir! It may not take a hour, but if I get back here before you do, I will jest wait here for you," said Old Proddy, as he trotted off after his two companions, who were some little distance in advance of him.

Mr. Gower turned into a winding walk, deeply shaded with forest trees, and followed it through all its turnings around the park.

He did not wish to go near the house, or expose himself to the view of any of the servants.

Like a ghost returned to the scene of its early life, he wandered about his own park, not daring to show himself, for an hour, and then returned to the gate, where Old Proddy stood waiting for him.

It required only a glance at the old man's distressed countenance to discover that his mission to his landlord had failed.

"I see how it is, Proddy; but take heart, my friend," said the young gentleman, as he joined the cobbler, and they walked to the gate together.

"Ah! your honor, how can I take heart, when to-morrow poor Tree's houseful of little children will be turned out into the street, and Penn's sick wife and old feyther and mawther, and the babies, too, without a ruff to cover them?" said the old man, ready to weep.

"And yourself, Proddy?" kindly inquired the young man.

"Oh! sir, as for me and the missus, we can pay for our lodgings in some of the cottages for a day or two while we turn ourselves around. No fear of us. It's the children I'm thinking on, and the old aged, and the sick, wot will all be withouten a ruff to cover them to-morrow night!"

"You don't mean to say that that man up there will push matters to such extremity as this?"

"I do mean to say that we will all be put out'n our house to-morrow, in default of the rent!"

"How much is this rent, Proddy?" inquired the young gentleman, after a little while, as they walked together along the highroad leading to Hawkeville.

"I owes two quarters, sir, which comes to three pun sterling. Tree owes for three, sir, which comes to seven pun ten, and Penn for two, sir, which comes to one pun ten. Twelve pun sterling altogether, sir."

"And for this three families, burdened with old age, sickness and infancy, are to be turned into the street?"

"Yes, sir; there's no help for it."

"You couldn't raise twelve pounds among your friends?"

"No more'n we could raise twelve hunder, sir," sighed the old man. "Oh! sich a thing never could have happened in the time of the r'yal nobility of the Hawkes!"

"And it shall not happen now if I can help it! Who else are to be ejected to-morrow besides yourself and your two friends?"

"No one as I knows on, sir. The other tenants in the willage and the farmers have managed to scrape together the rent, by hook or by crook, and paid it. The poor laborers are to be 'lowed until the first of September to pay, but if they ain't ready with the money by that time, they go."

"What does Traverse, the steward, say to all this? He is a humane man—or used to be. It must go very hard with him to enforce all these harsh measures."

"Mr. Traverse, sir! Your honor knowed him, then!"exclaimed the cobbler, in surprise.

"Oh, yes. I have been in this neighborhood before," laughed Hamilton Gower.

"To be sure! Has your honor, really?"

"Really! But about Traverse, the steward. Is he zealous in carrying out the new lord's policy?"

"Mr. Traverse, sir! Lord bless your honor, Mr. Traverse ain't the steward any longer! He was give his walking papers soon arter the use-uppe come into the estate."

"What! that faithful manager of the property discharged; the tenantry abused and oppressed! Oh! my folly is prolific in evil results that I never dreamed of! But it can last but a month longer! Scarcely a month longer!"exclaimed Mr. Hamilton Gower.

"Anan?" questioned Old Proddy, with a look of helpless and hopeless idiocy on his face, for he could by no means understand the drift of the young gentleman's words.

"What was the pretext for Traverse's discharge?" demanded Hamilton Gower.

"Beg pardon, sir?"

"What was Traverse turned off for, then?'

"Oh! because my lard chose to be his own steward, your honor, which was a pretty thing, wasn't it, for one who pretended to stand in the shoes of the r'yal nobility! No, your honor, if Mr. Traverse had not been turned off, he would ha' gone off hisself, rather than grind the faces of the poor, or do sich ha'sh deeds as is to be done to-morrow."

"Come here, Proddy! Let us sit down on this bank of gorse for a little while. You are not in a hurry?" inquired the young gentleman, leading the way to a grassy and gorsy ridge on the right-hand side of the road.

"Me in a hurry! Ah, your honor! Why should I be in a hurry to go home with bad news to the poor missus? News that will keep her awake the whole night! No, your honor, I am in no hurry," sadly replied Old Proddy, as he followed.

They sat down on the ridge, and then the young gentleman looked up and down the road, and seeing no one in shight, he unbuttoned his coat and drew from his breast pocket a thick morocco wallet.

Old Proddy watched the operation with curiosity and interest, wondering whether this pleasant-spoken young gentleman was going to give him a half crown, a crown, or a half sovereign.

"You said twelve pounds would settle the rent and save the ejectment of three of the Hawkewood tenants-y-our- self, Tree and Penn?" inquired the young gentleman, as he opened the note folder and displayed a pile of Bank of England notes.

"Yes, sir, I did," answered the old man, in a voice trembling with a newly awakened hope that seemed so extravagant he was afraid to entertain it.

"Here, then, Proddy, are two five-pound notes," continued Mr. Gower, drawing the slips from the pile, "and here are two sovereigns," he added, taking a couple of gold coins from a compartment and handing them, with the notes, over to the old man, who stared at them in his open hand, without daring to close his fingers upon the treasure.

"Put up the money, Proddy, or you will lose it. And go back this afternoon with your friends, Tree and Penn, to that self-appointed bailiff of Hawkewood estates, called Lewis Manton, and pay your rent and secure your homes. Don't fail to ask for a receipt, and don't trouble yourself to be civil to the brute. He shall not hurt you. I say it—Why, what is the matter now?"

Poor old Proddy was crying quietly

."You don't understand! This money is not a gift to you and your friends. It is a debt paid. And every shilling that has been extorted from the tenants on the Hawkeville estate, over and above the rent they have been accustomed to pay, shall be refunded to them again with compound interest. That is only just. So you need not feel under any obligation," continued Mr. Hamilton Gower.

The old man took his hand and kissed it, while tears dropped fast upon it.

"No, I don't understand, sir. I don't see how you has the power to do it; but I believe in you, sir; and I love you, the Lord knows I do, though I never saw you before this day, sir—I love you like my own son, sir, if your honor will excuse me for taking the liberty," sobbed old Proddy.

"'Excuse,' my old friend? Why, my heart accepts and rejoices in your affection! And now let us go on," said Mr. Hamilton Gower, rising.

Old Proddy helped himself up by means of his staff and followed his benefactor.

They walked on together until they came to the stone bridge across Demondike.

Then the young gentleman paused, and said:

"You are going to the village, I suppose, Proddy."

"Yes, your honor. Yes, dear sir, I be going straight to the willage to make glad the hearts of Tree and Penn and their poor, scared families! And, oh, I wish your honor could look upon them and see their faces of joy as I shall tell them I bring them glad tidings! Couldn't your honor manage it? It would be better than the circus, sir!" pleaded old Proddy.

"No, I couldn't manage it; I have something else to do. But you shall tell me about it, for I shall see you again," said Mr. Gower, with a smile.

"Oh, I hope so, sir! I hope so, your honor!"

"Well, now, good-morning. My way lies over the bridge."

He shook hands with old Proddy, who detained his hand to kiss it and to cry over it a little longer, and then they parted.

Old Proddy trudged off toward the village with wonderful speed for one of his years—his feet being winged with the delight of giving delight.

Mr. Hamilton Gower crossed the bridge, and, following the course of Demondike, walked toward the sea.

When he reached the Ruined Tower he found the two Nans, Ham and Lona waiting for him.

Dinner was ready—an excellent dinner, beginning with a bit of fine turbot, followed by a haunch of South Down mutton, with the proper sauces and vegetables, roast pheasant with guava jelly and celery, and, finally, tropical fruits and nuts, and champagne, and port wine, and mocha coffee.

Mr. Hamilton Gower was truly amazed to see such a dinner set forth amid such rude surroundings.

Ham Gow laughed at him, and whispered:

"You needn't have any qualms of conscience on the subject of your bill of fare! The fish came honestly out of the sea! The mutton, without a doubt, from the Hawkeville market; and the pheasant—a little out of season, to be sure—from the Hawkewood preserves! As for the fruits and wine, the worst that can be said of them is that they never paid duty!"

"A repast provided by poaching and smuggling! Hardly meat to say grace over; eh, Ham? However, 'travelers must be content,' as Shakespeare, or some one else, said, or might have said," laughed Mr. Hamilton Gower.

The party sat down to dinner and enjoyed themselves greatly. Even Old Nan, who presided in a blue cotton gown and a red bandanna head kerchief, was mollified and gracious under the benign influence of the viands set before her.

It was while they were still at table that Ham Gow said:

"We have heard it all from Mrs. Crook, sir! There is no longer a doubt on anyone's mind that the present Earl of Hawkewood 'made away with' his predecessor, as they put it."

"Indeed! Is that true?" inquired Mr. Hamilton Gower, slyly.

"True as—true! The late countess knew all about it, and either confessed it on her deathbed or else betrayed it in her delirium—it is hard to tell which, for both these statements are afloat."

"Why is the present earl not arrested, then?" inquired Mr. Hamilton Gower.

"Ah! there's just where it is! Nobody seems to have the pluck to go before a magistrate and openly accuse him. Why, they say that from the bold way in which his lordship carries himself he cannot have any suspicion of the dreadful rumors that are abroad concerning him!"

"No, that he has not," put in Young Nan, who was tackling the wing of a pheasant with her hands and teeth.

"But they say summat has come out lately that aggravates the case so it'll fetch things to a head and the false yarl may be took up any hour now!" added Old Nan.

"What is this 'snmmat,' then?" inquired the young gentleman.

"I don't rightly know. Nobody seems to. If so be he be brought to trial for the murder of the late yarl, be you coming forward to save his neck, sir?" demanded Old Nan, turning suddenly upon her guest.

"I—what do you mean, m'am ?" inquired Mr. Hamilton Gower, in some confusion.

"Oh, nothing much! You are Mr. Howilton Gammer. Well, maybe you are! Gimmy the breast o' that other pheasant, wi' a-plenty o' white sauce and guava jelly, Ham!" said Old Nan, rising and stretching her arm quite across the board to hand her plate to the carver.

No more was said on the subject of the possible trial.

When dinner was over, Mr. Hamilton Gower and Mr. Ham Gow lighted their pipes and strolled out upon the beach, leaving the women to "clear up."

The beach was deserted. If it had not been so, the two men would have turned their steps up along the banks of Demondike.

"We must start for town to-night, Ham," said Mr. Gower, as they sauntered along, "for you know it is absolutely necessary that we should be in London to-morrow morning, ready to receive the first possible news from our detective."

"Yes, of course, I see that," assented Ham Gow.

"Besides, it is not safe for our plans for us to stay here a day longer. Old Mrs. Crook already suspects me," continued Mr. Gower.

"Oh, she is a witch! She is even more of a real witch than she pretends to be," said Ham Gow, as he stuffed some fresh tobacco into his pipe, drew a match on his boot and lighted it—the match, not the boot.

"Ham," gravely inquired Mr. Gower, "what are those two women to you?"

Ham Gow lighted his pipe, drew a whiff, slowly expelled the smoke, removed the pipe from his lips for a moment, and replied:

"You asked me that question years ago, when we used to rob orchards—your own orchards—together."

"I know I did, but you could not give me any satisfaction then."

"And I cannot now! I knew nothing then, I know nothing now, about the matter. I was taught to call the elder woman granny and the younger one mammy, in my infancy; but later in my boyhood I came to learn, though I do not know by what means, that these terms really mean nothing, and that I had no claims of kindred on the women that brought me up."

" Have they never spoken to you of your parentage?"

"Never directly. Some extravagant hints have been dropped by Old Nan, but I consider them nothing more than vague surmises that had better not be entertained."

"Did you never question them on the subject?"

"Yes, but never got anything in reply but what I have told you—hints, surmises, absurd and extravagant Only one thing is certain: the two women have always loved and cherished me as devotedly as if the elder had really been my grandmother and the younger my mother, and I owe them the duty and affection of a son," warmly added the young man.

"A debt that I feel sure you will faithfully discharge," earnestly declared Mr. Gower.

"I mean to do so henceforth, sir, if I have never done so before," said Ham Gow.

They strolled on, smoking, in silence for a little while, and then the ex-tramp, taking the pipe from his mouth, burst into a loud laugh.

"What is up now?" inquired his companion.

"I was thinking of the 'yarl,' as granny calls him; and how if he were arrested for this supposed murder, it would cap the climax of absurdity!"

Mr. Gower echoed the laugh in which Ham Gow's words began and ended.

"If now such should be the case, and the 'yarl' should be arrested, and cast in prison, charged with your murder, would you put in an appearance to save him?"

"Not one day sooner than I shall do so under any circumstances. In fact, I should feel tempted to lie perdue a little longer, to give 'my lord' full opportunity of enjoying his new position, before going forward to save his neck and take his title!" said Mr. Hamilton Gower.

"Ha! ha! ha! I fancy he would be glad to have his neck saved, even at that price! That reminds me of what Granny Crook asked you—whether in the event of the 'yarl' being brought to trial for the murder, you would come forward to save his neck! Strange she should have asked you that question."

"She either recognized me or strongly suspected my identity. I don't know which. She would not explain her meaning when I asked her for it, nor, indeed, did I wish to push the inquiry too closely. I am glad we are to leave the neighborhood so soon."

"You don't want a premature discovery, sir."

"By no means!"

They sauntered on, smoking, for an hour longer, and then, as the sun was sinking beneath the western waves, they returned to the Ruined Tower, and entered the strong room, which the women had now restored to order, and where the neat tea table was set.

After tea, the three visitors took leave of the two women at the Ruined Tower, and set out by starlight to walk to Hawkeville to take the evening train to Penzance en route for Southampton.

As the night was fine, the road good, and their spirits were light, they stepped on briskly, talking cheerfully and laughing gayly, so that the time and distance seemed short when they entered the village of Hawkeville.

They would have to pass entirely through and beyond the village to the railway station that was half a mile out of town.

As they passed down Market Street, which would have been dark but for the lights in the shops that were still open, they saw groups of villagers here and there, and caught fragments of conversation, sweet enough to the ears of Mr. Hamilton Gower, but quite unintelligible to his companions.

"Ah, yes, sonnies," said the wheezing voice of a very old man, who was holding forth to a little group of men, women and children that stopped the way before a locksmith's little, dingy shop. "Ah, yes, sonnies, a perfect gentleman he was, as well as a perfect stranger, who didn't give his name to Mr. Proddy, but told him he had come down from Lunnun town a purpose to see us righted. And it's my opinion as he is the prince hisself, or some o' the r'yal family of England as has heern of our wrongs."

"Wan't yer s'prised, Granddady Penn ?" inquired a voice from the little group.

"S'prised? Ay, lad. When Mr. Proddy come inter the shop where Phil was a-sitting wid his head in his hand looking like a man gone crazy, and the women a-crying and the children scared to death at they didn't know what, and I trying to comfort 'em all by telling on 'em as they'd be sure to like t'rough it all, in comes old Mr. Proddy looking like a angel, with his face all shining, and a gloriole round his head, and says he:

"'Peace be unto this house, and unto all that are in it,' same as if he had been the parson come to pray over the sick. And then he holds out his hand with bright gold money in it, and says:

"'Cheer up, Philly Penn! Here's money to pay your rent, and Jim Tree's and mine, and all our troubles is over!'

"Then, sonnies, I was proper scared, for I t'ought as poor old Mr. Proddy had been so left to his own devices as he had committed highway burglary in his desperation, and we'd all be sent to Bottommy Bay for it. But when I looked at him ag'in, and saw his face shining like a angel's, I knowed he couldn't ha' committed no crime, and then I t'ought—"

But what old Grandfather Penn thought was lost to the three travelers, who by this time with difficulty pushed their way through the crowd and passed out of hearing.

A little further down the street a woman sat on the sill of her front door, expatiating on the same subject to several of her neighbors, who were standing before her.

"I had e'en a'most lost my faith in everythink, and was ready to give up and die, when down comes this relief as suddenly and as unexpectedly as if it had dropped out'n the clouds! What I say is—"

But what she further said never reached the ears of the travelers, who had again passed out of hearing.

At the end of the town they came upon a crowd of children before a long, rambling house, with a tan-yard in the rear.

One of the little girls was telling a story with much vehemence, and evidently with great exaggeration.

She was saying:

"How he didn't wonder as men went raving mad and burned ricks and housen, and mother cried, and cried, and cried, and cried tubsful! And just then Daddy Proddy come in with his pockets crammed full of golden guineas! Oh, I tell you all what—"

What she had to tell them all was never heard by the wayfarers, who hurried on beyond the sound of her voice.

"What on earth are they all—men, women and children—talking of so excitedly?" inquired Ham Gow of the universe at large.

"Of some one who seems to have paid their rent and saved them from ejectment," said Mr. Hamilton Gower.

"Oh, that is it—is it? Well, I suppose it is! Come! we must hurry, or we shall miss our train."

The three walked rapidly on, and reached the station just in time.

"Take a whole compartment for ourselves, Ham. We don't want company," said Mr. Hamilton Gower.

The compartment was engaged, and the travelers entered it.

It had three seats behind, and a sofa in front. The sofa was given up to Lona, who gladly stretched herself upon it to rest and sleep, while the two men, her traveling companions, occupied the seats in the opposite corners.

They had scarcely got comfortably settled before the train started.

Twice only during that night's journey were they disturbed—to change train at Penzance for Southampton, and to change at Southampton for London.

They reached Paddington Station at sunrise, stopped to take breakfast at the Grand Southwestern Hotel, and then took a carriage to go to their lodgings at the Crown and Anchor, at the opposite end of London.

As soon as they reached the inn, Mr. Hamilton Gower went to the office to inquire for letters.

"No letters, sir, but a telegram came about five minutes ago. Here it is," said the clerk, handing the sealed envelope.

Mr. Hamilton Gower tore it open, and read:

"Benjamin Hutchings, Rosedale, Yorkshire, to Mr. Hamilton Gower, Crown and Anchor Inn, Gaunt Street, London: Most important discoveries, only to be communicated in a personal interview. Leave this within an hour. Expect to reach London by the 10:30 P. M. train. Meet me."

CHAPTER XIV
THE HAUNTED WELL

MR. HUTCHINGS, the most skillful of the secret detectives on the force, had other and more ostensible ways of making a living than his hidden calling of tracking criminals.

Outside of the "Force" he was not known as a detective, or even suspected as one.

But his name in white letters on a black signboard over the door of a small shop in the Borough, informed all and sundry that he was a "Fancy Stationery and Newsdealer."

And here behind the counter he was generally to be found when the secret service of the "Force" did not require his presence elsewhere, on which occasions his wife, son or daughter supplied his place in the shop.

Mr. Hutchings was also the agent for the sale of the patent needle threader, an ingenious little instrument for enabling the oldest eyes and fingers to thread the finest needles with perfect ease; and for the patent knife sharpener, which would put the keenest edge on any piece of cutlery, from a razor to a woodman's ax.

These two agencies were of great service to Mr. Hutchings in his calling as a detective.

They introduced him into families, schools, stores and workshops, and put him on the most confidential terms with men and women, boys and girls.

What woman or girl could resist the patent needle threader, price only one penny, and such an invaluable assistant to weak eves or clumsy fingers?

What man or boy could resist the patent knife sharpener, price only twopence? Why, its saving in profanity alone was inestimable!

Then, again, these specimens were very light and portable. The agent could carry in his pocket a dozen gross of each without inconvenience.

Armed with these useful articles, "which no family should be without," this detective could go anywhere unsuspected, and, while teaching some old woman the perfect, simple and easy method of threading her needle with the patent threader, he could, if he wished, turn her mind inside out and shake it free of any information she might be able to give him upon any subject in which he might be interested.

On the termination of Mr. Hutchings' first interview with his new employers at the Crown and Anchor, he hurried off to his shop in the Borough and startled Mrs. Hutchings, as that worthy stood waiting for customers behind the counter, by saying that it was necessary for him to raise a certain sum of money by the first of the ensuing month, and that he should take a quantity of the patented articles for which he was agent and try to sell them wholesale to the country dealers through Yorkshire, a locality through which he had never traveled with them before.

Mrs. Ben was accustomed to these sudden and unexpected departures, so she only said:

"As I have often remarked before, it is very strange you can't foresee these things so as to give me time enough to get you up comfortably for your journey. All your best shirts are in the wash, and—"

"Never mind, my dear. Common shirts are best for a journey, anyway. Put me up a couple; I shall not want more. Only be quick about it. I want to catch the four-thirty express," said the agent for the patent needle threader and patent knife sharpener, as he went behind the counter and proceeded to take down from the shelves grosses of these articles, and to pack them into a japanned tin box with a handle in the top.

In twenty minutes he was off to catch his train, leaving his wife to mind the shop, and without a suspicion that her husband had gone to Yorkshire on any more serious business than the one he had given as the object of his journey.

He caught his train, and was soon speeding by express toward the city of York.

He arrived there early in the morning, and had time to get breakfast before leaving by another train for a certain village about forty miles west of the city.

Short as the distance was, he had to change trains twice, and at each change there was a delay of two or three hours, so that it was afternoon before he reached his destination, and then he had a ride of three miles by stage to the hamlet of Rosedale, which was to be the scene of his operations.

He finally reached the quaint little place just as the sun was sinking to its setting in the western horizon, and the shadows of isolated houses and trees were lengthening over the broad moor in a dent of which the little hamlet nestled.

The stagecoach by which he had traveled from the last railway station drew up before "Campbell Arms" — a pic- turesque little inn built of dark-red bricks, with a very steep roof of many gables, and very large windows with very small panes, and very high twisted chimneys with hoods on their heads to prevent them from smoking the in-mates of the house.

There was a swinging sign in front, on which was painted the "Campbell Arms"-hieroglyphics which no one but a professor of heraldry could have understood. And there were large trees, under which stood benches, where the rustic customers often sat while regaling themselves with pipes and beer.

Behind the house were stables with red roofs, and there were brown hayricks, and a few apple trees in an old-fashioned garden; all of which made a pleasant rural picture fully appreciated by the Londoner.

As the stagecoach drew up before the door the landlady herself came out to welcome any chance guests.

But besides Mr. Hutchings there were only three other passengers, countrymen, who got out and went into the tap-room to call for mugs of beer, and who, after drinking, went off to their homes.

Hutchings walked into the parlor of the inn, and asked if he could have a room and tea.

The landlady, a brisk little body, with black eyes, black ringlets, a black alpaca gown and a cap trimmed with red ribbons, answered that he could be promptly served with all that he should be pleased to call for, and anything else.

Could he have his tea in that parlor? he wanted to know.

Certainly; there were no other stopping guests, and he could have his tea in that parlor.

And would the landlady pour it out for him?

The landlady would pour it out for him with pleasure; but first she would send the chambermaid to show him his bedroom.

Exit the landlady and enter the chambermaid—a stout, high-complexioned country girl, in a blue dress and white bib apron, and a white cap with blue ribbons.

She stood and courtesied silently, and then turned and opened a back door and looked around at the guest.

The latter understanding by this pantomime that he was expected to follow, arose and followed his conductress through a labyrinth of narrow passages and up a corkscrew of winding stairs to a quaint little room, ending in a gable, with one white-curtained window and a small, white-curtained bed, with a rug laid down beside it, and a three-cornered washstand, with a towel rack on one side and a looking-glass on the other. Plain, neat and clean was all that could be said of it.

Having shown the guest into this room, the silent girl retreated.

There was at least plenty of pure water and fresh towels.

The traveled treated himself to a good wash and a change of linen, and went down into the parlor, where the landlady stood presiding over a neatly spread little tea table.

"Hope you feel refreshed, sir," said the landlady, blithely, as she lifted and rang a little hand bell that stood upon the table.

A waiter in a white apron brought in, in answer to the bell, a tray on which stood the teapot, a stack of dry toast, a rack of boiled eggs, and a covered dish, from which emanated an aroma of mutton chops.

These were all neatly arranged on the table, and the landlady sat down to pour out the tea.

"Much travel in this direction?" inquired the guest, as he received a full cup from his landlady.

"Dear me, no, sir! The house depends mostly on the neighborhood. If it had depended on travelers it would 'a' gone into bankruptcy long ago, sir. You see, the place is out o' line o' travel, sir."

"But tourists? Don't they come around in the summer and autumn?"

"Hardly one in a year, sir! Why, there is nothing to attract them in these moors, sir."

"Nor artists?"

"Lor', no, sir! What should fetch 'em?"

"Why, have you no picturesque ruins, or interesting old houses?"

"No, sir; naught of the sort—though, now I think of it," added the landlady, after a thoughtful pause."

"Well—now you think of it?" questioned the traveler, waiting for an explanation.

"I was a-going to say our own manor house, sir—"

"Well—your own manor house?"

"Rose Hill, sir."

"Rose Hill? Is that your manor house?"

"Of course it is, sir. The seat of the Campbells, sir. They owned all the hamlet of Rosedale, sir, which this house is the Campbell Arms, sir."

"Yes; so I observed! What were you going to tell me about Rose Hill?"

"Why, sir, I thought if you were on the lookout for interesting places, I should think that would be an interesting place to visit. At least, so it had been considered ever since it happened," said the landlady, with grave significance.

"'It happened?' What happened?" inquired the guest, pausing, with a bit of mutton chop on his fork.

The landlady looked at him with surprise and incredulity, as who should say, "Is there a living man who has not heard what happened?"

"Was it a fire? Was it a flood? Was it a riot? Or—what was it?" pursued the traveler, as he put the bit of mutton chop in his mouth.

"Can it be possible, sir, as you haven't heard what happened at Rose Hill Manor House five years ago?" inquired the astonished landlady.

"Let me see," said the guest, putting his right forefinger on his right eyebrow with the air of a man trying to recall a circumstances vaguely remembered to full memory. "It appears to me that I do recollect hearing of some tragedy connected with the name of Rose Hill? What was it, again, now? Oh! A man poisoned his wife there, didn't he?"

"Dear me, no, sir! naught of the sort! It was a young girl, sir, who strangled her infant cousin, the heir, partly in revenge for the cruel treatment of herself by his mother, and partly in covetousness of his estates, to which she was the next heiress. Surely, sir, you must have heard of the trial of Margaret Campbell!"

"Oh, ay, yes! to be sure! I remember all about it now. What a dreadful thing that was!"

"Oh, I tell you, sir! And we had crowds down here then. It was in my late husband's time, rest his soul, for he was a good man. No complaint of want of custom then, sir. Why, while the search and the inquest were going on at the manor house it took all the hamlet to wait on the customers here, sir. And for days and weeks afterward."

"It must have been an exciting time," said the traveler, cracking one of the boiled eggs.

"It was, sir! And while it lasted the house here was as full as it could cram both day and night. But when it was over the custom fell off again, and the house got to depend on the neighborhood for its support."

"There were three other travelers, besides myself, came by the coach."

"All from the neighborhood here, sir! Went to Stockstone this morning by the stage, and came back this afternoon. No, sir! No stranger ever comes here but a commercial traveler, or bagman, as we call them here. You'll be something in that line yourself, sir?" inquired the landlady, dubiously.

"Yes, something in that line! I am traveling for the sale of the patent needle threader, price one penny, invaluable aid to dim eyes or awkward hands, enabling an old woman of ninety, or a child of three years, to thread a needle 'with neatness and dispatch,'" quoted the traveler.

"A needle threader! For pit-tee's sake! What will they be getting up next, I wonder! I thought, when the sewing machine and the baby jumper were invented, they could not go beyond that unless they had invented a boy spakner, which might 'a' been useful. But a needle threader! For pit-tee's sake! I'd like to see the instrument!" said the landlady.

"I am pleased with your interest in this invention ma'am, and you shall see it, and learn how to use it the moment I have done tea, if you can spare me the time said the traveler.

"Oh! I can spare the time well enough. One barmaid waiter can attend to all the customers we have, and play half the time, as they do, the lazy things!"

The traveler soon finished his tea, and the landlady rang for a waiter to take away the service.

When the table was cleared and covered with a neat red cloth, and the landlady and traveler were seated at it, the latter drew from his pocket a small pasteboard box, containing about a gross of the new instrument.

Drawing one out, he handed it to the landlady, saying:

"You see it is as simple as the needle itself! And you can tell by merely looking at it how to use it."

"Why, so it is! Why, so I can! Now, ain't it strange that no one ever thought of inventing such a simple thing before, as long as needles have been in use, and wimming have been worritting their eyes out of their heads, trying to thread fine ones?" exclaimed the landlady, in delight.

And the needle threader was, in fact, the very simplest and most obvious of instruments.

It looked like a coarse number one needle, with a large, funnel-shaped eye, but it was in reality a hollow tube, and the needle to be threaded was to be shoved up the tube, until its eye was even with the eye of the funnel, and then no matter how fine the needle might be, or how dim the eyes, or awkward the fingers that guided the thread, the end could be easily passed into the funnel and was bound to go right through the eye of the needle, for it could go nowhere else.

All this Mrs. Keene saw at a glance, and she quickly whipped a housewife from her capacious pocket, unfolded it and selected the finest needle she could find and threaded it in an instant with the needle threader.

"Well, there! I might ha' been five minutes trying to do that with my own eyes and wouldn't ha' done it! Sir, I'll take a shilling's worth o' these patent needle threaders; so if I should happen to lose one I would have others to fall back upon, for I'll never be without one — never!" she exclaimed.

"Madam, allow me to present you with a dozen. And if you can recommend the article to your neighbors I shall be more than repaid," said the gallant traveler, offering to the landlady a paper of the instruments marked one dozen.

"Oh, thank you, sir! Recommend! I should think so! Why, I don't believe there's a woman in the village that won't buy as many of them as she can afford, for fear she should get out of them and couldn't get any more! Yes, sir, I shall recommend them everywhere!"

"Do you think the family at Rose Hill would patronize me?" inquired the traveler.

The landlady paused thoughtfully.

"The family at Rose Hill, sir," she said at length, "live in the strictest retirement, and have lived so ever since it happened. There is no one there but the widow and her two daughters, and one of 'em is afflicted."

"Ah! you mean the one who gave the most important testimony against the accused young lady? You see, I begin to recall the circumstances of the trial, now, since you have mentioned it."

'"As why shouldn't you, sir, being face to face, as one might say, with an eye-witness of the tragedy; leastways, of the great fuss that was made about it! Yes, sir, the same poor, afflicted girl lives there still with her mother and sisters. Some do say they haven't got any right to live there at all; because when the poor baby was murdered Margaret Campbell was the next heir; but as she is a conwick for life, her estates perverted to the crown, which means to the queen, I suppose! But, anyways, it seems her majesty must be too good-hearted to turn 'em out, for there they be still, living all to theirselves and keeping no company. A needle threader, for pit-tee's sake!" exclaimed the landlady, suddenly breaking off in her discourse to contemplate her new treasures.

The traveler recalled her wandering attention.

"Perhaps some of the old domestics there might patronize my wares."

"I beg pardon, sir?"

"Maybe the old servants might buy my needle threaders."

"Oh, yes! to be sure! Now I think of it, Granny Keene—my late husband's sister-in-law, she was, sir, and she keeps the gate lodge at Rose Hill now—she might like to have some of them! You could tell her I recommended you to her, and she would show you over the place, sir! Over the grounds, I mean, of course, not over the house, though that is a fine show place, too, with the picture gallery the room Queen Mary Stuart slept in one night, and other interesting places; but the family being there, you can't see the inside of the house now, sir. But you can see the grounds, and the well where the child was found. Oh, sir listen!" And here the landlady dropped her voice to a mysterious whisper. "They say it's haunted!"

"Haunted!" exclaimed the traveler.

"Yes, sir."

"What, the house?"

"No, sir; the well!"

"What, or who, haunts it?"

"The ghost of Margaret Campbell carrying the murdered child in her arms."

The deep solemnity with which the woman spoke drove the incipient smile from the lips of the traveler.

"How can they say the ghost of the murderess haunts the well, when she is a convict several thousand miles away?" he inquired.

"Oh, sir, they say she must have died out in them foreign parts! She must have died, else how could her ghost haunt the well, carrying the murdered child in her arms?" solemnly inquired the landlady.

"But how do you know her ghost does haunt the well? Who says it does? Who has seen her?" demanded the traveler, with natural incredulity.

"Oh, sir! Plenty of people have seen it! Why, the old coachman as has been in the family forty years, man and boy, he seen it so often that he couldn't stand it, and he has given warning, sir! he has, indeed, after forty years' service! And one of the young grooms run away without giving any warning, and lost half a month's wages! You see, the dry well is near the stable yard, sir, and the stablemen see the most of the ghost! And there was my own dear departed husband's own dear sister-in-law, sir—Granny Keene, as keeps the gate—she was sitting along of the coachman's wife in the stable cottage one night and stayed late, and, as she was going home, with one of the stableboys carrying a lantern to light her way, she came face to face with the ghost, in a long, white sheet, and carrying the child, all swathed in white! And Granny Keene fell down in a fit, and the boy dropped the lantern and ran, yelling, back to the cottage, and told the tale in such a wild, wandering way that nobody could understand it; and the coachman and all the stableboys ran out to the dry well, but they didn't see any ghost there, only Granny Keene lying down among the damp weeds in a dead faint. And they lifted of her up and toted of her to the coachman's cottage, and laid her on the bed, and burned feathers underneath her nose, and poured rum down her throat, and worked on her ever so long before they could fetch her to! And then they had to get out the pony chaise to take her back to the gate house. Oh, sir, you see, there can't be any mistake about it! The ghost of the murderess haunts the well with the murdered child in her arms."

"Do the family tolerate such a report among their domestics?"

"I beg pardon, sir?"

"Sho! What do the widow and her daughters say to all this?"

"There ain't but one of her daughters capable of saying anything to it, sir! The other one is afflicted, as I told you. And I don't know what they say to it. Granny Keene and the coachman's wife don't see much of the ladies, and so they don't know how they take this dreadful thing, and, of course, they can't tell me," continued the landlady.

"How far is Rose Hill from here?" inquired the traveler.

"Why, sir, not more than a mile. This is a part of the estate; this whole village is. I rent from the steward, as my husband did before me, and his forefathers did before him."

"Which road should I take to go there?"

"Why, sir, when you walk right straight out of this house, you turn to the left and keep right straight on, past the mill and past the church, and the parsonage, and the patch of wood, and then you come to the park gate and the lodge. Granny Keene keeps the lodge, as I told you before, and if you mention my name, I am sure she will be glad to see you, and if you show her the patent needle threader, I am sure she will be glad to buy a lot of them. Goodness! why, every time I go to see her she makes me thread dozens of needles and stick 'em into a big, round pincushion ready for use. She will be glad enough of the needle threader always at hand!"

"I will be sure to submit them to her approval."

"I beg pardon?"

"I'll show her the instrument."

"Yes, sir; do."

The traveler arose and took his hat.

"You don't mean to walk, sir?" inquired the landlady.

"Certainly. It is only a mile. I may stay late—late enough to see the ghost. How long do you keep open?"

"Oh, we close at eleven, but you can get in at any hour by knocking."

"Thank you," said the traveler, as he left the room.

CHAPTER XV
THE SPECTER

WHEN Mr. Ben Hutchings, secret detective from Scotland Yard, ostensible agent for the sale of the patent needle threader and the royal knife sharpener, and best known as stationer and newsman in the Borough, stepped out of the Campbell Arms, he paused for a moment to look up and down the quaint little village street—if street it could be called, which seemed only a country road, grass-grown on the sides and flanked by scattering little shops and houses of various sizes, built of stone, brick, or wood, or a mixture of all three, and all except the shops, which were even with the sidewalk, standing back from the street, and having little vegetable and flower gardens before them.

But the last faint glow of the long twilight was fast fading on the western horizon, and the full moon was rising in the east, and Mr. Hutchings, seeing that he had no time to lose, turned to the left, as he had been directed, and walked rapidly down the street, with the twilight glow behind him and the rising moon before him.

He passed the blacksmith's forge, the wheelwright's shed, the saddle and harness maker's shop, seeing on the opposite side the village doctor's office and surgery, and the grocer's store, where also the post office was kept.

He passed the mill, and the rustic bridge that spanned the mill race, and he passed the old Gothic church of St Asaph's, which had a long, romantic history of its own, and the picturesque rectory, seeing on the opposite side rustic huts and gardens, with long shadows thrown toward him by the rising moon.

And finally he passed on until there was nothing but the vast rolling moor on the right and left, with its boundaries lost in the obscurity of the distant horizon.

At length, as the road began to ascend one of the swells of the moor, he saw before him on the height, crossing the scene, the high stone wall of a park, with an iron gate and a lodge on its right, to which this road directly led.

He walked slowly up the gradual ascent until he reached the great iron gate of the walled park.

The place looked solitary and deserted. Above the high wall could be seen the tops of stunted evergreen trees. On the right of the iron gate was the little Gothic lodge, with a solitary light gleaming from a tiny window in the gable end of the roof.

The traveler found the gate fastened, though it was as yet quite early in the evening.

He rang, and waited, but received no response to his first summons.

He rang again, a louder and a louder peal.

Then a window on the ground floor was cautiously opened, letting out a little stream of light, and a trembling voice inquired:

"Who's there?"

"A friend from the Campbell Arms, with a message from Mrs. Keene," replied the traveler, in cheery tones.

"Eh! then wait till I send the lad to open the gate," said the voice within, and the window was closed, and the door of the lodge was opened, letting out a stream of light upon the shrubbery, and a boy came forth and unlocked the small side door of the gateway that was used by passengers.

As the lad opened the gate and stood in the line of light from the cottage door, the traveler saw that he was a sandy-haired and freckled-faced little fellow of about twelve years of age.

Mr. Hutchings passed through, leaving the boy to fasten the gate, and walked up to the lodge door, where he was met by a little, thin, old woman with a fair, pale face, and scant, gray hair, surmounted by a high-crowned, white muslin cap. She wore a dark calico dress, with a white handkerchief crossed over her bosom, and a white apron tied around her waist.

She welcomed the visitor in a friendly manner.

"You come from Peggy Keene, do you, my man? Now, what do Peggy Keene want of me at this time o' the evening?" she inquired, bending rather sharp blue eyes upon the speaker.

Then, seeing that he was not one of the servants from the inn, and that he might be a gentleman, she hastened to say:

"I beg your pardon, sir. Please walk in. Any friend of Mrs. Keene is very welcome to me."

The traveler bowed to the old dame with as much respect as if she had been a duchess, and stepped into a neat room with sanded floor, whitewashed walls, white-curtained windows, clean, oaken chairs and tables, a tall corner cupboard, a tall corner clock, and between the two last a red chimney-place, in which burned a little fire, and over which sang a little copper kettle.

A little table stood in the middle of the floor, and on it was arranged the frugal supper of bread, cheese and cold corned beef.

The old woman drew forward her own armchair, and begged her visitor to be seated.

"Do not let me interrupt your supper," said Mr. Hutchings, as he took possession of the chair.

"Eh, sir! that can wait. The lad, Zach, helps in the stable up at the great house, and he have just come in to his supper; but he can wait. He is my grandson, sir, and a great trial, too. And he lives with me, in course. Now, please—if it be no offense—what did Peggy Keene want?"

"She wished me to show you a curious little instrument called a needle threader, by which the poorest eyes can thread the finest needle," replied the traveler, taking the little box from his pocket, selecting an instrument, and handing it to the dame, who looked at it curiously, understood the way of using it at sight, and exclaimed:

"A needle threader! Well, well! I thought when kerry-sene and lucifers was inwented, we had got to the werry end of inwentions! But—needle threaders! Well, well! They must cost a sight of money!"

179

she said, longingly contemplating the little instrument that she held between her finger and her thumb.

"No, indeed! They cost only a penny apiece!" exclaimed the agent.

"Only a penny apiece! Bless and save the man! does he think a penny is not a sight o' money for the likes o' me?" sharply inquired the dame, who had lost half her reverence for the visitor on discovering that, after all, he was only a traveling agent for the sale of a patented article.

"If you think the price too high, madam—" commenced the agent, in a conciliatory tone; but she interrupted him:

"I'm not saying the price is too high for other folks! for Peggy Keene, now, who makes lots of money from her public! But for me, now! Why, how much do you think a I have got to live upon, anyhow?"

"I am sure I don't know, madam. I hope it is enough."

"Well, it ain't, then. I get the free use of this house for tending the gate, and that's all I get! And the boy, there, gets three shillings a week for helping in the stables, and that's all he gets! And out o' them three shillings a week we have got to buy meat and bread, and tea and sugar, besides hats and shoes and trowsies for him, and everything else in the world."

"Your lines are hard, ma'am," said the detective, in a sympathetic tone.

"Ay, they just are, then!" assented the dame.

"In that case, pray permit me to present you with a box containing a dozen of my best needle threaders," said the agent, in an insinuating tone, offering her a small packet.

"Ah, sir, you are too good!" exclaimed the old dame, with all her respect for the vendor reviving.

"Nay, do not hesitate to accept my little offering, which I make with great pleasure! Ah ! I was once blessed with an aged mother myself!" added the detective, with a sigh.

"Was you, indeed, sir? Just see that, now!" exclaimed the old dame, in a tone of great surprise at such a strange coincidence. "An aged mother yourself! Well, there! Yes, sir, I'll take the thread needlers, and thank you, too, seeing as you had an aged mother yourself."

"And perhaps this young gentleman here would like to possess a patent knife sharpener, warranted to put the sharpest edge upon any piece of cutlery, from a razor or a penknife to a spade or an ax," suggested the agent.

"Oh, just wouldn't I, though! Oh, my eyes!" exclaimed the youth in question, who was not troubled with bashfulness. "But I haven't got no knife to sharpen," he added, with rueful remembrance.

"That is a pity; but perhaps that misfortune may be remedied! Perhaps I may be able to find a knife, as well, as a knife sharpener, to reward a smart young chap who works to help his grandmother."

"And round a haunted old well as is enough to curdle your blood and make your hair stand up straight on yer head!" put in the "young man," to augment his merits.

"'Haunted?'" repeated the detective, catching at the one word with an air of curiosity and interest that was not altogether assumed.

"Yes! haunted! haunted awful! Arks granny, if you don't believe me," returned Master Zach.

"Oh, my dear sir! Far be it from me the sacrilege of casting incredulity upon the statements of a pious youth who supports his aged grandparent," solemnly replied the detective.

"Well, then, you just arks granny, if you can't believe me! Just arks her. Ah! she knows! She just does!" exclaimed the youth, resentfully, misunderstanding the words of the detective, and imagining himself to be doubted and reproached.

The detective turned an inquiring glance toward the old dame.

He was very anxious to get to the bottom of this ghost story, for he saw in it the means of elucidating the mystery of that murder for which Margaret Campbell had been condemned to transportation and penal servitude for life.

"Oh, yes, sir," said the old dame, with a deep sigh, "it is too true! the boy tells the truth! The well is haunted, sir! it is horribly haunted! There's a-many people as don't believe in ghosts, but if they had seen what I saw at the well one dark night last month, they'd never again misdoubt as the dead do walk!"

"I never misdoubted it! I have heard too much and seen too much to misdoubt it!" solemnly replied the detective.

"Ah, sir, but I'm glad to hear you say that! It is good to meet a sensible gentleman sometimes! So many don't believe! There's our minister, though he is a learned man and a good Christian, he don't believe in the ghost I saw that night, what turned my blood to water and my bones to jelly, so that I fell down for dead! But if he'd seen it! Ah! if he'd seen it!" sighed the old dame, clasping her hands and raising her dim, blue eyes.

"Has anyone else seen it besides yourself?" sympathetically inquired the traveler.

"Oh, yes, sir! This boy here, he was with me at the time, carrying a lantern to light me through the yard. I had been sitting with the coachman's wife, sir"-and here the dame told the story of her fright at the well just as the traveler had already heard it from the landlady of the Campbell Arms.

"Has the apparition been visible since that night?" inquired the traveler.

"Anan?" questioned the dame.

"Has the ghost been seen since?"

"Oh, yes, sir! Yes! Every night between midnight and morning that ghost has been seen by anybody that happened to be about at that hour; and always wrapped in a long white sheet that trailed upon the ground, and always carrying the murdered baby in its arms and weeping over it—oh! weeping as if its heart was broken, and fit to break anybody else's heart, as well as to scare 'em to death!"

"I didn't tell you before, sir! I didn't like to! But of course we all on us knows whose ghost it is! It's as plain as daylight!" said the old dame, in an awful whisper.

"Whose?" inquired the detective, in the same hushed tone.

"Why, of course, hers, sir! Margaret Campbell's! She must have died out there on Bottommy Bay, and now her spirit is condemned to come back here and wander every night and go through the motions of her bloody deed, all in dumb show! And no wonder her spirit can't rest! In course, you have heerd of Margaret Campbell, sir?"

"Oh, yes! I think most people have heard of her—in these realms!"

"Yes, sir, to be sure they must have! Well, sir, it's Margaret Campbell's ghost as haunts the dry well, carrying the murdered baby in her arms and weeping over it fit to break your heart."

"I have no doubt of it in the world! And I should like to see it above all things."

"Oh, sir, wouldn't you be affeard?"

"Why, no; why should I be? What harm could the ghost do me?

"But the sight of it, sir, would turn your blood to water!"

"The sight wouldn't affect me in that way! You say it can be seen every night between midnight and morning?" inquired the traveler.

"I say it has been so seen whenever anybody has been near the old dry well at that hour to see it," explained the old dame.

"Look here, ma'am! I have the very greatest curiosity and desire to see that wonder, with my own eyes! Now, if you could manage it for me so that I would not be considered a trespasser, I would make it worth your while to the tune of two guineas," said the traveler, placing two gold sovereigns and two silver shillings on the table before her.

"Two pun-two? Great Heaven!" gasped the old dame; "more than Zach could yarn in two months! What is it you want me to do, sir? I would do anything in the world—honest—for two guineas."

"I only want you to guide me, or to send some one else to guide me to the dry well, or to some spot from which I can have a view of the well between midnight and day," said the traveler.

"To-night, sir?" gasped the old woman, turning pale.

"To-night," answered the traveler; "I wish to test this matter for myself."

"And—would you want—anybody—to stay there till they saw the ghost?" faltered the old dame, who was powerfully shaken by the conflict between her fears of the ghost and her desire for the guineas.

"No, I only want some one belonging to the place to go with me to the spot to quiet the dogs, who would bark at me as a stranger, and to prevent me from being mistaken for a trespasser, who am only an inquisitive commercial traveler. My companion might then leave me to watch alone for he apparition."

"There, now! that's what I call fair and above board! Zach, my son, you will go with the gentleman, like a good boy," said the old dame, in persuasive tones.

"No! I wunnot! I dunnot want to see the ghost again," answered the boy, with his hair on end.

"But if I give you one of the shillings, Zach, to spend as you like."

"No!"

"If I give yer both shillings, Zach! Come, now," coaxed the dame.

"No! I wunnot! I dunnot want to see the ghost, not at no price!" answered the boy, intrenching himself behind a mulish obstinacy.

"But if I give you a four-bladed knife, with a patent knife sharpener, such as no boy or man in the whole neighborhood has got—if I give you these in addition to the two shillings your grandmother has promised you, how then?" inquired the traveler.

The boy hesitated. The battle between his terror and his cupidity was wonderful to behold.

"I'll—I'll take you to the withered pear tree and stay till the dogs stop barking; but I won't take you no nigher nor I won't stay no longer," he said.

"But where is the withered pear tree? inquired the detective.

"It is right outside the stable yard. The stable gate is locked, so you couldn't get in there, anyway, but you can have a full view of the old dry well and the fir wood where the ghost walks from the pear tree."

"It is a bargain, then. You shall take me to the withered pear tree, introduce me to the dogs as a friend of yours, so that they won't eat me, or even object to me, and then you may leave me there alone to watch for the ghost."

"All right, and you'll give me the four-bladed knife and the pattink sharpener, and granny'll give me the two bob?"

"Yes, assuredly," replied the traveler.

"But we needn't go till nigh midnight, nohow. It were arter midnight when me and granny seen it, that time she had been a-sittin' up long of the coachman's 'oman, which was ill," said the boy.

"Very well! We will not go until near midnight, if Mrs. Keene will give me houseroom until that time," the traveler.

"That I will, sir, and welcome! And now, as you are to stay, won't you take a bit of supper with us?" inquired Mrs. Keene.

The traveler declined, but begged that Dame Keene and her grandson might sit down and sup without ceremony.

They followed his advice.

After they had finished their meal and the dame had cleared the table, and set the two tall tallow candles in brass candlesticks upon it, she said:

"Now, sir, if you will excuse me, I will go upstairs to bed, on account o' my rheumatics; and you and Zach can sit here until it is time to go to the haunted ground. You'll excuse me, sir?"

"Certainly, ma'am! Pray do not stand on ceremony with me," said the traveler.

"Thank y', sir. And mind, Zach, when you go, lock the front door and take the key with you," she added, turning to the boy.

"And leave you locked up here? 'Spose there was a fire or anything, and you wanted to get out?"

"I could unbolt the back door, of course!"

"Oh, so you could! I forgot that!"

The old dame courtesied to the traveler and went upstairs to the little room above, where, for about five minutes, she could be heard walking, and then she was heard to get into a bed that creaked under her light weight. And finally all was silent.

The traveler and the boy sat at the oaken table, opposite each other, with the two tallow candles in the brass candlesticks between them.

The clock struck ten.

The boy opened his mouth and yawned fearfully, supernaturally, and said:

"Yer wunnot mind if I go to sleep, master, will yer? I am so"— another phenomenal yawn—"awfully dead beat!"

"Certainly not. Go to sleep. I will wake you when it's time to start," said the traveler.

But the permission was superfluous; the boy heard not a word of it; he was snoring with his head upon his folded arms on the table, before the sentence was completed.

The traveler sat for a little while thinking over what he had heard, and drawing certain conclusions from the story, and then he began to feel bored, and to wonder how he should pass the two hours before it would be time to start for the haunted well.

He got up and looked around the room. He discovered a few books on a hanging shelf against the wall, and he went to them and examined them one by one—the Book of books, the Holy Bible, a common prayer book, a volume of religious tracts, the "Pilgrim's Progress." Such was the collection.

Hutchings had not seen the "Pilgrim's Progress" since he was a Sunday-school boy, thirty years before.

He now felt some curiosity to look into it. He took it to the table, sat down, opened and began to read it.

He was soon so absorbed in the adventures of Christian as to become deaf to the snores of Master Zach—who, sleeping in an uneasy position, with his arms and head on the table, blew his trumpet with unusual force and volume—and oblivious to the passage of time until the loud striking of the clock startled him.

It tolled eleven.

He then closed his book and restored it to its place on the shelf.

"I shall not wait here until twelve," he said to himself, "for it may be just possible that the 'ghost' may take it into its head to 'walk' before midnight, in which event I should miss it by delay! I will, therefore, rouse our heroic friend here, and proceed to the withered pear tree at once! Heavens! how weird and unearthly all this seems to be!"

CHAPTER XVI
THE HAUNTED WELL AT MIDNIGHT

ALL was still as death within and around the lonely lodge. The boy still slept soundly, with his head laid upon his arms on the table.

The detective went to his side to arouse him. Taking him by the shoulder, he shook him gently.

It was no easy matter to awaken this sleeper, however, for if he was shaken up one instant he was down again the next.

At length, by repeated efforts, the detective succeeded in arousing him and restoring him to some sense of the situation.

"Now, then! Do you know where you are?" demanded the traveler, as he stood the boy up on his feet and held him fast to keep him from falling.

"Yezzur," drowsily replied the lad, reeling.

"Do you know who I am?" inquired the man, steadying the boy.

"Yezzur," gaped the latter, rubbing his knuckles into his eyes.

"Attend to me! Do you know what you promised to do?"

"Yezzur," yawned Zach, coming slowly to his senses, "yer promised to gimmy a four-blade knife and a pattink sharpener and two bob."

"Oh, ay, to be sure! But that is not the question! What did you promise to do to earn them?" demanded the detective.

The boy yawned fearfully and shuddered; but that might have been caused by his having been so rudely aroused from his sleep.

"Come, come! Do you know what you promised to do to earn the four-bladed knife, the patent sharpener and the two bob?" impatiently demanded Hutchings.

188

"Yezzur," gaped the boy.

"What was it, then? Come, speak up!"

"Yer promised—I promised to go with yer and—to go with yer to the withered pear tree and—and show yer the haunted well—where the ghost walks-Ur-r-r-r-r!" shuddered the boy.

"All right! That is what you promised to do," assented Hutchings; "and now it is time to be off!"

"But, mind you, I ain't a-gwine no nigher nor the dead pear tree; and I ain't a-gwine to stay no longer nor to still them dogs—no, not at any price," said Zach, as he reeled off toward the corner cupboard and took his old hat from a hook at its side.

"All right! You shall not be required to do more than you have agreed upon," laughed Hutchings.

"And ye're to gimmy the four-blade knife and pattink sharpener and the two bob, true and faithful," added the lad, who was now at length fully awake.

"True and faithful," agreed the detective, as they left the house together.

Hutchings locked the lodge door on the outside and withdrew the key, as Zach had been ordered, but had forgotten to do.

The full moon was at the zenith and shining brightly down upon the grass-grown avenue, along which they walked with stealthy steps, and upon the old trees that flanked it.

The two went on in perfect silence, the man before, the boy close at his heels, shuddering, stealthily looking over his own shoulders and starting fearfully at every dead bush or crooked tree that happened to be more grotesque than usual.

So they went on for about half a mile, and then the boy stopped abruptly.

"What now?" inquired the man, also pausing.

"This here path leads to the corner of the stable wall where the old gateway used to be; but it is walled up now," said the boy, pointing to a blind path on the right that struck into a thicket so dense as scarcely to admit a ray of the bright moonlight which was flooding the atmosphere."

"Well?" inquired Hutchings.

"Well," repeated the lad, "the dead pear tree is there agin' the wall at the other end o' this here path."

"Very good! Let us turn into it, then. Why do you stop?" inquired the detective, seeing that the boy did not budge.

"Yer go fust. I'll foller," cried the boy, with chattering teeth.

"All right! Come on!" cheerily exclaimed Huthings striking into the narrow, tangled thicket, now damp and dark with the dews of an August night.

"Ur-r-r-r-r-r!" shivered the boy, as he followed. "Mind, I ain't a-gwine no nigher nor the dead pear tree, nor I ain't a-gwine to stay no longer nor to still them dogs !"

"Of course. I understand that," replied his employer.

"Not at no price!" added the boy.

"No, 'not at no price,'" assented Hutchings.

"And ye're gwine to gimmy the four-bladed knife and the pattink sharpener and the two bob, as yer promised?"

"Upon my sacred honor, I will."

"True and faithfurl?"

"'True and faithful,'" solemnly replied the detective, as he pushed on through the dark and dense thicket, pressing aside the mingled branches of the trees to the right and left, and crushing the brushwood under his feet.

They went on so for about an eighth of a mile, when suddenly they emerged from the thicket and came out upon an open space, like a disused road, that ran along on the outside of an old, dilapidated stone wall that stood before them.

Apparently a row of fruit trees had once grown there; but now nothing remained but one dead tree, whose skeleton branches stood out as if traced in ink upon the gray surface of the stone.

"There! Ur-r-r-r-r! There's the dead pear tree! Ef yer'll go to it and climb upon the rubbish, yer kin see the paddock 'tween the stable yard and the fir wood, and the old haunted well in the paddock where the ghost walks," said the boy, with his teeth chattering like a pair of castanets.

Here the dogs began to bark vociferously, and the boy plucked up a little courage, for there is something very antighostly in the hearty bark of watchdogs.

"Down, Fly! Hush yer tongue, Tip! Shut up, Buck! Hold yer jaw, Wool! Be quiet, can't yer?" he called, first to one, then to others in turn, finally to all; and so, as they recognized his voice and his presence, he succeeded in quieting them.

"Now yer kin go up to the wall," said the lad.

But Mr. Hutchings had his doubts whether the watch-dogs would keep quiet after the boy should have gone and only himself be left, and so he said:

"You—what are you going to do?"

" Oh, now, master, don't go to try to do me! Yer know I told yer I wurn't gwine no nigher 'an the dead pear tree, nor stay no longer 'an to still the dogs! No, not fur no price! And yer 'greed! And now them dogs is quiet as lambs, and here's the dead pear tree, where yer kin stand and see the ghost when it comes to the haunted well. Ur-r-r-r-r-r! And I'm gwine home right off now!" cried the boy, turning to run.

But Hutchings laid hold on him.

"Lemmy go! Lemmy go! I wunnot stop for no price!" cried the boy, struggling.

"Ohe moment! I want to ask you a question."

"Lemmy go!"

"Are you going home through that dark thicket?"

"Yes! Lemmv go!"

"By yourself?"

"Yes! Lemmy go! Lemmy go!"

"Suppose you were to meet the ghost in the path?"

"Ah-h-h-h-h-h-h!" yelled the boy, dropping on the ground, appalled by a possibility that had not before occurred to him.

"You can go if you like, you know," said Hutchings, kindly.

"I darn't! Oh, I darn't! I darn't stay here! I darn't go away! Oh, wot wull I do? wot wull I do?" cried the boy, rolling over and over on the wet ground, and kicking in his impotent excitement.

"I tell you what I would do if I were you."

"Wot? Oh, master, wot?"

"I would go and stay with the dogs. It is well known to all men that ghosts never go near dogs! Now, I would go and stay with the dogs if I were you. Hear! They are beginning to growl! They'll burst out barking again if you don't go to them."

"I jes' believe I will, marster. It'll be the best way! Ye're sure ghosts don't 'pear to dogs?" inquired the boy, somewhat recovering from his abject terror.

"Sure and certain! I would take my affidavit to the fact! There, now, go! or they will be in full blast again."

The boy gathered himself up and crept off to the kennels which were at the end of the wall—on the right hand.

The dogs then became perfectly quiet, and the boy also must have calmed himself in their company, for no sound was heard from the kennels.

Ben Hutchinge went up to the withered pear tree, climbed upon a pile of broken stones and thence up into the tree. Seating himself in the fork between two strong limbs he looked over the stable wall.

A weird scene met his view.

The full moon, shining broadly down, revealed every object with clearest distinctness.

And this was the picture:

On his extreme right stood the dark, massive stone building of the stables, the carriage houses, the coachman and grooms' quarters, and the kennels. Nearer, but still on the right hand, was the stable yard. Just below him and straight before him was a hurdle fence dividing the stable yard from a small paddock that lay immediately to the left. In the midst of this paddock stood an old dry well, of which, nothing above ground remained but a moss-covered circular brick wall about breast high. On the extreme left of the paddock stood the dark fir wood, and behind it arose the white chimneys of the manor house.

In the background, straight before him, past the stable yard and paddock, were fields and barns and hayricks.

But it was upon the paddock with the old well that the attention of the detective was directed.

The paddock, lying between the stable and the old fir wood, was bathed in moonlight.

Hutchings, from his perch in the dead tree, watched it closely.

The Test of Love

What did the detective expect to see?

A ghost? A spirit? A thing of air?

Not he. He claimed to be a realistic man of the nineteenth century, and he lived a very real life, and followed two or three very matter-of-fact callings.

He expected to find in this so-called "ghost" a material being, a guilty creature pursued by an avenging conscience, and driven in her sleep to haunt the scene of her crime, and nightly react its horrors.

Such were his expectations. And he resolved that his conduct in the premises should be guided by circumstances. He might feel constrained to awaken the somnamubulist, and to surprise her into a confession of her crime, or he might only observe and remember, and leave the denouement to another day.

While debating this matter in his mind, a faint, glimmering light from the body of the dark fir wood drew his attention. It was as if a moonbeam were breaking from the deep green thicket.

But as he gazed the soft light arose to the height of about five feet, and gradually condensed and crystallized into the form of a woman, wondrous white, with pale, yellow hair streaming over her bare shoulders and over her white and flowing drapery.

As the detective gazed on this marvel, strange, powerful electric thrills shook his whole strong frame.

The form advanced slowly, without a step, but with a gliding motion, and her wild, bright eyes had a wondrous shining light that seemed to send rays before them.

Hutchings gazed spellbound, awe-stricken.

The spirit glided nearer and nearer, and now it could be seen that she carried in her arms—not a mimic child, a puppet of rags and paper, such as the detective had expected to see in the possession of the somnambulist, but—a babe, as beautiful as one of the cherubim

194

of heaven, with a halo of light around its form; and now, also, it was evident that it was this light only that illumined the woman's form.

Yet still the detective could not move a limb or utter a word, nor even withdraw his gaze from the radiant form of the spirit-woman and babe.

The vision had now advanced to the well, and with her back to the entranced spectator, and with the babe to her bosom, and her head bent until all her shining hair fell forward over the form of the child, she leaned and looked down into the deep, dark shaft below them.

"By all that is most holy!" cried the detective, by a mighty effort breaking from the spell that bound him—"by all that is most holy! spirit or flesh, she shall not throw the child into the well!"

And so saying he swung himself over the wall by a branch of the tree, and let himself drop into the paddock below.

The fall was a shock to his frame, but he quickly picked himself up and ran reeling on toward the well, where still stood the radiant form of the woman, with the beautiful babe clasped to her bosom, her shining hair veiling it as her head was bent and her eyes were fixed on the pit below.

Hutchings ran impetuously forward, intending to seize her from behind and whirl her with the child from the brink of the well. But—

She swayed around as on a pivot, and fixed upon him a pair of wild, bright eyes that glowed from a cavernous, white face half veiled with flaming yellow hair.

He cast his arms around her, and clasped—an electric shock that threw him violently back upon the ground, left him in a state of unconsciousness.

CHAPTER XVII
WITHIN THE MANOR HOUSE

WHEN the detective recovered his consciousness, the moon was sinking toward the west, and the dawn was rising in the east.

His clothing was damp with the dews of that autumn night; his limbs were stiff, and his head was heavy.

He gathered himself up with a groan, and began to collect his faculties.

The scene aided his memory; there was the paddock with the old dry well in the midst, and with the stable yard and the stable on its right, the dark fir wood on its left, and the fields, hayricks and barns beyond. The only difference was the lengthened shadow of the stable cast half across the yard by the descending moon on the right and the white light of the dawn tipping the dark fir wood on the left.

"What have I seen? What have I discovered? Was it a dream? Was it a reality? or was it a trick? It seems I have been worsted in this quest, and caught—nothing but the rheumatism, probably! How strange all this is! Nothing like it ever happened in my experience before! Let me think," said Hutchings to himself, as he stood by the broken wall of the old well, and, with his hand to his head, tried to clearly recall the adventures of the night that were but dimly present to his mind.

"Let me see! I came down here to investigate the facts of that five-year-old murder of a child at Rose Hill, for which Margaret Campbell was condemned—unjustly, as her friends say—to transportation and penal servitude for life!

"I reach this place and hear the story of a ghost-the ghost of a woman with a child in her arms—who haunts the well and has been seen by too many people to leave a doubt, even on my practical mind, as to there being some solid foundation for the story.

"I draw my own conclusions, however! I believe the ghost to be no other than a material woman—the same woman seen by the traveler at the well with the child on the night of the murder—a guilty creature tortured by remorse, driven by conscience and compelled to walk in her sleep, haunting the scene of her crime, and re-enacting it in her dreams!

"I resolve to go at midnight to the 'haunted' well and watch for the 'ghost,' or somnambulist, as I am convinced she is.

"I go and watch, and what do I see? An unearthly vision—yes, my soul!—an unearthly vision!—a vision of woman, carrying in her arms a child, emerges from the wood and glides across the paddock.

"Spellbound, I gaze upon the vision until it reaches the well. Then— to prevent a catastrophe—I make a supreme effort, break from my trance, and rush forward to clasp and whirl her away from the brink of destruction.

"I clasp—thin air, and receive a shock that annihilates sense and reason for hours! I come at length to myself and here I stand in the paddock, and there is the haunted well before me. But where is the haunter?"

Here Hutchings walked up to the circular wall around the well and looked down into its depths. He saw nothing but a bottomless, black pit.

Then he turned and walked to the fir wood. It was a tangled, impenetrable, pathless thicket, through which scarcely a hare could have found its way.

"And yet from its depths the vision of the woman the child came!" said Hutchings to himself, as he retraced his steps.

He was now anxious to get out of the paddocks and to return to his lodgings, to think over all that had occurred at his leisure.

Unfortunately he could not jump from the ground to the top of the wall as easily as he had dropped from the top of the wall to the ground.

He looked around for other means of exit, for he did not wish to be found trespassing on private premises by any of the stablemen, who might now soon be astir.

Finally he climbed over the hurdle fence that divided the paddock from the stable wall, and seeing a gate bolted on the inside, he went and unbolted it and passed through.

He found himself now on the road outside the stable wall where he had parted from his boy guide a few hours before.

Even if he had not recollected the circumstance, he would have been reminded of it now, for all the dogs began to bark.

"That will arouse the stablemen, anyhow; and I wonder what has become of my heroic young friend? Has he remained all night with the dogs, or has he found courage to go home?" Hutchings mentally inquired.

His question was practically answered by a familiar voice:

"'Old yer tongue, Buck! Hush yer jaw, Tip! Stop yer noise, Fly! Down, Wool! Will yer then, yer idiwuts?"

It was the voice of little Zach "stilling" the dogs, whose vociferous barking at the approaching intruder had roused the boy from his sound sleep.

Zach now came out of the kennels, with straws in his hair and his knuckles in his eyes.

"Hello!" exclaimed Mr. Hutchings. "Did you stay all night with the dogs?"

"Yezzur," drowsily answered the lad.

"How came you to do that?"

"I dunno. Yes, I does, too. I wur waiting for you, and yer never come for me," answered Zach, who was waking up faster in the fresh outer air of this morning than he had been able to do in the close atmosphere of the lodge on the previous night.

"Well, I came for you as soon as ever I waked up. I have been asleep—or something, myself," said Hutchings, good-humoredly.

"Us hed better get along back to the lodge. Mr. Merry-winkle, the coachman, or some on um, will be coming out yere to see wot hev been the matter of the dogs," advised the boy.

"True. Come along; let us hurry," assented Hutchings, leading the way to the entrance of the blind path that led through the plantation thicket to the main park avenue.

"Did yer—did yer—see it?" inquired the boy, in hushed tones, as they passed in.

"See what?" demanded the detective, pretending not to understand the question.

"Oh, yer know—the ghost—but I recking yer didn't see it, or yer wuddn't arks—Wot?"

"No, I did not see it," coolly replied Hutchings.

"Not!" exclaimed the boy, stopping and staring.

"No. Come along. We have got the key of the lodge, you know, and your granny may be wanting to open the front door. See, the sky is getting red in the east, and the sun will soon be up."

"And so wull granny soon be up, and hur will wop me ef I ain't thar to 'elp 'ur! And yer didn't see it?" again inquired the boy.

"No."

"Well, I thought yer didn't, or yer wouldn't arks-Wot? But it's mons'us queer yer didn't see nothink."

"Oh, I went to sleep on my post. I reckon that was the reason why," Hutchings explained.

"I reckon so, too. Yer wouldn't do fur a sojer, would yer, now? And mind, yer hev got to gimmy that bladed knife and pattink sharpener, and them two bob, ef yer didn't see nothink! Yer hev got to give um to me, whether or no!" said the boy, with the air of one upon whom it would be no use to try any tricks.

"Oh, of course, of course," readily assented the traveler.

"Yes, but when are yer gwine to give um to me?"

"Just as soon as we get back to the lodge."

"Well, come along, then! Le's hurry! Granny'll be wanting of the keys, yer know!" exclaimed the boy, stimulated by the prospect of winning his reward at the end of his walk.

They soon emerged from the thicket out into the broad avenue, where both breathed more freely.

A rapid walk of twenty minutes brought them to the lodge.

"Oh, granny's up! See the smoke comin' out'n chimbly," said the boy.

Mr. Hutchings drew the key from his pocket and gave it to Zach, saying:

"Run around the back way and hand this key to your grandmother, that she may let me in, if she likes."

"Why can't yer unlock the door and let yerself in, long as yer hed got the key?" inquired the boy.

"Because that would not have been quite polite to your grandmother," replied Hutchings.

"But nobody don't think it no use to be perlite to the likes of old granny," said Zach, as he ran off with the key.

Two minutes later the front door was opened by the old woman, who confronted the visitor with a face full of interest and curiosity.

"Zach says as yer never saw nothink, sir!" she said, in an incredulous tone.

"No, I never did," replied the detective, who had his own reasons for keeping his secret and his own method of quieting his conscience.

"Now that there is werry strange! But, Lord save us, sir, how bad yer do look, tew be sure! W'y, ye're pale as a corpse and wet tew the skin!" exclaimed Granny Keene, as she looked more closely at the traveler.

"Well, not quite wet to the skin, but damp on the surface. The dews were very heavy last night," smilingly replied Hutchings.

"As the jews are apt to be on August nights," assented the old woman; "but come in! come in, sir! Bless us, ye're not gwine any farder this morning until yer hev dried yer clothes and got a good hot cup o' coffee!" she added, stretching the door wide open and placing her armchair forward for the guest.

Hutchings, well pleased at the prospect of rest and refreshment, entered and seated himself.

Granny Keene added a bundle of faggots to the little fire, and then filled a small copper kettle and hung it over the blaze, and drew out an oaken table and spread a white cloth over it preparatory to breakfast.

Zach sidled up to the visitor and whispered:

"Yer know wot yer promised me, master."

"Oh, yes," said Hutchings, putting his hand deep in the pocket of his coat and drawing out a handful of its contents. "Here is your four-bladed knife with a buckhorn handle." (It was the man's own familiar pocketknife; but he gave it up for the sake of peace, promising himself another and a better one in its place.)

"Oh!—ain't this just the bulliest knife as ever was!" cried the boy, in an ecstasy of delight over his new possession.

"And here is the patent sharpener," added the agent, producing the instrument.

"Oh! Ah! Eh! Gimmy the thing! I know how to use it! I see how to use it—look!" exclaimed the boy, seizing the tool and beginning to test its powers upon the largest blade of his knife.

"And here are two 'bob'! And now we are quits!" said Hutchings, laying a couple of bright new shillings down on the table before the boy.

"Yes! now we's quits!" admitted Zach, pocketing the coins.

"And don't yer never get in debt to a boy ag'in, as long as yer live, sir! for yer'll never have no peace of yer life till ye're outen it," said the old woman, as she placed a large loaf of brown bread on the table.

"No, I never will!" solemnly replied the visitor.

"And I think, Zach, yer might be taking the gemplan upstairs where he'll find soap and water and towels to wash hisself before breakfast. Wouldn't you like to, sir?" she inquired, turning to her guest.

"Yes, indeed, very much!" replied the man, rising to follow the boy, who led the way upstairs and probably wondered that anyone should want to wash his face when he had the option of leaving it alone.

While the two were upstairs the old woman made the coffee and fried rashers of bacon and fresh eggs.

When the traveler returned he found breakfast ready.

"This is really very kind of you, Mrs. Keene, to provide so liberally for a poor wayfarer," said Hutchings, with hearty and sincere appreciation, as he seated himself at the table.

"Lawk, sir, ye're kindly welcome! And sure this is not much to do after yer liberalality to the boy and me!" replied the dame, as she handed him a large cup of coffee.

"Ah! that is nothing to what I hope to do to show my sense of your worthiness, ma'am!" politely replied the guest as he received a cup from her hands; "but tell me, do you not think the ladies up in the manor house might like to look at my needle threaders?"

"Well, sir, I don't think as yer'll get to see the ladies nohow! But still there's nothing like trying, and there can't be no offense in trying. I might go up to the house with you, sir, and go in first, as they'll not object to seeing me, and I might talk 'em into takin' a look at yer thread needlers," suggested the dame.

"Oh, I wish you would! It would be very kind of you!" eagerly exclaimed the agent.

"Then we will go directly after breakfast, sir; but, dear me, sir, it do seem to me, as selling them things at a penny apiece, or a shilling a dozen, yer'll make very little profit on 'em! Hardly enough to make it worth yer while to travel down in these yere parts with 'em," said Granny Keene.

"Oh! my dear ma'am, it is not for what we make now. We are only introducing them. No, it is not now we expect to make money; but when every man, woman and child in the civilized world—every human being—either in the family or in business, as milliners, dressmakers, embroiderers, book stitchers, glovers, saddlers, harnessmakers, shoemakers, and all who use needles, will require needle threaders, and we sell them by hundreds of millions of packages—then we will make a profit—then we will make colossal fortunes!" said the agent, with enthusiasm.

"Oh, lor'! how I wish I could 'went somethink!" exclaimed Zach, staring with great, round eyes.

"If you don't ''went' your way to the stable, Mr. Merrywinkle will 'went a way to make yer sorry for it!" sharply replied the dame, as she arose from the breakfast table, which her guest had already left.

"Well, I'm gwine as soon as I get my grub," replied the boy.

"Sit down there and get it, then," ordered the old woman. "And now, sir," she said, turning to the visitor, "I will just go and put on my bonnet and shawl, and wait on yer up to the great house."

She went upstairs, and took rather more time with her toilet than was expected; but when she came down she appeared in her best black alpaca gown and shepherd's plaid shawl and black silk bonnet.

Zach, meanwhile, had bolted his breakfast, and filled his pockets with all the bread and bacon that he could not eat; and he was ready to go with his granny and her guest.

The three left the house together, the old woman locking the door after them, and putting the key in her pocket.

They walked on silently until they reached the spot where the blind path branched off from the avenue through the thicket toward the stables; there the boy left them and turned into the path on his way to the scene of his daily work.

Mr. Hutchings and Mrs. Keene continued their way along the avenue.

"I always understood that this property was entailed upon the heirs—the males taking precedence—and on the failure of the males the females inheriting. How is it now? There seems to be no heir or heiress of the Campbell family in possession; only the widow is there, with her children by a former husband. Has she any right to be there?" inquired the traveler.

"Well, sir, I dunnot know about any right. They do say as the poor creature, Margaret Campbell, as was sent across the seas, was the next heiress after her little cousin, as she was accused of killing. And then ag'in some do say as a conwick for life can't own no property, which if they do, it goes back to the crown, which means to the queen? But I do reckon ef it is so, as her majersty be too kind-hearted to mislest this poor widow and turn her out'n doors! Hows'ever, one says one thing, and one says another, and I don't know nothing about it, for sartain."

"Ah!" muttered the traveler, and they walked on in silence a little further. Then—"

Do the ladies attend the parish church?" inquired Hutchings.

"Eh! no, sir; they be Romans and go to St. Dominick's chapel, up by Huxton, a score o' miles from here, when they go anywhere," repeated the dame.

A turn in the avenue now brought them in sight of the house—an old, oblong, redstone building, with many latticed windows, gable roofs and twisted chimneys. The walls were partly overgrown with ivy, and the whole house heavily shaded by large forest trees.

The avenue led them up before the front door, a double-leaved portal of black oak, which was reached by half a dozen large, moss-grown stone steps.

"I'll go round to the servants' door if yer'll wait here, sir," said Mrs. Keene, turning off toward the right.

"Very well! I'll go with you! Being only a sort of peddler, the ladies might take it as a liberty if I was to stop at the other door," said the traveler.

"As yer please, good sir," assented the dame, who was not able, in her own mind, to fix the social status of the stranger.

She led him around to a small door in the rear of the building, and rang the bell.

A grave-looking woman, in a black stuff gown and a white cap and apron, opened the door.

"Eh, how do yer do, Sairy?" exclaimed Granny Keene. "And how is the madam and the young ladees? Eh! wench, let me come in and sit down, for I'm that spent with walking from the lodge to the house here that I can hardly stand!"

"Come in, then!" said the woman, in a very inhospitable tone, as she moved aside to let the old woman pass.

Hutchings followed without an invitation.

They found themselves in a back passage, or hall, furnished with a few chairs.

The two visitors sat down without waiting to be asked to do so.

"Who is that you've got along with yer? You know very well as strangers ain't allowed into this house!" said the servant woman.

"Eh, then, let me sit down and get my breath a minute before I'm called to answer questions," panted the old woman, as she settled herself in her chair and untied her bonnet strings.

"This gentleman," she resumed at last, "have got the most wonderfullest inwentions for threading all sorts of needles and sharpening all sorts of razors and knives and things as ever was seen or heerd tell on in this world! And as I hev tried the thread-a-needler and found it good, I thought, Sairy Ann, as it 'ould be a godsend to you to gin yer a chance to get one for yourself. Only a penny apiece,and yer might never hev another opportunity as long as yer lived."

"Well, I don't mind if I look at the thing—though I know it's a humbug! I don't believe in new-fangled things, nor likewise take no stock in 'wentions! But I'll just take a look at the cantrip!" said the woman, surlily.

"Certainly, ma'am! Look at it! We are only introducing the article now, and if you will oblige me by accepting a couple and giving them a trial, I would be very grateful," said the agent, with extreme politeness, as he produced a packet, selected from it two needle-threaders and handed them to the woman.

Curiosity prompted the latter to look at the little tool, and she, like others, saw at a glance how easily it could be used, and what a great convenience it would be

She pocketed the needle threaders and thanked the donor—though with an ill grace, for politeness did not come naturally to her.

"And now, if you would be kind enough to take this packet to the ladies of the house," he added, proffering the little parcel.

"Yes, I will take it, and maybe the mistress will deal with you, for they be great needlewomen, be our ladies," said the woman, as she received the paper and disappeared through a door on the right.

"Oh, dear! Sairy Ann Johnson is a crusty piece!" said Mrs. Keene, half to herself.

Hutchings made no reply.

In a few minutes the woman returned, saying:

"You are to go up to the ladies with your needle threaders. They want to see all the varieties you have got."

Hutchings arose to follow the servant who was waiting to conduct him.

Mrs. Keene also arose to accompany them, but Sairy Ann arrested her intention by saying:

"Granny Keene, you are to stay just where you are, or to go home, just as you please; but you are not wanted upstairs."

"Eh, dear, the imperance o' 'pampered' mediums!" muttered the old woman, sinking back in her seat.

Mr. Hutchings followed his conductress through the door on the right, and thence down a long, narrow passage that led to the great hall, thence up the grand staircase to an upper hall, from whence many doors opened into suites of rooms.

The woman opened one of these doors on the right and admitted the visitor into a small, oak-paneled parlor, in which were seated three women—all in mourning, or half mourning.

The elder was tall and handsome, though somewhat past her prime; she wore a black dress and a widow's cap.

The second in age, a girl of about twenty-five, was a beautiful brunette, and wore a white Swiss muslin dress, with blue ribbon sash and bows.

The third was a pale blonde, with dim blue eyes and dull straw-colored hair, and wore a sort of loose white wrapper carelessly fastened about the waist with strings of the same material as the dress.

These three women were gathered around their worktable. The two beauties. evidently mother and daughter, were engaged in embroidery. The invalid was sitting in perfect idleness, with her hands laid straight on her lap and her eyes fixed upon them.

As the visitor entered he was at once struck by the strange expressions on these women's faces.

That of the mother betrayed a depth of anguish and despair that caused the spectator to turn shuddering away from its contemplation, wondering the while that its owner could suffer so much and live!

That of the dark-eyed daughter displayed an excess of discontent and irritability.

That of the pale blonde expressed a depth of gloom and terror bordering on the horror of insanity.

Surely these were three strange-looking women to find in this oak-paneled parlor of the quaint old manor house! Any visitor, unacquainted with their antecedents, might naturally ask what fearful tragedy had happened there to impress upon the faces of two, at least, this indelible expression of anguish, horror and despair!

For a moment Hutchings glanced from face to face, and then his gaze became riveted on the face and form of the cold, deadly pale blonde girl!

And well it might, for she was the perfect counterpart of the woman he had seen in the midnight vision at the haunted well—wanting only the beautiful child and the supernal illumination!

CHAPTER XVIII
"WEIRD WOMEN"

"COME here," said the elder lady—who wore a widow's dress and cap—speaking in a strange, hollow, unnatural tone, as she beckoned the stranger to approach the table at which she and the two girls were seated.

But the detective scarcely heard her—his attention being still riveted upon the pallid, silent, motionless creature whose phantom he had seen in his midnight vision at the haunted well.

Excepting the addition of the beautiful child she had carried in her arms, and the supernal illumination of her whole form of air as seen in the vision, it was the perfect image of this pale, stony, immovable girl.

"Come here," repeated the lady, in a sterner tone.

"I beg your pardon!" exclaimed the man, with a start, as he recovered himself and obeyed the summons by stepping up to the table.

"Sit down," said the widow, in the same peremptory tone, pointing to a vacant chair.

The detective dropped into the seat and tried to recover from the unprecedented panic into which the sight of that girl had thrown him.

He had discreetly withdrawn his eyes, but his thoughts still dwelt on her, or circled wildly around her.

"This form of flesh," he said to himself, as his gaze once more furtively sought the girl—"this form of flesh seems like a body from which the soul has fled, and that form of air seemed like a disembodied spirit."

Then suddenly pulling himself together, as he would have expressed it, he took himself to task, mentally saying:

"Come, come, Hutchings, it is all queer enough, but don't you go mooning over things you don't understand; but just attend to the lady."

The widow was, in fact, speaking to him.

"I asked you to sit down; for Keene has told me that you came on foot all the way from Rosedale—a long walk and all uphill," she said, in the same strange, hollow but now not unkindly tone.

"I thank you, madam. Yes, I walked from the village," said Hutchings, respectfully.

"And you have something new in the appointments of a workbox to show us, I understand?"

"Yes, madam, if you will allow me; a needle threader that will enable anyone, no matter how weak the sight, or how nervous the fingers, to thread the finest needle in one instant, without the least trouble," said the quasi patent agent, taking a little box from his pocket and opening it to display his wares.

He handed one specimen to the elder lady and one to the pretty brunette girl, and a third to the pallid, stony creature who had not once lifted her eyes from the crossed hands upon her lap, or in any other way given any sign of life.

The widow and the elder daughter received the little tools and examined them with interest; but the cadaverous blonde took not the slightest notice of the offering.

"Will you not honor me by trying one of these little instruments, miss?" inquired the agent, bending toward her and pressing the article upon her acceptance.

But his words and acts had no more effect on her than if he had been a dressmaker's dummy.

"Do not disturb that young lady. She is not in good health," said the widow, in a stern voice.

"I beg pardon, madam," respectfully answered Hutchings, recoiling into his place.

"You may leave a dozen of these, and I will recommend them to our friends," said the lady, laying down a shilling on the table before the agent.

"I thank you, madam," said Hutchings, with a bow, as he handed over a packet of needle threaders and pocketed the shilling.

"That is all, I think. We will not detain you longer," said the lady, with an unmistakable manner of dismissing her visitor.

The detective arose and bowed; but he could not go without another look at the death-like form in the low chair, and another effort to attract her attention, to make her raise her eyes to his eyes, as her phantom had done in the midnight vision by the haunted well.

As he passed her he stooped and laid a little parcel on her motionless hands, and said:

"I wish you would kindly favor me by examining these."

She started, and looked up, and then, with a sharp cry, covered her face with her hands, exclaiming, in agonized tones:

"Oh, no, no, no, no, no! Oh, no! it was not so! It was never, never so! Oh, great Heaven, why didn't I die? Why didn't I die?"

The elder lady was at her side in an instant, with her arms around the excited girl, expostulating with her.

"Malvina! Malvina! Behave yourself directly! Do you want me to— Behave yourself, I say!"

But the poor creature fell to the floor in a fit, and began to foam at the mouth.

The detective sprang forward to assist in raising her; but the lady stretched out her arms to repel him, saying, sternly:

"Leave the room, sir! and leave the house instantly! How dared you to speak to this young lady again, after my having told you that she was out of health? Lavinia, my dear, help me to lead your sister to the sofa," she added, turning to the beautiful brunette, who had dropped her embroidery and was already standing over the fallen girl.

The two ladies raised the fragile creature to her feet, and supporting her on each side, guided her to the sofa and laid her carefully upon it.

The detective lingered at the door until he saw this feat successfully accomplished, and then he went downstairs by the way he had come up, and reached the back hall leading to the servants' entry.

The same woman who had admitted him first, now hearing his footsteps, came out of the kitchen to open the door for him.

"Granny Keene have gone around to visit the coachman's wife, and says how, if yer would look in at the stable quarters, yer might sell some o' yer needle threaders there," said the woman, as she opened the door.

"Thank you," replied the man, in a noncommittal manner, as he passed out.

He did not care to sell any more of his wares. He had accomplished all that he had intended in coming down into the neighborhood, and more than he had expected. He had nothing to do but to return to London and report to his employer.

And yet he was not fully satisfied, and, as he walked along the deserted old avenue that led from the house to the lodge, he anxiously communed with himself.

"That pallid, stony, death-like girl is the guilty party, but how deeply is a question. She is guilty, and suffers in her conscience. And her mother knows that she is so and suffers with her. Great Heaven! how that mother suffers! 'To know that her daughter is guilty of the murder of her little brother—of that mother's own infant child—a crime for which the girl should suffer death on the gallows-and to know that another, and a most innocent young creature, is now suffering punishment in her stead, by transportation to the penal colonies for life! To know all this, and to have the hideous alternative of harboring this most guilty secret, or else of denouncing her own daughter to the law and its terrible penalty! No wonder that look of anguish and despair is indelibly impressed upon that woman's face!"

Here Hutchings reached a rustic seat on one side of the avenue, and he sat down on it, drew his handkerchief from his pocket, and wiped his forehead.

"And the stupor of that girl during the whole of my interview with her mother. She seemed to me—ay, and she was, totally unconscious of my presence in the room until I went up close to her, spoke in her ear, and touched her hand to make her look up at me, as the phantom had looked in the midnight vision by the haunted well.

"And her sudden, overwhelming terror as she met my eyes. What could that mean? Did she recognize me as anyone she had ever seen before? Was it she whom I saw at midnight by the well? Was she sleepwalking? Did she awaken and see me, and having seen me at the well, did she recognize me again this morning?"

"It seems likely. It seems absolutely certain. But—but—the form I saw carried in its arms a babe! Not a doll, not a puppet, but a babe as beautiful as one of the cherubim, and it was illumined with a supernal light that shone like the sun, though in a limited sphere. And when I went to throw my arms around this image, and clasp it, I clasped only empty air, and at the same time received an electric shock that hurled me to the ground, and left me unconscious for more hours than I care to count.

"No, if that form I saw at the haunted well was this Malvina Mattox in the flesh, where did she get that beautiful cherub? Where did she get that radiant, supernal light? And why, when I threw my arms around her form, did I clasp nothing but thin air? And why did I receive an electric shock that hurled me to the ground as if I had been struck by lightning? Who can answer these questions? And, on the other hand, if this image was not Malvina Mattox in the flesh, how came it to resemble her so closely, and why should she have been overwhelmed with terror on meeting my eyes this morning?

And, finally, if that form seen in the midnight vision by the haunted well was not Malvina Mattox in the flesh, what was it?

"Ben Hutchings! Ben Hutchings! you are out of your depths now, if ever you were in all your life; and I advise you, Ben, not to tell this story of the ghost in Scotland Yard. It would not be good for your reputation, Ben.

"It is enough for you that—setting the ghost aside—you have seen and heard sufficient to corroborate the testimony of Mr. Ham Gow as to the really guilty party in that Rose Hill murder."

With these, sage reflections the detective arose and walked on toward the lodge.

The cottage was shut up as he passed it, but he easily unbolted the gate and let himself out of the park, and then walked along the turnpike road leading down the hill toward Rosedale.

He soon reached the Campbell Arms, before the door of which he saw the stagecoach for the Stockstone railway station standing, and several passengers getting out and passing into the barroom. It had apparently just arrived with travelers by the early train.

"How soon do you go back to the station?" inquired Hutchings of the driver.

"In half an hour, sir," answered the latter.

Hutchings passed into the barroom, where the landlady herself was behind the counter helping the barmaid to wait on the customers brought by the stagecoach, and who seemed to belong to the neighborhood, for as soon as they had drunk their beer they went their way.

"Eh—bless us!" exclaimed the Widow Keene, as soon as she saw her guest. "Sure, I was feared some ill had come to you, sir, by your not getting back last night."

"Not at all. Nothing but good came to me, I am thankful to say," blithely replied the detective.

"Oh! I am glad to hear you say so, sir, though I did expect you back last night, and told Jim Sims to sleep with one ear open so he could hear you if you came back late," replied the landlady, with a shade of resentment in her voice.

"But I found such favor in the eyes of your relative at the gate, for both myself and my wares, that I spent the night on the estate, and breakfasted at the lodge this morning," good-humoredly explained Hutchings.

"Eh! then if so be, Granny Keene has took to entertaining travelers, she had better get the madam's consent, and hang a sign out," sharply commented the landlady.

As Hutchings did not know what to reply to this outburst, he contented himself by asking for his bill, adding:

"And you make it out up to the present hour, for though I did not occupy a bedroom, I certainly engaged one, and shall pay for it."

"Yes, sir, certainly; that is as it should be," said the landlady, who, finding that her bill was not to be disputed, became mollified at once.

The last of the stagecoach passengers had just received his mug of beer from the barmaid's hands. When he had quaffed it and left the house, the landlady stooped toward the detective, dropped her voice to a confidential, low key, and inquired:

"Did you have the good luck to show any of your wares to the ladies, sir, if one might ask?"

"Oh, yes! Old Mrs. Keene was so kind as to go with me to the house this morning, and get me an interview with the ladies. They were pleased with my patent needle threaders, and bought a dozen."

The landlady stared in astonishment for a moment, and then exclaimed:

"Well! though I asked you the question, I didn't expect you to answer it in that way! I could hardly have believed that you would have got in where no one is ever allowed to go! But I suppose it was just because you were a stranger from a distance! No one from this neighborhood would ever be allowed to enter into that house, now, I can tell you."

"I do not see why," said the detective.

"Neither do I; but it is just so! And so it has been ever since the house was cleared of the police and law officers after the verdict of the coroner's jury and the committal of Margaret Campbell for the murder. I'll dare to say as you are the first man, barring the doctor, and the priest, as has been received into that house these five years past."

"Well! I had no trouble to get in."

"It must have been because you was a stranger from a long distance, and couldn't be thought to know or to remember what had happened there five years ago."

"Perhaps so."

"And did you really see the madam, now, sir?"

"Of course I did."

"And—her oldest daughter, the beauty, Miss Mattox?"

"Yes."

"Ah, poor girl, I pity her!—for it is not likely as any man will ever venture to marry her " sighed the landlady.

"Why not?" demanded the inquisitive detective.

"Oh, sir! And insanity and epilepsy and what not in the family!" exclaimed Mrs. Keene.

"'Insanity!'—'epilepsy!'—I don't understand you!" said Hutchings.

"Did you see—the youngest girl, sir? the afflicted one?" inquired the landlady, lowering her voice to an almost inaudible key.

"The one that has fits? Yes, I saw her," answered the detective, in as careless a tone as he could assume.

"They say she never was quite right in her head, and ever since that terrible tragedy she has been altogether wrong, quite crazy."

"Yet, if I remember rightly, she was the principal witness against Margaret Campbell?"

"That she was, sir! and, therefore, one might think she couldn't be quite as crazy then as she was cracked up to be, else the judges wouldn't have listened to her. I say, sir—did you—did you—see or hear anything about the ghost of the haunted well when you were at the place last night?" inquired the landlady, in a low whisper.

"I heard a good deal about it from old Mrs. Keene and the boy," replied Hutchings, evasively.

"Beg pardon, master; but if so be you expect to go to the train by this coach, you'd better look sharp! She starts in about two minutes " said the stage-driver, putting his head into the barroom.

"One moment!" exclaimed Hutchings, and he hastily paid his bill, caught his valise from a porter, bade good-by to the landlady, and ran out and took his place in the coach.

An hour later he had caught the train at Stockstone, and, seated in a second-class carriage, was being whirled on toward York.

He reached that ancient cathedral city early in the afternoon, and had only time to send a telegraphic dispatch to his employers before he had to rush on board the express train just starting for London.

He had telegraphed to Mr. Hamilton Gower that he should arrive by the ten-thirty express, and requested that gentleman to meet him at the station.

CHAPTER XIX
THE DETECTIVE AND THE WITNESS

THE train was five minutes ahead of its time. It was just twenty-five minutes past ten when it "slowed" into the White Cross Station.

Nevertheless, Mr. Hamilton Gower and his shadow, Ham Gow, were already on the spot, and were the first two men the detective saw on leaving his seat.

"What is your news?" impetuously demanded Mr. Gower, taking Hutchings' arm and drawing it within his own. "But I forget, you cannot tell me here. Let us go immediately to some quiet inn and take a room where we can talk. You must know of one somewhere near at hand?" he added, on reflection.

"Yes, sir, the Mitre, within a short walk. How do you do, Mr. Gow?"

Ham Cow replied by lifting his hat lightly, and the three men walked out of the station and across the street, and turned a corner into another street that led them a few paces to the Mitre.

Here Mr. Hamilton Gower took the lead by walking into the barroom and asking for a private parlor and ordering a supper for three.

The bartender beckoned a waiter, who ushered the guests into a snug private parlor, and then went out to attend to their supper.

"Now, then," exclaimed Hamilton Gower, "is your news of vital interest to our case? Have you succeeded in gather- ing any evidence of sufficient weight to support the testimony of Mr. Gow as to the guilt of this girl, Malvina Mattox?"

"I think I have. I may say that I feel sure that I have. I have seen and studied the girl. She is still with her mother, the widow of Duncan Campbell, of Rose Hill, who is still living in the manor house on sufferance. The girl Malvina appears to me as one who is crazed by remorse, or some other deeply concealed trouble. I think it is remorse. I also think that she might be surprised or frightened into a confession of her crime. She suffers fearfully. So does her mother, who evidently now knows as much about the matter as the girl herself. Another view of the case is that if Malvina could be withdrawn from the influence of her mother, she would—without being surprised or frightened into the measure—confess her crime, from sheer inability to bear the burden of the secret. But I do not think she would ever have to suffer the extreme penalty of the law. She is evidently too much of an imbecile for that."

"What, then, would be her fate?" inquired Ham Gow, in a grave and compassionate voice.

"Seclusion 'during her majesty's pleasure' in the Asylum for Criminal Lunatics, at Hanwell," replied the detective.

"The conviction of this guilty woman is absolutely necessary to the vindication of the innocent young girl who is now bearing the penalty of this woman's crime! The charge of murder should be brought against Malvina Mattox at once! With the testimony of Gow, here, supported by the evidence that you may be able to gather, she can be brought to trial! And every hour's delay in bringing the guilty to justice is a heinous wrong to the innocent! Let us lose no time in this matter, but go to Yorkshire by the next train," said Mr. Hamilton Gower, in a stem, relentless, determined manner.

"I beg your pardon, sir," interposed Detective Hutchings. "But such haste would ruin our cause. Or it might do so. If we should succeed in bringing this woman to trial on the evidence that we have got, it is very doubtful whether we could convict her on it. Mr. Gow is ready to swear that he saw Malvina Mattox at the well on the night and at the hour of the murder. Very well! But, on the other hand, the old groom who was awakened by a noise that same night and hour, swears that he saw Margaret Campbell at the well! There, you see, is oath for oath!"

"Yes," impatiently interrupted Mr. Hamilton Gower. "But don't you know that the groom was old, purblind and at some distance from the well, whereas Ham Gow, a young, sharp-eyed man, was on the spot?"

"Still there would be contradictory testimony, and without stronger evidence than we have got to support Mr. Gow's, it would not be advisable to bring the charge against Malvina Mattox; for if she should be arraigned on that charge and not convicted our cause would be finally lost. Malvina Mattox would go free, and Margaret Campbell, with the stigma of a crime upon her name, must remain in penal servitude for the term of her natural life."

"What, then, would you advise us to do?" demanded Mr. Gower, in a voice of despair.

"For the present wait and watch for an opportunity to surprise or terrify the girl into a confession of her crime."

"But—would that be lawful?"

"By some means, no; by others, yes."

"But what reason have you, Mr. Hutchings, for supposing it to be possible that this most guilty woman could be either surprised or frightened into confession?" demanded Mr. Gower.

"My own experiences and observations, while investigating the case at Rose Hill. I had better give you the full particulars of my visit, and then you will be able to judge for yourself, and I am sure you will agree with me! But here comes the waiter to lay the supper. After we have got rid of him I will tell you the whole story, and one part of it will astonish you!" said Hutchings, nodding with a peculiar gravity.

The entrance of a man, bearing a great tray on his head, imposed silence on the three guests until he had placed the supper on the table and stood waiting orders.

"You may go. If we should want anything, I will ring," said Mr. Gower.

The waiter withdrew, and Ham Gow arose and locked the door after him.

"There! Now we are alone, I will just dispose of a slice of bread and beef and a glass of ale, and then tell you all about it! I can't before, because I am famished and must feed, and I never would talk and eat at the same time," said Detective Hutchings, as the three sat down to the table.

"Pray take your own time," observed Mr. Gower, somewhat coldly.

Hutchings made haste and ate and drank fast, however; and when he had satisfied his hunger he drew a little away from the table, settled himself comfortably in his chair and began his report.

He told his attentive listeners of the ostensible business that he traveled upon, as agent for the patent needle threader and knife sharpener, and how easily it introduced him into all houses.

He related his gossiping interview with the landlady of the "Campbell Arms," at Rosedale, and of her account of the murder at Rose Hill and the sensation and excitement that had drawn such crowds to her inn and put so much money in her till.

He told them that the impression of the neighborhood seemed to have been then, and certainly was now, that there had been no mistake at all made in the person of the convicted criminal and that Margaret Campbell had been justly condemned.

He told them, further, of the strange reports in the neighborhood as to the strict seclusion in which the widow and her family had lived since the tragedy, and of the rumored illness and insanity of the younger daughter, who had been the principal witness against Margaret Campbell.

He told them of his evening visit to the old lodge keeper of Rose Hill, and of his passing the greater part of the night in her little parlor, where he heard, subsequently, the same account of the secluded family at the manor house that he had already heard from the landlady of the Campbell Arms.

He purposely omitted all mention of the ghost story, or of his own strange adventure at midnight near the haunted well, leaving that episode for the last; and he went on to tell of his morning visit to "the three weird women" in the seclusion of their own private sitting room.

"The 'needle threader' was the talisman that procured my admittance 'behind the scenes,'" he remarked, in passing, "though I have reason to believe that even that talisman would have failed had it not been presented by a stranger from a long distance, who was supposed to know nothing, or to have forgotten everything, about the tragedy which had been enacted there five years before," he added.

And then he went on to describe from personal observation that indelible expression of intense pain and hopeless sorrow on the face of the widow, and of the chronic stupor of despair in which the younger daughter seemed so deeply plunged as to render her unmindful, if not absolutely unconscious, of all.

"From all these circumstances, added to what we had both heard from Mr. Gow, and also from what I heard in the village, I drew the same conclusions that you will now draw—namely, that Malvina Mattox, however irresponsible by reason of her insanity, was the consciously guilty party in this child murder, and that she was suffering deep and dull remorse in semi-idiocy which had stupefied her for the last five years; and that she must have long since unburdened her soul by confession had she not been closely watched, and perhaps constantly drugged with opiates, by the mother, who had discovered her secret, and who was grimly determined that that secret should not be made public," said the detective.

"But what a cruel, what a criminal course for that woman to pursue, knowing her daughter to be guilty and allowing an innocent girl to suffer in that daughter's place " exclaimed Mr. Gower, indignantly.

"Cruel and criminal indeed. No doubt she feels it to be so, and she too, suffers acutely; her face shows her suffering; but her conduct is not unnatural—for the criminal is her own daughter and the innocent girl is nothing to her, and she has not the Roman courage to give her own child up to justice to vindicate an alien. I am afraid few women, or even men, would have," said the detective.

"I burn at the stake until justice can be done!" vehemently exclaimed Mr. Gower.

"We must surprise or frighten this woman into self-betrayal or confession. I tried a little experiment on her when I was about to withdraw from the room, after having had the interview I have just related. She had been sitting on a low chair, with her hands clasped on her lap, her head bowed and her eyes fixed. She had never once spoken, looked up, or moved in the slightest degree. She was as pale as death, and might have been dead for any sign of life there was about her. I went up to her as I was leaving, and laid a packet of my needle threaders on her hands and spoke close to her ears to insure her attention. I only said:

"'I wish you would be so good as to look at these articles,' or words to that effect.

"But she sprang up as if suddenly stung and began to wring her hands, and to cry out incoherently:

"'It is not so! It is not so!' over and over again, as fast as she could speak, and then: 'Why didn't I die? Why didn't I die?' until she fell into convulsions.

"I stooped to raise her from the floor where she had fallen; but the mother, who had darted to her assistance, dismissed me with sharp words, and I left them—to draw my own conclusions, as you will now draw yours," said the detective.

Mr. Hamilton Gower reflected for a moment, and then said:

"But did not that wretched girl's incoherent words—what were they?—'It is not so! It is not so !'—savor more of denial, of passionate, obstinate denial, than of confession?"

"No; for no one had ever accused her. No, indeed—not as I understand them, from her manner. It was the sudden utterance of brooding remorse. 'It is not so!' meant, to my apprehension, that Margaret Campbell never committed the crime for which she is suffering the penalty."

"Good heavens! Yes! that must have been the meaning of the outburst!" said Mr. Gower.

"And yet the words would certainly bear two meanings—either a denial of her own guilt, or of Margaret Campbell's," put in Ham Gow.

"You would not think so if you had heard and seen her. And now I come to the strangest, the most incomprehensible of my adventures at Rose Hill," said the detective, solemnly; and then he paused and looked gravely from one to the other of his hearers.

"Go on. We are all attention. Let us hear your adventure, if it has any bearing on the case in question," said Mr. Gower.

"It has a very important bearing on the case," replied the detective; "but, mind, I intend to give you the facts in all their supernatural seeming, but I do not intend to try to account for the unaccountable mystery. I may, indeed, advance a theory, but I certainly will not insist upon it."

By this time Hutchings had thoroughly aroused the curiosity of his two hearers.

And now he began by telling them of the strange rumor that had met him on the very day of his arrival at Rosedale—a rumor that had gained credence throughout the neighborhood—that Margaret Campbell, the convict murderess, had died out in the penal settlements of Van Dieman's Land, and that her lost spirit haunted the scene of her crime, and might be seen every night at midnight standing over the old dry well, or walking around it, with the shape of the murdered child in her arms.

"A mere vulgar ghost story, such as would be likely to be invented by the lower classes in a neighborhood where such a tragedy had been enacted," said Mr. Hamilton Gower, contemptuously.

The detective looked at the speaker with a quizzical expression for a moment, and then said:

"Ah that is your opinion, is it? So was it mine when I first heard the story from the landlady of the Campbell Arms. But I had soon good reason to change my mind, and to confess that there must be a material foundation for the general fright."

"A material one, perhaps, but scarcely a spiritual one. But, however, tell us your modified opinion," said Mr. Gower, with an incredulous smile.

"My opinion was, that the supposed ghost—the haunting spirit of the old dry well—which had frightened away every midnight prowler more effectually than the fiercest watch-dog could have done, was no other than the material person of Malvina Mattox, who, pursued day and night by remorse, epileptic, somnambulic, was driven each night to walk in sleep around the scene of her terrible crime."

"That may have been likely, you know," put in Ham Gow.

Mr. Gower said nothing, but became more attentive.

"This story, I must remind you, came to my ears before I had actually seen the girl, but not before I had heard sufficiently of her disturbed mental condition to be enabled to suspect her of sleepwalking. With this suspicion on my mind I determined to gain admittance to the premises that night, and to watch beside the haunted well, and if the sleepwalker should appear, to seize and awaken her, at all hazards to her own safety, for the purpose of surprising her into self-betrayal and confession."

"Well, well," eagerly demanded Mr. Gower.

"I got the confidence of the old portress at the lodge, where I passed the early portion of the night, and guided by her grandson, I went a mile or so through the old wooded park to the rear of the manor house, where the stables, kennels, paddock and so forth, were situated."

"Yes; go on," said Ham Gow.

"The scene of my adventure lies as plainly before my mind's eyes to-night as it lay before my bodily eyes last night. My path through a dense thicket had brought me up to an old stone wall and under the branches of a dead tree. It was midnight, and the full moon was shining broadly down from the zenith. It was almost as bright as day. I climbed the dead tree and looked over the wall."

The detective paused for a moment to drink a draught of ale, and then continued:

"And this is what I saw under the broad, bright moonlight: On my right, the large, dark group of stone buildings, comprising stables, coach houses, grooms' quarters and kennels, surrounded by the stable yard. Just before me an open paddock, with an old well in the midst, and hayricks and barns beyond. On my left an obscure, dense fir wood, from far behind which the chimneys of the manor house arose."

The narrator paused to take another drink, and continued:

"Now, my dear sirs, you need not think, though it was midnight, that I dreamed what I am about to tell you; for remember, that I was up in the fork of an old dead tree, and I was even uncommonly wide awake, both from a sense of the danger of my position, should I forget myself for an instant, and also from a vivid anticipation of an immediate encounter with a sleepwalker."

"We understand the situation," said Mr. Gower.

"Well, then, as I sat, with my eyes roving over the whole scene—the stable yards and buildings, the paddock, with the old dry well, and the dark fir wood—suddenly out of that dark wood streamed a ray of vivid white light, like nothing that I ever saw in the natural world. This light arose and condensed into the form of a woman—a fair, fragile woman, who steadily advanced—not step by step, but gliding as light glides—into the paddock. I was so much amazed by what I saw that I became spellbound and unable to withdraw my eyes from the vision. She continued to advance, and I saw that she carried in her arms the form of a fair and beautiful child, and that it was the halo which emanated from the radiant child that illuminated the woman's form as by a borrowed light.

"I remained spellbound, to gaze upon the vision until it approached the old dry well and bent over its brink.

"Then, in the sudden feeling that the woman was about to drop the child into that perdition, I broke from the spell that bound me, swung myself over the wall by the limb of the tree in which I sat, and dropped into the paddock below.

"It took me a moment to recover from the shock of the fall, and then I arose and ran toward the woman, who was clasping the form of the child to her bosom and gazing down into the well.

226

"As I approached she raised her head and turned around and met my gaze with a pair of strangely blue, blazing eyes that seemed less human eyes than inward fire flaming through their sockets.

"Thinking only to save the child, awaken the sleepwalker and surprise the criminal into self-betrayal, I threw my arms around her and clasped —"

"What, what?" demanded Ham Gow, while Mr. Gower only listened in silent wonder.

"Empty air! And at the same instant received a shock as if a thunderbolt had struck me to the earth where I fell and remained in a state of unconsciousness for several hours.

"It was daylight when I recovered and found myself lying under the wall of the old well. As soon as I collected my scattered faculties I examined the ground, but found no signs remaining of my nocturnal visitant or vision! There, gentlemen, I have given you the facts! Make of them what you please!" concluded the detective.

"How very extraordinary," commented Ham Gow.

"You have given us the facts, you say, and inexplicable enough they seem! But you promised us theories! What are they?" inquired Mr. Hamilton Gower.

"None that are satisfactory. The most plausible is the one to which I have frequently alluded in the course of my narrative."

"And that was?"

"That the midnight apparition at the haunted well was no other than the conscience-tortured, sleepwalking criminal, Malvina Mattox. And I tell you also that there was a circumstance that singularly favored this theory."

"Ah! and that —"

"It was this strange coincidence, that when I saw Malvina Mattox, the same day, I found in her an exact counter-part of the woman seen in the midnight vision—excepting only the presence of the radiant child and the supernal light."

"Well, but is not that the most likely of all theories in regard to the apparition?"

"It would be, but for some objection! If the vision at the well had been that girl in the flesh, I should have clasped a material body, and not a form of empty air! I should have awakened a sleepwalker, and not have received an electric shock that struck me as by lightning to the earth, and left me there in a state of unconsciousness for hours! Besides, if the vision were only the girl herself, whence came the radiant child and the supernal light?"

"From your own overheated imagination, possibly!"

"I have no imagination."

"Then you abandon the theory of the sleepwalker?"

"No, I don't; it may be the true one! I am only puzzled and in doubt."

"Oh! well, I have another theory to offer!" said Mr. Hamilton Gower.

"What is that, sir?" inquired the detective, with a look of interest.

"My theory of the apparition is this—that while you were perched up in that tree with your mind brooding over the expected meeting with the somnambulist, you fell asleep and dreamed the whole affair straight on to the moment when you attempted to start forward and seize the form of the apparition, when you say that you clasped empty air and received an electric shock that struck you as by a thun- derbolt to the ground, where you lay in a state of unconsciousness for several hours; but—when I say that in starting out in your sleep to catch the form of your dream, you simply lost your balance and fell from the tree to the ground with a shock that stunned you into insensibility, from which you were very fortunate to recover at all. There! that is my theory."

"A very likely one, too!" admitted Ham Gow.

"With only one objection, gentlemen, that it is not, and cannot be, the true one. I was not asleep. I was not even the least sleepy. I was wider awake, more vividly alive to my surroundings, more keenly expectant of events than I am at this present moment; and of this I assure you by my word of honor and by all my hopes of happiness in this world and the world to come," said Hutchings, with so much solemnity that his two hearers found nothing more to say on the subject.

"Well, what is our next move?" inquired Ham Gow, at length.

"To take the early train to-morrow morning to Yorkshire, and go down to Rose Hill," replied Mr. Gower.

CHAPTER XX
FLIGHT AND PURSUIT

"OUR next move will be to take the first train to Yorkshire, eh? Is that your decision, sir?" inquired the detective, dryly.

"It is," answered Mr. Gower.

"Then let us see when that train goes," murmured the detective, drawing a Bradshaw from his breast pocket, and referring to the London and North Western Railway route. "Ah! here it is. The York express leaves London at 1 A. M.—reaching York at 8 A. M. There you are, sir! Will you take that?" asked Hutchings, as he marked the line and passed the guidebook over to his employer.

"Certainly we will take this one! I did not know that there would be one before daylight, but I am glad there is! The sooner we are off the better," replied Mr. Gower, as he examined the route.

"Do you wish me to go with you, sir?" inquired Hutchings.

"Of course! Why not? Why do you ask the question?" demanded Gower.

"Because it would not be polite for me to reappear in the neighborhood so soon after my departure from it," replied Hutchings.

"You mean at Rosedale?"

"Yes, sir."

"Well, I see the objection! Your immediate return with two strangers in your wake might excite suspicions and lead to precautions which would baffle us! And yet we should need your presence, too," ruminated the young gentleman.

"There's where it is, sir! But I will suggest this-that we all go together to Yorkshire as far as Stockstone, which is the last terminus of our railway journey; and that you, sir, and myself remain at Stockstone, while Mr. Gow goes on by stage to Rosedale to reconnoiter."

"A good plan. We will adopt it. But in a gossiping little country neighborhood like that, Gow would need some pretext to roam about Bose Hill. What should it be?"

"I might go as a vagabond artist in search of the picturesque," suggested Ham.

"'Twon't do," briefly replied Detective Hutchings.

"Why won't it?" demanded Ham Gow.

"Because as traveling artist you would have no pretext for pushing yourself into the presence of the ladies of Rose Hill! And I think one of your first enterprises should be to contrive to get face to face with Miss Malvina Mattox, to identify her to your own satisfaction as the young woman you saw throw a parcel into the well on the night and at the hour in which the child was cast there."

"Certainly," said Mr. Gower, "that should be your first and principal object in going before us to Rosedale; and,as Mr. Hutchings justly observes, your traveling in the character of an artist in search of the picturesque would never help you to the attainment of that object."

"Well, then, will somebody please to suggest something better, something that will do?" said Ham Gow. in a tone of pique.

"Go as a peddler. You needn't burden yourself with a large pack. Go with a small assortment of ribbons and laces, cords and tassels, combs and brushes, and such like! Go as a peddler and you can get into any country home you like," said Hutchings.

"Got no license," said Ham Gow.

"Never mind! We will have time to fix all that when we get to York. I see by the Bradshaw that if we go by the 1 A. M. train, which reaches York at 8 A. M., we shall have two hours to wait for our branch train, and that will give time enough to buy your pack and license both."

"But, I say," interrupted Mr. Gower, "if we don't make a move soon we will not catch our train."

"Oh, there's time enough; but we may as well ring for the bill," replied Hutchings, as he arose and pulled the bell cord.

"Bill!" said Mr. Gower, to the waiter who answered the summons.

The account was presented and settled, and the three men left the house to walk the short distance between the Mitre and the station.

They were in full time to catch the express train for York, after having telegraphed from the station the fact of their sudden journey, to Lona, at their inn.

Mr. Gower engaged a first-class compartment for his party, and when they entered it he said:

"Ham, you and I will ensconce ourselves in these comfortable corners, and leave the sofa opposite for Hutchings. He has been going day and night for the last forty-eight hours, and must need rest."

Hutchings thanked Mr. Gower for his thoughtful kindness, and stretched himself on the sofa, and before the train left the station he fell into a deep and dreamless sleep.

The train moved slowly out, and gaining speed at every minute, was soon rushing northward from London.

Mr. Hamilton Gower and his faithful "gillie," snugly ensconced in opposite corners of the back seat, alternately listened to the heavy breathing of the sleeper on the sofa before them, or gazed from the windows out on the open country through which they were rushing, with its sleeping villages and darkened farmhouses looking weird and spectral at this silent and deserted hour of two o'clock in the morning.

"I say, Mr. Gower, I think you needed to stretch your limbs at rest as much as Hutchings here! Surely, you have been moving about as much in the last forty-eight hours! If he has been traveling in

Yorkshire we have been traveling in Cornwall. So I think you need that sofa as much as he does."

"Speak for yourself, Ham! I never felt fresher in my life."

"Speak for myself, indeed! As if moving about were not my normal condition—my 'vital breath,' my 'native air'! But with you the case is different. You do look both pale and fagged."

"I am very anxious, Ham, that is all. I wish to do something definite, and have something of value to say to my friends in Tasmania before I write to them, as I shall do by the next Australian mail."

"That doesn't go for ten days yet! Courage! You shall have something to tell them !" said Gow, hopefully.

"If you could get sight of that woman, Malvina Mattox, you might surprise her into self-betrayal, and you would be far more likely to do it than anyone else," said Mr. Gower.

"How so?" demanded his companion.

"Oh, Ham! You never were cut out for a detective. How so, indeed? Don't you see? Look here! Did you not tell me that on the night when you saw that woman throw the parcel into the old dry well— the parcel that you then supposed to be waste paper, or something quite as worthless—she turned around and met you face to face, and saw your features as plainly as you saw hers?"

"Yes! and she looked frightened enough at seeing me, too!"

"At seeing the unsuspicious witness of her crime. Now, do you suppose that she has ever forgotten your face, or that she will ever cease to fear its reappearance before her? Then, if suddenly you should come before her, especially if at the same time you should give her a significant look, or a significant word, do you not suppose that she might be startled into self-betrayal?" gravely inquired Gower.

"By George! I should think she might, indeed! But I hope it isn't on the cards that I shall have to hang that wretched girl, after all!" exclaimed Ham Gow, uneasily.

"Even if it should come to that, it would still be your solemn duty to give the testimony that should convict the guilty in order to vindicate the innocent," said Mr. Gower.

"Yes, I know that, and I should not shrink from my duty; but still I hope it will not come to hanging," said Ham.

"Never fear! She is too much of an imbecile for capital punishment. Imprisonment in the Hanwell Asylum for criminal lunatics will be the utmost penalty she will have to suffer. She will be kindly treated there; quite as well off—indeed, much better off than in her mother's house, and very much happier than she is now, with that guilty secret weighing on her conscience, and the horrible fear of the death penalty always over her."

"I am glad you think they won't hang the poor girl," said Ham Gow, with much feeling.

"'Think?' Nonsense! I don't 'think.' I know they won't! They don't hang idiots in the nineteenth century," said Mr. Gower.

The slowing of the train, the flashing of the lights along the platform, and the bustling arrival of the express at a great branch depot, put an end to the conversation.

"Hitching! Change here for Cambridge, Bedford and Leicester!" bawled a guard, bustling noisily the carriage doors.

This woke Detective Hutchings up.

"Hitchin Station, is it? We are thirty-two miles from London, and I have slept like death all the way!" he exclaimed, sitting up and shaking himself.

But the express was off again.

Mr. Hutchings did not lie down again, but implored his fellow travelers that one or the other should take his turn.

Ham Gow declared that it was only recently he had become reconciled to riding on a railway train; but as to sleeping on one—well, he would see the whole world further first!

After a little persuasion, finding that no one else would occupy the sofa, Mr. Hamilton Gower lay down on it and went to sleep.

Ham Gow and Detective Hutchings, reclining in opposite corner chairs, talked until they grew drowsy, and then dozed. until they reached the old cathedral city of Peterboro'.

There they waked up.

Day was dawning. They slept no more.

Mr. Gower arose refreshed from his sofa. There was a delay of ten minutes here that allowed the three travelers time to go into the station and refresh themselves by washing their faces and heads, after which they returned reinvigorated for their journey.

The train started again, and the three companions, now fully aroused, wide awake, talked with each other on the subject that brought them to the North, or they watched the beautiful dawning of the morning over the broad moor through which the express was rushing.

The sun was an hour high when they reached Newark-upon-Trent.

There they got out of the carriage, and drank some coffee and ate some rolls at the refreshment counter of the station, and so reinforced for the last stage of their journey, resumed their seats just as the train was moving off again.

At eight o'clock they reached York.

There they learned the truth of Hutchings' former statement, that there would not be a train for Stockstone before ten o'clock.

They, therefore, had two hours before them to attend to whatever they had to do.

They took a cab and drove around to the largest stores, and bought miscellaneous articles for Ham Gow's peddler's pack.

As they bought from necessity at retail stores, they had to pay retail prices, and so they could not expect to make much profit; but as we know that profit was not their object, we are sure that the circumstance was of no consequence.

As soon as the public city offices were open for business, they went and bought a peddler's license for Ham Gow.

Also here the three travelers had to purchase two extra valises and several changes of clothing, and other necessaries for their journey, which their hasty departure from London had prevented them from providing in that city.

When all this business was accomplished, they returned to the railway station, where they enjoyed a substantial meal, which might have been called either breakfast or luncheon.

After which they entered their train and were on their way to Stockstone, where they arrived about noon.

The stagecoach that ran between the market town of Stockstone and the village of Rosedale was at the station, waiting for chance passengers.

"We had better not seem to know each other here," whispered Detective Hutchings to Ham Gow, before they left the compartment which the three had occupied alone together.

"Just so! I will go immediately and get into the Rosedale coach with my pack, and I will write and report to Mr. Gower, as arranged," whispered Ham Gow, in reply.

"Can you recommend any inn here?" hastily inquired Mr. Gower.

"Yes, the Cat and Fiddle is the best. Never mind the name. It is the best, really. We can walk thither," replied Hutchings.

The carriage door was opened by the guard, and the three men got out and parted on the platform as if they did not know each other— Ham Gow going into the stagecoach for Rosedale, and Mr. Hamilton Gower and Detective Hutchings walking up Market Street, bound for accommodations at the Cat and Fiddle.

We must follow Ham Gow.

While Mr. Gower and Detective Hutchings were seated comfortably at dinner in the little coffee room of the Cat and Fiddle, the largest inn in Stockstone, situated in the busiest part of Market Street, Ham Gow, with his pack, was being jolted along the turnpike road over the moors toward Rosedale.

He was the only passenger by the stagecoach on this day, which did not chance to be market day.

Ham was glad of the solitude and did not mind the jolting. He put his pack upon the opposite seat, crossed his arms over his bosom and leaned back to enjoy at once the threefold luxury of silence, isolation and passive exercise; nor did he change his position until the coach rattled over the rocky street leading into Rosedale and drew up before the Campbell Arms.

Then he paid his fare, took up his pack, and marched into the taproom and called for a mug of "'arf-and-'arf."

While he stood drinking his beer, the landlady approached him— attracted by his pack; a peddler from London, as she supposed him to be, would produce novelties not to be found in Rosedale.

"Can I have a room here, ma'am ?" inquired Ham, meeting her advances half way.

"Yes. How long will you want one?" inquired the little widow, her black eyes turning from the peddler to his pack, and snapping with eagerness to get into it.

"Well, that depends on how I dispose of my wares, ma'am," answered Ham, with a laugh.

"Oh! you are a peddler?" exclaimed the landlady, just as if she had not known that all along.

"Yes, ma'am—a peddler. Will you take a look at my wares—some of the newest and prettiest things out—"

"Say," whispered the landlady, interrupting him, "take up your pack and follow me."

Ham Gow set down his empty mug, lifted his merchandise, and followed his leader into a little parlor behind the bar, where they found themselves alone.

"Now, then, put your pack on that table, and sit down in that chair while you open it at your ease. But," she said, lowering her voice to a whisper, "first tell me, are you a smuggler?"

"Oh, ma'am!" exclaimed Ham Gow, in a scandalized tone, as he fumbled in his pocket for his peddler's license.

"Oh, now, you needn't go off at a tangent! I have nothing to say against smuggling. I believe in free trade—I do,—and in getting a silk gownd for two-and-six the yard, instead o'paying four-and-six, which the duty and the rest of the cheating makes it."

"But I am not a smuggler, ma'am," put in Ham Gow.

"Oh, I see you don't believe me. You think I am trying to entrap you to hand you over to the excise men; but I am not, indeed! I wouldn't do such a thing for the world! I believes in free trade; and, as I had no voice in making the laws ag'in smuggling, I don't feel bound to obey them! I try to keep the ten commandments, and that is about as much as I can do. So trot out your French silks and Brussels lace."

Ham Gow "trotted" out his peddler's license instead, and laid it before her in triumph, which was a little dashed when she exclaimed:

"Oh, yes; I see that, of course! You are obliged to have that, anyway, smuggler or no smuggler. It's a blind to most people, but it don't blind me—not much! Now, then!"

Ham Gow had opened his pack and spread the contents all over the table before her.

It was the miscellaneous assortment of the ordinary peddler's pack.

Ham Gow sold her a black silk dress, a pair of black kid gloves, and a lace collar and cuffs; all of which she bullied him into selling at half price, because she insisted that he had never paid duty on them.

And then the barmaid, and chambermaid, and cook, ands cullion were called in and permitted to make purchases on the same easy terms—the landlady still whispering confidentially to each:

"He's a smuggler, so you must make him let you have the things cheap; and you needn't mind dealing with him. Women never had anything to do with making the laws agin' free trade, and they ain't bound to respect them."

So Ham Gow had to see linen handkerchiefs, cotton lace and gilt jewelry go at about half what he had paid for them; but he did not care—the loss was not his, and profit was not the object of his present employer.

"Do you think of going out with your pack this afternoon?" inquired the landlady, as Ham Gow, having sold them all they wanted, was busily engaged doing up his merchandise.

"Yes; I do," he replied.

"Then, I'd advise you to strike out into the country. You won't sell so much in the village here, because we have shops, you know."

"I see! But could you advise me as to the most profitable route to take?"

"Yes. There, you women, you have got all you want, now go!" said the landlady, suddenly turning to her four handmaids, who thereupon gathered up their belongings and departed.

She closed the door after them, and turned to the peddler, and resumed:

"Yes, I can advise you where to go. You go fust to Rose Hill. It is a straight road from this to the park gate, where my mother-in-law keeps the lodge. Tell her I sent you, and tell her you have got a heavy blanket shawl such as she would want, and you can sell it to her at about half what she would have to give in the village shops, I know."

"Thank you, ma'am! I'll take a bit of dinner and then go! Rose Hill? Let me see! Rose Hill? Didn't I hear something dreadful about that place once? What was it, again? Oh, I know! A jealous husband shot his wife and shot his rival, and then cut his own throat—didn't he?"

"No! nothing of the sort! Not at Rose Hill! It was a young girl as dropped her little cousin down a well, so she could come in for his fortune; but she was conwicted for it, and would have been hunged ef it hadn't been she was such a child herself. She was sent to Bottomy Bay to pick oakum for life; but she's dead now, sure enough, and her ghost walks every night around the haunted well!" said the landlady, mysteriously.

"Good gracious! Does anybody live in the house?"

"The Widow Campbell lives there with her two daughters, leastways with only one daughter now—the eldest, Miss Lavinia; the youngest one, Miss Malvina, which is afflicted have run away."

"Who has run away?" inquired Ham Gow, now very much interested.

"Miss Malvina, the afflicted daughter. I will tell you all about it. Day before yesterday there came down a chap as was agent for a pattink needle threader. And he went over to Rose Hill to try and sell some of them there—which I must say they are a real blessing to any woman, and no fam'ly should be without. Hows'ever, he went, and got word with the ladies, and few there are as ever do that; for since Miss Malvinia has been so afflicted they never sees any strangers."

"How is she afflicted?"

"Apple-ipsy they call it. I say it is nothing but fits! Hows'ever, whether it was because she wasn't used to seeing strangers, or what not, I can't say; but while the needle-threader chap was there in

240

presence she fell into one of her worst conniptions and from out'n one fit into another—crying all the time:

"'It was not so! It was not so! It was not so! Just as if anybody ever said anything was so, to cross her, until, as Sarah Ann, the parlor maid, told my old mother-in-law, it was enough to drive everybody in the house demented!'"

"The girl is crazy, then?"

"Crazy, or-something. Anyways, it was hours before she sank into quietness and then into a deep sleep, such as the madam thought from past experiences would last all day and all night. So they drew the window curtain and shut the door and left her alone.

"The ladies went to luncheon. Half an hour afterward, sir, when the madam opened her door to see how she was sleeping, she was gone!"

"'Gone!'" echoed the peddler.

"Gone! The madam was surprised, but at fust she was not alarmed. She thought the poor girl had waked up and wandered off to some other room in the house, and she and her eldest daughter went in search of her; but, sir, the afflicted one could not be found, neither in the house, nor in the grounds, nor in the neighborhood. Neither had anyone seen her or any sign of her since her mother left her sleeping soundly in bed when she went to luncheon."

"She had disappeared," said the peddler.

"Yes, she had disappeared. And naturally the poor mother thought of that terrible time when her other child disappeared and was found dead at the bottom of the old dry well. And she sent to the village and had a man go down into the well to search it, but nothing was found there but a lot of old bundles made of nothing but wastepaper. Well, now, to make a long story short, the whole country have been beat up, yesterday, last night and this morning, and no trace of the lost girl has been found."

"How could she have vanished so suddenly and so completely?"

"Ah! how? But the woods are thick around Rose Hill, and I should not wonder yet if she were found dead in some of the thickets."

"Heaven forbid!" exclaimed Ham Gow, who felt that in such a death of Malvina Mattox all hopes of the vindication of Margaret Campbell, upon which his friend, Mr. Hamilton Gower, had so set his heart, would also die.

"Ah! Heaven forbid, indeed, for the poor madam's sake! Ah! they used to say that she did not care for her poor, afflicted girl, and was ashamed of her, and would rather have her out of the way than in it; but they ought to see her now, as my old mother-in-law describes her, just mad with distress and anxiety. But I'm keeping you from your dinner. You mentioned dinner, I think?"

"Yes, anything that you have got handy. I'll not wait to have anything cooked now, for I must 'make hay while the sun shines,' you know. I'll just take a cold bite, and make up for it at supper time," he said.

"Then you can have that cold bite in here, if you like," said the landlady, as she arose and left the room.

In a very few minutes she returned, followed by a waiter bearing a tray laden with all that was required.

The table was spread, and the peddler sat down and, made a hearty repast of cold beef, bread and cheese, and beer.

Then shouldering his pack he left the house, and being directed by the landlady, he marched out of the village by the road that led to the Rose Hill lodge, and reached it in good time.

CHAPTER XXI
HIDDEN

HAM Gow stopped for a moment to gaze at the high, moldering old stone wall, now covered with moss, lichen and other parasitical plants, that had changed its original surface of stone-gray to a variegated marble hue of red, green, brown and yellow, and on the crowded trees that reared their lofty heads above it.

Then he tried the small gate on the right of the great one, and, finding it open, he rang the bell at the little Gothic lodge.

The door was opened by the old dame, who, seeing a peddler there with his pack, gladly welcomed him with the words:

"Oh! Ah! You have got summat to sell. Come in! Come in! I'll take a look at it."

Ham Gow nodded and smiled as he entered the cottage, and sat down in a chair placed for him by the dame.

"Your daughter at the Campbell Arms recommended me to come and show you my goods," said the peddler, as he proceeded to open his pack.

"Ah, yes! she's a good daughter enough. She allus sends me anything likely that comes in her way! Day before yesterday she sent me a thread-needling fellow, which I wouldn't be without it now for double and treble its worth, let alone other profits as I made out'n him! Ah! that's what I want! That would just suit me—if it's anything like a reasonable price!" exclaimed the dame, seizing on the heavy blanket shawl of dark-gray color and holding it up.

"Your daughter thought it would suit you."

"Ah! she knowed it would! It isn't whether the shawl would suit, it's whether the price would suit! That's the question," said the old woman, cunningly.

"I think I can make the price suit," replied the peddler.

"I hope so, I'm sure! Yer see, here's where it is—I dida sarvice for that needle-threader chap, which he paid me princely in two guineas; which, if it hadn't been for that, I shouldn't never ha' been able to buy a warm shawl for the winter as I wanted worse kind. I know I shall never see two more guineas the longest day I live in the world! So, yer see, I ain't gwine to give all my fortin for a shawl, bad as I want it!"

"Oh, no, ma'am, certainly not! You shall have this shawl for one guinea. And, really, I only make one shilling profit on it," said Ham Gow, telling the exact truth.

"Do yer expect me to believe that? Guinea, indeed! Set yer up with it! I'll give yer no sich extorbitting price," exclaimed the dame.

"Well, then, what will you give?" inquired the peddler.

"I'll give yer ten and sixpence, and not a ha'pennymore!"

"Oh, ma'am! I could never let the shawl go for half price!"

"Well, then, yer kin keep it yerself! Half price, indeed! Yer know very well as yer never give more'n eight shillings for it! Yer smuggled of it! All you peddlers be smugglers—or worse!"

"Oh, ma'am! This could not be a smuggled shawl! It is home manufacture—"

"Oh, yes, yer made it yerself, or your missus did!"

"It is from the woolen factories of—"

"I don't care where it's from, I won't give more'n ten-and-six!"

"Say fifteen shillings and the shawl is yours! And I assure you I lose five shillings on it."

"Set yer up with it! I'll—well, I give you ten and nine-pence and not a ha'penny more!"

After a little more chaffering, which Ham Gow sustained on his side more for keeping up his character as a peddler than for any other purpose, the shawl was sold for twelve shillings, with a clear loss of eight shillings upon the cost.

And old Dame Keene afterward confided to Sarah Ann at the manor house that she knew the peddler had either smuggled the shawl or stolen it, else he never would have sold it for twelve shillings, when it was worth every bit twenty-five!

But this is a digression.

When the purchase had been effected and a further investment of two shillings had been made on a pair of brown doeskin gloves, and the dame had declared that she would spend no more money that day, the peddler asked her if the gentlefolks up to the manor house would not like to look at his wares.

"No! no, young man, they wouldn't! And if yer'll take a fool's advice, yer'll not go a-nigh the house! They won't see yer, the ladies won't, and any servant as let yer in would be sure to lose her place! Why, yer don't know what's happened there, do yer?"

"I heard in the village that one of the young ladies had disappeared."

"Yes, she have, and the madam's purty nigh distracted, and all the house is upsot! And they say it all happened through letting that thread-needling fellow into the house!"

"Why, do they think that the sales agent ran away with the girl?"

"Oh, no! not that; but she were afflicted, were Miss Melwiny, and he were a stranger, and they all will have it as the sight of the stranger unsettled her. Anyway, she's been gone ever since yesterday arternoon."

"And no tidings of her yet?"

"Yes; I reckon as they have got summat like tidings at last."

Ham Gow pricked up his ears.

245

"Something like tidings, did you say?"

"Well, yes; summat like that. Now, young man, ef I tell you something, will yer promise me not to tell Susan, nor any of them gossiping people at the Arms?" inquired the old dame, who dearly loved to impart news.

"Yes, I promise, sacredly," answered Ham Gow, thinking to himself: "I am glad she does not want me to promise not to tell anybody out of the village."

"Well, now, then I'll tell yer."

"'Bout noon to-day—I was just a-sitting down to dinner with Jacob, which it were bacon and black-eyed bean soup—when the gate bell rung. The same side yer came through yerself, only it was locked then; and who should I see but one of the feythers!"

"One of the feathers!" exclaimed Ham Gow.

"No! man alive; one of the feythers—one of the priests of St. Sepulcher, to be sure, where the madam goes to church, when she do go. You know St. Sepulcher, don't yer?"

"No, I do not."

"Well, it is about fifteen miles from here, and no railroad nor stage line. So I court'sied down to the ground, and let his reverence in. And he only bowed, with his queer-topped hat on his head, and went walking solemnly up the avenue, with his black gown tied around his waist, and hanging all the way down to his heels Did yer ever see one o' them rigs, sir?"

"Yes, I have."

"Well, it is a sight to see. And, as I was a-saying, he walks solemnly up the avenue; and says I to myself: 'Summat's afoot,' says I."

"The priest was afoot, anyway," laughed Ham Gow.

"So he was, sir; but I didn't mean him," solemnly replied the old woman, who had no mirth in her soul. "I meant summat was up consarning Miss Melwiny!"

"Ah!"

"Yes, sir; that was it. So I went in and put on my things, and went up to the house. But, lor'! the priest had got there long before I did, and he were closeted with the madam at that present speaking. And Sary Ann, she was nowhere to be seen. But I could guess very well where she was. I knowed very well if there was any secret parveling and marveling in a room with closed doors Sary Ann would be at the key. So there I stayed in the kitchen a-waitin' for what would happen next. Eh, dear! what a world this is!" muttered the dame. And she went off into reverie.

"What did happen next?" inquired Ham Gow.

"Eh! nothing much, just at first. The missus rang her bell, after a bit, and ordered wine and biscuits brought up, and half an hour or so later on I heard the priest come down and leave the house. I didn't consider of it needful for me to go back to the lodge then, for I had left the gate open for his reverence to pass out; so I waited till Sary Ann come down. Then the cook up and 'tacked her.

"'And wot fetch the priest here this morning?' says the cook, says she.

"'And how do I know, 'less he come to comfort missus in her trouble, as a good Christian minister ought,' says Sary Ann, says she.

"'Well, I do reckon as that was his business sure enough,' says the cook, who was a onsuspicious soul as ever lived.

"'And now, Sary Ann, my dear,' says I, 'if so be as you'll walk a bit back with me, I'll give you a couple o' my needle threaders.'

"And Sary Ann ris right up at that, and said she would go.

"And we walked along the avenue toward the lodge.

"'And now, Sary Ann,' says I, 'you and me be old cronies, who don't have no secrets from one another, and likewise we is two descreet wimming as don't go a-gossiping here and there! So now I want you to tell me true—what did the priest come for this day, and do he know anythink about Miss Melwiny?'

"Now, I seed Sary Ann were fairly a-busting to tell me all about it; but says she:

"'If I tell yer, will yer swear never to tell no huming being?'

"And I promised faithful, never to tell no huming being, an' no more I won't, sir, never; for I don't count telling you, as ye're a perfect stranger, as will go away ter-morrer or next day, and forget all about it! But mind, yer mustn't mintion it to a soul in the willage while here you stay!"

"Never!" exclaimed Ham Gow, emphatically.

"Well, then Sary Ann, she up and told me all about it! How the priest had told the missus as Miss Melwiny were at the Convent of the Holy Sepulcher, which the pious sisters were taking good care on her at that present speaking.

"'Seems like, from wot I could hear,' says Sary Ann, 'as she 'rived at the convent last night, and begged to be taken in; and she was took in, because it was seen at once that she was a poor needlet as it would be dangerous to turn away. And this morning, when the priest seen her, he recognized her as one of the Miss Mattoxes—that is, the afflicted one. And he came over here and told the missus.'"

"It was a long walk, fifteen miles," said Ham Gow.

"Bless you, he didn't walk all the way. He rode a horseback, it 'pears, far as a parishioner which is sick and wanted spirituous consolation, and he left his horse there to feed and rest, while he walked here, which is a short walk. Leastways, that's wot Sary Ann says he told the missus, when she offered to have the pony chay brought around for him."

"So the young lady is at the Convent of the Holy Sepulcher?"

"Yes; but don't you go and tell anybody in the willage."

"No, I won't; but I don't see any reason why it should be kept secret."

"Don't yer? Well, then I'll tell yer! It is because, if it got out now, the missus would be sure to think as somebody had been a-listening! Missus is so wery suspicious."

"Ah, and is the young lady to be left at the convent, do you know?"

"That's just what I arksed Sary Ann, when she said, it 'peared, from all she could make out, as the poor afflicted gal was to stay there for the present."

"Where is that convent?" inquired the peddler, with assumed carelessness.

"Oh, west of this! 'Way down by the sea."

"Ah, well, poor girl, I hope she will be taken care of. And now. dame, as I cannot sell you anything more—"

"Which I think I have spent money enough for one day, I do."

"And as you think it would not be advisable for me to go up to the manor house—"

"It would be worse nor useless, sir."

"Then I think I will bid you good-by, and return to the village. It is getting late."

"So it be, indeed! And these roads over the moors be uncanny for strangers after sundown, which if once they miss their way on 'em it ain't so easy to find it again; not as there's any danger to you so long as you keep straight on this road, and keep out'n public houses."

"Thanks! I'll take your advice, dame. Good-afternoon."

"Good-afternoon! Gi'e my love to my darter-in-law, Susan, at the Arms, and tell her as how I'm obleeged to her for ree-commending you to me. I'm proud o' the shawl, though I do think as yer charged me too much fer it! Will you tell her?"

"With pleasure. Good-night."

"Thanky'! And mind, don't yer tell anybody in the willage what I told yer about Melwiny Mattox!"

"Not a word, on my honor! Good-night."

"Good-night."

The sun had set, and the afterglow was fast fading from earth and sky as Ham Gow passed through the park gate and turned into the road that led back to the village.

He had obtained all the information he could find at Rose Hill, and it was so very important that he resolved to go on that very night to Stockstone to impart it to Mr. Gower and Detective Hutchings, that they might take counsel on the situation.

He walked rapidly over the ground that separated him from the Campbell Arms.

He did not know whether the Rosedale and Stockstone stagecoach was to make another trip to the Stockstone station that night, or, if it should. at what hour it would go; or, failing the stagecoach, whether he could get any other conveyance from the village to the market town; but he knew that opportunity might be missed by delay; and nothing could be lost by haste.

So he walked at his utmost speed, notwithstanding his heavy pack; and it was well for his enterprise that he did so; for, just as he came in sight of the Campbell Arms, he saw the stagecoach moving on.

He ran and shouted to the driver.

"Hello! Stop! Stop!" he cried, waving his hat in his left hand, while his pack was held fast in his right one.

"Hello, yourself l What is it?" shouted the driver, in reply, as he drew up.

"A passenger! Double fare if you'll wait two minutes!"

"Hurry up, then!"

Ham Gow ran up, ran into the Campbell Arms, dropped down his pack before the landlady, saying:

"Keep that for security of my bill until I come back! Have got to go to Stockstone to look after something I have left behind and feel uneasy about!"

And before the breathless landlady could recover her wind, Ham Gow had rushed out, jumped on board the starting coach and was off.

The alarmed landlady recovered her breath, and expressed her sentiments.

"Humph! We'll never see him ag'in, unless it's in the hands of the perlice! As sure as eggs is eggs, he stole these things, and he's running from the perlice! Here! Peter! John! Susan ! Mary! Listen what I say ! That peddler what put up here has left his pack and gone off in the coach to Stockstone! Now, I want you all to bear witness as I'm no receiver of stolen goods! Let that pack lay right there where he drapped it, and don't any of you lay finger on it to put it away. I'd send it to the perlice station if there was any nigher than Stockstone, but as there isn't, why just let it lay there and nobody touch it till the perlicemen come to look after him, as they will come soon, you bet!"

Meanwhile, Ham Gow, happily unconscious of the dark suspicions against him, and brimful of the news he had to tell his companions in this quixotic adventure of righting the wrong, was jolted on his way to Stockstone, where he arrived at the hour which old-fashioned housekeepers used to call "early candlelight."

He went straight to the "Cat and Fiddle," and inquired for his friends, and was at once ushered into a private parlor, where he found Mr. Gower and Detective Hutchinqs, quietly reading the country papers.

"What news " exclaimed the former, starting up.

"A sack full of news!" replied Ham Gow, throwing himself into a chair.

And then and there he eagerly told his story.

"Fled to a convent, has she? Now, then, our bird is so certainly netted! She leaves the convent only to stand at the bar of justice!" exclaimed the detective.

"Explain yourself," said Mr. Gower.

"The Assizes are to be held here in ten days from this, and Malvina Mattox shall be arraigned at them to stand trial for the murder of Stuart Campbell. And of that I pledge you my official word of honor."

"But I do not understand! Explain, I beg you."

"I have a plan that is sure of success. "

CHAPTER XXII
RUN TO COVER

"WHAT is this infallible plan of yours, then?" inquired Mr. Hamilton Gower of the detective.

"A very simple one. Mr. Gow here tells us that when he discovered the girl, Malvina Mattox, at the well, that night, the moment after she had committed the crime—which he did not understand at the time to be a murder—they stood for an instant face to face with each other, gazing at each other, fully taking in every feature of each other," said Hutchings.

"Well?" inquired Gower.

"Do you not suppose that, under the circumstances, an indelible impression of the other's face was made upon the memory of each?"

"Yes, I do."

"Do you not suppose that girl's guilty conscience is haunted with the secret fear of seeing the face of that witness again appearing some time to accuse her?"

"I think it more than likely."

"Then, let Mr. Gow, here, go at once to the Convent of the Holy Sepulcher, and, upon some pretext that we must invent, ask to see the girl. When she shall be brought in the visitors' room to see him, let him ask her if she remembers the occasion of their first meeting at midnight by the old dry well, some five years since—and—the result, mark me, will be her self-betrayal!"

"Ah-h! I see," muttered Hamilton Gower.

"For, you see, by all that we can judge from what we have heard, she has been tortured by remorse for the last five years, and has, doubtless, betrayed herself to her mother, and must certainly have done so to others, had she not been closely watched by that lady. Even my visit, for some reason that I do not understand, disturbed her to such a degree as to throw her into convulsions, and later to cause her flight from her home and her taking sanctuary in the convent. Judge, therefore, what the effect will be when she shall find herself face to face once more with the only mortal witness of her crime!"

"I see! I see! Let us lose no more time in talking! Let us go at once to the Convent of the Holy Sepulcher! Now, then—what train should we take? And what is the nearest station?" hastily inquired Mr. Gower.

"There is no train leading anywhere near the convent, and this is the nearest station, and it is nine miles off! So I learned by inquiry at Rose Hill. The Convent of the Holy Sepulcher is one of the most secluded of the religious houses in the realm. We shall have to take a private conveyance," said Hutchings.

"All right! I will go and get one!" exclaimed Ham Gow, rising and running out.

"Hold on, if you please!" called out the detective.

Ham Gow ran in again, inquiring:

"What is up now?"

"It is too late to do anything to-night, you know!" said Hutchings.

"Not so!" impatiently exclaimed Hamilton Gower. "We shall not be able to gain admittance to the convent to-night, it is true; but we can go on and stop at the nearest public house, and be ready for as early a visit as the rules will allow in the morning. So time will be saved, and time is precious."

"That is so, if you choose to go to so much extra trouble and inconvenience," assented Hutchings.

"I would go to any trouble—suffer any inconvenience!" exclaimed the young gentleman.

"You speak and you work as if you had a very heavy stake in this game, sir," said the detective.

"I have a very heavy stake in it, my friend," replied the young gentleman.

Ham Gow stood looking from one to the other, waiting orders, as it were.

"Go on, Gow, dear fellow, and engage a carriage with a pair of good, fresh horses, and while you are at it inquire more particularly into the whereabouts of the convent, and the best way of getting there," said Mr. Hamilton Gower.

The ex-tramp needed no spur, but ran out of the room again, and used such expedition that in less than twenty minutes he returned with the announcement that the carriage was at the door, and that the Convent of the Holy Sepulcher was situated on High Moor, ten miles north of Stockstone, and was to be reached only by a labyrinth of country roads.

"Ten miles! That is one mile more than we bargained for, to begin with, and the distance doubled by winding ways! However, it does not matter so much, since we could not get into the convent by any means before morning," said Hamilton Gower, as he made hasty preparations for departure.

In five minutes the three men were seated in the carriage, bowling along the road toward High Moor.

It was a hazy night; but the moon, a little on the wane now. was shining through the thin clouds, making their road over the seemingly boundless moor clearly visible.

"I would like to have some faint idea of where we are to sleep to-night; not having been in bed for the last three nights, the subject is an interesting one," said Hutchings with a grim smile.

"Oh! I asked about that," returned Ham Gow, "and I find that within a quarter of a mile of the convent stands the old inn of the Great Black Bear, on the old London Road—an inn almost as ancient as the convent itself, which—if you believe the Stockstone folk lore—must have been built on a rock in the sea, long before this island formed around it."

Hutchings laughed at the tramp's hyperbole, but Mr. Gower gravely said that—all jokes aside—the convent was certainly of very ancient date.

Their horses were in good condition, and went so well that, notwithstanding the winding ways, at about ten o'clock they drew up before one of the oldest, quaintest and most picturesque country inns that the travelers had ever beheld.

It was a large building, or rather a large cluster of buildings, of graystone, red brick, peaked and tiled roofs, and latticed windows, and with stable yards, corn cribs and hayricks crowded behind it. On the right and left great forest trees overshadowed it; in front, from a high pole, the sign of the Great Black Bear swung and creaked in the night wind.

And over all the moor there was not another building of any sort visible, though the driver of the carriage, pointing with the handle of his whip to a mass of black shadows on the horizon, opposite the inn, told the travelers that there stood the Convent of the Holy Sepulcher, supposed to be the oldest of its class in England.

At the sound of wheels, a man with a lantern in his hand emerged from the silent and solitary-looking inn and came up to the carriage.

"Can we have accommodations here for the night?" inquired Mr. Hamilton Gower.

"Ou, ay, no doot, your honor," answered the man, with a very low bow.

The three travelers alighted, and followed the waiter into the house, while the driver took the carriage around to the stables.

"What would your honors hae for supper?" inquired the waiter, as he ushered his guests into the best parlor.

Ham Gow whispered to his "feudal lord":

"No matter what you order, they will give us bacon and eggs and bad beer, or worse wine."

"Anything will do; whatever you have in the house, so that it is cleanly served," answered Mr. Gower.

The waiter bowed and withdrew, and his exit was soon followed by the entrance of the chambermaid, who courte- sied and conducted them to their rooms—three little chambers in a row, opening upon the same passage.

Sweet little rooms, with white dimity curtains and bedspreads, all smelling of dried lavender; three-cornered washstands with blue stone basins and ewers, and dressing tables draped with white muslin and surmounted with swinging glasses.

By the time the travelers had refreshed themselves with a good wash and had brushed their hair they were called down to supper, which was laid in the best parlor, the same into which they had been first introduced.

The supper was not what Ham Gow had prophesied that it would be—bacon and eggs, with bad beer and worse wine—it was cold ham and beef, fine cheese and butter, good bread and prime Scotch ale.

After enjoying a hearty meal, the tired travelers retired to rest, and— as neither of them had been in bed for three nights—they each and all dropped into a deep and dreamless sleep that lasted until morning.

Mr. Hamilton Gower was the first to wake. The level beams of the rising sun, streaming in between the middle opening of the white window curtains, struck him full on the eyelids, and, with that kiss of light, aroused him.

He started up, collected his faculties, and went and looked out of the window.

The moor stretched away on every side until its boundaries were lost in the distant horizon.

Not a house or a tree was to be seen in the vast expanse, except that group of dense black shadows under the horizon straight before him which the coachman had pointed out on the night before as the buildings of the Convent of the Holy Sepulcher.

"The last refuge of the conscience-stricken murderess who has left an innocent girl to suffer in her stead," said Hamilton Gower to himself, as he gazed upon the mass.

He was in no mood to incur delay by the somnolency of his fellow-travelers, so, before beginning to dress himself, he walked out into the passage and beat a "reveille" upon the door of the room occupied by Ham Gow, which soon aroused the latter from his profound slumber.

"Hello! what the—" growled Ham.

"It is I! The sun is up, and so should you be! I am going to order breakfast. We must be off in an hour! Hurry!" exclaimed Mr. Gower, as he left the door of Ham Gow's room, and went to that of Mr. Hutchings.

But the noise had already aroused the detective, who called out that he was awake and about to rise.

Mr. Gower returned to his own chamber, and rang for the waiter, who promptly appeared.

"Breakfast in half an hour, and the carriage at the door in three-quarters," he said.

The waiter touched his forehead and vanished.

Mr. Gower dressed himself and went down into the parlor, where he found the breakfast table set, and where he was soon joined by his two traveling companions.

"Let our coachman get his breakfast and be ready to attend us," said Mr. Gower, as they took their seats at the table.

The waiter went out to give the required order, and then returned to serve the guests.

As soon as breakfast was over, the three travelers entered the carriage, and gave the order:

"To the Convent of the Holy Sepulcher."

Their way lay across the barren moor. A quarter of a mile of country road brought them to the high, gray wall that surrounded the convent grounds and inclosed the convent buildings.

Above the high wall could be seen the top of the main edifice.

Had a full view been afforded from the outside, it would have been observed that the structure was in that style of architecture that might be called composite, since it was a blending of the Roman with the early English style.

This Convent of the Holy Sepulcher, if it was not what it was said to be, the oldest in the kingdom, yet was certainly very ancient.

It was founded in the reign of Edward the Confessor, by a Saxon princess of great piety, who renounced the world, endowed the house with all her worldly wealth, and lived and died within its cloister—not its abbess, as she might have been, but one of its humblest and most submissive nuns; for all of which, in later days, she was canonized by the church.

Enriched by the gifts and endowments of princes and nobles, the Convent of the Holy Sepulcher steadily increased in power and splendor, through five centuries of prosperity and then, all in one year, came adversity and destruction.

Henry, the cutthroat, wife killer and church burner, in his greedy raid upon the religious houses of his kingdom, sacked the rich convent, and drove the helpless sisterhood out to beggary or starvation.

The house, given to a court favorite, passed through many hands in successive generations, until, in the year the Catholic emancipation, it came, by purchase, into the possession of a wealthy Catholic gentleman, who, dying unmarried, bequeathed it to a community of Carmelite nuns.

The Test of Love

It was now restored after its model in the medieval age.

The carriage containing the three travelers drew up before a small, heavy, oaken door, that was the only object which broke the monotony of the long stone wall.

"Have you made up your mind what pretext to advance for seeing the girl? You know they won't let you see her without a satisfactory reason," said the detective, as Ham Gow was about to leave the carriage.

"No! I have not thought of anything yet! I must trust to circumstances, or the inspiration of the moment," replied the tramp.

"You might say that her mother sent you to see her," suggested the detective.

"Oh, I hate to lie, even in a good cause," said the tramp.

"But in such a case as this the end justifies the means," said Hutchings.

"Can't see it. I shall trust to circumstances," replied Ham Gow, as he got out of the carriage, leaving his two companions seated, while he went to the little door in the wall and rang the bell.

A small panel in the door slipped aside, and an old woman's face in a nun's veil and muffler appeared.

"I have come to see Miss Malvina Mattox," said the visitor.

The portress silently opened the door, which closed behind him with a clang as soon as he had passed the threshold.

The silent portress, without leaving her niche beside the door, pointed in the direction of the convent, and immediately, with bowed head, resumed the counting of her beads.

Ham Gow found himself in a courtyard where the ground was covered by coarse grass, shaded by large trees and intersected by gravel walks.

Following one of these gravel walks, he approached the main entrance of the building, and found himself facing a flight of broad steps that led up to a pair of heavy, oaken doors.

Here he rang a second bell.

A second panel opened, and a second old woman's face in a nun's coif and veil appeared.

"I have come to see Miss Malvina Mattox," said Ham Gow.

This second door swung open, and closed behind him with a clang as soon as he had crossed the threshold.

Ham Gow found himself in a vestibule with three inner doors—one on the right, one on the left and one opposite—straight before him.

The right-hand door led into the den of the second old portress, who had already turned her back on the visitor and disappeared from his view.

While Ham Gow was wondering what he should do next, the door straight before him opened, and a nun came out with a bunch of keys in her hand.

She never raised her eyes to the visitor, but silently unlocked the door on the left, and by a gesture indicated that the visitor was to enter that room.

Ham Gow entered the room, and the door clanged behind him as the other doors had done.

His attendant had disappeared as her predecessors had.

Ham Gow found himself alone in a small, square apartment, with bare floor, whitewashed walls and four oaken chairs. There was a grated window in front, and an iron grating instead of a wall at the back.

While the tramp was wondering what would happen next, a soft, sweet voice stole upon his ear.

"You have been sent to see Miss Malvina Mattox?"

Ham started in a sort of panic, and turned in the direction of the sound, to see a lady of majestic presence and surpassing beauty, which even the nun's ugly dress could not spoil, seated on the other side of the grating; but her eyes were fixed upon the ground, from which she never raised them. "Yes, miss! Ma'am! My lady! Your holiness!" replied Ham, in utter confusion.

"You have been very prompt. We did not expect you to bring Malvina's wardrobe for some hours yet. You have left Rose Hill very early this morning," said the nun.

"I—left Rose Hill last evening, my lady—your reverence!" gasped Ham.

"Ah, you did."

"Yes, ma'am—your holiness, and I put up at the Black Bear—and—if you please, my lady—your reverence—I would like to see Malvina Mattox, according to the wishes of them that sent me."

"Exactly. Mrs. Campbell would wish you to bring a report of her daughter's condition from personal observation. I know—I understand that this course would be the most satisfactory to the mother. Remain here, and I will send her in to you," said the beautiful nun, as she arose, and without once lifting her eyes from the ground, passed away into the shadows behind the grating.

"There! I said I hated to lie! I said I would trust circumstances, and circumstances have favored me. She takes me for some one else— some messenger that was expected here with the girl's clothes— Ah!"

This exclamation burst from Ham Gow as his soliloquy was cut short by the opening of the parlor door and the entrance of Malvina Mattox, attended by an aged and venerable-looking nun, who, like her predecessors, never raised her eyes from the floor, but silently led her charge to a chair, placed her in it, and stood with arms crossed and hands hidden in her wide sleeves, and eyes cast down upon the floor.

The unhappy creature whom she had brought into the room sat fixed in her seat more like a corpse than a living being. She was clothed in a white cambric wrapper, with a white Berlin wool shawl thrown loosely around her shoulders. But her attire was no whiter than her pallid, fleshless face, that looked like a skeleton face with the skin drawn tightly over its bones. Her hair, faded to the palest flaxen, hung neglected over her shawl. Her light-blue eyes from their cavernous sockets stared straight before her into vacancy. Her hands hung down each side listlessly, forgotten, like those of some idiot.

A pang of pity shot through the heart of the tramp as he gazed upon the young human wreck before him.

"You see what she is," said the nun, without raising her eyes or changing her position. "You see what she is, and you can report to madam, her mother. That lady had better come and see her in person. We can do nothing with her. She sits always so. It is not likely that she notices your presence. You had better speak to her."

Ham Gow desired nothing better. Although the aspect of the poor creature filled him with the profoundest pity, it also relieved him of one sickening dread—that of being instrumental in consigning a wretched girl to the gallows!

He saw at a glance that this half-idiotic creature would never be considered a proper subject for the death penalty.

He had, therefore, the less reluctance to try his experiment upon her.

He arose and bowed to the nun—who, by the way, with her downcast eyes, was perfectly unconscious of the courtesy—and went and stood before the stupefied girl without attracting attention.

"Good-morning, Miss Mattox," he said.

She gave no sign of hearing.

"How do you do, Malvina?" he inquired, taking one of her limp hands, raising it and holding it in his own.

She slowly lifted her eyes to his and her ghastly face began to change. It could not grow more pallid, but the sharp chin dropped, leaving the mouth wide open, and the dull eyes dilated and fixed themselves upon his face with a stare of amazed and horrified recognition.

Ham Gow saw in an instant that she knew him and that she remembered when and where they had met; saw that she recognized in him the secret witness of her crime.

He pressed the hand that he held, and that she seemed to have no power to withdraw, and he said:

"Don't be frightened of me, Miss Mattox. This is not the first time we have met. Don't you remember that damp, drizzly night by the old dry well at Rose Hill?"

Her staring eyes began to flame with terror.

"It was between midnight and morning, you know, and you had just—"

"Don't! don't! don't! don't!" screamed the wretched creature, suddenly breaking through her trance of horror, snatching her hand from his clasp and clapping both hands before her eyes as if to shut out some hideous vision; and before he could intervene to save her she fell to the floor in strong convulsions.

"You see!" said the nun, as she arose and raised the stricken creature from the floor. "You see, she is a subject for a lunatic asylum, not for a peaceful convent! Tell madam, her mother, this! Go now, your presence has excited her too much! You can leave her clothes with the portress."

Ham Gow bowed again and left the room.

As he opened the door a little bell rang, at the sound of which the nun with the keys appeared from the middle door, and unlocked the front door and let the visitor out.

He walked through the grounds to the gate, thrilled with pity and horror at what he had witnessed, yet fully satisfied now that the guilty and wretched creature might be brought to conviction, though not to punishment.

As he reached it the aged portress silently unlocked it and let him pass out.

He immediately joined his companions, who were anxiously awaiting his return, seated in the carriage.

"Order the driver to go on," he said, "and I will tell you all about it as we proceed."

The order was given, and the carriage started.

Then Ham Gow described to his eager listeners the scene that he had just passed through with the miserable and half-idiotic young criminal.

"The time is ripe," said the detective; "there must be no further delay, lest the girl should die, or become hopelessly imbecile! With the evidence now in our possession we must return to Stockstone and lay the case before the bench of magistrates who meet to-morrow."

This course was immediately agreed upon.

The travelers stopped at the Great Black Bear only to pay their bill and feed their horses and then set out for Stockstone.

CHAPTER XXIII
IN THE CONFESSIONAL

FATHER BENEDICT, priest of the chapel of the Holy Sepulcher and confessor of the sisterhood, sat in the little cabinet on the right of the altar, called the confessional.

The priest was very aged. He had seen four score years and five, and on this day he was weary, for it was Saturday, and nearly all the sisterhood had come to him in turn to make their confessions and obtain absolution, preparatory to receiving the Sunday morning's sacrament.

No very grievous sins had as yet been confided to his ear by the harmless nuns; only such peccadillos as the wanderings of their thoughts during prayer, irritability of temper during pain, little passing angers or envyings, or, at most, intrusive doubts of the divine mercy toward such sinners as themselves.

Such and such like were the heinous sins and misdemeanors to which the good old man had been compelled to listen all day long, and for which he had prescribed the terrible penances of a little self-denial and a few short prayers.

And now that the day was nearly done, he was weary of it all, as he sat upon his hard bench in the close, dark nook, and he was thinking of withdrawing, when a sound fell upon his ear that at once fixed his attention.

It was a most distressing moan, as of some dumb animal in pain, and it came from the other side of the little panel, through which his penitents, unseen, had breathed their confessions.

The moanings were repeated, until at last the kind-hearted old man could wait no longer for a voluntary communication, but felt compelled to break his prescribed silence, and ask:

"What is the matter? What can I do for you? Speak freely."

"Oh, father! father!" wailed the voice of a woman from behind the screen.

"You are in sorrow, my daughter. Confide your trouble to me, without fear, and I will comfort you, if I can," gently whispered the old man.

"But—I am—the blackest of sinners!" burst with a gasp from the lips of the unseen woman.

The old priest started and shuddered. It had never happened to him in his long, harmless life to receive the confession of any great criminal, and there was that in the tone of the unseen woman, who spoke through the little opening in the panel, which convinced him that her words were the morbid exaggeration of a self-accusing fanatic, but the preface to some terrible revelation of crime. For a moment he could not speak.

"Ah, you shrink from me already! What will you do when you hear what I must tell?" moaned the woman.

"I do not shrink from you, my daughter. Who am I, that I should dare to shrink from any? I wait to hear what you wish to say," gently replied the old man.

"I must relieve myself—of the secret—that oppresses and suffocates—my soul!" said the voice behind the screen, speaking with difficulty and in gasps.

"I listen, my child," murmured the old man.

"I have borne the burden—so long—so long that it has—nearly maddened—or killed me! I wish it had done one—or the other!"

"Nay, nay, my daughter! Say not so! But why bear the burden of your sin, when you could lay it down at the foot of the cross?" gently inquired the priest.

"Oh. I was not permitted to confess! I was watched, guarded, day and night! My mother would not let me out of her sight—until—by an artifice—by affecting a deep sleep—I eluded her vigilance and fled here! For I must confess, or die, or go raving mad!"

"Speak out, my child, in the name of Heaven!" said the priest.

"I am—that wretched creature called—Malvina Mattox!" spoke the penitent, in gasps.

"I thought as much. I knew that unhappy one sought refuge in the convent. Go on, my child."

"You-remember—the awful death—of the babe—at Rose Hill—five years ago—"

"I remember."

"And Margaret Campbell—was convicted—of the murder."

"Yes, upon your evidence," said the old man, solemnly.

"I was forsworn! She was innocent—I alone was guilty of that crime!" said the voice of the woman, in a dying cadence.

The good old man started and shuddered.

"Miserable one," he said, as soon as he could command his voice, "what led you to such a crime—to such a tissue of crime?"

"I don't know! I don't know! Oh, don't betray my secret! Don't betray my secret! I had to tell you, but don't you tell anyone!" wailed the woman, in a voice of agonizing entreaty.

"You know that the seal of the confessional is on my lips, and it may not be broken for any cause whatever. You know that what passes here will never transpire through me," gravely and sorrowfully replied the old priest.

"I know! I know! And yet I fear! I fear! Oh, father! what shall I do?" cried the woman, wringing her hands.

"Make a full confession, in the first place! Tell me what instigated you to such a course of crime."

"I say I do not know! I had no malice against the child or against anyone! I liked the child! Indeed I did! I used to like to play with him, for he was my baby brother, you know, and I really liked him."

"Are you telling me the truth? Remember that to tell a falsehood here is more than falsehood, it is sacrilege!" said the priest, in a solemn voice.

"I am telling you the truth, as Heaven can bear me witness! I had no malice against the child! I liked him! But listen! One day, in the same summer that he was born, I had him in my lap playing with him; I suddenly put him in my mother's arms and ran out of the room. Afterward they all asked me why I acted so strangely. I did not tell them. I could not tell them; but I will tell you, father!"

"I am listening."

"It was because I was suddenly seized with an unaccountable, irresistible impulse to throw him out of the open window! It would have killed him! And to prevent doing so I had to drop him in his mother's lap and run out of the room! And I had no ill will to the child either!"

"It was a possession of the devil, against which you should have struggled with fasting and prayer," said the horrified priest.

"I was afraid to tell anyone of that dreadful visitation which grew upon me from that time. I was afraid to be left alone with the child for a moment for fear I should do him some harm. I hated myself for these visitations that I could not foresee or resist—for they came upon me suddenly, unexpectedly. I never could trust myself near the child, and everyone thought I had taken a dislike to my baby brother. But they were all mistaken! I loved him, but I feared that I was doomed to destroy him! Oh! the horror of it all!"

The miserable girl paused, and shuddered, and let some moments pass before she resumed:

"This malady grew upon me until I became a terror and a horror to myself. I could not sleep nor eat; and I grew weak and thin. They said my health was failing, and I hoped it was."

"My child, that was a sinful hope, to be repented of," said the old man, in a warning voice.

"Was it? I could not help it any more than I could help the rest of it. I wished to die before I could do my baby brother any harm. But though I grew thin and weak, I did not die. I feared I could not die. I feared that I was fated to live, and to do the deed I so much dreaded. Oh! the horror of it! —the horror of it!"

The wretched girl shook as with an ague, and at length continued:

"At last I was tempted to commit suicide."

"Oh, my unhappy daughter!" groaned the priest.

"I could not help it, I say, any more than I could help the rest. I was tempted to kill myself to keep me from hurting the innocent, helpless child. But I could not nerve myself to do the act. I wish I could have done so. Oh! how I wish I could! Oh! that I had taken my own life rather than his!"

"My child! —my child you speak wildly and wickedly! I must not listen to you if you speak so!" exclaimed the old man.

"Bear with me! Bear with me! I am so wretched! No lost soul in the depths is more miserable than I am!" wailed the girl.

"Speak on, poor soul! I have nothing but pity for you now," said the priest, in a gentle tone.

"The visitations increased upon me fearfully; day and night that horrible, fratricidal impulse beset me with irresistible power. I began to walk in my sleep, and to haunt the nursery door at night—an infirmity of which I was totally unconscious until my roommate, Margaret Campbell, discovered it and told me of it. She also took to watching me, following me, waking me up, and leading me back to my bed."

Here the old priest sighed deeply, for he was thinking how foully the guilty girl before him had repaid this friend for all this kindness.

"And now I come to the fatal night. I had been pursued and tortured by that terrible impulse all day long. At one time my mother brought the baby into the parlor where I was sitting alone, and told me to take care of him while the nurse went to the village on an errand; but instead of obeying my mother I screamed with terror, and ran out of the room and out of the house. I was scolded and beaten by my mother for what I did, yet I dared not tell her why I had fled from the child, and so I became more nervous and ill than before."

"You should have told her. She might have consulted a physician. All this trouble might have been saved," said the priest.

"Ah, yes! but what is the use of saying this now? What's done is done!" moaned the penitent.

"True," acquiesced the old man.

The unhappy girl continued:

"At night I went to bed and fell into the deepest sleep I ever experienced. I fell into that deep sleep while I held Margart Campbell in my arms; for, as I said, she was my roommate and my bedfellow, and my mother scolded her as well as me, and we had a common cause of complaint that united us in sympathy. So, with Margaret Campbell in my arms, I fell into a deep, dreadful sleep, and dreamed—a fatal dream!"

"'A fatal dream!'" echoed the priest.

"Yes. Father, I am going to tell you the strangest experience that ever happened to any human being—I am going to tax your credulity, perhaps, to the utmost," said the girl.

"Speak on, poor soul!"

"I say I dreamed a fatal dream! I did not know it was a dream then. I thought it was reality! I thought that my bedfellow, Margaret Campbell, withdrew herself from my arms, got up and unlocked our door and left our room, taking the key with her. I thought I arose and followed her, and saw her kneel down at the nursery door, which was locked on the inside, and push the key out of its socket until it fell on the nursery floor, and then insert our key, which fitted the lock, turn it, open the door, and walk into the room, lift the sleeping child from its crib, and bring him out."

"What are you telling me?" demanded the priest.

"A dream, which, at the time, I took to be a reality," answered the girl.

"Go on."

"I thought that Margaret Campbell closed and locked the door and withdrew the key with her right hand while she held the sleeping child to her bosom with her left arm. And then she walked out of the back door, I following her. She went out, as I thought, into the paddock, where the old dry well had been left uncovered—that spot which had possessed such a horrible fascination for me. I followed her, horrified, but unable to stop her, or to call out, or to do anything else but follow. I followed her then to the verge of the dry well, when suddenly she and the child sank into the ground before my eyes, and in their place arose a strange, wild-looking man with a shock of black hair and beard.

"We gazed in a panic at each other for an instant, and then I turned and fled to the house. When I regained our room I found Margaret Campbell sleeping quietly in bed!

"I was so puzzled by all that had happened, or had seemed to happen, that I slept no more that night.

"The next morning— Oh, father, do not ask me recall the agony of the days that followed—the disappearance of the child; the anguish of the search; the horror of the discovery when his body was found in the well; the inquest; the trial and conviction of Margaret Campbell!

"One other thing was strange. I had temporarily forgotten half that dream which I had believed to be a reality, and I remembered only that part of it which related to Mar- garet Campbell's rising and leaving the room, taking with her the key which unlocked the nursery door, and of her being back again when the clock struck three.

"And thus I gave in my evidence both at the inquest and on the trial.

"Oh, father, it was not until weeks had elapsed after the transportation of Margaret Campbell, that one night, while I was walking in my sleep, I was followed by my mother and awakened on the brink of the old dry well, while I was in the act of dropping into it a puppet baby. And in that awful moment full memory flashed back upon me, revealing all the horrible truth, that I—I—in the homicidal mania that haunted even my sleep and governed even my dreams, had committed the atrocious crime for which the innocent Margaret Campbell had been condemned to transportation and penal servitude for her life."

CHAPTER XXIV
THE FIAT

"IN the homicidal mania that haunted even my sleep and governed even my dreams, I had done the deed!"

The priest heard these words faintly breathed into his ear, and he shuddered.

Never had it happened to him, in his gentle and monotonous life, to receive the confession of a great crime. And now he felt overwhelmed by grief, horror and the magnitude of the responsibility thus thrown upon him. He seemed unable to utter a word, though his penitent evidently paused to give him the opportunity and waited to hear him.

"Oh, father! speak to me! Speak to me! Counsel me! Tell me what I ought to do, while I am sane enough to understand you!" cried the girl, in a voice of anguish, as she knelt there, wringing her hands.

"Poor, miserable child! You made this discovery years ago! Why did you not then do your obvious duty? Why did you not go at once and confess your crime and vindicate the innocent one who was suffering for your sin?" demanded the priest, in a voice of pain.

"Father, she would not let me!" wailed the girl.

"'She?' Who? You should not have allowed anyone to hinder you in the discharge of a duty so vital!"

"But she was my mother. She had authority over me. She made the discovery in the same moment in which I made it. I knew it at the time that she did! I knew it by the look of horror and terror that came over her countenance when she met my eyes!"

"What did she say?"

"Nothing at first. It was I who spoke. I said—for I could not help saying it, the words rushed from my soul—I said:

"'Oh, mother! mother! I did that deed! I—'

"But she seized my elbow and shook me, as she hissed into my ear:

"'Is it not grievous and horrible enough that I should have my baby murdered, without having my daughter hanged! You never did that! You have had a nightmare! Or you are crazy! Go on with you to the house!'

"And she drove me before her, until we reached the house and my room, where she locked me in! From that time I was a prisoner. It was my mother who prevented me from explaining my sin and vindicating the innocent," moaned the girl.

"You are not here to accuse your mother, but to accuse yourself! I am not here to audit your denunciation of the sins of another, but your confession of your own," said the priest, with gentle firmness.

"I know! I know! And I do not wish to criminate my mother, but I must tell the whole truth of the circumstances under which I lived, or you will never understand my action," meekly replied the girl.

"Go on, then, poor child, only avoid mentioning other sinners as much as possible."

"I will try! Well, then, without mentioning names or persons, I must tell you that every mental and material means were taken to deter me from confession and to keep me quiet. I was never left alone except when I was securely locked in my own room. My mind was subjected to daily terrors by tales of the horrors of imprisonment and the tortures of a public execution. No dreadful, blood-curdling story of death by public strangulation on the gallows was ever published that was not read to me—with additions and exaggerations, as I do now believe—until I screamed with terror, and shrank from exposing myself to such a penalty."

"Poor girl! Was not the sense of remorse, then, strong enough to overcome the sense of fear?"

"Sometimes it was, father Sometimes the thought of my crime caused me such anguish that I felt willing to face death in any form so that I might expiate my sin, be forgiven and find peace! Then I cried and wailed to be let out to go and give myself up to justice!"

"And then?"

"Then opium was given to me! Opium, that plunged all my senses in a fool's paradise of serene enjoyment."

"Ah! what sin!" breathed the priest.

"And this went on for years and years! I did not get a chance or an opportunity to speak to anyone, even to my own sister, even to a servant. She waited on me herself and gave out that I was crazy, and that it was not safe for others to attend me. At last I felt that I was really going crazy."

"Were you at this time a sleepwalker?" inquired the priest, who had heard the neighborhood rumor of the "ghost" that haunted the old well, and who hoped to get at some elucidation of the mystery.

"Within the limits of my own room I may have been a sleepwalker, but not beyond it, for you see I could not get out. My room was at the top of the house and I was locked in every night. It had but one door, of which she took the key, and but one window, with a sheer descent of eighty feet to the ground. Why did you ask me that question, father?" inquired the girl, in a low, earnest whisper.

"I will tell you. Because an absurd rumor is now disturbing the minds of our rustic population. This rumor is to the effect that an apparition is nightly seen to hover about the old well which was the place of the tragedy. It occurred to me that if anything of the sort has really been seen, it must have been yourself walking in your sleep," frankly replied Father Benedict.

"It was not I! At least it was not I in the flesh!" breathed Malvina, in a low, mysterious voice.

"Why do you say, 'at least it was not I in the flesh?'" wistfully inquired the priest.

"Because, father, I could not leave my prison chamber, for the reasons that I have told you, to go anywhere in the flesh during the night. I was locked fast in. But, father, here is a mystery. I seemed to be driven to go to the scene of my crime—in the spirit—every night," whispered the girl.

"How say you?" demanded the bewildered priest.

"I say that there are mysteries about myself in my abnormal state that I cannot penetrate or understand."

"Explain yourself, my daughter."

"I cannot. I will tell you all I can, however. Every night, when I was locked in my room and covered up in bed, I fell into a deep sleep and had a very vivid dream."

"Ah!"

"I always dreamed of rising in my bed and passing out, of the door—not out through the open door, but through the closed door, as if its solid timbers had been only a shadow, and so on through every material barrier, as if they had been shadows and I had been the only substance. And so passing through the house without opening a door—through the lawn and into the plantation without opening a gate, and through the thick plantation, where scarcely a fox could have gone—through the tangled brushwood as if it had been but a mesh of shadows, and so into the paddock, and so to the old dry well. And, oh, father!" she suddenly exclaimed, with a startling change of look and tone.

"What is it, daughter?"

"In my dream the child came to me, living—warm, living, loving, joyous! In my dream I had not hurt it!" she answered, with a thrill that visibly shook her whole frame.

"And what do you gather from that dream, poor girl?"

"I think my spirit left my body and entered that world which lies all about us, invisible—that world where matter is shadow or is nothing, and spirit is substance and everything; that world in which the child whom I loved and whom I never wished to harm, and never really had the power to harm, still lived, and understood, and felt, and pitied, and came to comfort me. No; I never harmed the child!"

"Unsound! Unsound!" murmured the priest.

"It is not the thought of the child that tortures me! The child is an angel in heaven, and he knows that his poor afflicted sister loved him! No! it is not for the child I grieve, but for the poor girl unjustly convicted and sent to the penal colonies for life—it is of her I think!"

"Yes, of her you should think! Of her who suffers for your crime," said the priest.

"She shall suffer no longer than I can help! Father, I wish to tell you what precipitated my flight from Rose Hill."

"Speak on, my daughter."

"Three nights ago I had the strangest dream, or vision, or experience—call it what you will—that I ever had in my life."

"What was it, my child?"

"I dreamed that I rose from my bed, passed through the closed door as a substance passes through shadow, and passed out and on until I found myself in the paddock, with the beautiful child in my arms, on the brink of the old well, when—oh! it was terrible!" suddenly exclaimed the girl, throwing up her wan, white hands and covering her face.

"Compose yourself and go on," said the priest, in a voice of calm authority.

"Oh, it was terrible! terrible! for I suddenly stood face to face with a man who attempted to seize me!"

"My daughter!"

"Yes, father, and in my agony of terror my spirit flashed back again into my body and I woke up in my bed! I was so distressed that I arose and tried to get out of the room, but the door was securely locked and I could not escape!"

"But, my poor, unhappy child, to what purpose do you recall and recount these nightmare dreams?" demanded the priest.

"Nightmare dreams, do you call them, father—only nightmare dreams?" wistfully inquired the girl.

"Only nightmare dreams, perfectly natural under the circumstances of a sin-troubled soul (and an unsound mind),"he added, mentally.

"Only nightmare dreams " she murmured, thoughtfully.

"No more, at all! Why do you recall them?"

"Because you told me to speak out. Because I wish to explain the circumstances that drove me to this sanctuary."

"Go on, then!"

"I could sleep no more that night! I was sick with ter- ror of—I know not what! I walked the floor of my room. I rapped and called at my door. All to no purpose! No one heard me ! No one slept on the same floor, in fact! So passed the remainder of the night! And now, father, listen to what happened the next morning, and see if you can explain that, for I cannot!"

"I listen."

"I did not go to bed again, but walked the floor until the day broke and it was light enough for me to see to dress. When my mother came to unlock my door and let me out, she saw my terrible situation. I would have told her the cause of it, but she would not let me talk. She gave me a dose of morphine, which quieted and stupefied me, but did not put me to sleep!"

"My daughter, let me interrupt to remind you that you must not use names or refer to other persons more than necessary," gently said the priest.

"I will try to avoid doing so. I could eat no breakfast, and after we left the table, my mother, sister and self went into our morning sitting room, where they occupied themselves with needlework, and I sat in a half stupor, until I was terribly aroused from it! A man had come into the room."

"Ah!" breathed the priest.

"At first I was only dimly conscious of his presence, of—of his being a sort of peddler or patent agent, who was trying to sell something to my mother and sister; but I took no notice of him, for I was not interested in what he was doing, until at last he came boldly up to me, spoke to me, put something in my lap, and so compelled me to look up at him, when—oh, father!" cried the girl, shuddering and covering her face with her hands.

"What? what, my daughter?" cried the excited priest.

"Oh, father! in him, this peddler, I recognized the man I had seen in my fearful dream of the previous night, who had attempted to seize me!"

"And what happened next?" inquired the astonished priest.

"I hardly know! But was it not strange, was it not horrible that I should meet this man face to face, in the flesh, after having met him in that terrible dream?"

"It was, indeed, passing strange! But compose yourself, my child, and tell me what next occurred."

"I say I hardly know! I remember trying to pour out a confession then and there, but I believe I soon became incoherent, and fell into convulsions. I know that I finally lost all consciousness of my surroundings, for when I came to my senses again I found myself in bed, in my mother's chamber. I was quite alone. My mind was singularly clear—clearer, indeed, than it had been for many years. I determined then to try for liberty. I arose and went to the door, but found it locked on the outside. I was locked in. Then I went to the window, which was fastened on the inside. I unfastened it and got out on the roof of the veranda, and climbed to the ground by the aid of the old knotted branches of the honeysuckle that grew over it. Then I fled! Father—"

"Well, my poor child!"

"My fate pursued me even here. I fled hither for sanctuary, for confession, for counsel; but my fate pursued me even hither!"

"I do not understand you, my child."

"You know—or at least I know—that a messenger was sent to let my mother know where I was."

"Yes."

"And she was persuaded to leave me here for a time."

"I know."

"And she promised to send my clothes to-day."

"Yes."

"Oh, father! while I was expecting only a messenger from my mother, I was told that a visitor wished to see me in the parlor. I went down with Sister Olympia, thinking only of seeing one of our own servants; but, father, conceive my terror when, for the first time since that fatal night, I stood face to face with the witness of my crime! Oh! oh! it was overwhelming! He used I know not what words to remind me when and where we had met before. And— convulsions, chaos and unconsciousness on my part followed. Father, this happened this morning! When I came here I eluded the vigilance of Sister Olympia, and left the infirmary to steal hither and make this confession. Father, I killed my baby brother, though I did not mean to harm him! I alone am guilty of that crime for which another suffers in my stead! Father, what must I do?" pleaded the penitent, with clasped hands and beseeching eyes.

"My poor daughter, your conscience has already told you what you must do. You must make a public confession of your crime to clear the innocent! Think what it has been to leave a guiltless girl to suffer an exile to the penal colonies for these five long years!" mildly spoke the priest.

"She cannot have suffered as I have, and she should not have suffered if I could have had my liberty before this; and she shall not suffer longer than I can help. But tell me what I shall do?" inquired the girl.

"I have told you—your own conscience has told you; you must make a public confession! You will have no forgiveness, find no peace, until you cleanse your soul by a public confession. Be sure of this, my daughter."

"But—I thought—that you could give me absolution—could make me at peace with myself," faltered the girl.

"No, no, nothing can be done for you without a public confession that shall acknowledge your own guilt and vindicate the innocent."

"Ah me! ah me! how can I make such a confession? I cannot go upon the housetops and proclaim my crime!" cried the girl, wringing her hands.

"You can go to a magistrate and give yourself up as the slayer of the child for whose murder Margaret Campbell was transported to penal servitude for life."

"Oh, Heaven! And witness the horror with which everybody will regard me! They will think I am the cold-blooded murderess who destroyed my own little brother and then allowed an innocent girl to suffer in my place! They will not know the very truth of the case! Oh, it is too hard, too hard!" exclaimed the wretched girl, wringing her hands.

"Yes, it is hard, but it is absolutely necessary as your most imperative duty. I will not try to convince you otherwise," said the priest.

"And oh! to be imprisoned in a dreadful jail; to be brought to be public trial!" wailed the girl.

"Yes, it will be grievous; there is no denying that all this will be very grievous; but, my child, it is no more than Margaret Campbell innocently suffered in your stead. Think of that, and brace yourself to do her justice."

"And oh! the end of it all—the public execution—the shameful, cruel death! Oh, I cannot bear it! I cannot bear it! I could risk my soul sooner!" she wailed, in utter woe.

"My daughter, all this would be no more than many a tender woman has endured before you, nor near so much as some have suffered— ay, some of the best women that ever lived have suffered the most cruel deaths, and suffered bravely in the cause of justice, liberty, patriotism, or religion! You, if it should come to the worst with you, would not suffer much. But it will not come to the worst in your case. You will not have to suffer death as the consequence of your confession."

"What? What? Not suffer death, when I did destroy the child?" exclaimed the girl, in amazement and perplexity.

"No, for you did not wish or intend to harm the babe."

"No, I did not mean to hurt the child! I tried not to do it! I succeeded in not doing it during my waking hours! But an evil spirit seized me in my sleep, and I did the deed in a dream! Oh, I am willing to suffer for it! Glad to suffer imprisonment, transportation, penal servitude— everything else, only I shrink from the gaze of people, and I shudder at the thought of the public, ignominious death!" she gasped, shaking from head to foot.

"You will not be called to suffer it. Daughter, can you not confide in me?"

"Oh, yes, yes!"

"Then believe me that you have no reason to fear the extreme penalty of the law. You are not a subject for it. Come, my daughter! Rouse yourself to do your duty. I will do all that I can to sustain and support you during the trial. Will you do this, my child?"

"Oh, yes, I will, I will!" fervently replied the girl.

"And now return to your cot in the infirmary. Rest to-night, and to-morrow you will do your duty. *Benedicite*, my daughter," murmured the priest, and the penitent arose and glided away in the darkness.

CHAPTER XXV
THE FATE

MALVINA MATTOX crept back to the infirmary and sank down upon her cot bed in a state of utter collapse.

The great strain upon her nervous system that had kept her up so long was now relaxed, and a rapid reaction set in.

Sister Olympia, the head of the infirmary, came in with a cup of tea and a piece of dry toast, which she set upon a little stand beside the cot as she said:

"You must take some food now. I brought it to you an hour ago, but you were not here. You should not have left your bed. You are much too weak. Where did you go?"

"I went to the chapel. I went to confession," faintly replied the girl.

"You need not have done so. Father Benedict would have come to you here. Your mother has at length sent the messenger with your clothes. They have just come. Your mother sends word that she will be here to see you to-morrow."

"Then she will not see me," sighed the girl.

"What do you mean by that? Why will your mother ,not see you?" questioned the sister.

"Father Benedict knows. He will tell you when he thinks fit," replied Malvina.

Sister Olympia bowed her head and slightly changed subject.

"The man who was here this morning to see you in the parlor, and who frightened you so badly, was not your mother's messenger, as it appears. Who, then, was he, and how did he frighten you?"

"Father Benedict knows. He will tell you when he fit," sighed the girl.

285

Again Sister Olympia bowed her head, and finding that she could learn nothing from the fast failing girl, ceased to question her.

"Drink your tea," she said, at length.

Malvina obeyed, but found the liquid difficult, and the solids impossible, to swallow. After a few sips of tea she put down her cup and pushed away her plate, and dropped back upon her pillow exhausted.

"You must do better than that," said the sister.

"I cannot—I cannot swallow anything more. I am dying," sighed the girl.

"Nonsense, you are low-spirited."

"No, I hope I am dying."

"You must not talk like that. If you do I shall call our mother superior to you."

"No, do not. I will say no more. But please leave me in peace," pleaded the girl.

"I must leave you for a little while to go to benediction, but I will not be long away; and I will not have any more nonsense talked about dying. Do you hear me?"

"Yes," sighed the girl.

The sister took up the cup and saucer and plate and carried them out.

Malvina Mattox closed her eyes and clasped her hands above her head, and yielded herself up to rest, or sleep, or death—she cared not which.

She lay perfectly quiet until an hour later, when she was aroused by the entrance of the infirmary night nurse, who insisted that the patient should undress and go regularly to bed.

Malvina obeyed, and gave no more trouble to anyone that night.

Early the next morning, however, she arose and began to put on her walking suit, though she was still so weak and ill that she tottered as she walked, and dropped things as she handled them.

Sister Olympia, coming in from first matins, found her patient in this condition, and ordered her immediately back to bed.

But on this occasion the usually manageable girl refused to obey.

"No, I cannot stay in bed. I have an engagement with Father Benedict that I must fulfill," she explained.

"Father Benedict again! Well!" exclaimed the sister, somewhat emphatically, but quickly recollecting herself, she bowed her head and became silent.

A few minutes later a message came up from the portress: "Father Benedict and Dr. Pullen are in the parlor, asking to see Miss Mattox."

"They have come for me—they have come for me, though I did not expect the doctor!" exclaimed Malvina, as she took her bonnet from its hook and put it on her head.

"You will not go down before you get your breakfast, and here it comas," said Sister Olympia, as one of the attendants brought in a waiter and set it on the stand.

Malvina drank some coffee and tried to swallow some bread, but finding it impossible to do so, she gave up the attempt, and said that she was ready to obey Father Benedict's summons.

"Where are you going in your bonnet and mantle?" inquired Sister Olympia.

"Father Benedict knows. He will tell you when he sees fit," replied the girl.

"How oracular all that sounds!" exclaimed Sister Olympia, as she followed her charge from the room, and down through many corridors and flights of stairs to the bare convent parlor, where the confessor and the physician of the sisterhood awaited her.

Father Benedict immediately came to meet her at the door, and said, in a low voice:

"I have a carriage at the gate to take you on your errand, my child; and it is proper that Dr. Pullen should go with us; but he goes only as your physician; he knows nothing of the secret you confided to me, and nothing of the special business that takes you to the squire's."

Having said this, the old priest bowed, and stood aside to let her pass to a seat.

She greeted the convent doctor and then sat down.

But the latter looked at her attentively, arose and took her hand and felt her pulse, and then, turning to the priest, said, earnestly:

"Sir, this young lady is not in a condition to go out. I make my protest against her doing so. She must go immediately to bed."

"My dear doctor, it is a matter of much more importance than life, or death, that she should take this drive. Understand that there is no alternative. She must go," said the priest.

"It is as much as her life is worth!" murmured the doc- tor, lowering his voice, so that his words should reach the ears of the priest only.

"And the matter at stake is much more than her life is worth. She will tell you so herself," firmly replied the father.

"Listen to me. She is dying now; actually dying," whispered the doctor.

"Dying?" muttered the old priest, with a slight start. "Oh, you mean that she has some mortal malady from which she can never recover, as we say of an invalid that he or she is dying of consumption, or cancer, while they may live for years—dying surely all the time. That is just what you mean, I suppose."

"I mean that death is upon her now; her pulse counts one hundred and forty; her breath is labored. She will not live to see the sun set," earnestly replied the doctor.

"Holy Mother! is this true?" exclaimed the father, crossing himself.

"It is true. You see now the urgent necessity of her being placed in bed."

"Yes," said the priest, and he crossed the room and whispered to his patient:

"The doctor thinks that you are not well enough to go out, my poor child. You must return to bed and we can send for the squire to come here and take your deposition."

"No! No!" exclaimed the girl, with startling energy for one so weak-"No! There will be no time to send a message and fetch the squire! No! I must go! I must go in person! I must tell my story, if I drop dead after ending it! Oh!" she gasped, laboring for breath, "I caught some words of your conversation! I heard the doctor say I was dying! I knew it before! I have been dying since last night! Oh, yes, thank Heaven, I am dying! But I must use the last hour of my life to do that justice which should have been done many years ago! Help me to the carriage, Father Benedict!"

In vain both priest and physician earnestly endeavored to dissuade her from her purpose.

Her dying self-will and energy was something frightful to encounter. Her eyes blazed like coals of fire from the white ashes of her sunken face, and her impetuous words came in gasps with her laboring breath.

"Doctor," said the priest, deferring to the authority that he recognized as superior in this case, "doctor, do you not think that we had better let her go, since we cannot reconcile her to the idea of staying? Will not this excitement caused by our opposition to her will do her even more harm than the journey would?"

"Yes, I think so! The choice is between two evils. In any case, she cannot outlive the day. Let her have her way," concluded the physician.

It seemed impossible that the girl could have overheard these words, which were whispered at the front window some distance from the chair on which she sat, panting; yet she spoke as if their meaning, at least, had reached her, when she said:

"I shall go and tell my story to the squire, and I shall not die till then! Lead me to the carriage."

The doctor gave her his arm and supported her whole weight as he led her out, followed closely by the priest, who was ready to lend assistance when it should be needed.

They took her through the convent grounds and through the outer gate and to the spot where the carriage stood waiting.

They placed her in it, supporting her on every side by the cushions and then gave the order to the coachman:

"Drive very slowly to Squire Storkridge, at Croft Court."

Then they placed themselves on the seat fronting the dying girl, and each held a hand of hers, rubbing and patting it gently to impart some vital force to her failing system.

Squire Storkridge was one of the justices of the peace in the shire, and had been chosen by Father Benedict as the recipient of his penitent's deposition, not only because the squire was a clear-headed, kind-hearted old man, but because his seat, Croft Court, was in easy distance from the Convent of St. Sepulcher.

Twenty minutes' slow driving brought them to the outer gate of the park, and five more to the door of the huge gray stone house that the squire called his hereditary home.

The dying girl was not so much exhausted by her drive as they had expected her to be. The mental satisfaction of having her own way had done her good.

The Test of Love

"Rest here for a few minutes, my child. The doctor will remain with you. I must see the squire alone," said the priest, as he opened the door of the carriage and stepped out.

As he walked up on the old moss-covered stone steps that led to the front door, intending to knock for admittance, that door was suddenly opened by a gray-haired servant in livery, who was showing out a tall, dark-complexioned, black-bearded young man, who looked as if he held a doubtful social position between that of a gentleman and that of a yeoman.

The young man raised his hat to the priest and passed on.

The eyes of the latter followed him with involuntary interest that made him, for the moment, forget his business; for, in fact, he recognized the visitor to the squire as the person who had gone to the convent on the preceding day to inquire for Malvina Mattox, and whom the nuns had mistaken as her mother's messenger, but whom she at once remembered as the secret witness of her crime, whose presence in daylight and in dreams had lately afflicted her so deeply—in a word, the tramp, Ham Gow!

What business had he with the magistrate? Had he come to denounce Malvina Mattox as the murderess of the little Stuart Campbell, her infant brother"

While he was asking himself this question, the gray-haired servant waited respectfully, and then inquired:

"Did you wish to see my master, sir?"

"Yes! yes!" exclaimed the priest, rousing himself. "I wished to see the squire. Is he at home?"

"Yes, sir; please walk in. I will take your card."

The priest drew a blank card from his pocket, wrote upon it, with a pencil:

"Benedict Riordon, S. J.," and handed it to the footman, who first showed him into a small reception room and then left him.

In what seemed but a moment, the man returned and said:

"The squire will see you at once, sir, if you will please to walk into the justice room, where he is engaged at present, but will soon be at liberty.

"The priest—trembling with impatience at the thought of the vital interest then at stake, which a few minutes of delay might ruin forever—followed the footman down the hall to the rear of the building and through an oaken door, to a long room, comfortably carpeted and curtained, and having a raised platform at one end covered with a green drugget, and provided with a long writing table, behind which, in a large, leather-covered armchair, sat Squire Storkridge, busily writing and closely attended by a constable.

As the priest walked toward him, the squire looked up, nodded, sighed deeply, and handed a folded paper to one of the constables, saying:

"Take this, go at once to the Convent of St. Sepulcher, and ask for Malvina Mattox. When you see her, serve the warrant, and bring her hither. Stay! You must take a carriage. The girl is in bad health. What can I do for you, Mr. Riordon?" then inquired the squire, turning abruptly to his new visitor.

"Recall your officer, Mr. Storkridge. If he bears a warrant for the arrest of Malvina Mattox, his errand will be a vain one. She is not in the Convent of St. Sepulcher," said the latter.

"She was there no later than yesterday," said the old squire, bending a glance full of suspicion upon the face of the speaker.

"Yes, she was there yesterday and she was there this morning, not an hour ago—but now—"

"Where is she now?" demanded the magistrate.

"In a carriage at your door."

The squire stared.

"Waiting to come in and accuse herself of the crime she committed five years ago; to accuse herself, that she may vindicate the innocent girl who has for all these years been suffering in her stead—to accuse herself before she dies, for she is dying," solemnly declared the priest.

And the squire stared.

"There is no time to explain further. Will you see this girl now?" inquired the visitor.

But the squire stared.

Father Benedict turned to go his errand, and when he had reached the door the squire spoke:

"Come back, if you please, Mr. Riordon! This is all very strange, sir, that you tell me! Come back! I don't understand all this."

The priest turned to retrace his steps.

"Be I to go and sarve the warrant?" inquired the constable, who had been hesitating all this while.

"No! You are to wait here for the present! Come back, Mr. Riordon! Ah! you are coming! Well, sir, what is all this you are telling me?" demanded the squire, as soon as the priest stood before him again.

"I tell you, sir, that the girl whom you have sent to arrest has forestalled your warrant by coming voluntarily to give herself up, and that her physical condition is such as to render all delay in taking her deposition dangerous to the cause of justice," said the priest.

"Unaccountable! Here, an hour ago, comes to me a young man, one Gow, from Somerset—no, from Cornwall, and more recently from Australia—who tells me that he was an eyewitness to the murder of little Stuart Campbell, of which he charges Malvina Mattox—and tells so straight a story that I felt constrained to issue a warrant for the girl's apprehension. And now you come to tell me that the girl herself comes forward voluntarily to give herself up to justice. I say these two circumstances, taken together, are very strange."

"They will seem less so, squire, when you hear the girl's confession, which I implore you to lose no time in doing. Her physician declares that she cannot outlive the day," earnestly declared the priest.

"Ah! a deathbed repentance and a dying confession! I place little confidence in either!"

"No; this is no mere deathbed repentance. The girl has been for years suffering from remorse and eagerly longing to confess her crime, but she has been confined and watched, and prevented. You must hear her story. She is not so guilty as appears," urged the priest.

"Send her in," said the squire.

"I will bring her," replied Father Benedict, as he turned and left the room.

In a few minutes he returned with Malvina Mattox leaning on his arm, and supported on the other side by the doctor.

They carried her to a chair in front of the magistrate's table and placed her in it.

She bowed to the magistrate and sank back, panting.

The priest stooped and whispered:

"Tell your story, my child, not with as much detail as you used with me, but as briefly, as clearly, and in as few words as possible. Then answer any questions the magistrate may put to you."

"I—wish to be put under oath. I—want every form to be used to insure that justice shall be done," gasped the girl.

The oath was duly administered to her, and she told again the strange story of her involuntary crime, committed during somnambulism, utterly forgotten for a time, and then suddenly remembered when she was abruptly awakened out of a similar fit of somnambulism at the scene and hour of the tragedy. She spoke with difficulty, while her whole aspect revealed to the most careless observer that not her hours only, but her minutes, were numbered.

The magistrate's clerk took down her deposition in writing, and when it was finished he presented the paper for signature.

Three times the pen dropped from her relaxing fingers before she completed it, and then she sank back in her chair, laboring for breath.

The doctor took her wrist in his hand, felt her pulse, and then dropped it with a sigh.

All the persons present signed the deposition as witnesses.

Then the priest inquired of the magistrate:

"What will be your next move? You will not commit this dying woman to prison?"

"No, poor soul! she would not reach there alive. Doctor, how long will this last?" inquired the magistrate, in a whisper, as he glanced toward the panting girl.

"A very few minutes," murmured the physician.

"Then, doctor, pray do as you see fit. You may take her away, if you think she is strong enough to bear removal; or you may lay her on a bed in this house, if you choose. I will ring for my housekeeper," said the squire, kindly.

"No; don't, don't ring. Look!" replied the doctor, pointing to the girl, whose eyes were fixed and glazed and whose labored breathing had ceased, and over whose head the priest ,was extending his open palms and murmuring some prayer in Latin.

A great awe fell upon the company, but the poor, sinning, suffering and repenting soul of Malvina Mattox was at peace.

CHAPTER XXVI
VINDICATION

THE old squire was the first to break the awe-stricken silence that fell upon the death of Malvina Mattox.

"Poor creature!" he said, compassionately, "this is the very best thing that could have happened to her and for all connected with her. What a strange, tragic phase of mania was hers! She should have been placed in a lunatic asylum, under medical treatment, years before she had any opportunity of doing harm. Doctor, you can, of course, give a certificate of death from natural causes to forestall the inconvenience of an inquest?"

"Certainly," replied the physician.

"And I, if you will permit me, must go immediately to Rose Hill to break the news to the family there; though, ah me! I can easily understand how this event will be more of a relief than a grief to the widowed mother and the sister," sighed the priest.

"I will attend to the removal of the remains, if you will instruct me as to where they shall be carried—to Rose Hill, or to the Convent of St. Sepulcher," said the doctor.

"I thank you. To the Convent of St. Sepulcher. I will bring the mother thither; and, gentlemen, it is not now necessary, I hope, that the afflicted lady should ever know anything about the painful scene that has transpired in this room," suggested the priest.

"No, it is not; though she may unhappily hear of it by accident," said old Mr. Storkridge.

"That is scarcely possible. She goes nowhere, she receives no visits; and even should any servant of hers hear of this day's work, he or she would not dare to mention it to the mistress," said the priest.

"Well, gentlemen, if I or my establishment can afford you any assistance in this sad affair, command us. We are entirely at your disposal," said the old squire.

"We thank you very much, but need not trouble you, sir. Upon second thoughts, I will join the doctor in taking the remains back to the convent and go from thence to Rose Hill to notify the family," replied the priest.

"Will you not want another carriage? The break, or the wagonette, or any other in the coach house is quite at your service," persisted the squire.

"I thank you, no; we can take the body back in the same carriage in which we came. But, squire, it is not only in the departed soul that I feel deeply interested, but in the innocent, living, suffering young girl serving out the term of her natural life in the penal settlements of Van Dieman's Land! It is of her that I am thinking now! With the best haste that we can make it must be six or eight months before justice can reach and relieve her."

"I shall lose no time, Mr. Riordon. I shall act promptly, you may be sure. These documents shall go up to London to the Home Office, this day, by a special messenger, who shall urge them upon the attention of the secretary for immediate action. There is not a doubt but that the order for the discharge of Margaret Campbell will go out with the next mail to Hobart Town," warmly responded the old squire.

"This contents me. I knew the girl, and through my relations to her as her spiritual director, I knew that she was innocent, though I did not know who was guilty."

"Kelsy!" said the squire, turning somewhat abruptly to the constable who still held the warrant, "oblige me by destroying that paper! You cannot serve it on a dead woman, you know. And go and see who that is that Oxton is bringing in."

"It be Tom Rorke, your worship, cotch a-poaching ag'in," answered the officer.

"Go turn him back. Tell Oxton to keep in the strong room until I call up the case. You see how I am engaged now," said the magistrate.

"Yes, yer worship, I do. I will turn 'em round, yer worship," exclaimed the constable, stumping off on his errand.

"And I see that you are busy, squire, and that we are hindering you. I think I can carry this poor little light-weight out to the carriage without assistance," said Dr. Pullen, as he went to the body and drew the black mantle around its form and let down the veil over its face, and lifted it in his arms as if it were only a fainting girl, and carried it out and laid it carefully in the carriage, without even exciting the suspicions of the coachman that a corpse and not a swooning woman had been returned to the cushions.

Then, after having carefully closed the carriage door, the doctor returned to the justice room to take leave of the squire.

And when the physician and the priest had said good-by to the kindly master of Croft Court, they went out and re-entered their carriage, and drove back to the Convent of St. Sepulcher.

At the gate of the convent the doctor again lifted out the body, and carried it in his arms through the grounds to the door of the building.

"Holy Mary!" cried the portress at the outer gate, as she crossed herself. "The poor child has fainted dead away! She never ought to have been taken out to drive in her weak state."

And words to the same effect were uttered by the portress at the house, as the doctor bore the body into the main building.

Not until they reached "The Room of the Dead" at the back of the infirmary, and had laid the body on one of the slabs, did the priest, leaving the doctor on guard, go to inform the mother superior of the convent about the death, and even then he told that lady of nothing but the death, and having dispatched her in haste to "The Room of the Dead," he re-entered the carriage and drove to Rose Hill, to notify the family there of what had just occurred.

On arriving he sent up his card to the lady of the house, and was at once admitted to her presence in the upper sitting room, which was her usual morning retreat.

"You bring ill news, father," she said, on observing the deep gravity of the priests aspect.

He bowed solemnly and in silence, as he seated himself on the chair that she drew forward for his accommodation.

"My unfortunate child! How is it with her?" anxiously demanded the lady.

"It is well with her," gravely replied the priest.

"You mean—you mean?" breathlessly inquired the lady.

"That she is at rest," responded the priest, reverently bowing his head.

"Dead!"

"Passed to her eternal home."

A look, not of grief, nor even of regret, but of infinite relief, came into the mother's face. Every feature expressed what her tongue only forbore to speak:

"Thank Heaven!"

It was with a deep sigh of satisfaction that she inquired:

"When did it happen?"

"Not an hour ago—suddenly, too suddenly to have you notified in time."

"I knew it would come suddenly when it did come. I was warned of that by our family physician. Did the poor girl suffer much at the last?"

"Not at all. She passed away very quietly. I am here to offer any assistance on my own part, and on the part of the community of the Holy Sepulcher. The sisterhood are giving all requisite attention to the remains, but, of course, we wait your orders. We would know whether you would have the body brought hither, or interred in the convent .cemetery."

"Oh, in the convent cemetery by all means, if the sisters of the Holy Sepulcher will be so good as to allow it," said the lady.

"Then it shall be so, and the sisterhood will willingly extend to yourself and your daughter the hospitalities of their house in this time of trouble."

"They are very good. I would like to go to the convent immediately."

"There is nothing to hinder. There is a carriage at the door."

"I will speak to my daughter," said the lady, as she arose and left the room.

A few minutes later Mrs. and Miss Campbell reappeared arrayed for their ride, and the priest attended them downstairs and out to the carriage.

When they reached the convent the two ladies were received with the most tender sympathy by the mother superior, who did not suspect and could not have understood why the death of the girl should have been such a great relief to the mother and the sister.

Mrs. Campbell felt that her wretched daughter was at last safe from the imminent danger of a public trial, and possibly a public execution, and she was very glad that this should be so.

She suspected nothing of the dying deposition made by the girl, nor did anyone enlighten her on the subject, which would have overwhelmed her with pain and shame.

To the questions of Mrs. Campbell the nuns replied that Miss Malvina had arisen and dressed herself in the morning, and, with much excitement and obstinacy, had insisted on taking a drive; that the physician thought there would be less danger in gratifying her wishes than in opposing them. Accordingly, she was allowed to take the drive, attended by the physician, who kindly volunteered his services. But the girl had expired in the carriage.

This was the impression the nuns had received, and though it was not in all respects exactly true, yet it was honestly believed and uttered as truth.

Mrs. and Miss Campbell remained three days at the convent.

At the end of the third day the obsequies of Malvina Mattox were performed in the chapel, and her body was laid in the cemetery.

And on the morning of the fourth day Mrs. Campbell made a munificent present to the convent, and then returned with her daughter to Rose Hill, where they fell into the monotonous routine of their secluded lives.

In the meantime other events of importance to the destinies of our friends were rapidly transpiring elsewhere.

After Ham Gow had laid the formal charge of murder against Malvina before Squire Storkridge, and had seen the warrant made out for her apprehension—that warrant which was destined never to be served—he returned to the little wayside inn where he had left Mr. Hamilton Gower and the detective waiting for him.

He found them in the private parlor—the only one the little inn could boast.

"Well?" demanded Mr. Gower, eagerly.

"All right. The squire received the charge and acted on it immediately. An officer, armed with a warrant, has been dispatched to the Convent of the Holy Sepulcher to arrest Malvina Mattox on the charge of having murdered her infant brother," replied Ham Gow, speaking to the best of his knowledge and belief.

"When will the preliminary examination take place?" inquired Mr. Gower.

"It is set down for three o'clock this afternoon, which, I suppose, will be immediately after the squire's luncheon, and will give ample time for the officer to have the criminal before the squire, and for me to return and meet her there as her accuser and the principal witness for the crown."

"Very well. I shall attend that examination. You, also, Hutchings, must go with us to give your evidence in regard to the scene you witnessed in the boudoir of Mrs. Campbell on the morning of your visit to Rose Hill," said Mr. Gower.

"Of course, I will go," replied the detective.

"I hope it will not go very hard with the poor, crazy creature! This hunting a poor, half-witted girl to disgrace and death is not at all to my taste, even in the cause of justice," sighed Ham Gow.

"But it is to rescue another, a most innocent and most grievously wronged young lady, from a degradation worse than death that you must do this," said Mr. Gower.

"And it will not go hard with her; never fear. She is too crazy to be amenable to the laws, though she will probably be shut up in an asylum for criminal lunatics, to keep her from further acts of violence," added the detective.

How little they suspected that they were discussing the fate of one who had already passed beyond the power of human tribunals!

"Hope you will excuse me for saying that I am hungry, gentlemen! S'pose we have some dinner, and then set out for Croft Court to attend the investigation?" suggested Ham Gow.

"Agreed," said Mr. Gower, touching the bell pull.

The dinner was ordered and a carriage engaged.

And half an hour later, when they had well dined, they entered the vehicle and soon found themselves rolling over the moors toward Croft Court.

They arrived a little before three o'clock, but were immediately shown into the library, where they found the squire alone, enjoying his pipe.

"Well, sir," said the old man, on recognizing Ham Gow, "of course, you expected to find me at my duties in the justice room, ready to preside over the preliminary examination of a prisoner charged by you with murder."

"Yes, your worship, certainly I did," replied the young man, with a respectful though puzzled air.

"And these," added the squire, indicating Gow's two companions, "are other witnesses that you have brought?"

"Mr. Hutchings here has testimony to give," replied Ham, with a wave of his hand toward the detective, who bowed to the squire at this informal introduction.

The squire nodded briefly, in response to this courtesy, and then turned an inquiring look toward Mr. Gower.

"This gentleman—Mr. Hamilton Gower, lately from Australia—has no direct evidence to offer, but, being deeply interested in the case, wishes to attend the examination of the accused," said Ham Gow, in explanation.

Mr. Gower bowed to the squire, who returned the salutation, and then said:

"But, gentlemen, there will be no examination, which is the reason why you find me here instead of in the justice room."

"No examination!" exclaimed the three men in a breath, as they looked from the squire toward each other.

"Has the accused woman escaped, then?" inquired Mr. Gower.

"She has—entirely beyond the power of magistrate or man to recapture her. She has gone to the judgment above," gravely replied the squire.

"Dead!" exclaimed Ham Gow.

"I am not surprised," remarked Detective Hutchings.

"What a misfortune!" exclaimed Mr. Hamilton Gower.

"No, sir; it was a very fortunate event for all concerned," said the squire, replying to the last speaker.

"But in what manner now can the innocence of Margaret Campbell be established?" inquired Hamilton Gower, with a bitter sigh.

"By the dying deposition of that unfortunate girl, taken down from her own lips in my presence, and duly signed and witnessed," replied the squire.

"She confessed, then!" exclaimed Mr. Gower.

"I told you so!" said the detective.

"I thought she would," added Ham Gow.

"Yes, she confessed," answered the squire. "The poor creature, at her own earnest desire, was brought here in a carriage, accompanied by her physician and priest. She was dying, and by what seemed a supernatural effort of will, she lived—gasping, panting, fainting and rallying—until she had made and signed her confession; and five minutes afterward she expired in her chair."

Silence fell upon the men who heard this statement.

Mr. Hamilton Gower was the first to speak.

"You will take steps immediately to bring this case before the Home Secretary, that no time may be lost in doing justice to Margaret Campbell," he said.

"I wish to communicate with the secretary immediately. I could send the documents up by mail, but in that case they would have to go through the hands of so many underlings before they could reach those of the secretary—if they ever should reach them—that at best there would be great delay, and the order for the liberation of that most deeply, wronged young lady could not go out, as it ought to do, by the next mail steamer to Australia. Therefore, I wish to find a responsible messenger, which is not a very easy matter, just in a hurry," said the squire.

"Allow me to be the bearer of these dispatches. I am, for certain reasons which I should be perfectly willing to explain to your worship, if there was time, the most deeply interested of anyone in the vindication of Margaret Campbell. Allow me to bear the dispatches!" eagerly exclaimed Hamilton Gower.

The old squire looked somewhat surprised and seemed to hesitate.

"My great reason for returning to England at this time—though I had other and very important interests to draw hither—was to vindicate the innocence of Margaret Campbell. Though I am a stranger to you, sir; and though I do not come to you accredited; and though I have no time now to lose in procuring credentials, yet, surely, you cannot hesitate to trust me with those papers, which no human being would find any interest in embezzling or misappropriating. Or if you have the slightest doubt on that subject, pray intrust me only with the copy of the attested confession, and give me a letter from yourself to the secretary, and I will leave for London to-night," vehemently declared the young man.

There was no possibility of doubting his earnestness and sincerity.

"You are, perhaps, a near relation to this unhappy young lady?" said the squire.

"I am her betrothed husband," answered the young gentleman, "and not a ticket-of-leave man, though I have just returned from the penal colonies," he added, with a smile, as he met the scrutinizing gaze of the magistrate.

"I did not suspect you to be one. I will let you take the papers, and give you a letter to the secretary. I believe you to be trustworthy, and even if you were not, you could have no temptation to betray this trust, since to do so would not advantage you in any way. I need not detain you while I write a letter to the secretary. I have the letter already written, and waiting for a messenger to take it. I have only now to put your name on the lower left-hand corner of the envelope. Let's see," said the squire, dipping his pen in ink, "it's Mr.—Mr.—"

"Hamilton Gower," explained the young man.

"Oh, ay, yes, to be sure! Any relation of the great ducal house of that name?" inquired the old man.

"I have not the remotest claim to such an honor," replied the young man, with a smile.

"Here you are, then, my young friend. And Heaven speed you!" said the squire, as he put into his hand a long envelope containing the attested confession of Malvina Mattox and his own letter to the secretary.

"And now, sir, if you wish to catch the London train, we must get back to our inn as soon as possible," suggested Detective Hutchings.

And the three men arose and bade good-by to the squire, and re-entered their carriage to drive back to the market town.

They stopped at the Cat and Fiddle only to pay their bill, and then continued their journey on to Stockstone, where they were so fortunate as to catch the night express to London.

CHAPTER XXVII
SUCCESS!

HAMILTON Gower and his companions reached London about seven o'clock the next morning, and then took a cab and drove to their inn, the Borough.

They found Ham Gow's young wife safe and well, though a little impatient at having been left alone for three whole days and nights.

"Which, if it hadn't been for the friendliness of Mrs. Bounce, the landlady, in taking me out sometimes, it is moped to death I should have been before this," she said, as she sat down at the head of the breakfast table to pour out the coffee, in the private parlor of the party.

"But I telegraphed you every day, Lona," said the young husband, deprecatingly.

"Oh, what is a telegram with nothing in it but 'All well, be home soon, take good care of yourself,' or some such, when I wanted you, or else a long letter every day," complained Mrs. Gow.

"But, my good child, we were all on a mission involving more than life or death—involving justice and mercy. We had no time to eat or sleep—at least with any satisfaction to ourselves—much less to write letters!" said Ham Gow deprecatingly.

"I'd like to know what that business was that took you off at a tangent, and kept you three whole days! I am sure if it hadn't been for the telegrams the landlady would have thought you had abandoned me, and I might have thought so, too!" said Mrs. Ham.

"Oh, no! Oh, no! you never could have done me that injustice, Lona!"

"I don't know! But tell me what that wonderful business was that made you leave London as suddenly as if you had been running from the police."

"Other people's secrets, my good little woman, that I dare not divulge," said Ham Gow, so seriously that Lona ceased to tease him.

As soon as breakfast was over Mr. Hamilton Gower changed his dress, made a very careful toilet, ordered a first-class hansom from a livery stable, entered it, and taking with him his documents, drove to Somerset House, in the fond, fallacious hope of finding the home secretary at his office and of being admitted to his lordship's presence.

Perhaps, if he had presented himself under his proper name and title, he might have commanded some respect and attention; but appearing simply as Mr. Hamilton Gower, though that name was a good one, too, and bearing a letter from no more important a person than an obscure Yorkshire squire, he met nothing but coolness, snubs, rebuffs and delays, all the way up, through porters, footmen, messengers, pages and clerks of all grades, until he reached the corridor of the anteroom to the office of the private secretary of the home secretary.

After difficulty and delay, he obtained one minute's interview with the great man's great man, who told him that "his lordship" was not at the office that day, nor was it certain when "his lordship" would be there. Would the gentleman leave letters?

"No," said Mr. Gower, "they are to be delivered to his lordship in person. They contain matters concerning life or death."

"So many letters of that sort come to the minister. Good-day, sir," replied the great man's great man, smiling "superior" as he dismissed the applicant.

It would be tedious to tell how many times young Hamilton Gower presented himself at Somerset House, without succeeding in his attempt to see the secretary.

At length, after three days of vain effort, he wrote a note, in which he briefly stated the urgent claims of justice and mercy that had brought him from Australia, and lastly from Yorkshire, to seek a personal interview with the home minister. He marked this letter private, and addressed it to the town house of the secretary, and then waited the course of events.

The following morning he received a note from the private secretary of the minister, saying that "his lordship" would receive Mr. Gower at the "office" that same day at twelve o'clock noon.

Hamilton Gower rejoiced, for he now considered his cause as good as gained.

And he was right.

He once more made a very careful toilet, engaged a first-class hansom, and drove to Somerset House.

Here his reception was now very different from what it had been on the occasion of his former visits.

The gentleman who presented himself by appointment to be admitted to the august presence must certainly be treated with the utmost respect, not to say reverence and veneration.

The underlings were obsequious, and passed the visitor on from one to another with bows and scrapes, until he found himself before the awful potency that represented the throne in its dominion over life and death. The great minister, was in point of fact a gentle and unassuming old man, who might have been the beloved pastor of some simple country congregation; and yet he was one of England's most eminent as well as most Christian statesmen; while his high, full, broad forehead, thoughtful eyes, and calmly compressed lips, quietly folded hands and easy attitude showed all an intellect as serene in its integrity as it was benevolent in its aims and potent in its strength.

His manner at once put the young visitor at ease.

With a low, respectful bow Hamilton Gower laid the letter and documents before his lordship.

"Sit down, young sir, while I look into these papers," said the minister, taking up the packets.

Hamilton Gower took a seat at a short distance and glanced from time to time at the face of the secretary, who was now reading the letter of Squire Storkridge.

The young man now fully appreciated the act of the great minister in giving his personal attention to a matter that might have been referred to some of his numerous assistants.

"This is the most cruel case of the kind that ever came under my notice," said the home secretary, as he finished reading the documents.

The young gentleman bowed in respectful assent, and the elder one continued:

"Measures shall be at once taken to redress this great wrong, so far as it can be redressed; but what can compensate to that unhappy girl for the injuries she has suffered—the distress of her trial and conviction, the misery of five years of penal servitude? Not certainly the mere order for her discharge from custody. I would there were some better way of compensating to her, and to all victims of circumstantial evidence, for the great wrong done to them in their conviction."

And the minister bowed his head upon his chest with a deep sigh that revealed the painful sympathy of his soul.

"I wish to say to you, my lord, since your lordship so kindly takes some interest in this case, that the young girl, since her arrival in Tasmania, has had no suffering to encounter, beyond that of exile— exile softened by the presence and companionship of an aged relative, who preceded her out to the colony, made a home for her there, and received her on her arrival in the only way in which he could do so, as his assigned servant, nominally, as his adopted daughter really."

"I am glad to hear it. I know such arrangements are sometimes made in the penal colonies. I am glad this has been done in the case of this unfortunate girl. Mr. Gower, the order for Margaret Campbell's discharge from custody shall go out in the steamer that sails for Melbourne on the tenth of September."

"I—beg your lordship's pardon. I had supposed the ship would sail on the first," said the young gentleman, respectfully.

"The time of sailing has been changed," quietly responded his lordship.

The first feeling of Hamilton Gower on hearing this news was one of disappointment—a delay of even ten days seemed very grievous to him; but his next feeling, following almost instantly upon the first, was one of delight at the thought that this very delay would enable him to be the bearer of the order for Margaret Campbell's release, if only the minister would permit him to become so. He felt that he was beginning to trespass a little too long on the golden minutes of the home secretary; yet he could not help saying:

"Again I beg your lordship's pardon and forbearance, but—I am going out to Australia by the steamer of the tenth, and I should be very happy to be intrusted with the order for Margaret Campbell's discharge."

The minister reflected for a moment, and then said:

"At present I see no objection to the plan. You came to me accredited by Mr. Storkridge, of Croft Court, with whom I have some acquaintance. Come here again at this hour on Monday next."

"I thank your lordship deeply. I have the honor to bid your lordship good-morning," said the young man, who, feeling that the interview was at an end, thus took leave and departed.

His face was radiant when he went back to his inn, where he found Ham Gow alone, smoking a pipe and reading a paper while he waited for his friend.

Mrs. Ham was out shopping with her friend, the land-lady.

"No use to ask you what news! Your whole face is beaming with good news!" exclaimed Ham Gow, withdrawing the pipe from his mouth and smiling.

"Oh, yes! Glorious news! I am to take out the order for Margaret Campbell's honorable discharge by the next mail steamer for Australia!" joyously replied the young man.

Ham Gow stared.

"You?" he exclaimed. "Why, you have got to go down on the first of the month to claim your estates in Cornwall, to celebrate your majority at Hawkewood, and to kick Lewis Manton, neck and heels, out of Hawke Hall. Now, how can you do that and sail for Australia all in one day?"

"I cannot do it, of course."

"Then you mean to sacrifice your own interests for the present, at least, and leave the usurper in possession for another year?" said Ham Gow, in a tone of disgust.

"I mean nothing of the sort. I shall go down to Hawkewood on the last of this month so as to be early on the ground at Hawke Hall on the first of next month, when I shall have the pleasure of shaking hands with my old tenantry and showing Mr. Manton the door."

"You cannot do all that and sail for Australia on the same day to save your life and soul!" persisted Ham Gow.

"I know I cannot. I told you so," replied the young man, with his eyes twinkling with amusement.

"I don't understand you at all," said Ham Gow, resentfully.

"Of course you don't, old fellow, because you have not got the key! Here it is, however: the time of the sailing of the mail steamer is changed. She sails on the tenth. I shall go down on the first, do all I have to do in Cornwall, and be ready to embark on the tenth. Now do you comprehend?" inquired Mr. Hamilton Gower, with a laugh.

"Whe-ew!" cried Ham Gow, withdrawing his pipe from his mouth and sending a spiral column of smoke that resolved itself into a white cloud above his head.

"And now," exclaimed the young gentleman, gayly, "let us do something pleasant to pass away the time. We have been forced to neglect Mrs. Ham a great deal—and she the only lady of our party! Now, what do you say to our taking her to the theater to-night? They are playing 'The Lady of Lyons' at the Princess. I am sure she would like that."

312

"I know she would. Thank you, we will go," said Ham Gow.

Mrs. Ham returned soon after, and was very much pleased with the proposition to go to the play, and immediately began to make a grand toilet for the occasion.

They went, and were so well entertained that they resolved to indulge themselves in the same pleasure at some other theater on the succeeding night.

Still, to the eager spirits of Hamilton Gower, the time hung very heavily until Monday noon, when he again went by appointment to Somerset House.

On this occasion he did not see the minister, but was met by his private secretary, who placed a sealed packet in his hand, directed to "His Excellency, Viscount Seyres, Governor of Van Dieman's Island," and having printed on the left-hand upper corner the words: "On Her Majesty's Service."

Hamilton Gower bowed his thanks, put the precious packet carefully away in his breast pocket and came out.

When he returned to his inn, he found Ham Gow occupied precisely as on a former occasion, smoking a pipe and reading a paper while waiting for his companion's return.

"You find me alone here again, you see! Mrs. Ham has gone out with the landlady to see Madam Tussaud's wax works! London sights have turned that young woman's head; and, as for Mrs. Bounce, who goes gadding with her and at her expense—well, it is fortunate there is a landlord and several grown-up sons and daughters to look after the interests of the house, or the business would go to the bow-wows," laughed Ham Gow.

"Well, leave Lona to enjoy herself, poor girl, and tell me what you think of this?" exclaimed Hamilton Gower, taking the long packet from his pocket and laying it on the table, just under the eyes of his friend.

"I think," said Ham Gow, drawing his pipe from his mouth and bending his head to scrutinize the superscription, "I think—in the inelegant but expressive language of my boyhood—that it is bully!"

Before another word could be spoken, the door was suddenly opened and two policemen unceremoniously entered the room.

The two men who were seated at the table looked up in surprise.

"Have you not mistaken the room?" inquired Mr. Hamilton Gower, on seeing the officers approaching them as if they meant business.

"No, I think not," said the foremost policeman, referring to a printed paper in his hand, and then looking attentively at Ham Gow.

"Then, what is your business here?" demanded Mr. Hamilton Gower.

"Our business, sir, is with this gentleman," replied the ,policeman, and going up to Ham, who was staring with all his might, he laid his hand on his shoulder, and said:

"Ham Gow, I arrest you in the queen's name! You are my prisoner!"

"Me! In the name of all the dees, what do you want of me?" demanded the ex-tramp. Then, with a sudden light breaking all over his dark face, he exclaimed: "Oh, I see! I see ! By the Lord Harry! but this is too funny!"

"You will not find it very funny, I am afraid, my fine fellow! You have eluded justice long enough, but now we have got you, and the charge against you is a very serious one," said the policeman, as he drew a pair of handcuiffs from his pocket, and, quick as lightning, snapped them upon Ham's wrists.

"Upon what charge do you arrest my friend?" gravely inquired Mr. Hamilton Gower; for though he divined at once the nature of the accusation against the prisoner, he chose to hear it stated in distinct terms.

"Upon the charge of being an accomplice of Lewis Earl of Hawkewood, in the murder of Horace, late Earl of Hawkewood, on the morning of Wednesday, September 1, 18—, at Hawke Hall," replied the policeman.

To the astonishment of that officer, the prisoner burst into a loud laugh, in which he was joined by his companion.

"Has the earl been arrested?" demanded the young gentleman.

"Yes, sir. His lordship was safely stowed in Hawkeville jail this morning," replied the policeman.

"Well, I'm blessed!" exclaimed Ham Gow. "I don't mind being accused of a murder or so now and then, but to be charged with being an accomplice of Lewis Manton's!"

CHAPTER XXVIII
HAM GOW'S GREAT GRIEVANCE

THE two policemen were preparing to take Ham Gow away.

"Where are you going to carry him?" inquired Mr. Hamilton Gower, curiously divided between a sense of humor and a feeling of annoyance.

"We shall take him down to Hawkeville, sir, and lodge him in jail, alongside of his principal in the charge, leastwise in another cell it will be, hows'ever; for it is ordered as the accomplices be kept apart," answered the policeman.

Ham Gow made a wry face—such an awfully wry face that Mr. Hamilton Gower hastened to say:

"I am very sorry for this inconvenience to you, old boy!—though it will last but a day or two. Tuesday, you know, is the first of September, when all this mystery of our own making will be cleared up. Have patience, old fellow, until you can turn the tables on your persecutors."

But Ham Gow screwed up his handsome face into the likeness of a nut cracker, and made no answer.

"Really, I would do anything in the world that I could do to relieve you of this inconvenience, but I cannot possibly do anything now, or here! Suppose, for instance, I should declare myself—who would believe me? There is no one here to identify me, except yourself, and you would not be believed under the circumstances! Nor even if we should succeed in convincing these officers of the truth, could they act upon their convictions? They have made the arrest, and they have to take their prisoner to Hawkeville. They have no discretionary power. Come, dear old boy, brace up! brace up! This will soon be over!" urged the young gentleman.

"Oh, you misjudge me altogether!" laughed Ham Gow' "Do you think I mind being arrested on the charge of murder, even such a murder? Oh, ye great, great guns and little whistles!—or a few days' imprisonment, which shall end in such discomfiture and ridicule of the Hawkeville Dogberries? No, indeed! I don't mind in the least being charged with a murder or so, now and then! Many a better man than Ham Gow has been so charged before this! But what grieves and humiliates my soul, oh, friend of my youth, is that I should be taken for an accomplice of Lewis Manton!"

"That is mortifying," gravely assented Lewis Manton's enemy.

"'Mortifying!' Mortifying isn't any name for it! Look here, Mr. Hamilton Gower! You have known me ever since we were little shavers together, and you will know what I am going to say to be the truth. I should have been poor, ragged, hungry, homeless and friendless, but for you, a good part of my life, but I never did keep bad company! And ,now to be pointed at as an accomplice of Lewis Manton, so-called Earl of Hawkewood, is—a little too much of the monkey!" complained the ex-tramp, with a very much injured air.

"Never mind, old fellow. You will disprove that charge as well as the other," said Mr. Hamilton Gower, cheerfully.

"Oh, yes! I shall disprove that charge and all the others. But when so much mud is thrown, and such black mud at that, some will stick. I shall go back to the colonies after this."

"Gentlemen, we don't want to be disagreeable, but we must take off our prisoner if we are to catch the down train to Penzance," said the policeman who had made the arrest.

"I will go down to Hawkeville with you, Ham," said the young gentleman.

"No, dear old man; please don't think of it! Pray stay here, and look after my wife a little. She will be coming home from the wax works presently, and will be frightened out of her senses if she should miss me and then hear what has happened. You wait here and meet her. Tell her I have left town on important business. If she should chance to hear of the visit of the policemen, explain to her that they have taken me off as an important witness for the claimant of an estate— for that is what they really are taking me for, whether they know it or not," added Ham Gow.

Mr. Hamilton Gower nodded.

"And when you come down on the thirtieth bring her with you, and take her to Demondike."

"I will do so," said the young gentleman.

"We must really be off! We have not five minutes to lose!" said the policeman.

"I am ready! And, indeed, old man, I am anxious to be off, before my wife returns here to discover these men, and to be frightened out of her wits! You can send my traps down by express," added Ham, as he wrung the hand of his friend, and turned to accompany the two policemen.

"Oh, see here!" impulsively exclaimed Mr. Hamilton Gower, forgetting all his former reasoning as soon as he saw his friend being led off. "This is supremely ridiculous, you know! You have arrested that man for the murder of one who is still living! Horace, sixteenth Earl of Hawkewood, is no more dead than I am!"

"Oh, come now, sir; that is a little too thin!" replied the policeman.

"But it is true, I tell you!" persisted the young gentleman.

"Beg pardon, sir; but if any other than a gentleman had made that statement I should think he was a fool, or took me for one!"

"Horace Hawke is still alive and well, I say, and is in London at this present time."

"All right, let him produce himself!"

"He can do so immediately. I am Horace Hawke, for whose murder you have arrested that man," earnestly declared Mr. Hamilton Gower.

"Oh, I dare say you are my granny, who has been dead this twenty years!" insolently laughed the policeman, who was fast losing respect for the "gentleman."

"I repeat that I am the Earl of Hawkewood, who was supposed to have been murdered. Your prisoner knows that I am so."

"You are chaffing us, sir, and we know it; and, begging your pardon, this is no subject for chaffing!" said the policeman, joining in the discussion for the first time.

"Ham Gow! Who am I? Tell these blockheads!" exclaimed the young gentleman, losing patience.

"You are Horace Hawke, sixteenth Earl of Hawkewood, my lord!" answered the prisoner.

"You hear?" said the young nobleman, turning to the two officers. Both those persons burst into a simultaneous laugh of derision.

"All right," said the elder one, ironically. "You prove that to the sitting bench of magistrates at Hawkeville to-morrow, and the charge against the prisoner will be instantly dismissed. For the present, we have got to do our duty and take away our prisoner, though all London were here to declare you to be the nobleman you claim to be! Come along, Gow!"

"You see, it is no use, my lord, I must go; but don't you mind it, for really I do not! It will all be right in a day or two," said Ham Gow, cheerfully.

"I knew it would be of no use to declare myself here; I felt that it would be wrong not to do so. However, will go down with you to Cornwall, and find a-plenty to identify me there."

"I beg you won't, sir ! Remember that the impression of you having been murdered has been so deeply stamped upon the minds of men that nothing but proof positive of the trick you and I played in changing characters will ever bring them to acknowledge you as the living earl who was supposed to have been murdered in his bed."

"Well, we will give the explanation!"

"But we cannot prove it without Delaplaine! You, being the claimant, would be an incompetent witness. I, being under arrest for the earl's murder, would be another. We must wait for Delaplaine, who is to meet us on the first at Hawke Hall."

"I believe you are right. I will not fail you on the first," said the young earl.

"And, meanwhile—poor Lona—my lord!"

"Yes, I will see to her."

"Now, good-night, my lord."

"Good-night, Ham ! God bless you, old fellow!"

"You, too, my lord."

The two policemen laughed incredulously at this dialogue, which they supposed to have been got up for their especial edification, as they led their prisoner off.

They had not been gone fifteen minutes, when Lona came running into the parlor, radiant from exercise and sight-seeing.

Finding Mr. Hamilton Gower alone she demanded:

"Where is Ham?"

"He has been suddenly called out of town on most important business. He left me here, Lona, to tell you so," explained the young gentleman.

"That is just the way he went off before!" impatiently exclaimed the young woman, sitting down and jerking off her gloves.

"You must not blame him, Lona. He was obliged to go," said the young gentleman.

"Why was he obliged to go off so suddenly without giving me a word of warning, just like he did before?"

"My dear girl, I would rather not tell you."

"It is another secret, I suppose, like the cause of his sudden night journey to Yorkshire."

"Yes, it is a secret for the present."

"I hate secrets, especially between husbands and wives!" said Lona, petulantly throwing off her bonnet.

"So do I; but they cannot be told, when they are other people's secrets, you know! But, never mind, you shall know all about this one in a day or two."

"Where has he gone this time? Up into Yorkshire again?"

"No; down in an opposite direction."

"When is he coming back?"

"Not for a week; business will detain him in the neighborhood that long at least; but I am to take you down to him to-morrow."

"Oh! what time to-morrow?"

"We can leave by the nine-eighteen express from Paddington."

"Oh! but where are we going?"

"Down to Southampton—first."

"Whatever business can Ham have in Southampton? If he had only prepared me!"

He had not time. He was called away too suddenly. He did not even take his valise with him. Asked me to express it to-night."

"Well, if we are to leave by the nine-eighteen, I must go and pack up. Are we to take our sea boxes?"

"I do not advise it. Leave them here in the care of the landlady. Take only a valise."

"Very well."

"And see here, my dear girl! The first thing you do will be to pack your husband's valise as quickly as you can, and let me have it. I must send that off to-night. He will want it the first thing in the morning."

"Very well," said Lona Gow, again, as she seized her bonnet and vanished from the room.

The young man lighted his meerschaum and began to smoke while he read the evening papers—a bad habit-not the reading, but the smoking, which he had picked up in the Australian gold fields and fastened upon himself on shipboard.

In a very short time, Lona Gow entered the room, bringing a well-packed portmanteau, which she placed upon the table before the young gentleman, and then, with a few words of earnest thanks for the trouble he was about to take on her husband's account, she left the parlor to resume her own preparations for the next day's journey.

Mr. Hamilton Gower put on his hat, took up the portmanteau, and conveyed it to the office of the Royal Parcel Express Co. (Ltd.), and there sent it off to Ham Gow, care of the governor of the Hawkeville House of Detention, as the county prison was called.

He returned to his inn to join Lona Gow in a *tête-à-tête* supper, after which they bade each other good-night, and separated to retire to rest.

Very early in the morning, Mr. Hamilton Gower was astir.

On entering the parlor he found Lona Gow already there, quite prepared for her journey, and the breakfast table waiting.

Lona returned his kind good-morning, and then rang for the coffee and accompaniments, which were promptly brought by the waiter.

Lona, eager as any child for a holiday, was too much excited by the thought of her journey to eat much.

She speedily dispatched her morning meal, and seemed to feel aggrieved that Mr. Hamilton Gower should take more time over his muffins and chops than she had done.

"Won't we miss the train, Mr. Gower?" she asked at length.

"Possible!" exclaimed the gentleman, starting up.

At the same moment the waiter entered and announced the cab that had been ordered to take them to the railway station.

In ten more minutes they were seated in that cab and bowling rapidly toward Paddington.

They caught their train. It was the express, which in the course of a few hours rushed them rapidly down toward Southampton.

Lona Gow was more aggrieved than ever. Mr. Hamilton Gower, wishing to indulge in his own thoughts, had supplied his companion with papers, magazines, cakes and fruits, and had left her to enjoy herself with them while he ensconced himself in a corner and gave his mind to reverie.

But Lona was no reader, and so she could not occupy herself with literature, nor could she munch cakes or suck oranges forever, so she sat there, sometimes staring out of the window at the fields, farmhouses and forests that seemed to rush past her as the train went on, and sometimes casting furtive glances at her silent escort, and putting questions, which he answered absently in monosyllables that were not always to the point.

So, when they reached Southampton, Lona heaved a great sigh of relief, and said:

"Now, then, let us go and find Ham! Perhaps he is on the platform waiting for us."

"Why—did you expect to see Ham here?" inquired Mr. Hamilton Gower, in surprise.

"Of course I did! When I asked where you were going to take me, you said to Southampton, and I expected to find him here, since we were following him," said Lona.

"And we are following him, but this is only the first stage of our journey. We are to go on to Penzance."

"Will we find him there?"

"No, my dear Lona; your husband is at Hawkeville."

"Then, why didn't you tell me so at first, Mr. Gower?"

"I thought I did tell you so. I had no intention to do otherwise. We will take the train for Penzance in a few minutes. Are you tired, Lona?"

"No, I am not tired of anything but of these sudden journeys of Ham! I am tired enough of them."

"Never mind! Courage! This will be the last one, I hope!" said Mr. Gower, as they stepped out of their compartment to the platform.

"I hope so, too!" answered Lona.

In a few more minutes they were on the express train for Penzance, where they arrived late that night.

There was no train for Hawkeville until the next morning. In fact, there were but four trains in the twenty-four hours on that little branch railroad, and the last one for the day had gone.

There was no alternative for the travelers but to put up at the Railroad Hotel for the night, which they reluctantly did.

At eight o'clock the next morning they entered upon "Hawkeville Special," and were soon flying over the last stage of their journey.

They reached the Hawkeville station at half-past nine. They happened to be the only passengers that got out there, before the train went thundering on its way further down the coast.

CHAPTER XXIX
THE BIRTHDAY

THIS was the morning of the first of September, and the twenty-first anniversary of the young Earl of Hawkewood's birth.

He cared no longer to continue the masquerade he had been enacting for the last two years.

To-day he would throw off all disguise, declare himself, prove his identity, claim his estates and vindicate the accused prisoners from the charge of his murder.

He stepped gayly off the train, handed his companion out, and, seeing no carriage at the station, inquired:

"Lona, do you think you can walk as far as Demondike?"

"Of course I can. Is Ham there?"

"No, Lona; Ham is probably at the court room in the town hall now—"

"Oh!"

"You remember that I told you he was called down here to attend a trial."

"Oh, yes, I remember," said the unsuspicious young woman.

"So I shall take you to Demondike and then walk over to see how the trial goes, and send Ham back to you when the court adjourns."

"I thank you very much, sir. Bother the court! When do you think it will adjourn?"

"It may not do so before a late hour in the afternoon."

"Very well; then you will send Ham to me, sir."

"Oh, yes!"

They were walking as briskly as young and strong muscles could carry them on the road to Demondike, where the earl, as we shall henceforth call him, chose to take Lona Gow, in preference to leaving her in the village hotel, where she would be in danger of hearing from some indiscreet gossip the present situation of her husband, and without the key to the mystery, would be terrified out of her senses at his apparent danger.

A brisk walk of three-quarters of an hour brought them to Demondike, where they found the old ruined watch tower looking just the same as it had looked on their last visit—as it had looked, in fact, for the last hundred years, and would look probably for the next hundred.

But this description refers only to the outside, which presented the base of a fallen tower situated on the edge of the cliff at the mouth of the raging torrent.

They opened the door and entered the strong room, where they found Old Nan seated in her big armchair, smoking a short pipe, and Young Nan busily engaged in packing.

The latter started violently on seeing the intruders; but on recognizing them she shut down the lid of the trunk she had been filling and advanced toward them.

The earl made her a sign to be on her guard, and then said:

"I have taken the liberty of a friend of the family to bring Mrs. Gow here to wait for her husband, who is attending a trial at the town hall."

"As a witness, you know, Nan. You don't mind my coming in this offhand manner, do you?" inquired Lona.

"No, child; no, I don't," replied Young Nan, with a tremor in her voice, for she knew that Ham Gow was arrested for murder, and she considered him in extreme danger.

"And she will not have long to wait. I pledge you my word to send Ham to you as soon as the court shall adjourn this afternoon," said the earl, to reassure Young Nan as well as to comfort Lona.

"Eh! What's that you say? Come here, you!" cried Old Nan, in a peremptory voice, as she took her pipe from her mouth, and struck her stick sharply upon the floor.

Laughing, the earl went to her, while Lona Gow still stood near the old woman, trembling, for she was very much afraid of Old Nan.

"Well, Mrs. Crook, here I am! What is your will with me?" inquired the earl, still laughing.

"Come here, you! I know you! And I knowed when you was here a month ago! You're the Airl o'Harkwood, you are!" said the old woman, snappishly.

"You are right, Mrs. Crook. I have no disposition to deny your statement. No! I thank you for recognizing me," said the earl, gravely enough now.

"You're the Airl o' Harkwood lawfully; but you're not the airl justly! No!" exclaimed the crone.

"Who, then, is the rightful heir, Mother Crook?" good-humoredly inquired the young earl.

"Your elder brother, my lord! Ham Gow!"

The young earl started violently and flushed to the top of his forehead.

However strongly he might have suspected his own relationship to the companion of his childhood, ever since hear- ing the story told by John Hice, it was terrible to have his suspicion confirmed so suddenly.

The crone continued to speak, regardless of her hearer's agitation.

"Yes! Ham Gow, the oldest living son of the late airl, by his first marriage with Radiance Gow! Ay! it was a gypsy marriage, you'll say, and not binding on the airl; but I say it was binding on the man! Ah! Ham Gow, if he had his just rights, would now be Airl o' Harkwood, and you, my lord, would be only the airl's younger brother, the Honorable Horace Hawke," said Old Nan, sharply.

The young earl found nothing to say to this tirade.

Old Nan continued:

"But law and justice is opposed to one another in this case, as they often is in others, sich as the law of excise and the justice of free trade, the law of landholders and the justice of free sile, the law o' game preserves and the justice of poaching, and so on, and so on, forever till the day of judgment!" fiercely exclaimed this old communist.

"But I could not reverse this order of things if I ever so ardently desired to do so," said the young earl, deprecatingly, glad that the subject had assumed a general, in place of a particular, character.

"Oh, I know you can't do nothing to alter it! If you was to try to put Ham Gow in your own shoes to-day the law wouldn't let him wear them. So Ham Gow must remain Ham Gow, and Horace Hawke must reign at Hawke Hall as the Right Honorable Airl of Harkwood!"

"I will do all that I can for my brother! Does he know his relationship to me?" inquired the lord.

"You may take your affidavy to it that he does! He has known it ever since he was a baby! I told him!"

"How did you know it?" now inquired the young earl for the first time.

"How!" exclaimed Old Nan, with a harsh laugh. "Wasn't I present at the marriage of Capt. Hawke and Radiance Gow? Didn't I know 'em when they lived at Brighton? Didn't I see 'em often and often at Boulogne? Wasn't I aboard o' Pierre Moreau's schooner *La Belle Femme*, lying at anchor just off the coast, when we saw the child carried off by the current, and Pierre offed with his pea-jacket and flung hisself overboard, and fished it out o' the sea and brought it to me?"

"And that child was Ham Gow?" inquired the young earl.

"It was Ham Gow, in course."

"Why did you not restore him to his father?"

"Why? That's a good un! The *Belle Femme* had a cargo o' French silks and brandies as we wanted to land on t'other side before daylight, and to be quick about it, too! And we didn't want to draw no partic'lar attention. Pierre Moreau upped anchor and steered for the English coast in about ten minutes after fishing the child out of the sea. It was a week or more before we heard how the child had got into the sea. Seems like the poor mother and her two children had got into one o' them shallopy boats what the 'longshoremen have for hire, and it was upset. The boatman saved the eldest boy, but the youngest, Ham, was carried out by the tide and picked up by Pierre Moreau, as I said, and the poor mother was drowned. It would ha' been well if Jack had been drowned, too, for he only lived to come to a worse fate!"

"You have heard the end of John Hice, then?"

"Haven't I? One of our boys in the free trading line o' business—I don't mind mentioning of it now, seeing as we have been druv to giv' it up, all along of Lewis Manton's interference—dog him! I'm glad he's going to be kicked, neck and heels, out'n Hawke Hall, and if you hadn't come back to do that, something better still would ha' happened to him, and he would ha' been hanged for your murder, and sarve him right! I wish you had kept dark, my lord, till the vilyan was hung, then you might have come back and claimed your own; but nothing could 'a' brought him back. That there's a mistake as can never be remedied If you'd only kept dark till he was hung for your murder, my lord!"

"But that would have sacrificed Ham " said the young earl, laughing despite the gravity of the subject.

"So it would. Ham would ha' had to swing alongside of him. I'm glad you have come back to kick Lewis Mantoa out."

"You were saying that you had heard of the fate of John Gow, known as Jack Hice—from one of your friends, I believe," suggested the young earl, who was desirous of finding out exactly how much of this history was known to the old woman.

"Yes, I was saying one of our boys who was sent over for seven years on account of his contempt of custom house, came back on the *Labrador*, after honorably sarving out his time, and he told me all about John Gow, and where he died and where he was buried. Well, he's at rest, anyway. But poor Ham!"

"I will do the best I can for my brother," said the earl.

"You're a good un, I'll say that for you, lad, though you do belong to an order which I ain't got much respects for, noway! 'Lords,' indeed! The imperence of 'em! When the youngest Sunday-school child knows as there ain't but one Lord over the heavens and the earth."

"I said before, Mother Crook, that I cannot reverse the order of society, if I wished to do so," said the young man, good-humoredly.

"No more you can't as I said before."

"Mother Crook, I have a few more questions to ask you. In the first place, why, when you discovered that the child you rescued was mourned as lost, you did not send word to the bereaved father that he was safe?"

"Mixed motives, such as rules the most of us. You see, we was on this side when the news was brought by a fishing smack that a boat had upset with a lady and two children, and that the eldest boy was saved, but the lady was drowned, and her body recovered, but as the youngest lad was drowned and his body washed out to sea and not found. This were full two weeks arter the ewent. I knowed well enough who the child was when I first seed him. That wasn't no news to me. But, you see, in those two weeks I had got fond of the lad. I allus had a fondness for chillun, like some people have for cats and dogs, and besides which I had a spite agin' Capt. Hawke for not making that gypsy marriage lawful by a Christian one; and so, partly out'n fondness for the boy and partly out'n spite agin' the father, I kept the child and never let on that he was alive."

"How came you first to the ruined watch tower?"

"Lor' bless you! the old tower, with the caves under it, had been used by the free traders for time out o' mind! And when I heard that Capt. Hawke had turned into the Airl o' Harkwood and married a dook's darter, I moved right over from St. Rosalie, where I had been living, and settled right down into this strong room and made it comfortable, and I kept guard over the smugglers' secrets."

"And did my—did the late earl ever find out that his son had been rescued from drowning?"

"Of course he did! Ah! I went and told him! But he was married then, as I said, and expecting of a legal heir every day. Ah! he would ha' taken the boy away from me, but I threatened exposure of him and his gypsy marriage. And so he left the lad with me, which was nothing but a baby anyway, you see! And he promised, when the lad was old enough, to see to his education and his setting up in life; but, lor', he died too soon to do anything for poor Ham."

"Did my—did the late earl suspect the smuggling operations in which you were engaged?"

"I reckon he did! And winked at 'em! Why, he were our best protector! He muzzled the steward, old Traverse, who had his suspicions, and would ha' set the constables on us an' it hadn't been for the airl putting of a muzzle on his mouth! And he'd ha' kept his word and edicated Ham if he'd lived long enough! Poor Ham!"

"I repeat that I will do the very best I can for my brother! But Ham is in no want of help. He was very successful in the gold fields. He is a rich man."

"Glad to hear it! But he is sorely in need o' help now, my lord! If it hadn't been as he is accused of murdering you, I don't know as I should ha' let on to you as I knowed who you was this time any more than I did the last time you was here, and I knowed you then!" said Old Nan.

The young earl arose and said:

"I must leave you now. I must hurry back to Hawkeville, and present myself as a witness at the court room."

"Werry well! And maybe when you have time you'll tell me how you come to be alive when we all thought as you were dead, and whose body that was as was thought to be stole and cut up by the doctors, and, most of all, why you vanished, and where you have been these two years!" said the old woman.

"I will leave Ham to tell you all that!" said the young earl, looking around for Lona.

But the two women had disappeared.

"They went out, just as you came to me. Did you think that I'd ha' spoken so free to you, if them wimmen had been listening with all their four ears cocked? Not likely! Didn't you know they were gone?"

"No, I never thought of them until this moment. Tell Lona that I will send Ham to her as soon as the court shall adjourn. She knows nothing of the accusation against him. She thinks he is there as a witness, and so he really is, though it was not as a witness that he was summoned, or, rather, arrested," said the young man.

And he once more turned to leave the room; but the evidences of impending removal, seen in the packed and half-packed boxes and trunks through which he had to pick his way, attracted his attention and excited his curiosity.

"Are you going to leave Demondike, after all these years ?" he inquired of the old woman.

"Yes! Didn't I tell you as Lewis Manton—may the fiend fly away with him!—broke up our free trading here? Ain't four of our boys caught and waiting their trial at the next assizes? Ain't Dennis Prout lost his situation as coast guardsman? Not as anything in this world can be proved agin' Dennis! But they charged him with neglect of dooty, and suspicioned him o' favoring the smugglers, and so they turned him off. Hows'ever, Dennis has saved a pretty penny, as we all has, for the matter o' that! And him and Nan is going to be married at last, and we are all a-going over to the Newlighted States of Americky, where there ain't no lords acknowledged, 'cept the One Lord as rules the universe! But, my lad—or my lord, if it must be so—hadn't you better be off to the courthouse?"

"Yes, yes; good-morning! I will see you again to say good-by before you go. By the way, when do you leave?"

"Next Monday."

"Oh, there'll be time enough, then. Good-morning."

"Good-morning. Go along now! You have wasted half an hour here."

The young earl walked out into the sunlight. He saw Young Nan and Lona Gow sitting down on an old boat on the sands, talking confidentially.

He merely raised his hat as he passed them, saying:

"Good-morning! I shall be sure to send Ham to you as soon as the court adjourns."

"Oh, do!" cried Lona, but her words scarcely reached his ears, he had walked on so rapidly.

He was absorbed in anxious thought. The strange revelations made to him by Old Nan Crook had disturbed him greatly, notwithstanding his long secret suspicion of the real relationship existing between himself and his beloved "tramp." But mere suspicion is one thing and assured knowledge another. Strong as was his attachment to this half brother, he felt glad to remember that Ham Gow had declared his intention to return to Australia and make that, prosperous colony his home.

Besides this, he had great source of anxiety in the continued silence of his late valet, Henri Delaplaine, who, as one of the chief witnesses to his identity, could scarcely be spared on this day; for a man whom the law, represented by a coroner's jury, had declared to have been murdered two years ago, and whose titles and estates had passed to his successor, would require something more than personal likeness to the earl who was supposed to have been assassinated, and the testimony of his accused assassin, to establish his identity and restore his rights.

He had written to Delaplaine before leaving Australia, and he had written again since arriving in England. He had directed his letters to the only address left him by the valet—"M. Henri Delaplaine, Barbièr et Coiffeur, Rue du Rivoli, Paris."

But no response in person or in writing had been received.

Now, suppose the ex-valet should be dead, or lost? How awkward for the young earl! Instead of being at once acknowledged as the Lord of Hawkewood, he might be looked upon as a mere adventurer, whom an accidental likeness to the murdered earl had tempted to take his name and claim his estates, and his very witness, Ham Gow, who was in custody for the murder of the earl, might be considered as his accomplice in the intended fraud. He might be put through endless and ruinous lawsuits, he might even be prosecuted in the criminal courts for fraud!

He might have to pay very dearly for his two years' frolic.

Heaven only knew how it would all end, unless Mr. Henri Delaplaine would come forward to identify his late master, and tell the story of his masquerading exchange of character with Ham Gow!

But where was Mr. Henri Delaplaine, and why did he not come or write?

Why?

"Heaven of heavens!" exclaimed the young earl, as the answer came with the shock of a terrible revelation to his memory!

Had he not heard in that story told by the camp fire in the gold diggings, by Ham Gow, that the valet, Henri Delaplaine, had been accused of being an accomplice with Gow in the earl's murder? Was not Henri Delaplaine even now a fugitive from justice?

Could he be found?

And even supposing that he could be produced, would not his place be in the dock, rather than on the witness stand?

The young earl wondered how he could have forgotten this circumstance.

And now his position seemed to him to be very doubtful and difficult.

He was dead in law, and his witnesses were accused of his murder. Should he come forward now and declare himself to be living, and call upon them to identify and tell the story of the little comedy they had all enacted together on the night of his birthday ball, he would be considered an impostor and they his accomplices!

The prospect looked so dark and threatening that the young man turned pale and cold, and walked slowly on, dragging one foot after the other, with a gliding motion.

Verily, he looked like the ghost of himself! He had shaved off his heavy black beard, and now wore only a light mustache upon his upper lip, and he had trimmed his hair and gotten rid of the sunburn of the sea voyage, and he looked at this moment the very facsimile of the sickly youth who had changed characters with the tramp and run away two years ago.

But he did not realize this! He walked, or rather glided, on along the beach, with his head upon his breast, his hands in his pockets, and his mind absorbed in painful reverie so deeply that he was unconscious of the approach of others, until his ears were assailed by loud voices—though they were not speaking to him.

"Promised to go and see the women 'fore they left for, 'Meriky!" said the voice of Penn, the locksmith.

"Well, I thought, being an idle day, as I'd stroll over and see how they was a-takin' of this new misfortin'. I don't think as they'll be going off to 'Meriky, leaving poor Ham in the lurch, till he's hanged, or 'quitted, or somethink," drawled the deep tones of Tree, the tanner.

"I was only gwine to offer my sarvices, if belike I could be of any use," piped the wheezing whistle of little Old Proddy, the cobbler.

But all these men, whatever other individual motives they might have had for visiting the Ruined Tower at this crisis, were simultaneously moved by curiosity.

The young earl raised his pale face and looked at them.

There was a unanimous yell and flight.

"Lord betune us and harm!" cried little Penn.

"Hail Mary, full of grace!" rapidly intoned Tree, as he scudded away after Penn.

"Lord spare my life this time, and I will try to be a better old man!" whimpered the little cobbler, Proddy, falling upon his knees, and hiding his panic-stricken face in his hands.

This incident made a revolution in the spirits of the young earl.

"These men have recognized me fast enough; only they have taken me for a ghost," he laughed, as he strode rapidly away.

He would have stopped to speak to Old Proddy, only he was afraid of frightening the old man into fatal fits before he could succeed in convincing him that the supposed disembodied spirit was incased in solid flesh and blood, and besides, he was in a very great hurry to reach Hawkeville.

Ten minutes later he entered the village, which he found in the highest excitement over the great event of the time.

There was no pretense of doing any sort of business or work.

Men were gathered at street corners, and women at each other's door step, and all were eagerly discussing the arrest of the Earl of Hawkewood for the murder of his predecessor.

The young nobleman made his way rapidly through all this hubbub, occasioning a shriek now and then from some woman who fancied she saw his ghost, and so at length he reached the town hall, where the bench of magistrates were sitting.

He pushed through the crowd that surrounded the building, and told the officer who guarded the door that he was a witness for the defense, and must have way made for him to the witness box.

"You will please pass around to the side door, sir, which will lead you right where you want to go," civilly replied the man.

The young earl followed this direction and went down an alley that led to a door in the side of the building.

To the man on guard here he told the same story, and was at once admitted.

This door opened directly into the crowded court room, where the magistrate was holding the preliminary examination of the accused prisoners.

But the first object that struck the sight of the young earl was the dock, in which stood, side by side, Lewis Manton, called Earl of Hawkewood, Ham Gow, and-Henri Delaplaine.

CHAPTER XXX
AMAZEMENT

COMING from the broad daylight into the semi-darkness of the crowded court room, the dazzled vision of the young nobleman could at first perceive nothing but a floor of heads so close together that one might have walked over them without tottering.

The first distinct figures that he recognized were those of the three prisoners, whom he only saw plainly because they were in the dock a few feet above the level of the crowd and on the opposite side of the room, and in a direct line with the door by which he entered and through which a bright sunbeam fell upon them.

But when the door was closed, and the light was excluded, all the scene became obscure again until his eyes grew accustomed to the half light.

"I am a witness for the defense," he said to an officer, who was in attendance.

"Then, you are the only one, I'm thinking, sir; but this is just the preliminary examination before the justices, you see," replied the man.

"I am aware of that. Where shall I sit?"

"Here, if you please, sir."

The young earl took the indicated seat.

As the scene cleared before him, he perceived three magistrates on the bench, the presiding one being old Mr. Oliver Ball, whose round, white head and round, red face were easily recognized. The two other magistrates were strangers to him.

There was a discussion going on in a rather low tone that prevented its purport from reaching his ears.

Turning his attention from the bench to the dock, he took careful note of the prisoners there.

Lewis Manton, so-called Earl of Hawkewood, looked as pale as death, kept his eyes fixed upon the floor and shuddered with every appearance of conscious guilt. If he were not a criminal, he was certainly a coward.

Ham Gow, on the contrary, stood erect, not with defiance, but with a face full of fun, as if he exceedingly enjoyed the joke, and he never looked down except in the effort to suppress an explosion of laughter. If the ex-tramp had not been there upon the gravest of all charges, he might have been committed for contempt of court—that is, if a man could be committed for the inward laughter that gleamed from the corners of his dark eyes and bearded mouth.

Henri Delaplaine, evidently taking courage from the guilty looks of the "earl," as well as from the merry aspect of the tramp, stood up in rather a theatrical attitude of heroism, with his chest thrown out, his arms folded, his head thrown back, and his eyes rolling calmly over the scene.

Withdrawing his glance from the dock, the young earl turned it upon persons seated nearer to himself. In a form directly in front of him, and with their backs toward him were seated the Rev. Paul Laude; Dr. Ellis, the family physician of Hawke Hall; the Rev. Mr. Vincent, rector of Hawkeville Old Church; Stepney, a footman formerly in the service of the "late" earl; and two stout matrons, servants from the Hall. These were the witnesses for the prosecution, he knew, and what an array there was to prove that Lewis Manton had murdered a man who was at that moment sitting behind them, alive and well.

Evidently the trial or investigation had already made some progress, the charge upon which the warrants for the arrest of the accused were issued had been read, and had been met by denial on the part of the prisoners; probably the minutes of the coroner's inquest which had sat upon the body of the "murdered earl" had also been read, and followed by the little discussion that was going on between the justices on the bench when the young earl had entered the court room and taken his seat.

Now, that discussion was over, and the oily voice of the bullet-headed Justice Ball was heard to say:

"Let the Rev. Dr. Paul Laude take the stand."

The doctor slowly arose, and reared his tall, grand form, until it towered above the highest head in the room, and stepped forward.

The oath was duly administered, and then Mr. Ball said informally— for this was but a preliminary investigation:

"Dr. Laude, you will please tell us all you may happen to know of the homicide at Hawke Hall."

"I know nothing whatever of that homicide, beyond the patent fact that my ward, the late Earl of Hawkewood, was certainly murdered there on the morning of the second of September, 18-, two years since," answered the doctor.

"Oh! you know that, do you?" said the young earl to himself, while in the dock Lewis Manton shuddered, Ham Gow chuckled and Henri Delaplaine twirled his mustache.

"Then," said the magistrate, "tell us something of your connection with the house, and any circumstances bearing, directly or indirectly, upon the homicide that may have come to your knowledge."

The reverend doctor cleared his throat, and began:

"My name is Paul Laude; my age is sixty-eight years; I am a clergyman of the Established Church; I took my degree twenty years ago, at Old Trinity, Oxford.

"For fourteen years, and up to two years since, I was resident guardian and tutor of the late youthful Earl of Hawkewood.

"I remember the morning of the homicide. There had been a birthday ball on the night before, and the revelry was kept up until about three o'clock in the morning.

"When all the guests had departed except those who were to stay all night, I retired to my chamber in the bachelors' corridor. That was the place where all the guests who were single men were quartered.

"On that night no one was lodged in the bachelors' corridor except myself, my ward and Mr. Lewis Manton. My ward, the earl, had the rooms exactly opposite to mine. A few doors further up the corridor, and nearer the main upper hall, were Mr. Lewis Manton's rooms."

"On which side?" inquired the presiding justice.

"On the same side as the late earl's," replied the doctor.

"Proceed with your testimony," said Mr. Ball.

"Well, sir, about two hours after I had retired to bed, when all the household might be supposed asleep, I was roused from a light slumber by a slight noise in the corridor. If it had been a frank, pronounced noise I should have stirred to investigate it; but this was a low, cautious clicking, as of some one trying to pick a lock, or turn a key without being heard.

"I thought the sound a very suspicious one, and I got out of bed, threw on my gown and took a taper and went out into the passage. There I saw Mr. Lewis Manton standing outside the door of my ward, evidently trying to open it.

"He started when he saw me and muttered something to the effect that he had lost his way, and mistaken that room for his own. I directed him aright, and went back to bed."

"Do you remember how the prisoner was dressed on that occasion?" inquired the magistrate.

"Perfectly. He wore a crimson satin dressing gown and a black velvet smoking cap with a heavy gold tassel."

"How is it that you have such a perfect memory of this costume? Are you usually so observant of dress, reverend sir?" sarcastically inquired Lawyer Poinsett, who had been engaged to watch the case for the earl.

"Not usually. But on that occasion the richness and gaudiness of the dress attracted my attention, and, if you will have it, my disapprobation. I hated to see a young man in a Christian country dressed in the gaudy trappings of a heathen. That is the reason why I noticed and re- membered the costume. My ward and myself wore black serge or gray flannel gowns—when we wore any," replied the doctor.

"Ah!" exclaimed the lawyer, derisively.

"I think that this is really all that I have to give in evidence; at least it is all that I know even remotely bearing upon the case," said the doctor, addressing himself to the bench.

"Then you may withdraw from the stand, reverend sir; but oblige us by remaining in the room," replied the presiding justice.

Dr. Laude came down and resumed his seat.

"Charles Stepney will take the stand," called out the clerk, in obedience to the direction of the magistrate.

The footman from the Hall arose and went forward, and testified to having been the last servant up in the house that night, to the best of his knowledge and belief.

He said that the prisoner, Henri Delaplaine, had threatened, in his hearing, to make something handsome out of the earl that night.

That later on, when he thought the whole household had retired, and he himself had put out the last light, and was going upstairs with a bedroom candle in his hand, the candle had dropped out of its socket and in falling had become extinguished.

That he groped along slowly and cautiously in the dark until he reached the bachelors' corridor, through which he had to pass in going to his own attic chamber.

That when he reached the bachelors' corridor, where a dim light was burning at one end, he saw the valet, Delaplaine, steal cautiously along toward his master's door and open and enter the room, followed by another person whom he could not identify.

He said that he thought nothing of it at the time, nor did he, until after the murder had been discovered, understand the significance of what he had seen, when taken in connection with what he had overheard.

The footman was cross-examined by Mr. Poinsett, but without weakening his testimony.

Dr. Ellis was then called and testified:

"I was present when the late Countess of Hawkewood, then Lady Volante Belle Isle, gave her testimony under oath, to the fact that at six o'clock on the morning of the murder, as she was passing through the bachelors' corridor, she saw a man, in crimson satin dressing gown and a black velvet cap with a gold tassel, come out of the late earl's room. But she was not near enough to identify the man. The evidence of this lady was taken down in writing, and signed before several persons, who affixed their signatures as witnesses.

"This document is in the hands of the police authorities, and can be procured for reference," concluded the physician.

"Jane Carraway," called out the voice of the clerk, and one of the stout women whom the earl had noticed among the witnesses for the prosecution got off the form and waddled up to the stand.

Being sworn, she testified:

"My name is what the clerk called me by, and I have been housekeeper at the Hall this thirty years or more, being sixty years of age now, and not a-growing any younger.

"I memorize the murder of my dear young master, the late earl, and all I have got to say about that, as I know well enough who done it, though not being able to swear to the same, through not being allowed to swear what I know inside of myself, but only to what I have seen or heard, and hopes as the grand villyan will be hung, and wishes as he could be drawn and quartered as well, which he richly deserves to be burned up at the stakes! And—if I had my will of him, he should be tored by wild horses and gored by wild bulls!"

Here the torrent of the woman's words was arrested by the stern reproof of the presiding justice, and she was told to keep to what she had seen and heard in connection to the homicide.

"I never saw nothing but the dead body of my poor dear massycreed master!" sobbed the witness.

("Oh, you saw that, did you?" muttered the young earl to himself, with an inward laugh.)

"And what I heard," proceeded the witness, "was from the mouth of the poor, dear, departed countess herself, and she on her ill bed, as it might 'a' been her deathbed, with all she had seen and heard to break her heart and crack her brain, being tied up, till death do 'em part, along with a 'sassinator!"

Again the woman was severely reproved by the bench, and told to restrict her statement to facts.

"I am, your worship! Ain't it every bit a fact I'm telling of you, and me on my oath? Yes, sir, I do memorize the day as my new mistress, the late young Countess of Hawkewood, was brought home to Hawke Hall! I do memorize that of all the five hundred days in the year, it was the very day of the hamnaversly of my dear young master's murder, and they was to have a festywall on the grounds! But it didn't turn out to no good.

"That night, after all the visitors had gone home, except the duke and duchess, as were to stay all night, I was suddenly startled by hearing some one scream out most fearful!

"I was at my supper, but I ran up the back stairs as hard as I could go, and on toward the bachelors' corridor, where the screams came from.

"And there I sees the earl, with the countess in his arms, a-taking of her toward her room.

"'And is it highstrikes, my lord?' sez I.

"'I don't know,' he said, as he laid her on the bed. 'Stay by her and do what is proper, while I go to look for the duchess.'

"And he went out and left me alone with the lady."

"Did you notice how his lordship was dressed on that occasion?" inquired one of the magistrates.

"Ay, I did, sir! He were dressed in a flaming red satin gown and a black velvet cap, and a glistening gold torsel, all as one with any of them circus men, which I thought at the time was misbecoming of a Christian nobleman."

"Go on. What occurred when you were left with the countess?"

"I soon brought her to, sir, your worship, which I was allers well beknown for my skill with fainting fits and high-strikes. And which her ladyship's first words were wild enough, for she were like one distracted!

"'He was the man I saw coming out of the earl's room on the night of the murder! He was the assassin of his cousin!'

"'Who be your ladyship talking about, my lady?' for I did think as she were off her head.

"'Him! Lewis Manton! Him I charge with the murder of the late earl!' she cried, fierce-like, staring at me with her great black eyes.

"'Oh, dear, my lady, your ladyship don't know what you're saying of,' says I, feeling sure then as she was out of her mind.

"'What have I said? Oh, what have I said?' she cried, starting up and trying to fling herself out of bed.

"I had seen highstrikes afore then, but nothing like what followed that! It was awful, she flung herself about so! I could scarcely keep her in bed.

"But presently my lord came in with the duchess, and at the sight of him her ladyship went off worse than ever and began to charge him with some crime that she did not name then, and suddenly, from violent convulsions, she fell into unconsciousness.

"And then I was sent out of the room, and never saw my lady for weeks, and never heard her repeat the charge she made on that wild night. That is all I know about it, your worship; but there are some here as knows more."

This witness was freely cross-examined; but the process only strengthened her testimony, and brought out additional items that weighed heavily against the accused, for when Mr. Poinsett inquired:

"You say, witness, that when her ladyship came to her senses she never repeated the charge she had made in her delirium?"

"No, your honor, I didn't say anything of the sort, begging your pardon; but I said after that I never saw her ladyship for weeks, and never heard her repeat the charge," replied the witness.

"Ah! When did you see her ladyship next?"

"The day on which the duchess took her away to Belle Isle. My lady called me into her room and told me she was going away for a change, and said she meant to raise my wages, and she presented me with one of her own Ingy shawls, which was worth fifty pound if it was worth a shilling, and I was quite flustered with all this graciousness and couldn't return thanks enough, nor make courtesies enough to show my thankfulness, until my lady says to me; says she:

"'I hope, Carraway, that you have not repeated to anyone any words of mine that I might have uttered in my fever on the night when I was taken ill?' says she.

"And then I knowed what she meant, and I knowed, too, that she hadn't spoken them charges when she was off her head, for people never remember what they have said in such states, and I knowed also why my lady raised my wages and gave me her Ingy shawl; but I replies, very solemn:

"'I hope I know my place better than to indulge in such werry improper gossip.'

"'I am glad to hear it, and I hope you will never speak of this matter; it would be very wrong to do so; I shall depend on your discretion, Carraway,' says my lady.

"And I promised never to mention what had passed in the sick room that night, and I never would ha' done so, your honor, if I hadn't been fetched here on my oath," concluded the housekeeper.

"You may sit down," shortly exclaimed the lawyer.

Mrs. Possett, the sick nurse, was called, and, being sworn, testified:

"My name is Ellen Possett, my age forty years. I have lived in this neighborhood all my life. I am a sick nurse by trade.

"I was called on the third of September, one year ago, to attend upon the late Countess of Hawkewood at Hawke Hall. I was with her ladyship during the whole of her illness.

"I never saw her ladyship out of her head once while I was in attendance on her. She was nervous and excitable, but never insane. I heard her on several occasions, when she was very much excited, charge his lordship, the Earl of Hawkewood, with the murder of his cousin, the late earl.

"She never charged him with the crime to his face, but if he ever came into her room she would shriek and cover up her head to keep from seeing him; and then when he would go out of the room she would mutter to herself:

"The assassin! he knows that I know he murdered his cousin, Horace, and he dares to come here and torture me by his presence."'

"Were these strange charges ever made in the presence of a third party?" inquired Mr. Poinsett.

"Not when I was one of the three, sir. And I don't think she ever made them in the presence of her grace the duchess, who seemed to be all at sea as to what could have caused her ladyship's sudden hatred of his lordship."

"You were with the late Countess of Hawkewood in her last illness, I think," said the presiding magistrate. "Tell us what occurred on the last day of her ladyship's life."

"Yes, your worship. It was afternoon. My lady was very low. The little infant, Viscount Hawke, had died the day before, and he was lying in his little casket on a table at the foot of his mother's bed. She would not allow him to be removed.

"There were in my lady's chamber about half a dozen people—his lordship the earl, his grace the young duke, her ladyship the Lady Victoria Belle Isle, the attendant physician (Dr. Ellis), and the sick nurse, which was myself, your honors. And we were all watching and expecting that every breath would be her last, when all of a sudden she opens her great black eyes—and awfully large and solemn they looked in her thin, white face—and she said:

"'I desire that everybody shall leave this room except the doctor and the nurse.'

"And after a little consultation with Dr. Ellis, by his advice they all did go out, leaving me and Dr. Ellis with the dying lady. Then she whispered:

"'I have no strength to write, or to sign my name, or to make a mark; my hands are already cold and dead.'

"I took one of her hands and Dr. Ellis the other, and we rubbed them. After a little she whispered again:

"'I cannot go out of this world and take with me a secret which may leave the innocent to suffer for the guilty. Bend your ears, both of you, and listen to my dying words.'

"We stooped nearer, and she whispered:

"'The secret that has cost me my life and the life of my little child, is this—that I know the present Earl of Hawkewood murdered the late earl. I saw him leave the room of the murdered man in the darkness before day on the morning of the murder. I did not know it was he then, but I knew it later. A few weeks ago I charged him with the crime, and he denied it and attempted to explain his pres- ence

348

there; and his denial imposed on me for a while, but here on my deathbed the conviction is strong upon me that he did the deed. If any other man should be brought to trial for that crime, I charge you to make this my dying declaration public; but—otherwise—keep it secret still; I only wish to shield the innocent—and Gow and Delaplaine are innocent—I do not-wish to—'

"And then, your honors, she lost her speech forever. Dr. Ellis went to the door and called in her friends, who gathered around the bed. But her eyes were fixed and her breath coming in gasps, and in a few minutes she was gone," concluded the witness.

The effect of her testimony was electrical. The air became alive with the buzz of voices. It is true that rumors of this deathbed declaration of the countess had prevailed and gained ground for weeks past; for the sick nurse had probably not been so reticent as prudence might have dictated to her to be; so the people were in a measure prepared for the revelation; yet still to hear the rumor confirmed by evidence given under oath produced the most profound sensation.

The presiding magistrate gave an order that silence should be enforced or the hall should be cleared.

This order had the effect of striking the spectators dumb for the time being; and then Mr. Poinsett began to worry the witness on the stand.

"You have a most wonderful memory, Mrs. Possett, to be able to repeat, word for word, that dying declaration of the late countess— that dying declaration which was never taken down in writing! How is it that you can repeat this lesson so well?" he sarcastically demanded.

"Your honors, I have repeated the last words of the Countess of Hawkewood, to the best of my knowledge, and that is all I can do. But your honors have a better witness than me. There is Dr. Ellis, as also heard the words," replied Ellen Possett.

"Dr. Ellis will please to take the stand," said the presiding magistrate.

The Hawkeville physician came forward, and, after being duly sworn, corroborated in every respect the testimony of the previous witness; it is unnecessary to give his words here, as in substance they were but a repetition of those of his predecessor on the stand.

"What do you take to have been the mental condition of the late countess at the time of her making the dying statement?" inquired the presiding justice.

"Her ladyship was perfectly sane, though much distressed in mind," replied the doctor.

"Have you at any time seen any evidence of mental weakness or mental aberration on the part of the late countess?"

"Never, your honor, though I knew her ladyship from the day that she was born until the day that she died; having been the medical attendant of her family when they were at Castle Belle Isle the greater part of every year, for twenty years. And I must say this for her ladyship, that I never knew a woman of any rank or any age of a sounder, better balanced or more practical mind than was the late Countess of Hawkewood."

The doctor was then permitted to withdraw.

CHAPTER XXXI
A DARK DEFENSE

THE three magistrates consulted together in a low tone and then the presiding justice, addressing the chief prisoner, said:

"You have heard the charge and the testimony against you. What have you now to say in explanation or defense?"

The so-called Earl of Hawkewood arose in his place, every eye turned upon him.

He stood there with a face as pale as his very light, flaxen hair; his light-blue eyes bent upon the floor, his long, thin fingers clutching the front of the dock; his whole slight form trembling like a sapling in the wind.

His voice was low and quivering as he began to speak:

"Yes, I have an explanation to make—an explanation of the action and the motive of that action, which has placed me in this humiliating position—false position, I should say.

"To make this explanation clear I must go back to the days when I was traveling in the East, with my tutor-not a clergyman, as most traveling tutors are, but a man devoted to science and especially to what are called 'occult sciences'—to astrology as a matter of detail.

"We were in Aleppo, where, among other interesting persons to be seen, was an astrologer famous for the accuracy of his horoscopes. Even the deriders of his 'science' never called him an impostor.

"I went with my tutor to see this wonderful personage. Curiosity impelled me to have my future forecast.

"He told me, or he foretold me, of every event of importance that has since happened to me—of the early death of my father, who, indeed, died before my return to England; of my sudden and unexpected inheritance of wealth, landed estates and titles; of my marriage with a lady of great beauty and high rank; and finally, of a series of terrible misfortunes that would happen to me in the second year of

351

my marriage; of the loss of my wife and child by sudden death, and of a heavier calamity still—of my own apprehension and trial for the deepest crime known to the law—the heinous crime of murder.

"He either could not, or would not, tell me how that criminal trial was destined to terminate; whether I should be acquitted or convicted of murder; or even whether I should deserve the one or the other fate. He answered to all my questions in his professional jargon:

"'The celestial sphere is veiled, the seer can see no more.' And so he took his fee and dismissed me; but I looked on the dark side.

"You may wonder when I tell you that even then, before one of those predictions had been fulfilled to justify my forebodings, my mind was darkened and depressed, when in obedience to the powers of a magician, these

'Forthcoming events cast their shadows before.'

"But, then, I was superstitious by nature and by—training, I was about to say. At least, the constant association of a traveling tutor given to the study of the 'occult sciences' fostered a morbidly speculative disposition within me."

Here the speaker paused for a moment, passed his long, thin hand over his forehead, and resumed:

"Do you ask me what all this has to do with the crime imputed to me? You will soon hear.

"My father was in the prime of life, being scarcely forty-two years of age. He was of a very robust constitution and had the finest health, never having had a day's illness in his life. He had no dangerous habits, was not a fox hunter, was not a heavy feeder or a hard drinker. In fact, he had every prospect of living to be ninety or a hundred years of age. I could hardly believe in that portion of the astrologer's prophecy.

"Yet the first news that met me on my return to England was that my father had been killed in a railroad collision, when on his journey to meet me on my landing at Southampton!

"I will not speak of the sorrow that overwhelmed me at that time. It has nothing to do with this case. But I must speak of the horror that darkened my soul and obscured my reason, as I brooded morbidly over this unexpected fulfillment of the astrologer's prediction."

("Ah! ha! he's going to set up the plea of insanity! It won't do, my lord! That game is played out!" muttered more than one of the spectators, in these or other words to the same effect.)

"If the first unlikely prediction had been fulfilled, then all the others might be. But only one of these troubled me. It was not, you may be sure, that I was to come suddenly into the possession of wealth, land and title, nor was it that I should wed a lady of high birth and great beauty; for no one could object to such good fortunes as those; nor yet that I should lose both wife and child in the second year of marriage, for no one can become very deeply interested in an imaginary wife and child.

"No! that which oppressed my soul almost to melancholy madness was the prediction announcing the murder! It haunted my mind both day and night, took away my appetite, prevented my sleep.

"I became very morbid. I read nothing but murder trials past and present. I thought that no earthly prosperity would be of any worth to me if my short career was to end in the awful way foretold and foreshadowed by the astrolo- ger; for though he only foretold the trial, and could not, or would not, tell anything beyond, I felt that he foreshadowed what I cannot even breathe here in connection with myself.

"My mind was becoming diseased on this subject; the more so that I was obliged to brood over it in silence. Any other mental trouble I might have confided to my minister; any other bodily ailment to my physician. But this trouble, preying on both mind and body, I was compelled to keep to myself. I could not tell it to anyone.

"I sought forgetfulness in society, in travel, in wine, but found it never. It was about fifteen months after this prediction had been made, and about twelve months after the first part of it had been fulfilled in the death of my father, that I was invited to attend the birthday festival of my cousin, the late Earl of Hawkewood, and I accepted the invitation and went to Hawke Hall on that fatal occasion.

"Now all that I have told you leads up to the explanation of my conduct at that time.

"I was really glad to make friends with my cousin after a family feud of three generations. And I should have enjoyed the festival had I not been overshadowed by the astrologer's prophecy of evil.

"The ball was kept up, as you know, to a very late hour of the night, or rather to an early hour of the morning. I—according to a custom I was but too readily falling into—drank too much wine, and perhaps too much of stronger liquors.

"Thus it happened that when I left my room I lost myself in the labyrinth of halls and corridors on the second floor, and as there seemed to be no servants at hand, it was some time before I got back into the bachelors' corridor, where my room was situated.

"Then, by the most natural mistake, I went to my cousin's door instead of to my own, and was trying to open it cautiously for fear of disturbing my fellow lodgers, when I was startled by the sudden opening of the opposite door and the appearance of Dr. Laude.

"He saw the situation at once, told me I had mistaken the door, and directed me to my own.

"I went to my room and went to bed, but some hours later became so ill that I had to rise to seek relief. I wanted a bottle of seltzer water. I had no idea where to find one, or where to look for a servant who would get me one.

"I was too ill to stand on ceremony; so I arose, threw on my dressing gown and smoking cap, and went to my cousin's door to rap him up, and to ask him how I could get the seltzer.

"I could scarcely walk, I was so ill; but I reached his door at last and rapped. There was no answer. As I rapped a little harder, the door swung open. It had not been locked, or even latched.

"With the privilege of a kinsman, I entered the room. There was a night light burning on the mantelpiece, and its feeble rays fell directly on the bed, whose crimson satin curtains were festooned back.

"I approached the bed, calling Horace, softly. There was no answer. I drew nearer, and then beheld a sight that seemed to turn me into stone with its horror! There lay my cousin, dead, with a ghastly wound on the forehead, and his blanched face and black hair surrounded by a pool of curdled blood.

"I stood there for—I know not how long or short a time—congealed with horror! I took in the whole terrible truth at a glance! He had been murdered! He was dead beyond recovery!

"And then, with the rush of a torrent, came the consciousness of great danger to myself! I remembered that the law, in looking for the perpetrator of a mysterious murder, always casts its eyes first upon the person who was supposed to be the most to be benefited by the death of the murdered victim.

"Who, in this case, was to be most benefited by the death of Horace, Earl of Hawkewood? Clearly no other than myself, Lewis Manton, the heir presumptive of his estates! And had not the astrologer foretold that I should be tried for murder and foreshadowed that I should be executed for it?

"All these thoughts, I say, rushed through my mind with the force of a raging torrent. I lost my self-possession! I became, for the time being, distraught! Instead of giving the alarm as I should have done, I fled from the room and hurried to my own, lest anyone should find me near the scene of the homicide! I locked myself in, and fell upon my bed, where I lost all sense of bodily suffering in the mental anguish that consumed me.

"I confess it now! I was afraid of being accused of this murder, of being tried for it, doomed to death for it!

"I was haunted by the horrible fear that some night watcher, like myself, might have seen me enter or leave my murdered cousin's room, and that the fact would come out as soon as the murder should be discovered.

"I dreaded the morning, dreaded to face the assembled household as if I had really been guilty of that dark deed of which I so much dreaded to be suspected! I was the latest up that morning; I did not leave my room until I had been three times called.

"When at length I went downstairs I found the whole family circle assembled with the exception of the host, for whom they were waiting.

On my appearance, Dr. Laude declared that we should wait no longer for the laggard, and he sent Pelton, the groom of the chambers, to call him.

"But why should I recur to what many of you here know so well? You, Dr. Ball, were on the spot, as well as Dr. Laude and others. You all remember the terrible dismay and confusion that ensued upon the return of Pelton with the awful announcement that his master, the young earl, lay murdered on his bed.

"I was not guilty, yet I am sure I must have looked most guilty to anyone who might have had leisure to notice me.

"You all know what followed. The house invaded by the police; the investigation; the coroner's inquest; the verdict of willful murder against Gow and Delaplaine!

"I had shut myself up in the library with a bottle of brandy and another of soda water, and there I sat and drank all day, dreading, every time the door opened, to see an officer come in to arrest me for the murder of my cousin.

"But when, in the evening, the verdict of the coroner's jury was rendered, and warrants were issued for the apprehension of Gow and Delaplaine, I felt infinitely relieved. I came out of my retirement to assume my place as master of the house and to perform my duties as host. I inquired about the evidence upon which the two men, Gow and Delaplaine, had been accused, and, when I heard it, I believed then, as I believe now, that they, and they alone, were guilty of the earl's murder.

"I felt quite easy, on my own account, until a few days afterward, when the Lady Volante Belle Isle, who had been present at the breakfast table when the murder was announced, and had been so overwhelmed by the shock as to have been prostrated on a bed of sickness for nearly a week, recovered, and demanded to see a magistrate, and to make a statement to him under oath.

"You all know what that statement was. She had been twice in the vicinity of the bachelors' corridor on that fatal night, or morning, before daylight.

"On the first occasion she had seen the earl open his chamber door and dismiss Gow and Delaplaine, giving them full directions of the shortest route through the park, and she had heard him close his chamber door and lock it after them.

"On the second occasion, two hours later, she was again in sight of the door, which was again opened, and this time by a man in a crimson satin dressing gown and a black velvet cap and gold tassel—a man with a ghastly pale face and trembling form—who stole along the corridor with a most guilty air.

"She did not recognize the man, nor did she at the moment suspect him of having committed a crime. It was only after the discovery of the murder that she did know the full significance of what she had seen.

"But I knew that she had seen me, and I was filled with dread lest she should in some moment of mental illumination recognize and identify me, and I should be brought to trial and convicted of my cousin's murder under deceptive circumstantial evidence.

"She did not even suspect me, however. You all know that some months later I married this lady; but that moment of mental illumination which I had dreaded was destined to come.

"You have heard from several witnesses what occurred on the first night after I had brought my wife home to Hawke Hall.

"But I must tell it to you from my point of view. When all the festivities were over and our guests had retired to bed, and my wife was in her chamber, I went into my smok- ing room to indulge in a cigar. This smoking room, I need scarcely tell you, was situated in the bachelors' corridor.

"I happened there to find my old crimson satin wrapper and black velvet cap. I really had forgotten that I had worn these things on the fatal night of the murder, of which this night was the anniversary.

"I threw off my dress coat and put on the wrapper and cap and sat down to smoke. I felt so comfortable that my one cigar grew to two or three. I was still smoking when the sound of some one walking in the corridor outside, and opening and shutting doors, reached my ears.

"Knowing that all the household had long retired, I believed that a thief had in some way got into the house, and I wished to surprise him. So I took a revolver from its case, and instead of coming down the passage, I entered by a side door into the bath room connected with the late earl's suite of apartments, and passed through them all to its bedroom and then opened the door of that bedroom and stepped out into the corridor ready to cover the intruder with my pistol.

"But I suddenly came upon my wife, who, on seeing me, stared until her face grew white with horror, and then, with a piercing scream, she fell into a swoon.

"I dropped the pistol, and stooped to raise her from the floor. I heard steps rapidly approaching, and soon the housekeeper was by my side, and with many anxious inquiries that I was unable to answer, she followed me as I carried the countess to her bedroom and laid her on the bed.

"You have heard from other witnesses that after that night my wife could not endure the sight of me for weeks.

"Later on in the year, when I insisted on her giving me an explanation of her strange conduct, she deliberately charged me with the murder of the earl, declaring that she had recognized in me, on that night of our home-coming, the man she had seen issuing from the dead earl's room on the night of the murder.

"This was very shocking! But I gave her the explanation of my illness as the motive of my visit to the earl's room, and of the terrible shock I had received on finding him murdered in his bed.

"She seemed at first to believe my statement; but—perhaps because I did not make my explanation full enough, and did not tell her my reason for not rousing the house and proclaiming the murder—she still suspected me, and she cherished her suspicions with such morbid persistency that they grew into a monomania that possessed her mind and influenced the minds of others. My wife was my first accuser. Her suspicions, based on circumstantial evidence, though unjust, were sincere, for they broke her heart! Her accusation, though false, was conscientious, for it was made on her deathbed.

"Now, your worships, I have given you the explanation of my presence in the room of the murdered man on the night of the murder, and of my reasons for not rousing the household and proclaiming my dreadful discovery.

"If that explanation does not satisfy you, I have no other to give. If that explanation—taken together with a hitherto irreproachable character—does not constitute a sufficient defense, I have no other to offer. I have done, gentlemen," concluded Lewis Manton, so-called Earl of Hawkewood, as he resumed his seat.

The three magistrates consulted together for a few minutes, and then the presiding magistrate, Mr. Oliver Ball, said, mildly:

"Your explanation, my lord, appears to us as very plausible, your defense very reasonable. Nevertheless, however much we may be inclined to receive them, inasmuch as they rest on your own unsupported word, which, in your circumstances, cannot be received as legal evidence, we feel compelled, in the discharge of our duty as guardians of the public peace and functionaries of justice, to act in accordance with the law and the testimony. We are very sorry to say that we shall have to commit you to wait the action of the grand jury."

The concluding words of the justice produced a profound sensation in the hall.

The prisoner turned as pale as a corpse; the spectators seemed stricken dumb and motionless, for not even a murmur of surprise escaped anyone; and before they could recover from their panic, Lawyer Poinsett sprang upon his feet and began to say:

"I protest! I protest! I protest against this outrage on the person of my noble client, a peer of the realm!"

At this moment the lawyer felt a hand laid lightly on his arm.

He stopped and turned. A gentleman had stepped to his side. The stranger whispered a few words in the lawyer's ear. The lawyer started violently and stared like a mad-man.

Then a short, whispered conference ensued.

While this was going on the presiding magistrate turned to his clerk and directed him to make out a warrant for the committal of Lewis Manton, Lord Hawkewood, to the county jail.

"I pray a stay of the proceedings, your worship," said the lawyer, rising up.

"Upon what plea, Mr. Poinsett?" inquired the presiding magistrate.

"Upon the plea that a most important witness for the defense has just appeared."

"Let the witness take the stand, then," said the presiding magistrate.

The prisoner arose and looked toward the lawyer and the stranger, and with an exclamation of "Great Heaven!" sank down again.

Ham Gow nudged Mr. Delaplaine and laughed.

Mr. Delaplaine arched his eyebrows and "smiled superior."

The spectators stood on tiptoe and craned their necks to see what was going on now.

And in the meantime, Lawyer Poinsett took the stranger by the hand and advanced to the witness stand, with the air of a man who was about to introduce some eminent public speaker to an expectant audience.

"Your worship," he said, addressing the presiding magistrate, "you were about to commit my client under the charge of the willful murder of the late Horace Hawke, Earl of Hawkewood."

"Yes," replied the magistrate. "What objection can you bring against my doing so?"

"The objection I can bring, your worship," said the lawyer, presenting the stranger, "is the living Horace Hawke, Earl of Hawkewood."

CHAPTER XXXII
DISCHARGED

"THE living Horace Hawke, Earl of Hawkewood, stands before your worships to answer for himself, to assert his own rights to every legal, social and domestic recognition, and to vindicate the falsely accused prisoners from the preposterous charge of his murder," continued Lawyer Poinsett, as he handed the young nobleman up into the witness stand, right under the eyes of the magistrates.

And then he let his eyes rove over bench, dock and audience, with an expression strangely made up of mirth, sarcasm and triumph.

The effect of his announcement upon all persons within that hall was something stupendous!

All the audience stood up upon their tiptoes and stretched their necks to the danger of dislocation in their efforts to see and hear what was going on around the bench.

Of the prisoners in the dock, Lewis Manton, sometime called Earl of Hawkewood, stood and stared with his eyes starting from his head like those of a madman.

Ham Gow looked and laughed silently.

Monsieur Henri Delaplaine threw back his shoulders, arched his eyebrows, and twirled his mustache in the most supercilious manner imaginable.

But the effect upon the three sitting magistrates!

"It was a thing to see, not hear!"

They perfectly recognized the young man before them. There was no doubt about that. He had grown up among them from childhood to youth, and the last two years of his life had not made such a change in his appearance as to raise the slightest question of his identity.

362

So, as he stood there on the witness stand, facing the bench, with the full light of the great window above the bench falling directly on his fine dark face and slight, elegant form, they saw and knew that Horace Hawke, Earl of Hawkewood, stood before them!

But at the same time they remembered that Horace Hawke, Earl of Hawkewood, had been murdered in his bed just two years before this; that a coroner's inquest had sat upon his body and found a verdict of willful murder against two of the men there in the dock, and the body of the unfortunate young nobleman had actually been stolen and dissected by medical students!

How, then, could he be standing before them, though the evidence of their senses proved that he was, while the testimony of their memory assured them that he could not possibly be!

Stout old drinkers of "old brown stout" and portly bibbers of heavy port cannot be expected to have very clear heads. And now these worthy administrators of justice had their minds hopelessly muddled between the evidence of their senses and the testimony of their memories.

They sat perfectly motionless and dumfounded, staring at the young man on the witness stand for some moments, and then all three gave vent to their amazement in a simultaneous utterance of the bothered Briton's favorite expletive:

"Lord bless my soul and body!"

It was lucky just then that the old clerk was a well-regulated piece of clockwork, not to be put out of routine by any sort of surprise or jar, and that, seeing the pause, he stood up and asked:

"Shall I swear this witness, your worships?"

"Eh? Yes. Swear him!" answered Mr. Ball, with a start, glad to act upon any suggestion in the present obfuscated and bewildered state of his magisterial intellect.

The oath was duly administered, and the young earl looked around upon the audience, then bowed to the justices, and made his brief statement under oath.

"My name is Horace Hawke, my age twenty-one years this day. I am the sixteenth Earl of Hawkewood, being the son and heir of Roscius, fifteenth earl.

"Two years ago, on the morning of the second of September, in the hours between three and five in the morning, I formed a plan, with the aid of my tenant, Ham Gow, and my valet, Henri Delaplaine, by which I might escape from a tutelage that had long oppressed me, to the serious injury of mind and body, and travel free and unsuspected for the two years that would intervene between that day and this one of my majority and consequent independence.

"It was a wild scheme and fraught with much danger—unforeseen danger to my humble co-conspirators; but in all other respects it was an entirely successful one.

"My old comrade, Ham Gow, was my perfect counterpart in form, feature and voice—my perfect counterpart in appearance, with the exception of the length of his beard and hair, the tan of his complexion and the roughness of his dress.

"My plan was to change dress and characters with Gow, leaving him to enact my part as Earl of Hawkewood, and going off myself to try the life of a tramp. A wild scheme, I repeat, but yet not a criminal one.

"With the skillful assistance of Delaplaine, who had once been attached to an amateur theatrical company, the double metamorphosis was made—Gow, with his hair trimmed and dressed, his beard shaved off, leaving only a light mustache, his skin whitened by cosmetics, and his form dressed in delicate fine linen, was left in possession of my name, character and surroundings, to hold and enjoy for two years, if he proved able to play his part for that length of time.

"I, with my skin darkened by red oak bark, and in a false black wig and bushy black beard, clothed in Gow's rough suit and accompanied by Delaplaine, left the Hall that morning, and took a third-class passage in the early train from Hawkeville to London, having left Delaplaine to make his way to Castle Belle Isle, where his wife, known as Mademoiselle Labbé, lived as lady's maid to the Duchess of Grand Manors.

"I had for a chance companion to London the Rev. Mr. Traverse, who had known me and Gow from our boyhood up. He took me for Gow, without the slightest doubt and gave me plenty of good advice, and was so kind as to accompany me to the East India Docks and put me under the protection of the ship's chaplain and see me off to Australia.

"I sailed on September 3d for Melbourne, in total ignorance of the startling events then taking place at Hawke Hall.

"I have spent the last two years in traveling over the Australian colonies and in the voyages out and back.

"I sailed on the fourth of last April by the *Labrador* from Hobart Town to London. I reached London on the fifth of August, and purposely lingered about that city until this twenty-first anniversary of my birth should make me a free agent.

"Of all the strange events at Hawke Hall that followed my departure, I have, of course, no personal knowledge whatever. I have learned them from hearsay. But my confederates, Gow and Delaplaine, are competent to corroborate my testimony and to supplement it by a statement of their own.

"Your worships, I have done, unless anyone here may wish to question me," concluded the young earl.

"Lord bless my soul alive!" again simultaneously exclaimed the three magistrates.

"Mr. Ball, may I venture to ask if you recognize me now?" inquired the young earl.

"Eh?—I—Lord bless my soul and body!" exclaimed old Oliver Ball, in confusion.

"You seem in doubt. Will you allow me to call a witness who can identify me?"

"Eh?—I-yes—call a witness."

The Test of Love

"Then let Ham Gow be put on the stand," said the young earl, stepping down.

"Yes, certainly, let Ham Gow take the stand," said Mr. Ball.

"I beg your pardon," here interrupted his brother magistrate—a Mr. Leigh—"the prisoner Gow, being held undercharge of murder, is not competent to give evidence in this case."

"Eh?-Oh! Ay, certainly not! Bless my soul and body, what a bother!" exclaimed Mr. Ball, wiping his round, red face.

"Other witnesses should be called to identify or deny the pretensions of this claimant," said the third magistrate—Mr. Thoms.

"Eh? Yes, of course, other witnesses," assented Mr. Ball.

"Who are not under arrest for crime," added Mr. Leigh.

"To be sure, who are not under arrest! Do you hear—a—sir—Mr.—my lord?" blundered old Ball.

"Heaven and earth, gentlemen, are other witnesses at all necessary? You are all my old neighbors! You have known me by sight ever since my childhood, as I have known you! Surely no other witnesses besides your own senses are necessary," exclaimed the young earl, impatiently.

"It is not, sir, what we may believe you to be, but what you can prove yourself to be by the testimony of competent witnesses! Nor may it rest with us to give a final decision in this case. It may have to go to the higher courts—the Court of Chancery, for aught we know! This is, as you are aware, only a preliminary investigation of the charge against these prisoners who are held to answer for the murder of the late Earl of Hawkewood. You appear as a witness for their defense, claiming to be the living Earl of Hawkewood. I hope you may establish your claim to that name and title, but you must do it not by your own mere assertion or even by your statement under oath, but by witnesses who can swear to your identity."

"Of course!" exclaimed the presiding justice. "Besides, Lord bless my soul and body, man, you may look ever so much like the late young

Earl of Hawkewood, but we know that you—I mean the late young Earl of Hawkewood -was assassinated in his bed two years ago, and the coroner's jury that sat upon his body brought in a verdict of willful murder against one Ham Gow and one Henri Delaplaine, now held in custody under the charge, and here present, as any man may see! And we have every reason to believe that your—I mean the late Earl of Hawkewood's body was stolen and dissected by medical students! These are hard facts, you see!" concluded the justice.

"And it is a much harder fact that I, Horace Hawke—and so forth-stand bodily before you, and that you all know it! Therefore, it could not have been myself who was murdered in my bed and 'sat upon' by a coroner's jury. If Ham Gow were a competent witness, he could tell you who it was that was—not murdered, but—stunned into apparent death, pronounced dead by the doctors, and decided by a coroner's jury, to have been murdered, but who, in the early morning, recovered from his stupor, crawled through a low window, and crept on to the ruined watch tower, where he was concealed and nursed for some weeks by old Nan Crook."

"That is a very strange story, but it wants proof, and Gow, as we told you, is not a competent witness," said Mr. Leigh, while the two other magistrates stared more stupidly than ever.

The young Earl of Hawkewood turned about and faced the audience in the hall—the eager audience who had nearly dislocated their vertebra by standing on tiptoes and stretching their necks, and he called in a loud voice:

"Are there any here present who recognize and can identify me?"

He was answered by a high tide of exclamations:

"Yes, yer lordship!"

"Lord bless yer anner, my lard!"

"Yer lordship's Lard Harkewood, sure!"

And so forth.

"Order! Order!" cried the clerk.

"Silence this crowd, or clear the hall!"

"Order! Order!" cried the clerk again.

The noise subsided.

Then a gentleman stepped from the witnesses' seats and came and stood beside the young earl on the stand, grasped his hand warmly, and said:

"Welcome back to England, my lord! I recognize you at once. So do all here, though you look much stronger and healthier than when we saw you last."

"I thank you heartily, Dr. Ellis. And—I am glad to come back to you—though I must confess that I was also very glad to get away! Do you forgive me for my escapade?" laughed the young man.

"Your escapade saved your reason and your life, my lord! That is a sufficient answer," replied the doctor.

Then addressing the confused bench of justices, he said:

"Your worships, I wish to be put under oath."

"Administer the oath," said the presiding justice.

The clerk advanced and performed this function, and the new witness said:

"I recognize in the last witness Horace Hawke, Earl of Hawkewood. I have known him from his earliest infancy, and cannot possibly be mistaken in his identity. I am perfectly certain that this gentleman is what he claims to be—the Earl of Hawkewood, and—if additional evidence of his identity is needed—it is stamped on his person by nature's own hand! The infant Earl of Hawkewood had, as a score of men and women in this neighborhood can testify, a most singular birthmark—'the trail of the serpent'—on his right ankle. It is a slightly raised speckled green binding, as if a small grass snake had wound itself closely around the limb."

"Will your lordship have the goodness to bare your ankle, that this strange phenomenon of nature shall be exhibited to prove your identity beyond all future question?" demanded Mr. Leigh.

"Willingly," replied the "claimant," with a smile.

But as he stooped to comply, Mr. Henri Delaplaine skipped over the rails of the dock, before anyone could stop him, knelt before his late master and began to draw off his boot and then his hose.

"Thank you, Delaplaine. There is the mark, your worships," said the young man, planting his naked foot and ankle on the seat of a chair placed for the purpose in full sight of the bench.

The justices bent down to examine it. The bailiffs kept off the crowd that would have pressed around to stare at it.

It was no deformity; it was not even an ugly mark; it was, on the contrary, a very pretty one. On a lady's wrist it might have seemed a curious enameled bracelet in the form of a serpent.

While the justices were gazing at this rare, natural anklet, the group around the young earl was augmented by the stately form of Dr. Paul Laude, who laid his hand on the shoulder of his late pupil and said:

"Horace, allow me to welcome you back to England, and to say that I forgive you for running away."

"Thank you very much, Dr. Laude! I quite forgive you for driving me to run away!" laughed the young man, as he took and pressed his late tutor's offered hand.

And now M. Henri Delaplaine, who seemed to think that *les bourgeois* had stared long enough at his noble master's handsome foot and decorated ankle, began carefully to cover them with hose and boot.

Mr. Poinsett here stood forward and addressed the bench:

"I move that the prisoners, Lewis Manton, Ham Gow and Henri Delaplaine, held in custody for the murder of a man standing alive before you, be discharged from custody."

"Eh? Yes, to be sure! Let the prisoners be discharged! Bless my soul and body! whatever are they kept for, anyhow?" exclaimed old Mr. Ball, vigorously wiping his round, red face, as he added: "And let the hall be at once cleared. The sitting is adjourned."

Then the three magistrates came down from the bench and shook hands with the young earl, warmly congratulating him on his return home.

They were joined by the discharged prisoner, Lewis Manton, who seized his cousin's hand, and in a voice broken by emotion welcomed him to Hawkewood, adding:

"Never did an unconscious usurper so gladly give up his false position to the true occupant."

"I believe you, Manton, and I thank you!" heartily responded the young earl, warmly returning the hand grasp, as the last vestige of his animosity against the usurper vanished away.

Ham Gow now claimed his attention.

"Will you allow me at last to congratulate you now, my lord?"

"No, dear lad! I will not allow you to linger here any longer for any purpose. I promised to send you home to your wife just as soon as the court should adjourn. Now be off with yourself as fast as you can go to Demondike, where Lona is awaiting you! Hurry, now, or the poor woman will be thinking that you have already received your deserts and are 'comfortably' hanged!" laughed the young gentleman.

Ham Gow, regardless of the presence of the "Most potent, grave and reverend seigniors," and fearless of being committed for contempt of court, since "court" had adjourned, laughed aloud, threw up his hat, caught it again, and ran out of the hall.

The crowd had already left it, but they had not yet dispersed to their homes; they were waiting outside to make a demonstration in honor of their young lord; for, ten minutes later, when the earl appeared, accompanied by the magistrates, the two clergymen, the village doctor, and Mr. Lewis Manton, such a shout arose from the assembled villagers and tenantry and laborers as had never before been heard in Hawkeville, and cries of:

"Long live the young Yarl of Harkewood!" reverberated like articulate thunder through the air and was re-echoed from the distant hills.

A carriage had been hastily drawn by a dozen men from the stables of the Hawkeville Arms, and with shouts they lifted the laughing and protesting young nobleman into its body, and taking hold of its shafts, drew him in triumph along the road that led to Hawke Hall, preceded by a procession of runners hastening to herald the news to the domestics, and followed by an enthusiastic crowd of men, women and children that increased with every mile of journey.

CHAPTER XXXIII
THE TRIUMPHAL ENTRY

WHEN the procession reached Hawke Hall it was seen that the news had gone before them.

The outdoor servants were all assembled near the lodge gate, and as the carriage was drawn along the way every hat was doffed and every voice joined the chorus of:

"Long live our young lord!"

At this point the young earl ordered the carriage to be stopped.

Many of the older servants and tenants crowded around him with heartfelt congratulations.

And with all of these he cordially shook hands, giving each some words of kindness and good cheer.

"Ah! steward, is that you? How are you, old friend?" he said, to his land steward.

"Heaven bless your lordship!" responded the latter.

"Why, Moss! I am glad to see you! How does your garden grow?"

"Splendidly, my honored lord; as if it knowed your lordship was a-coming back!" responded the gardener.

"And how are my old friends, Penn, Proddy and Tree, who have nearly run their limbs off from Demondike to see me?"

"Hooray! your lordship," responded the three.

And the laughing earl ordered the carriage to move on.

Among those who had hurried on before was Lewis Manton.

And as the young earl alighted from the carriage he was met at the hall door by his predecessor, who came down the steps and grasped his hand, saying:

"Permit me to welcome you to your home. The ex-governor, I think, always receives and installs the new governor. Allow me."

And so saying he drew the earl's arm within his own, and conducted him into the hall, where the household servants were drawn up on each side to receive their lord.

These domestics were too decorous to set up a shout, or to indulge in any other loud or violent demonstrations of joy; but as the young earl recognized one and another, the clasped hands and tearful eyes, and earnest, low-breathed prayers and thanksgivings testified to the depth and fervor of their affections.

"Ah Pelton, is that you ?" he said, seeing the gray-haired groom of the chambers, who had been in the service of the family so many years.

"Ah! Lord bless your lordship, my lord, it is I. Left lingering here to see your return. Oh! but it is like a resurrection from the dead!" cried the old man, pressing the hand given him by his young master to his heart.

"How do you do, Bruce?" echoed the young earl, as the fat butler bowed before him.

"Ah, my lord, so much better for seeing your lordship. Long life to you, my lord!"

"Stepney, I see you. Why, you have grown four inches in height, and eight in breadth, since I saw you last. You haven't broken your heart after your master," said the young gentleman, as the Hall footman made his bow.

"Oh! my lord, indeed I have. I was so cut up by your lordship's death that I fell offen my feed and sleep, and j'ined the Bible class and the Brotherhood of St. James, and everythink, in hopes I might meet your lordship in heaven at last!" exclaimed the great boy, with the tears rolling down his red cheeks.

"Well, we have met at last, lad, never to part again, I hope," laughed the young lord.

"Yes—thanks be to Heaven, my lord!" cried the footman. "Why, Mrs. Carraway! The benevolent Mrs. Carraway, who used to pamper me in the nursery and in the schoolroom with cakes and tarts, when my excellent tutor would have kept me on a regimen of oatmeal porridge and buttermilk!" laughed the young earl, as he offered his had to the housekeeper, who grasped it, wept over it and pressed it to her heart and to her lips, as she said:

"Oh, my lord! this is the very happiest day of my life, just as the day I thought we had lost you was the unhappiest!"

And so through all the line of servants, with a cordial grasp of the hand and a pleasant smile and word for each, he passed into a reception room at the rear of the hall, and there he found Ham Gow and Lona awaiting him.

He gazed on them in surprise for a moment, and then, with a comic gravity, exclaimed:

"You here, my children! Why, Ham, by what sort of natural or supernatural magic did you get over the ground between Hawkeville and Demondike and fetch Lona in this short time?"

"By no magic at all. I have not been to Demondike. When you turned me out of the town hall in that sudden and summary manner, the first person I saw on the outside was Lona, whining around the building like a sick kitten!" said Ham, laughing.

"Oh, I grew so anxious! I could not stay at the tower, so I walked over to the town hall, and I hadn't been there more than five minutes at the most when Ham came out, and—he told me all about it, my lord, and then put me on old Farmer Perry's tax cart that was going on that way, and brought me here to be ready to welcome you home, my lord."

While these old companions were talking together they were joined by Dr. Paul Laude, Dr. Ellis, the Rev. Mr. Vincent and Lawyer Poinsett, who had followed the earl, in another carriage, from the Hawke Arms, and had just arrived.

"And now," said Mr. Lewis Manton, "as I have seen your lordship 'installed' if I may borrow the term, I will take my leave."

"Why, where are you going?" inquired the earl, in surprise.

"To the Hawke Arms, for a few days, while I see to the removal of my personal effects from Hawke Hall. I owe your lordship the revenues of this place for the last two years. It will be easy to pay them, for very little of those revenues has been spent—nothing indeed except upon the improvement of the property. My steward will see to a settlement. After which I shall retire to my place in Northumberland."

While Lewis Manton spoke the young earl looked at him with grave attention. When he ceased speaking Lord Hawkewood said:

"I beg that you will do nothing of the sort, Manton! I ask you, as a special favor to me, to remain here and make this house your home so long as business may detain you in this neighborhood, and as much longer as may be convenient or agreeable. Come, Manton! We are cousins. Accept my invitation as frankly as it is given! You will remain?"

"Yes, thank you, Hawkewood, I will, with pleasure," readily replied the earl's kinsman.

"Well, Horace, your friends here and myself have only dropped in to welcome you to your ancestral home and to say good-by," began Dr. Paul Laude; but the young earl interrupted him:

"You have come to spend the day, or the rest of the day, and to dine this evening, gentlemen. I will take no refusal from you. Our arrival is sudden and unprepared; but our old housekeeper and butler are people of resources! At any rate, you must stay and take what our plain neighbors,

"'The rude forefathers of the hamlet,'
and their descendants call 'potluck' with us to-day!"

The friends invited in this offhand manner signified their willingness to accept the young earl's hospitality.

"And now if you will excuse me, gentlemen, I must go out and speak to my steward. There are about fifteen hundred villagers, tenants and laborers outside to be provided for to-day, and as we have no floral works nor fireworks nor pageantry of any sort to amuse them, the deficiency must be made up in beef and beer, and cake and tea, and fiddle and bagpipes; and old Traverse and the butler and house-keeper will have to see to all," concluded the young earl, as he left the room to issue his orders.

His upper servants were, as he had said, persons of resources.

A dozen casks of ale were carried out into the grounds and tapped; all the bread, cheese, cakes, cold meat and pies that were in the larder were taken out and distributed, and messengers were sent off in haste to the village to buy out every baker and confectioner there, as well as all the cooked meat that could be spared from the Hawke Arms.

And in two hours' time a feast was spread in the grounds amply sufficient to feed the fifteen hundred people.

And before they had got through eating and drinking, the fiddle and the bagpipes arrived, and all the young people deserted the viands for the violin.

The gentlemen came out from the house to join in the merrymaking.

The earl, with Mrs. Ham Gow for a partner, led the dance, and Mr. Ham Gow, with the plainest young girl on the ground, was their *vis-à-vis*.

Ham said he always paid attention to plain girls, for three good and sufficient reasons: Firstly, because other men neglected them; secondly, because they were always so pleased and grateful for attentions; and thirdly, because they could never cause Mrs. Ham a pang of jealousy.

Good Ham Gow!

The dancing was kept up until the night necessarily put an end to it as an outdoor amusement. And then, as it was impossible to improvise lights or fireworks, the people, after a full chorus of cheers for their young lord-cheers that frightened all the fowls of the air on the roosts, and started all the dogs in the kennels to barking furiously-left the grounds and dispersed to their homes—to go to bed and sleep? No, indeed; but to sit late into the night talking over the strange events of the day.

The small, impromptu dinner party at Hawke Hall was a success.

After it was over, and at quite a late hour in the evening, the guests arose to take leave.

The young earl, in the easy, offhand manner that had characterized his conduct since his return, pressed his visitors to remain for the night.

They, however, excused themselves, and with the exception of Dr. Paul Laude and Mr. Lewis Manton, took their departure.

When these two last mentioned gentlemen had bid their host good-night, and Lewis Manton had retired to his own usual apartment, and Dr. Paul Laude had been marshaled by old Pelton, the groom of the chambers, to his room in the bachelors' corridor, the young host rang the bell, and desired Stepney, the footman who answered it, to inquire of the housekeeper what rooms had been prepared for himself (the earl).

For so much engaged had the young nobleman been that he had not once found time to ascertain.

The inquiry was answered by the appearance of Mrs. Carraway in person, who courtesied, and said:

"If you please, my lord, we have got ready the suite of rooms over the drawing room for your lordship, as those in the bachelors' corridor once occupied by your lordship have been shut up these two years."

"Quite right. I will find my own way now. That will do, Mrs. Carraway. Good-night."

"Good-night, my lord."

The young gentleman took a bedroom candle from a bracket near at hand, and went upstairs to the magnificent suite of apartments that were usually reserved for distinguished guests, and had last been occupied by the late Duke and Duchess of Grand Manors on the occasion of their visit to their daughter and son-in-law.

When Lord Hawkewood entered the bedroom, he found his ex-valet, the elegant Monsieur Delaplaine, laying out a dressing gown, slippers, fresh towels and other conveniences, as naturally as if there had been no interruption to their relations during the last two years.

For a moment the interval seemed as a dream to him.

"Where have you been since you left my service, Delaplaine?" he inquired.

"In America, my lord—in the city of Chicago, engaged in the hairdressing business there," replied the valet, with a bow.

"And the fair Madame Delaplaine, *née* Labbé?"

"She went with me, my lord. We had been married sometime before we left."

"Why were you not to be found at the address you gave me in Paris?"

"Pardon, my lord, I read the papers and knew there was a warrant out for my arrest on the charge of murder. I hastened with myself to the new world, my lord."

"Then, you never got my letters?"

"Non, my lord."

"How, then, did you come back?"

"I remembered me of my appointment with your lordship, and came back to keep it, well knowing that your lordship would appear that day that was promised; but no sooner do I my appearance make than I am seized and thrown into prison on the charge of murder of my master."

"That was hard!" said the earl, but he said it with a laugh.

"It was varray hard, my lord!"

"Is your wife with you?"

"She is with some old friends in the village, my lord. She was on the grounds this afternoon with the others, though your lordship did not see her."

"Ah! What do you intend to do, Delaplaine—to return to America?"

"*Non*, my lord, not if your lordship will condescend to take me into your service again. I like not the public hairdressing. An artiste cannot choose his patrons, and he is exposed to the too intimate association with *les nouveauz richès*. I like more the private service of my lord."

"You really wish to re-enter my service? Very well, then, I engage you from to-night! But how about your wife?"

"Ah, she will take service again also. We have no family, my lord! And in the future, when my lord shall bring a fair countess to the Hall, it may be that Mélanie may find favor with my lord's lady."

The young earl laughed, and as during this conversation he had thrown off his coat and boots, and with the assistance of the valet drawn on his dressing gown, he dismissed Delaplaine for the night and soon after retired to bed.

The next morning Lord Hawkewood requested Dr. Paul Laude to give him a private interview in the library.

When they were seated, and the door was closed, the young nobleman delicately led the conversation up to the doctor's affairs and indirectly learned that the aged clergy- man had, for the last two years, been living in cheap lodgings on the Westminster Road, with nothing to do and no other income than that derived from the small interest of his savings which were invested in the safe but poorly paying three per cent. consols.

That he had been brought down from London as a witness at the preliminary examination of the prisoners charged with the murder of the earl, and that he had been living for the last few days at the Hawke Arms.

Now, although the old doctor had been an austere tutor and guardian to his pupil and ward, yet he had stood almost in the relation of a father to the orphan boy, and now the young earl was surprised to find that he felt almost a filial affection for the stern, but conscientious old man. He felt a tender compassion for him as he looked on his pale, worn face, thin gray hair and rusty, threadbare coat.

He knew that he could make the aged bookworm's life as happy as it was capable of being made, and he determined to do it.

"Doctor," he said, "I answered you with inexcusable flippancy when you kindly expressed to me your forgiveness yesterday. I hope you will pardon me for that, and for all my other offenses against you."

"My dear Horace, I have said that I do. I have always had your true interests at heart, and have always tried to do my duty by you," replied the old man.

"Indeed, I know it, Dr. Laude. And now I am going to beg you not to desert me; not to leave me to myself. I believe that I shall now be a much more satisfactory pupil than I have ever been before."

"Do you wish to re-enter Oxford? Many an older man than yourself has done so," said the doctor.

"Oh, no; but I shall read—after a time. In the mean-while, dear sir, I wish you to be so kind, if you will, as to return to your old quarters here and resume your old avocations! Dear doctor, I wish you to remain with me here, at the same salary, looking after the library and leading the morning and evening worship—so long as we both shall live. Will you do this, dear doctor? You have no one in the world so near to you as the troublesome boy you have reared."

"Horace," said the old man, in a voice quivering with emotion, "I was never given to softness or sentiment in my youth. Do not make a child of me now. Do not make me shed tears. If—if I can be of use to you, I will very gladly remain, as domestic chaplain and librarian, for that, I suppose, is what you mean. Yes! I will acknowledge now, that for fifteen years I had grown into this old library as an oyster in its shell—and the leaving it was as nearly fatal to me as tearing from its shell would have been to the oyster."

"I thank Heaven that it was not quite fatal to you, dear doctor! I thank Heaven that you have lived to come back. And now you must never leave it again! Nay, indeed, you must consider that you never have really left it except for a holiday. And, by the way, the estate is in arrears to you for two years' salary, which I shall instruct my steward to pay. Doctor, you have been accustomed to issue orders here. Pray send a servant at once to the Hawke Arms for your luggage. Will you? And see to the removal of your effects from London at your earliest convenience. Will you do so?"

"Yes, yes, my dear boy, I will; but just now, if you will excuse me, I want to find that black letter copy of Polycarp which I have been longing to look up for months," said the doctor.

The young earl smiled, and arose and went out, leaving the old man mousing among the musty bookshelves.

The next few days were occupied by the earl in receiving congratulatory visits from friends and neighbors.

On the Friday, Ham Gow and his wife, Lona, came to the Hall, and asked to see the earl.

When they were admitted to his presence, the ex-tramp said:

"We have come to take a short leave of your lordship. Mother Crook, and Nan, and Dennis go up to London to-morrow, as they expect to sail for New York on Monday. Lona and myself are going to see them off, and also to lay in certain English goods, chattels and comforts to take back with us to the colony, for we have determined to return on the same ship that will take your lordship out, and that will sail on the tenth."

"I am very glad to know that I shall have your company for the voyage out. Remember me to the excellent Mrs. Crook and her daughter, and say that I wish them much prosperity in the country of their adoption," said the young earl, in a serio-comic tone.

"I will do so. We shall go to the same old inn, and, after seeing the old folks off to America, we will wait your coming there. I suppose you will be in town very soon?" said Ham.

"Yes, in a very few days. Just as soon as I can arrange affairs here for my long absence. The ship, as you say, will sail on the tenth; I shall certainly be in London on the eighth, at the latest."

"Yes, my lord. We only came to take short leave, and now we wish your lordship good-by," said Ham Gow.

And he and his wife, declining all offered refreshments, on the score of haste, shook hands with the earl, and went their way.

The next morning, according to arrangement, Nan Crook and her disreputable family vacated the old watch tower that had been their home for over twenty years.

Four days later the young Earl of Hawkewood, leaving his old tutor, Dr. Paul Laude, in charge of the Hall, and his faithful steward, Traverse, in charge of the estate, bade good-by to his friends, and started for London.

And on Saturday, the tenth of September, attended by Ham Gow and Lona, he sailed in the Norfolk for Australia.

CHAPTER XXXIV
LOVE'S LONG SUSPENSE

VISCOUNT SEYRES did not find the governorship of a convict colony situated far beyond the last "jumping off" point of the civilized world, very much to his liking.

His lordship's delegated sovereignty and vice-regal court, with all their attendant power and dignity, did not compensate to him for the loss—let us say—of the *Times* at his breakfast table every morning, and all his other newspapers and newsmongers at his club every noon; for his ride in Rotten Row every afternoon; for his seat in the House, or his stall at the opera in the evening; for Epsom, Ascot, or Goodwood races in their seasons; for bird shooting, fox hunting or deer stalking in their seasons; nor for the lost society of friends who had grown old with him, and places familiar from his childhood.

Viscount Seyres had been "deadly poor" before he married the beautiful heiress of the Princess Zavieski, and accepted the governorship of Tasmania. His seat in Ireland was half a ruin, his whole estate a bog, and his tenantry were starving on land for which they could not and were not required to pay any rent.

But poor as the old nobleman was, he did not marry the heiress for her money, but for love notwithstanding her money and he accepted the governorship of Tasmania because it would give him a salary by which he would be able to support his household in good style without touching a penny of his wife's fortune.

So he had come out to Hobart Town and brought his bride, who had accepted him partly from admiration of his person and character, and partly from ambition to share his rank and title; and she had consented to their emigration because it was not safe for her to venture into English society while yet that second will of her grandaunt-that will of whose existence she had no suspicion—had not been discovered.

But in this first year of their married life such a perfect mutual affection had grown up between the husband and wife, and made them so entirely one in heart and mind, that all morbid sensitiveness about living on her money was gone and forgotten.

The Test of Love

He discovered that she was equally anxious with himself to return to England, and, after a final consultation with her on the subject, he made up his mind to send in his resignation by the first homeward bound ship.

Then, to please his wife, he set himself to persuade their son-in-law, Cosmo Belle Isle, to sell out his commission and return to England with them.

Nothing could have pleased the young lieutenant more than to do that very thing; but he had his scruples—he hesitated.

"You know, my dear boy," urged the viscount, "that it is utter folly in a young man with fifty thousand pounds a year to be living the life of a subaltern officer out here in the garrison of a convict colony, and subjecting his youthful bride to the same dreary existence."

"Yes, I know," responded the honest lad, "but you see, sir, that I have hitherto been so vacillating, that I should be steady now, even if it be to my own hurt."

"And to other people's hurt, also? I don't see it. Look here, Cosmo! There is another point of view! You are holding a position that you do not need, and that some other brave fellow does. Sell out, Cosmo, and give the other poor lad, whoever he may be, a chance!"

"I know you would not advise me to do anything wrong. If you, my lord, say that I can sell out with honor, I will do so with delight," eagerly declared the lieutenant.

"Then, see to it without delay!" said the viscount.

"I will !" exclaimed the young officer.

This was joyful news to the viscountess and to her daughter, Isola, who both longed with an unutterable longing to return to their native land.

All this took place within a few weeks after the young Earl of Hawkewood and his humble friends had sailed in the *Labrador* for London, on that first of April.

By the *Eyre,* that sailed from Hobart Town just a month later, on the first of May, the viscount sent home his resignation of office, to take effect on the arrival of his successor, who, he prayed, might be appointed and dispatched to relieve him with all convenient expedition.

In any case, the homesick exiles knew that there must be a weary time of months to wait before they could get answers to these dispatches.

The holy and happy season of Christmas came and passed before the governor began to look for advices from home.

However, news came at last. The *Sea Gull,* from London on the tenth of October, arrived at Hobart Town on the first of February.

She brought dispatches to the governor announcing the facts that his resignation had been accepted, and that his successor would sail for Tasmania by the *Derwent* on the tenth of the ensuing November.

This was most delightful news to the viscount and viscountess, and to the young lieutenant and his wife.

The *Derwent,* with the newly appointed governor and his staff, might be expected to arrive on or before the first of March, at which time the retiring governor would be at liberty to return with his family to England.

They began to make preparations for the reception of the strangers, and for their own voyage home.

But while the governor's household were rejoicing, many other families in the town were beginning to suffer keen anxiety for the fate of the *Norfolk*—which had left London on the tenth of the preceding September, and had not been heard from since. She should have been in port by the first of February, and was now, therefore, overdue for a month.

The only news the *Sea Gull* brought of her was, that she had certainly left London on the tenth of September, a month before the *Sea Gull's* own departure.

All, therefore, who expected friends, goods, or letters by the *Norfolk* were suffering all the worries of hope deferred.

But if the delay of the ship caused anxiety in the town, how much more it must have caused in the Mountain Hermitage?

After the departure of the young earl on his long and perilous voyage, a gloom fell upon that bright mountain home such as had never overcast it before.

Even old Theobald Elfinstar painfully missed the genial youth who had been his guest for so many months, and then his almost daily visitor for so many weeks.

And as for Seraph Elfinstar, it required all the fortitude and patience she had learned from suffering to enable her to endure the severe ordeal of her lover's absence on a long and dangerous voyage, while her suspense would be unrelieved by any certainty of letters or of news from him for a period of from eight to ten months.

It is true that there was a possibility of news, but it was a mere possibility. If the *Labrador*, bound for London, should be fortunate enough to meet a ship in midocean bound to Hobart Town, passengers would be able to exchange letters on this highway of the sea, and her lover would surely write to her. If this should not happen she would have to wait the best part of a year for news.

By every ship that reached this port after the departure of the *Labrador*, Seraph Elfinstar hoped "against hope" to receive news from the sea; but ship after ship came, at the rate of one a month, and no news of the *Labrador* reached Hobart Town.

Four months passed in this manner, and then the waiting bride said to herself:

"Half the time has gone. If he has had a prosperous voyage he is in port now. And the next ship that shall come from London after this date will bring me a letter from my love! And it may bring my discharge, also, if my knight succeeds as he hoped to do."

The thought inspired her with courage to endure the remainder of her trial.

She sent her faithful old groom, Stackpole, to the office of the shipping agent in the town, to bring her a copy of the shipping list, and on referring to it she found the *Norfolk* gazetted to sail from London on September 10th.

"The *Labrador* expected to reach London about the first of August. If she did—and she is reported to be a good, fast sailer—he will have time to work out his plan for my vindication, and send me the result by the *Norfolk*. Only four months more to wait! The *Norfolk* should reach here by the first of January, in the new year! And, oh! if she should be very fortunate, she may reach port by Christmas"

From this time Seraph Elfinstar began to look forward with hope. And still she continued to expect a letter from the sea by every incoming ship, for she said to herself:

"He may have met an outward bound ship when very near the end of the voyage, and he would have written by her."

But though mail ships continued to arrive every month, no letter came from her lover.

Yet as the time drew near for the expected arrival of the *Norfolk* her spirits rose. She checked off the days of the last month in the year with great pleasure, and kept her thoughts fixed upon the end, when Christmas or the New Year would bring the *Norfolk* with news of her lover, and liberty for herself.

But Christmas came and passed without the *Norfolk*; and New Year came and passed without intelligence of the lingering ship.

For the first week or two, though everyone was impatient, no one was alarmed. Ships were often delayed by bad weather, and the *Norfolk* might have met with such.

But when a month had passed away, and the first of February brought the *Sea Gull* to port, with the news that the *Norfolk* had certainly sailed from London on the day set down for her, a full month before the *Sea Gull* had sailed, then, indeed, anxiety rose to fever heat.

Jonas Stackpole, who had gone to town to make his usual monthly purchases, brought the news of the arrival of the *Sea Gull* to the Hermitage, and though it was late in the forenoon, old Mr. Elfinstar at once set out for Hobart Town to ascertain if there were any news of the *Norfolk*, or any letters for the Hermitage.

There were no letters, and there was no news beyond that the *Norfolk* had certainly sailed from London on the tenth of September, bound for Hobart Town and Melbourne.

The old gentleman came home disappointed, yet determined to keep up the spirits of his drooping daughter.

"You know, my love, that in so long a voyage a month more or less is no ground of anxiety," he remarked, after he had told her the result of his quest.

"But, oh, my dear father, if the ship should be lost!"

"Tut, tut, my dear! there is not one chance in a thousand that she is lost. How many ships are delayed by rough weather! How few, how very few, are lost!"

But the old gentleman spoke, perhaps, more hopefully than he felt.

Seraph was not comforted.

Another weary month of almost intolerable suspense and anxiety passed slowly and heavily away, and brought the *Derwent*, with the new governor and suite on board, and also the young gentleman for whom Lieut. Belle Isle's commission had been purchased.

There was another great gala day in Hobart Town, during which the retiring governor went in state to meet his successor, and to escort him to the town hall, where his inauguration was to be celebrated, and where there was a very great crowd assembled to see the ceremonies and to hear the speech-making.

After this came the public dinner, ordered from the Royal Victoria, but laid in the largest room of the town hall, at which both governors, all the higher officers of the army and navy who happened to be present in the town, together with those of the civil service, were present, and where the revelry was kept up to quite a late hour.

This was followed by a ball, at which the "beauty and fashion" of the colonial city, as well as its "intellect and chivalry," were present.

Among the guests were, of course, the family of the ex-governor, consisting of the Viscount and Viscountess Seyres, and Mr. and Mrs. Belle Isle.

These were by special invitation to remain as the guests of the new governor, at the government house, until such time as the *Derwent*, by which they intended to return, should be ready to sail for England, which would not occur for some weeks, as the *Derwent* was going on a further voyage to Melbourne, and would only stop at Hobart Town on her return voyage home.

This day and night was a season of great rejoicing to all, except such as were especially interested in the fate of the *Norfolk*.

Among the latter were, of course, old Mr. Elfinstar and his daughter.

Again Jonas Stackpole, who was sent into the town now every day to glean news, came back with the announcement of a ship's arrival.

And again old Mr. Elfinstar had mounted his horse and ridden into the town to hear all that could be learned from the *Derwent*.

He witnessed the pageantry of the new governor's reception and inauguration, but he got no letters in the mail that was opened, and heard no news of the missing ship.

And he went home that evening to his desponding daughter with the heavy news that there was no news.

She had ceased to hope, indeed; but still it is very hard to have despair confirmed.

On the afternoon of the second day succeeding the new governor's inauguration, the father and daughter were sitting out on the front piazza, pensively looking over the magnificent panorama of scenery rolled out beneath them—their own beautiful terraced plateau, with its statues, vases, fountains, arbors, shrubs and flowers, and the wooded descent of the mountain, the bright river beneath, now flushed with the crimson glow of the descending sun; the wooded, flowery, undulating hills beyond it, and the distant mountains whose summits were lost in the gorgeous sunset clouds; they were in nature's own temple, gazing on her glories of form and color; inhaling her incense in the perfume of a thousand flowers; listening to her vespers in the low hum of innumerable insects and the subdued twittering of countless birds; yet they were very sadly thoughtful.

"Father," at last breathed the daughter, "where is my love now, do you think?"

The old man hesitated for a moment, and then replied:

"In London, waiting for us to come home—if he has succeeded in his enterprise, and secured your discharge, and sent it out by the *Norfolk*—he is there waiting for us, whatever may have been the fate of the poor ship."

"But if he has not succeeded in securing my vindication, dear father?"

"Then, he is at work for you, and he will never tire or stop until he does succeed!"

"Well, in any case, death will at last end all our troubles. Life does not often last over seventy years, and twenty of mine are gone, thank Heaven! Grandfather, dearest, are you not happy in the thought that your term of penal servitude, called life on this convict planet called the earth, is almost over?"

"I should feel very peacefully happy in the certainty that every day brings me nearer home, were it not for the thought of leaving you alone, my darling."

She raised his venerable hand to her lips, and kissed it, murmuring:

"Grandfather, I wish I was seventy years old, and ready to go with you."

"No, no, my child! Do not say so! You are but twenty, as you say, and I hope that you have fifty years of life before you—life that shall be so full of sweet affection and good works, and of the joy and peace they bring, that this planet shall seem no more to you a penal settlement, but a paradise."

She kissed his hand again and was silent.

Then she suddenly started up and bent forward and listened as if every faculty were merged in the one strained sense of hearing.

CHAPTER XXXV
THE SURPRISE.

"WHAT is it, Seraph? What is it, love?" gently inquired old Theobald Elfinstar.

"Oh, hush! hush! It is his step! It is his step! Or—I am going mad!" panted the girl, transfixed in listening.

"Impossible, dear child," tenderly murmured the old gentleman. "It is your fancy only."

But it was not "fancy only." It was the most joyful reality that ever burst unexpectedly upon a hopeless heart, lighting up the "darkest hour" of life into a blaze of sunshine.

For even as the old man spoke a firm footstep crunched over the pebble walk beneath the piazza, and—

"Seraph!"

"Horace!"

And with that cry of joy the girl sprang forward, and was caught to her lover's bosom.

A few moments of utterly silent bliss, and then a few words of inarticulate endearments, and finally the young man's hand held out to the old gentleman, with the broken words:

"All is well, dear friend! Margaret Campbell is vindicated! I bring the order for her release!"

"Thank Heaven! Oh, thank Heaven!" exclaimed old Theobald Elfinstar, fervently, grasping the hand that had been held out to him, and then sinking back to his seat, overcome by emotion.

"It is such an unlooked-for delight! Our wildest hopes did not suggest the joy of seeing you here. We had almost lost hope even of hearing from you! We feared the *Norfolk* had gone down, with your letters on board," said Seraph, as she drew her lover in and made him sit down on the bench between her father and herself.

"The *Norfolk* encountered foul weather and was driven far out of her course, and she reached port only at noon to-day, in a very crippled condition. I came directly from the ship out here to bring you the good news," replied the young man.

"Thank Heaven that we see you safe! But how is it that we have the great happiness of seeing you, instead of only your letters?" inquired Mr. Elfinstar.

"By a special Providence, I seem to think. The time of sailing of the mail ships for the East was changed from the first to the tenth, so that the business that would have detained me in England the first week in the month was satisfactorily concluded in time for me to sail in the *Norfolk*, and, having the opportunity, I could not resist the temptation to bring the order for release, instead of sending it. But, dear friends, I have a long story to tell you, which I must reserve for some future occasion."

"Tell me only this: As you say that Margaret Campbell has been vindicated, of course the real criminal must have been convicted! That wretched girl! What is her fate?" inquired Seraph.

"Malvina Mattox is at rest. She died of nervous exhaustion before she could be brought to trial, but not before she had made a full confession. She was not near so guilty as we imagined. Hers is a strange story of nervous and cerebral disease, that I must tell you some time but not just now," sighed the young man.

"Oh, no, not now," assented the old gentleman, "for you are doubtless weary and in want of refreshment. And hark! there is the tea bell! We will go in and have tea, and afterward we will talk. Only one question I will ask you as we go: How is it with that fine fellow who was your chief help in bringing the truth to light?"

"Ham Gow?"

"Yes, Gow!"

"He made up his mind to return to the colonies. He and his wife came out with me in the *Norfolk*. They are at the Royal Victoria now and are going on to Melbourne by the *Derwent*, which we found in port here."

"And not by the *Norfolk*?"

"No, the *Norfolk* will have to lie to for repairs. The *Derwent* will take her mails and passengers to Melbourne."

"Ah that is all I wished to ask you now. Come in to tea," said the old gentleman, rising, and leading the way to the dining room.

The young man gave his arm to the young lady, and they followed to the bright and cheerful tea table.

After tea, when they sat together in the pleasant parlor, they talked over their affairs.

First the young earl gave the father and daughter a candid account of himself, and his reasons for leaving home at the age of nineteen and remaining absent until he had reached his majority. He frankly related all the serious complications that had followed his youthful escapade.

The old gentleman listened gravely, but could find no word of blame for the young man who had shown such devotion to himself and to his beloved child.

Seraph listened with the closest attention and deepest sympathy.

Next the narrator passed on to the story of their pursuit and detection of the real criminal, for whose guilt poor Margaret Campbell had so innocently suffered.

He explained how necessary it was to find other evidence in support of Ham Gow's testimony, which, under all the circumstances, would scarcely have been received alone and on its own merits.

He related the means that had been taken to bring the guilty woman to the confession of that secret crime whose burden was bearing her to the grave.

He described the circumstances of her death, and his own prompt action and successful appeal to the home secretary.

Lastly, reverting to his personal affairs, he told them of his journey down into Cornwall to claim his inheritance, and of his opportune appearance in the town hall, where his quasi-successor, Lewis Manton, his friend, Ham Gow, and his ex-valet, Henri Delaplaine, were arraigned to answer the charge of his, the earl's, murder. He told of the triumphal acquittal of the prisoners and his own immediate entrance into his possessions.

"I had no time to write and advise you of these matters, dear sir, for I found by the change in the day of sailing that I should be able to go personally on the same ship, which, had she sailed sooner, would have taken only my letters with the official order for Margaret Campbell's release. And so, by coming in person, although I have had a some-what rough and tedious voyage out, I have met you six months sooner than I should otherwise have done. But I have wearied you with my long story," concluded the young man, with a smile.

"You have wearied yourself, poor lad, but you have deeply interested us. Now you must have a glass of wine and a biscuit and retire to rest," replied the old gentleman, rising to ring for the required refreshments, after partaking of which the trio of friends separated and retired for the night.

The next morning, after breakfast, the young earl, accompanied by his aged host, set out to ride into Hobart Town to deliver the order for the release of Margaret Campbell to the superintendent of convicts.

When the necessary form had been observed, they repaired to the Royal Victoria to see Ham Gow and his wife, and after a pleasant interview with that light-hearted man and his light-headed woman, they went to a house and land agent's office to advertise the Mountain Hermitage for sale or rent.

"I leave the colonies in about a month from now, and should like to dispose of my property just as it stands before I go; so much should I like to do this, that I will let the place go at some sacrifice," said the old gentleman.

Then, turning to the young earl, he added:

"I do not suppose that I shall be able to get rid of it so soon; but that shall not keep us in the colony a day longer than we can get away. We shall go to England by the *Derwent*, which will stop here on her return from Melbourne about a month hence, as usual—whether the Hermitage shall be disposed of or not."

"I think, sir, you will have no trouble in selling the property. The new governor has authorized me to look out for a country seat for himself away from the sea, in a hilly or mountainous district, and within ten or fifteen miles of the city. It seems to me your place, from what I hear of it, is exactly what the governor would like, and much better than he could hope to get, for I do not suppose there is another place like it in the colony," said the agent, looking up from the book he had been examining.

"Very well, then, negotiate with the governor, and take ten per cent. on the sale from me. I leave the matter in your hands," concluded Mr. Elfinstar, as he took the supporting arm of his young friend and left the office.

They returned to the "mews" where they had left their horses, mounted and rode off toward the Hermitage, at which they arrived in time for their early dinner.

Seraph was informed of the good prospect of disposing of the Mountain Hermitage, and rejoiced in it, because her father rejoiced.

The next morning they had a final discussion of affairs, in which it was decided that the young pair should be privately married in the colony, the bridegroom under his simple name of Horace Hawke, and the bride under her real name of Margaret Campbell. This was to be done in order to make the marriage strictly legal, after which ceremony they were to appear as before—merely as a betrothed couple. They were to go to England as such, and, afterward, in London, they were to be publicly married, the bridegroom under his full name and title, and the bride as Seraph, granddaughter of Theobald Elfinstar, Esq., of Thorndike.

"For," said the old man, "the name and memory of Margaret Campbell, even though she has been vindicated, must die, lest the world should visit upon her, and all connected with her, her misfortunes as crime. My granddaughter, your lordship's betrothed, must be known in England only as Seraph Elfinstar, the heiress of Thorndike. You understand me?"

"I do," replied the young earl, gravely, while Seraph took the old man's hand and pressed it.

"And that brings me to another point. By the death of that infant boy who was murdered by the lunatic, Malvina Mattox, Margaret Campbell became the sole heiress of Rose Hill. Now, as Seraph Elfinstar she could not claim her inheritance. She inherits it as Margaret Campbell, the last of the Campbells of Rose Hill. But as Margaret Campbell she must not be heard of in England. How, then, shall she manage to enjoy her inheritance? This is my plan: Let Margaret Campbell, before her marriage with your lordship, execute a deed, giving Rose Hill to me, Theobald Elfinstar; after which, at another office, I will execute another deed, giving Rose Hill to my granddaughter, Seraph, Countess of Hawkewood. Do you understand?"

"Perfectly!" responded the young earl, who, with the hand of his beloved clasped in his own, thought no more of these business details than any other ardent lover of twenty-one might do.

The next day, Thursday, Ham Gow and his wife rode out to the Hermitage to inform their friends that the *Derwent* would set sail for Melbourne that evening. They had all their traps on board the ship, and had now come to say good-by.

"When you have quite made your fortune you will come back to England, Ham, dear boy," said the young earl.

"I'll come back to visit before that, my lord; but I shall live out here. I like the free life of the colonies," replied the tramp.

Seraph Elfinstar begged the visitors to excuse her for a few minutes, and she flew upstairs and took a casket of rare jewels, earrings, brooch, necklace and bracelets of pure sapphires set in pearls.

She presented them as a parting souvenir to Lona Gow, who received them with frank surprise and delight, and an outburst of gratitude that provoked smiles from all that saw and heard her.

Soon, with many good wishes, the visitors took leave and went away, accompanied by the young earl, who, at the last moment, determined to return to town with his friends and see them off to Melbourne.

"But come back to-night, though it will be late. The moon shines, and the road is good, and—I will sit up for you," said Seraph Elfinstar.

He gave her a fond and grateful look that promised everything.

The month that intervened between the sailing of the *Derwent* for Melbourne and its return to Hobart Town was a very busy one.

In the first place, the new governor came out in person to inspect the property he thought of buying for a summer retreat. He liked the place very much, and at once signified his intention to buy it if the price should prove as satisfactory as the place.

The bargain was finally concluded, and the Hermitage—house, land, stock and furniture—was sold to the new governor, and possession was to be given on the first of the next month.

Next, Margaret Campbell executed a deed, bestowing all her right, title and interest in Rose Hill Manor, in Yorkshire, to Theobald Elfinstar, of Thorndike, Cumberland.

After this, the betrothed pair, under the auspices of the old gentleman, went to Launceton, a town in the interior, where they were unknown.

There the young lovers were privately married, every legal form having been carefully observed by the precaution of Mr. Elfinstar.

They returned to the Hermitage immediately after the ceremony was concluded.

The young Earl of Hawkewood had been in the colony full a fortnight before he found time to renew his acquaintance with his former friends, the Belle Isles, and others.

At length, however, he called at the quarters of the lieutenant and learned for the first time that he had resigned or sold out his commission and left the garrison for apartments in the Royal Albert, the fine new hotel on Prince Street, where he was awaiting the return of the *Derwent*, by which he was to go home.

The earl went to the Royal Albert, where he was heartily welcomed by Mr. and Mrs. Cosmo Belle Isle, who addressed him as Mr. Hamilton Gower.

He did not set them right.

"They must find me out for themselves when we get back to England, if they do not before. And then they will remember that noblemen, as well as kings, and less honest men, sometimes travel *incog.*, as I have done."

He told them that he was going to England by the *Derwent*, and they expressed much pleasure in the prospect of having his company on the long voyage.

"There will be an unusually pleasant company in the cabin, I understand," said Mr. Belle Isle. "The ex-governor and his wife, our father and mother-in-law, you know, are going, and I hear that a Mr. and Mrs. Elfinstar—who, by the way, are friends of yours, are they not?"

"Yes," responded the young gentleman, with a smile.

"Seemed to me that I had heard you mention them when you were here last year. Well, I suppose, then, you know all about the old gentleman having sold out to take his daughter to England, and that they are going by the *Derwent*."

"Yes," said the earl, as briefly as before.

Then they talked of the "gay and happy" Gows and of the two calls they had made on the Belle Isles, immediately on landing from the *Derwent*, and the one just before sailing for Melbourne.

After a pleasant half hour spent with his friends, the earl took leave and returned to the Hermitage in time to join his bride and her grandfather at tea.

In three weeks from this day, a happy party of voyagers embarked on the *Derwent*, bound for "Old England."

Of the voyage it is not necessary to speak. "Happy is that life—or that voyage—which has no history." Only this I must say, that in the intimacy of ship association, the real rank of the earl transpired, and nothing ever was thought of his having traveled *incog*. Also, it was strongly suspected that his lordship was engaged to Miss Elfinstar. But that was really all that was discovered or surmised concerning the young couple or the aged grandfather.

The *Derwent* was a new ship and a fast sailer, and in due time landed at the East India Docks, London, "with all well on board," according to gazette, and according also to facts.

Three weeks after this, in the last days of August, there was a brilliant wedding at Thorndike in Cumberland, which was attended by all the neighboring gentry, and at which Mr. Theobald Elfinstar, of that ilk, bestowed the hand of his granddaughter and heiress, Seraph, on Horace Hawke, Earl of Hawkewood, in Cornwall, and at which Mr. Elfinstar gave the bride, as a wedding present, the fine manor of Rose Hill, in Yorkshire.

Immediately after the ceremony, the bridegroom and the bride took the train for London, en route for the country seat of the earl, Hawke Hall, in Cornwall, where magnificent preparations were made for their reception, and where they arrived on the morning of September the first, the twenty-second anniversary of the earl's birth.

There was a gala day worth describing, in which a birthday *fête* and a bride's reception were merged into one-a day long to be remembered in Hawkeville.

* * * * * * *

Some years have passed, and now here is the present position of the principal parties who have figured in our story.

The Earl and Countess of Hawkewood live at Hawkewood, and have a son and daughter. With them resides old Theobald Elfinstar, who, at eighty years of age, bids fair to complete his century of life, and who is very happy in his great-grandchildren, and old Dr. Paul Laude, who is

"Planted unco right"

in the grand old library, and who takes great pleasure in teaching the little Viscount Hawke his catechism and his Latin grammar.

These old gentlemen have formed a close friendship, and smoke their after-dinner pipes together in the library.

Lord and Lady Seyres live at Seyres Castle, in Ireland. At the earnest desire of Lady Seyres a large portion of her fortune was well invested in the complete restoration of the venerable castle, in the thorough draining of the land, and in the erection of comfortable cottages for the tenants and the agricultural laborers.

They, at least, live in the midst of a healthy, prosperous, smiling and contented peasantry, whatever other landlords may be doing.

They are blessed with one son, whom the viscount calls the Isaac of his age.

Mr. and Mrs. Belle Isle live principally in London at the Palace Zavieski; but they have a country seat in Northumberland, and a seaside house at Torquay, and

"Many children around them grow."

'Ham Gow is one of the wealthiest merchants in Melbourne, and his town house and seaside residence are among the most splendid mansions in the colony. Lona is very much admired for her beauty and amiability.

No one out there knows, or would care, even if they did know, that the wealthy merchant king was once a poor tramp, who married a poor servant maid, for they live in a colony of self-made men and women, who have risen from the lowest ranks. They have a house full of children, in whom they take the greatest delight.

Our worthy friend, Dennis Prout coast guardsman and smuggler from Cornwall, has "fallen on his feet," so to speak, in one of our American cities—never mind which.

By what political *hocus pocus* the "ring" and the demon only know, he is in the enjoyment of a post of honor and emolument, with unlimited opportunities for stealing, in one of the most important custom houses. Mr. and Mrs. Prout—Dennis and his wife, Nan—are in very good society, and are considered an eminently respectable couple,; but they have no family, and they decline all open intercourse with Old Nan, on account of her peculiar line of business, although they are sociable enough with the old woman in private.

Old Nan's success is, perhaps, the most surprising of any related in this story.

She is no longer known as Old Nan. She is Madame de Crook, the seventh daughter of a seventh daughter of a seventh daughter through seven generations and is consequently, by birth and inheritance, the most wonderful astrologer, clairvoyant healing medium—and humbug—that the world ever rejoiced in.

She lives in a handsomely furnished French flat, has her meals supplied from a first-class restaurant, has a maid to wait on her, and a stylish colored man to open the door to her dupes. She wears a picturesque costume of black velvet with a turban of the same, and a brilliant brooch, which may be a solitaire diamond or a big bit of glass; there is no telling one from the other in these days, unless one happens to be a lapidary.

Old Nan Crook may fall into the hands of the police some fine morning, and spend the remainder of her long and misused life in the calm retreats of the State penitentiary.

But, in the meantime, she is making her own fortune by telling the fortunes of others, and—equally with our more worthy friends— enjoying a full share of health and prosperity.

CPSIA information can be obtained
at www.ICGtesting.com
Printed in the USA
LVOW12s0635170817

545365LV00001B/59/P